Advance Praise

"*Soul Jar* is a fantastical bullhorn for voices that so often go unheard. Dive into this captivating collection of narratives, crafted by authors intimately familiar with the complexities of living with disabilities. Vibrant characters come alive, navigating a range of experiences and emotions, while simultaneously illuminating the impact representation in literature can have. The stories in this extraordinary anthology will pull you in, show you a vastly under-explored area of the literary world, and leave you wanting more."

—Violet Lumani, author of *Foretold*

"The literary community is a landscape in which you can still hear artists, writers, readers, and creatives calling each other in, asking each to bear witness to our individual and collective truths. *Soul Jar* is no exception. This dazzling anthology of creative writing demonstrates an incredible constellation of talent, humor, and not-so-out-of-this-world dystopian possibilities through the pens and pages of authors living with disabilities. It also reminds the literary community of the importance of true representation, and the void of raw talent and imagination we create when we create without accessibility and sustainability at the forefront of our practices. The future is now. Open this book and read."

—Christina Vega, founder of Blue Cactus Press and author of the poetry collections *Vega*, *Decay*, and *Maps*

"A wonderfully curated selection of captivating stories that will stay with you. A must-have for every bookshelf."

—Sho Roberts, owner of Maggie Mae's Bookshop

"For those of us with bodies that look and function differently than the majority, reading science fiction and fantasy can be a means of feeling understood and seen, or being ever closer to a world that is more welcoming than the real one. I'm grateful to Annie Carl and the talented authors who make up the contents of *Soul Jar*—these vibrant, haunting, full-hearted tales are as necessary as they are entertaining."

—Mo Daviau, connective tissue-disordered
author of *Every Anxious Wave*

"The soul jar overfloweth in this radical anthology of mermaids, mechas, and rotten hyenas. Annie Carl's refined taste for the far out has unleashed a swath of writers who zone in on disabled joys and vexations. How refreshing it is to read from writers who get it."

—Jonah Barnett, author of *Moss-Covered Claws*

"Like disability itself, these stories are a myriad of things: rich, nuanced, furious, complicated, joyous, determined. They are wild howls of imagination that simultaneously manage to showcase a vast spectrum of true, lived experience. Let *Soul Jar* be an arrow sent out into the world."

—Keith Rosson, author of *Fever House, The Mercy of the Tide,*
Smoke City, Road Seven, and Folk Songs for Trauma Surgeons

Soul Jar

Soul Jar

Thirty-one
Fantastical Tales by
Disabled Authors

edited by Annie Carl

FOREST AVENUE PRESS
Portland, Oregon

Library of Congress Control Number: 2023940824

"Song of Bull Frogs, Cry of Geese" by Nicola Griffith was previously published in *Interzone* #48, 1991, and in *Aboriginal*, July 1991.

"Weightless" by Raven Oak was first published in *The Great Beyond: An Anthology of Classic Space Adventure Tales*, June 2020.

"The Definitions of Professional Attire" by Evergreen Lee was first published in *Factor Four Magazine*, July 2019.

"Things I Miss the Most" by Nisi Shawl was first published in *Uncanny Magazine*, Issue 24, 2018.

Distributed by Publishers Group West

Published in the United States of America
by Forest Avenue Press LLC
Portland, Oregon

Printed in the United States

Forest Avenue Press LLC
P.O. Box 80134
Portland, OR 97280
forestavenuepress.com

1 2 3 4 5 6 7 8 9

For everyone like (and not like) us.
We recognize you.
You are our future.

Contents

Earth in Retrograde

Gone Astray

Wild Space

Creature Feature

Glorious Symphony

Nicola Griffith

IN 2018 I PUBLISHED my first and most likely only novel about disability (as opposed to a novel with disabled characters). *So Lucky* is about a woman, Mara, realising that she needs a community—other disabled people—that doesn't exist; it's about how she finds her people and then begins to discover and help shape a new culture.

"I need it, so I'll have to build it" is where the queer community as we know it began in the fifties and sixties and the feminist community in the seventies. Both accelerated in the eighties. The HIV+ community did it in the eighties and nineties. The disabled community is doing it right now.

Whether a community does not yet exist or that you don't know how to find it, not having a community to lean on in times of need is terrible: alienating, Othering, and enraging. Finally finding your people and helping to create a life, a history, a path, plan, and sense of purpose together, though? That is blazing joy. So few people get to be part of the building blocks of a culture. So many of us are born into a sense of belonging and history, and never get to really discover our own perspective on the world. As individuals we change throughout our lives, but generally speaking, any paths we may follow are already well-trodden, ready-made with off-the-shelf options, and lined with music, books, films, fashions, and documentary history to match.

But when you get to make the art that builds the culture and grows the community that doesn't already exist, the art you create is fuelled by the emotional journey: the alienation and the homecoming, the fear and excitement, the rage and joy. It is rich with the delight of discovery, of making, of connection; filled with the warmth of belonging and building your own hearth.

In the UK in the eighties the lesbian feminist community experienced this. It was an incredible time; the music and art that flowered from it is part of what made me and certainly made my music (I fronted a band, Janes Plane). The sense of breaking rules—political, legal, social expectations of good behaviour—made our lives feel sui generis. So when I began to write about a woman entering a different phase of life as newly disabled, I reached for that sense of DIY culture. I threw out all received notions of genre and story structure and built someting uniquely suited to the story of a woman moulding her disabled identity.

So Lucky is about a woman with MS, written by a woman with MS. The first word of the book is *It*, and *It* is a monster. But the monster is not MS; the monster is ableism.

Ableism is the story fed to all of us, disabled and non-disabled, from birth: that to have intellectual or physical impairments makes us less, Other. It's the only story we get in real life or on page or screen. Ableism is a crap story.

For one thing, it's wrong. What disables a person in our culture is not impairment but society's attitude to that impairment. We're disabled by assumptions. By, for example, the bookstore owner who, when asked why there's no wheelchair ramp, says, with no trace of irony, "Well, none of our customers use a wheelchair." Or the editor who says to their author, "Can you make the disabled character a bit more lonely and sad, more authentic?"

Ableism is an inauthentic story told by those who have no clue. Next time you read a book about a quadriplegic—with all the money, a great career, and a loving wife—who kills himself because he can't bear to live in a wheelchair, next time you read about a blind woman whose happy ending relies upon a magic cure, ask yourself: Is the author of this story disabled?

According to the CDC, one quarter of Americans have a disability that has a serious impact on their life. One quarter. But how many of the five million novels extant in English (per the Stanford Book Lab) are by and about disabled people? In a just and equitable society, one in which various peoples are mirrored in the culture's art, you might hope to find over a million novels by and about disabled people, to hear a million disabled voices singing a glorious symphony of disabled stories in all their brilliant variety.

I would be surprised if there were five hundred novels for adults written in English by and about disabled people and absolutely shocked if there were five thousand. All those missing voices...

Ableism is a crap story. We can make a better one. But to do that we first need to see ourselves reflected in the stories we read. We need to hear our own voices. Our strong, beautiful, ordinary, disabled voices.

Here are some of them.

Introduction

Annie Carl

THIS ANTHOLOGY WAS EDITED, and this introduction written, on the ancestral lands of the Coast Salish People, specifically the Tulalip, Snohomish, Stillaguamish, and Sauk-Suiattle Tribes. I see you, respect your right to sovereignty and self-determination, and am committed to being a better listener and self-educator. I will continue to work as an ally for Indigenous rights, stories, and authors.

In October 2017, I went my first bookseller trade show. Hosted by the Pacific Northwest Booksellers' Association, it was the first time I was among large numbers of booksellers, bookstore owners, publishers, authors, and other industry professionals. I entered as a new store owner with no idea what I would discover at the show. It was huge and over-whelming, and while I recognized a few other booksellers, I didn't know many of the people in attendance. The hotel itself was huge and it was a feat for me to get from my room to the bookseller events.

The trade show was also amazing. I met so many new peo-ple, listened to authors and publisher reps talk about books, and attended panels for self-education. Something I didn't get a lot of in the day-to-day operations of my store.

One of the panels I attended changed everything. It was about how to support and celebrate diversity in independent bookstores. It was a wonderful panel for diversity and inclu-sion of people of color, different religions, gender, and sexuality. The panelists only left one community out.

Mine.

Disabilities were not discussed at all. I had my hand up before the call for questions from the audience.

"What kinds of information and support do you have for disabled booksellers and authors?" I asked, genuinely curious what the panelists would say.

The only answer I received were blank stares from the panelists. They had nothing for me or my community. No groups dedicated to disabled voices in books and publishing. No bookstores that specialized in books written by disabled authors. Not even a disabled store owner, bookseller, or publisher to talk to during the show.

The slow rise of anger at the panelists' silent confusion burned away any qualms I had about demanding more for myself and the disabled community. From the panel. From the book industry. From Western society at large.

My advocacy was born in that moment. Not the moment I turned twelve and really started to understand what it was to be "differently abled." Not when I went to college and struggled to fit in on the lacrosse team, no matter the fact that I couldn't (and can't) run. Not even when I was designated high-risk while I was pregnant because of my disabilities.

No, the exact moment I discovered my advocacy was during that specific panel. I kept hoping they would get to it. That someone would magically come out of the woodwork and start talking about all the wonderful, bookish organizations that supported the disabled community.

What actually happened was Laura Stanfill, publisher at Forest Avenue Press, came rushing over to me as I packed myself up in a huff.

"We need to talk," she said.

And we did. And we didn't stop talking about disabilities and books and our families and businesses. Laura and I became close friends, and I hoped she would be on board with an idea I had been mulling over for years. I wanted to shine a light on how disabilities fit in with science fiction and fantasy. How people like myself and others can and should exist in the future and magical realms.

I live in the worlds fantasy and science fiction create. As a child, recovering from operation after operation, these places and characters took me away from my reality. But these stories, until recently, have largely been written by able-bodied authors starring able-bodied characters. As I grew up and realized that very few of these stories contained people like me, I knew that had to change. Publishers—especially in romance, young adult, and children's books—are starting to release books with positive disabled representation. Disabled authors are finding more opportunities to publish their stories. Western society is beginning to understand, after centuries of ignorance, that the disabled community is like other minorities. We're made up of real people with real lives and real stories.

How, then, do we find ourselves in the future? In magical lands or distant worlds where anything can be healed with the movement of a tricorder or the casting of a spell? Many books gloss over the reality of disabilities with instant cures or outright death. Rarely are we allowed, let alone invited, to exist in these realms. The gatekeeping in the science fiction and fantasy industries is immense and completely unnecessary. We deserve to be ourselves in magical lands and aboard spaceships. This anthology is yet another call to empower disabled people and our representation within fantastical worlds and beyond.

Inclusion runs through these pages and stories, written by authors defying expectations of the disabled community in the publishing industry. These words are the answer to the question I asked at that long-ago panel. Within these pages you will find mermaids, dragons, mechsuits, spaceships, imaginary friends, and demons raised from cereal box toys. Readers will encounter how these thirty-one   disabled authors view the future, space, and magic. I truly hope you find yourself in these phenomenal tales of fantasy and nebulas.

—ANNIE CARL, OCTOBER 2023

Earth in Retrograde

There Are No Hearing Aid Batteries After the Apocalypse

Carol Scheina

ON THE NIGHT THE world fell apart, Kesslyn slipped off her hearing aids like she peeled off her skinny jeans and her damned wired bra. That audiologist was wrong; after four months of hearing aids, the things still chafed at her ears. She'd need to go back for another fitting, but that meant going back to the sitting room and staring at posters with smiling people proclaiming, "Hearing loss is more common that you think."

Kesslyn didn't like the *real* message those posters imparted to her. *You've changed. You're never going back.* She was supposed to be dating, going out for drinks with friends, and whatever else carefree young women did for fun. Not visiting audiologists. Not struggling to hear through hearing aids, creating a world where sounds were tilted and she was still upright trying to make everything fit properly in the catalogue of dialogue and music and noise. Sounds vanished the moment she turned her hearing aids off. Sometimes it was a relief. Sometimes it was a reminder.

On the night the world fell apart, Kesslyn fell asleep with salty-wet eyes, as she had so many nights before.

She didn't hear the world end.

She felt it, though.

When Kesslyn pulled herself from the dust and debris of her apartment building, she found her hearing aids miraculously intact. They slipped into her ears, chafing be damned. She had to hear. There could be voices calling. Someone else out there still alive.

She cried tears and heard silence.

The ground shook violently, sending Kesslyn to her knees, bloodying her hand on a sharp piece of broken metal. She watched a soda can bouncing about by her feet until it finally burst, sending fizzy sweetness toward her eyes.

The can had made no sound. The fizzing hadn't hissed in her ears.

Is anyone out there? she called, her voice missing.

Hands flew to her hearing aids. Had they broken? Kesslyn slipped them off, peered at the earmold, the tubing, the plastic casing, the battery compartment. The battery. No battery was lodged inside either aid. She took the batteries out at night. The batteries were connected to the on-off switch. Keeping the batteries out meant the aids wouldn't accidentally drain the batteries.

She no longer had sound.

Hands trembled as they inserted the dead aids back in her ears. She had to put them somewhere safe, just until she found new batteries, and her ears would work.

If anyone was calling for help, she wouldn't hear. Hands rubbed sweet fizz and salty tears out of her eyes. She'd need to see clearly, to spot any possible movement around her that signaled life, to map her pathway to somewhere safe.

The sky's hues shifted toward paler shades as the sun rose. The first day *after*.

Kesslyn stumbled out of the debris wearing nothing more than a tank top, pajama bottoms, and slipper socks. She stepped carefully.

THE WAY TO GO was out. Away from the remaining walls that continued to wobble and shed bricks and rocks, like dogs shaking drops from their backs. A man vanished beneath one falling fridge-sized rock, right before Kesslyn's horrified eyes. She stopped looking for others and frantically looked for the way out.

Signs of life appeared, some trying to move too-heavy pieces of building. Some hugging themselves, waiting for helicopters and fire trucks and people with megaphones to give directions on how to stay safe. A brown dog with ears flat against its head that darted off as Kesslyn approached. People with cell phones, tapping randomly with shoulders squared with frustration, leaving Kesslyn to wonder if the phones were broken or couldn't connect to a service.

The dust in the air was beginning to smell of campfire and the red-orange hues of dancing flames dotted the northern horizon. The ones who sought escape trudged south, toward the main interstate. Not all, though. Some stayed to dig. Some stayed for the rescuers.

Kesslyn picked up a pristine composition book on top of a pile of red bricks. *Jessica*, it said in young, crooked pencil script on the cover. The inside had three pages filled with pictures of pink flowers and a pointy yellow sun crayoned in a corner. She hoped Jessica would understand if she used the book. Just until Kesslyn got new hearing aid batteries. Just in case someone could call Mom and Dad for her and write down their responses. She'd find a pen somewhere. Jessica would understand. Right?

Armed with a composition book and useless hearing aids, Kesslyn walked out of the city for the last time.

THE FIRE SPREAD, FORMING a tornado of flame that spun through the city and wrapped its tendrils around those still digging, those waiting for rescue. The ones who made it out had wet faces and waited for people to wrap them in blankets and take them to safe places with food and water.

In the end, it wasn't the buildings falling apart or the flames or the death that let Kesslyn know the world has really fallen apart. It was when no one came. Mom and Dad weren't coming. Around her, she saw people waiting to hear someone say, "It's okay, we're here to help." They heard only silence.

Clarinet Man stepped into that silence, because even after the world ended, people still needed comfort. Music filled a need, first with small performances that grew, people drawn to the music and the safety of fellow survivors like finding water after crossing the desert.

Four months after the world fell to pieces, blankets, broken plywood, and tarps formed their campsite, with a clearing in the middle for their makeshift amphitheater. A bonfire blazing behind him, Clarinet Man played his music, twisting with the rhythm, a dance Kesslyn tried to read like notes dotting sheet music. When he finished playing, the creases around his eyes were streaked with sweat and tears, dripping down his thick beard.

The other survivors—maybe five hundred in all—held

hands and closed their eyes, shiny and wet. Some smiled, tight and forced, but still a smile.

How did music give them such hope?

In her pocket, she touched her hearing aids, feeling the familiar rubbery earmolds, the plastic bodies waiting for new batteries. Waiting for that moment when the sound would click on, and she'd hear a note, a voice, anything.

She was surrounded by people, hoping for one moment of comfort, of connection. Like those who held hands and hugged. Two pill-sized batteries held the power of all her hopes. Aid batteries lasted about one week, but in that time, at least she'd be able to talk to someone.

Just two batteries, and yet, when Kesslyn peeked at the ruins of her old city behind them, doubt creeped in. Where the hell did one find hearing aid batteries in this new world?

The night Kesslyn realized would be no more music, no voices, no connection—no batteries—she sat on the hard ground, just on the edge of their makeshift theater, and sobbed her own melody of grief as Clarinet Man played.

A tap on her shoulder. She looked up to see Clarinet Man, his fuzzy beard smothering any chance at lipreading.

Kesslyn shook her head. "I can't hear." She hated not being able to hear her own voice when she spoke, yet she still had to speak. She pulled out Jessica's composition book and a small twig with a blackened tip. "Write your words here."

Clarinet Man pulled out a battered blue-ink pen. *Are you okay?* he wrote, the letters nearly illegible in the faint light.

Kesslyn wiped at her face and shrugged. What could she say? She was surviving. "I'm making do."

He scribbled, *Can I do anything for you?*

Kesslyn shook her head.

He nodded toward her paper and mimicked tearing a piece

out. Kesslyn massaged one sheet out of the binding of Jessica's notebook and handed it to him.

The man ripped the paper into sixths and began to write. Kesslyn read the words over his shoulder: *For Amber Pearson. I'm alive. Camped outside city. Send word back. Love, Jessie.*

A note of hope. Maybe a loved one was still alive.

She knew from watching that people left the camp looking for other groups of survivors that might be out there, hoping loved ones were somewhere. She'd tried to send her own notes out to Mom and Dad, but she never knew who was going to leave, or how to get in touch with them. All that information passed by word of mouth.

Kesslyn touched Clarinet Man's arm: "I've got notes too. Can you help get them out?"

He nodded and wrote, *Keep the pen.* He pressed it into her hand, holding it tight there for a moment, his large hand warm around hers.

"Thank you." For the first time a song filled Kesslyn's heart, a light tune that sang of hope and kindness and traveled like a warm hug up to her mouth.

Clarinet Man smiled back.

HOW DID THE WORLD fall to pieces? No one knew. Kesslyn didn't know what was out beyond the camp. Surely if things were going well elsewhere, people would have come to help?

When people in camp left hoping for something better, Kesslyn stayed fearing worse.

Besides, the camp had organization. A woman in a blue shirt assigned teams to scavenge for food and supplies, making trips into the skeleton of the city smoking on the horizon. Kesslyn had been assigned to the group hauling creek water using old coolers and trash bins the scavenge team brought back. Another team sanitized the water with fires and plastic tarps for evaporation. One group worked on building new homes.

Kesslyn made a mental note that all the books and movies were wrong; the apocalypse didn't turn humans into beasts. If anything, it brought them closer together as they worked during the day, gathering to hear Clarinet Man play his music at night before the bonfire.

She watched it all, like seeing a television show play out before her, only she was stumbling about, unsure of what part she was supposed to play.

Sleep never came easily those nights. Kesslyn fingered her hearing aids, feeling the holes where batteries would be slipped in. Empty. Always empty.

IN THE MORNING, CLARINET Man was there with a younger woman, asking for paper and pen.

She's trying to find her husband and children. Can she write a note? Clarinet Man wrote.

Kesslyn nodded.

The woman's lips were soft and easy to lipread. *Thank you.* Shiny eyes told of all the emotions held back. The world was so different, sometimes it was overwhelming. Kesslyn knew the feeling.

She looked to Clarinet Man. "Do others need paper and pen to send notes?"

He nodded. *People want to send letters. So much burned up. They're ripping clothes, using bark.*

What would people do to communicate? Once, they could make a call from anywhere, with just a simple swipe of a cell phone. Now, voices were missing. People wanted the connection. Kesslyn understood all too well.

"I have paper and pen," Kesslyn said. "Send them to me."

The world still remained each morning, and Kesslyn would grab her blue-and-white cooler and begin to haul water before the day turned too hot. In the evening, Kesslyn doled out pages from Jessica's notebook, offering her gifted pen for those scribbles of hope, words to send out into the world in hope that someone, somewhere, would read them and write back.

Kesslyn saved Jessica's drawings for last, finally letting a teenaged girl with a faded emoji shirt write over the pointed yellow sun with the last few squirts of black ink in the pen. All that remained was the cardboard cover, rubbed soft at the edges and filled in with the words of those who had communicated to her in writing. Kesslyn fingered the indentations the black ink made in the black-and-white marbling.

She looked at the ground, worn to dust with so many feet tromping around. Perhaps she could ask people to write in the dirt using a stick?

Would anyone bother with her since she no longer had paper and pen?

Clarinet Man played his evening music, but Kesslyn didn't watch the twists and turns of the dancers. Her hands held her hearing aids, feeling the empty battery compartments. She was through watching faces, pretending she was part of the audience. The music wasn't for her. It had never been.

Her eyes stayed down as she walked to her tent and tried to sleep. She fingered the aids instead. Perhaps it was time to toss them into the creek. She'd been weighed down by their promise long enough. No hearing aid batteries were left.

A woman, hair covered with a faded pink bandana, was outside Kesslyn's tent in the morning. Kesslyn couldn't lipread well enough, but she figured the woman wanted paper.

"I don't have any more paper."

Instead, Bandana Woman held out her hand, dirt

highlighting the creases, and four shiny AAA batteries were nestled in the center like tiny bird eggs. She took Kesslyn's hands and pressed the batteries into them, then pointed to Kesslyn's ears.

For hearing aids? How did the woman know? Kesslyn stammered out a jumbled response—*those weren't hearing aid batteries, she couldn't use them*—but Bandana Woman squeezed Kesslyn's hand before walking away.

A young man, thin and stretching tall over Kesslyn, was behind Bandana Woman, and he held out a lithium battery from a cell phone. He spoke a long time, kneeling into the dirt with his finger tracing a design of a hearing aid with wires connecting them. She wasn't sure what the plans meant, but the man seemed excited so Kesslyn smiled back.

"Thank you."

I'll find wires, he wrote in the dirt.

An older woman approached shortly after. Kesslyn recognized her as having received paper from Jessica's notebook, who had written a note for her husband. The woman held out a button battery, the kind used in small remotes, and pointed to Kesslyn's ears.

Wrong size again, but the thought wasn't on Kesslyn's mind. She grasped the old woman's hands, papery and thin, to her heart. "How did you know about the hearing aids?"

The old woman tapped her eyes, then pointed to Kesslyn. *I see you*, the sign said. Then she pointed to everyone and her eyes once more. *We all see you.*

As the night's air cooled with evening, people piled on wood around the fire. Clarinet Man bent his body to the rhythm as sweat dripped off his beard. He winked at her, and Kesslyn wondered if she could ask him to shave so she could lipread him more easily.

Her fingers didn't reach for the rubbery feel of her earmolds in her pocket. Her mind was planning instead, wondering if she could develop a form of sign language. Or maybe someone in the group could ask if any in the camp or any incoming travelers knew someone who signed? Kesslyn had never learned before.

This was the world of after.

Holding Back

Danielle Mullen

HE STILL CALLS ME kid sometimes. As if I never stopped being that hungry, skinny little girl he caught picking pockets all those years ago. I don't think he means anything by it.

He just forgets the passage of time.

Or maybe he wants to forget? I used to envy him. The doc's magic elixir. The extra strength. The extra power and less pain. But nothing lasts forever and I suspect his body remembers all the broken bones now. His movements have a new stiffness. He's still fast but not as quick as he used to be. The results of all those years spent *Holding Back Night's Evil*.

Night's Evil. I used to tease him about that. If evil is real, then it's just as busy during the day. I suspect the individual words lost their meanings long ago. It's just a slogan or a catchphrase. What it means to him is what matters. Whatever he tells himself he accomplishes by tilting at muggers and third-rate gangsters.

He used to be something, you know? Scary. Strong. His mere legend enough to keep people honest. Or so some claim.

The crime rate was a little lower back then. But so were unemployment and homelessness.

Now it's rare he makes it all the way to dawn. Seems like he's always got an "early meeting." I never tell him I know he's lying. When he leaves I feel like the woman at the bar who brought home someone who refused to stick around for breakfast. A crime-fighting booty call.

To be clear, there was never anything like that between us. Sure, I've heard the rumors. I've even read some of the fanfic. It is hilarious. But he's not my type.

I know most people aren't interested in the truth. They just want to hear the story they're already telling themselves. I'd like to give an interview one day. Say what everyone got right and what they got wrong. He's killed people. Not many, but some. He's not funny at all. Dead serious at all times. But he does give the occasional dry chuckle when I say something he finds amusing. The so-called "Queen of Crime" and him? She flirted with him, a lot. But she flirted with me too. It's her way of disarming people. He never reciprocated or made a move. None of the women in his day life stuck it out for long. No one really wants to be with someone who won't tell them where they are most nights. I told my now-wife the truth when we were dating. It was a risk, but she'll always be worth any risk to me.

Even if he had found someone he felt comfortable being honest with? I doubt it would have worked out. He's far too devoted to what he considers his duty. I told him once he should slack off more. Focus on his charitable works and collecting art instead. He said, *If I don't do this, who will?*

The police? I shrugged.

Got more than a dry chuckle out of him that time.

Most nights when he heads home early I do too. This thing we try to do, I know it's nothing. Maybe we help a few people at one moment in their lives but it's not changing anything. When he took me off the street? That was real. That's what kept me by his side all these years and why I still show up every time he calls.

Sometimes I stay and wait on the dawn alone, wondering what I'll do when he can't come out anymore. Just stop? Live out the rest of my life in the daytime like most people? Or will I find another pickpocket and keep going? As much as I loved it, I don't think any kid should do the things I did by his side.

Sometimes I wonder if he always knew I was trustworthy, or did he just take a chance? Were there others before me? He never said anything and I never asked. I didn't want to know. I'll never admit it to him, but I don't always mind when he forgets and calls me kid.

Survivors' Club

Meghan Beaudry

THROUGH THE WINDOW I can see clear across the alley into the apartment facing mine. Mrs. Finch reclines in her armchair by the window, a hand raised in greeting. Rain or shine, she's always there. Silver hair whisked back into a bun. Usually with a book in her lap. Lately it's been a mess of yarn and a pair of crochet hooks, although she hasn't made much progress this month. Whoever's expecting that hat or scarf or baby blanket will just have to wait. Mrs. Finch is looking thinner. Then I look down at my own body—my ribs protruding under my pink sports bra, the winding river of my surgical scar. All of America is on a diet, whether we like it or not.

I grab an MRE from the kitchen. Chicken with egg noodles and freeze-dried vegetables again. As good a breakfast as I'll get. I unscrew the top of my prescription bottle, shake one small oval into my hand, then wash it down. I fight the urge to yet again count the pills I have left.

I flip open my laptop and log on. *Day 1572* flashes across

the bottom of my laptop screen. It doesn't feel much different than Day 1557 (my twenty-ninth birthday), or even Day 1000 for that matter.

You don't have to know the numbers to track the progress of the world's first *caelivirus*. Just listen to the sirens outside, all day and all night. Just read the headlines. During the first month of quarantine, after all the restaurants shut down but before the National Guard came in wearing hazmats, it was *10 Ways to Keep Your Kids Entertained in Quarantine*. Midway through stories like *10 Meals to Make out of Existing Supplies in Your Pantry* and *How Long Can Leftovers Last Before They're Unsafe to Eat?* made their debut. These days it's *Five Books to Read When You Feel Like Giving Up* and *How to Make a Homemade Ventilator out of Everyday Household Items*. Yesterday's death count from the virus was 3,017. And that's just in NYC.

I GLANCE OUT THE window. I can't help but look at the dropbox affixed to Mrs. Finch's door. It's delivery day. Soon the drones will glide by, like robotic Santas delivering MREs and in Mrs. Finch's case, medicine. Mrs. Finch has better insurance than I do. Premium Medicare instead of the crappy Health Choice everyone's on, in which one's only real choice is to shut up and die already. She takes the same medical steroid I do. I know because I helped her sign up online for drone delivery that first week of quarantine.

I tear my eyes away from Mrs. Finch's dropbox and back to the computer. You have to be careful what you share on social media nowadays. To be more precise, you have to be careful that you *do* share these days. Everyone knows looters comb social media, eyeing that account that's been inactive for a week or more. You want to post enough to show you're still alive, although not much else. Don't give away too much information,

like if you're sick or how much food you have left. I search
Google Images and settle on a meme of Mr. Rogers wearing a
hazmat suit. *It's a beautiful day in the neighborhood,* the text below
the picture says. Click. Post.

BACK WHEN WE COULD still go outside, before we were afraid even
to open our windows, I spent an afternoon perched in front of
Mrs. Finch's clunky PC—a gift from one of her grown children.

Twitter and Instagram had seemed too complicated.
Snapchat? TikTok? Yeah, right. I finally settled on Facebook,
which seemed like it would be the most accessible for her.

"It'll help you stay in touch with other people," I explained,
pointing out the newsfeed. I sent myself a friend request from
her account.

"Dear, that's what phones are for," Mrs. Finch smiled. Her
eyes crinkled behind her glasses.

"You should get an Amazon account, too," I told her. "What
if the stores stay closed for a long time?" It was before the gov-
ernor made the lockdown official, but not before we all knew
it was coming. According to the satellites, that deadly orange
cloud of debris and germs would reach our city in days.

Mrs. Finch just shrugged and smiled.

MRS. FINCH WAS THE first person I met when I moved here.
I'd rented this apartment the year after my lung transplant,
but struggled with the stairs, as I knew I would. After two
flights, I'd gasp for breath and my fingers would tingle. Most
people—particularly other late-twentysomethings, but really
people of all ages—took a step back when I told them about
my transplant. Literally, a step back, as if a plane of glass had
fallen between us to separate the young and healthy from the
young and damned. But not Mrs. Finch. She'd brought over a

tray of sugar cookies, cut into heart shapes and slathered with pink frosting.

"To celebrate your new heart," Mrs. Finch had said. I didn't correct her.

She's still in front of the window, reclining on her armchair. I log into her Facebook account. "Another beautiful sunrise this morning," I post, then log out. My mouth waters thinking about those cookies now.

By now everyone knows the story of the lab explosion, the smog, the plague that spread across the globe like a viral blitz-krieg. We can recite the symptoms like we recite our addresses: first there's the watery eyes, the hacking cough with blood. Then victims gasp their last breaths, often cracking their ribs in the process. The scientists tell us the germs can live for months on a hard surface like plastic or wood, up from the few hours they said at first. They tell us it adapts quicker than any virus they've ever studied. That every time they come close to a vaccine it mutates. That at first they thought the chances of sur-viving it were ninety-eight percent, but now they're less than twenty. They tell us everything except what everyone's dying to know: how to get rid of it. The world has seen coronaviruses, influenzas, SARS, but we've never before experienced a *caeli-virus*—the first virus to attach itself to air particles and travel, hostless, for weeks at a time, like some goddamn invisible air zombie. I glance outside as the wind tosses a leaf past my win-dow. What I don't see is the deadly germs floating along beside it. But that doesn't mean they're not there.

By now scientists have adapted filtration systems for AC, but not before entire buildings perished, ribcages rattling one last time as parents clapped their last masks over children's faces. Most of them are still there four years later, entombed in swanky Park Avenue townhomes cursed with central air rather than window units.

The first year of quarantine, there'd been impromptu hallway parties and sourdough starter swaps. But as food and money diminished, the camaraderie, unusual for New York, had hardened to suspicion, then naked greed. After the first neighbor tried to break in, I moved my dresser in front of my door, then sharpened a knife to keep by my bed.

WE'VE ALL RETREATED INTO the safety of the virtual world. Social media is all we have now. A mass of humanity clambering to be seen, to be heard, to share. None of it feels quite real, but we cling to it like it's our last hug from a loved one we know we'll never see again. Every one of us is desperate to connect. Too bad a hundred loud voices is no match for an assassin no one can see or hear.

A FRIEND FROM COLLEGE likes my post. A friend's mom has posted a cooking clip. Rachel Ray, that rogue survivalist. With only a few TV channels still functioning, she films her own show from her underground bunker. She'll make it out of this mess, most likely brandishing a makeshift tuna soufflé. I like the post, then keep scrolling.

The first wave of deaths sent everyone scurrying inside. Schools went online. Restaurants closed. Only the hospitals worked overtime. Six months later the second wave washed away thousands—mostly people who just couldn't take the isolation anymore. Conspiracy theorists who believed the virus was a hoax and wanted to be liberated from lockdown. Liberate themselves they did—right out of this life and into the next. Teenagers sneaking out at night, sharing beer or joints or even just conversation. Suzy Q. Homemaker lured to her death by the allure of a fifty percent off coupon. People who stepped outside, just for a few hours, lured by the siren song of "fresh" air and sunshine. I stand by the window and tip my coffee mug of hot water to the outside. The air and I stare each other down. Those sidewalks have no hold over me, I tell myself.

The fourth wave, which started late year three, was mostly suicides. People came up with all kinds of ways of ending it all. Leaping from their balconies. Swallowing kitchen cleaner. Going for a last leisurely stroll around Central Park. One woman licked her countertops after the virus took her husband and two children. Some of them streamed it, the last facial expression they'll ever make immortalized in a fifteen-second clip.

THE MOST DEPRESSED I've ever been happened well before quarantine. The year after my transplant, a childhood friend I'd met in the hospital died before she got her new lungs. Crippled by guilt, I hardly left my bed that month. I didn't shower. I barely ate. But my lungs kept inhaling, drawing in oxygen and transforming it into carbon dioxide. Lungs gifted from another's body to save my life. "Grieving doesn't mean giving up," I'd told myself.

I STAND ON A chair to unscrew the lightbulb above me so it lasts longer. Last year the one remaining bulb in the kitchen went out. In the rare event I cook, I unscrew a bulb from my bedside lamp and relocate it. If that bulb ever dies, I'll have to go full on Laura Ingalls Wilder and make myself an oil lamp.

BEFORE MY TRANSPLANT AND well before *caelivirus* was even a blip on the horizon, I used to think having a pile of cash was the key to survival. I'd slept on a friend's couch for months before the transplant and before my job at the firm, Medicaid hemming and hawing as the hospital bills bled me dry. No way in hell was I ever going back. I got hired as a paralegal at a big firm in Midtown as soon as I was well enough to work. I'd saved my money like crazy. My emergency fund bloomed into three months, then six months, then five years' worth. More now, since rent has been suspended indefinitely. All my colleagues at the law firm took taxis to their fancy townhomes and tossed back cosmos at swanky nightclubs. I moved into my cramped fifth-floor studio. I didn't know I'd be trapped here for years.

ON THE EVENING NEWS once a few months ago the police executed a handful of looters. They do that from time to time as a message to the rest of us. Toe the line. Stay inside and starve to death like good citizens. Not that they're wrong. The alternative is gasping your last breath on a ventilator. One of the looters was a white man in his fifties. Right before the bullet entered his chest I got a look at his face. Scott, the lawyer with an office down the hall from my cubicle.

Nobody thought this would happen in America. The years long martial law. The executions without trials. The suspended elections. But maybe we should have. For all our talk of democracy, we're not so different from the rest of the world. There's no depth people won't stoop to to take one last breath, no matter how miserable.

Those of us left are all part of the same club: the Survivors' Club. Mrs. Finch, me, whichever neighbors are left to peek through their window curtains. Membership comes with a measly government subsidy each month, not to mention a handful of MREs each week that taste like the foil they're wrapped in. Canned beans and rice that stare you down when you open the pantry, if you're lucky enough to have a pantry. Not to mention the dangerous gift of unlimited free time, even for someone like me whose chronic fatigue keeps them in bed half the day. Seven years after the transplant and I still need eleven hours of sleep, not to mention rest breaks throughout the day. As a chronically ill person, I thought I'd never see the day when the healthy people in my life were as limited as I am. Death has run its icy finger down our collective spine. No one here has been left untouched.

More than anything, membership in Survivors' Club requires adaptation. It's bending a knife into a makeshift screwdriver, then using that screwdriver to bolt your windows shut and pry open a three-year-old can of beans. You find yourself capable of doing things you never imagined.

DELIVERY DAY, I THINK for the hundredth time. Adrenaline jolts through my heart. I picture the package falling into Mrs. Finch's dropbox, the prescription bottle of little oval pills inside. She hasn't put down her knitting. She's so frail, her neck so thin you'd think it might snap.

I pull on some threadbare yoga pants and a T-shirt, then turn the TV to Fox News. I can only bear to watch for a few minutes, but I need to know what they're saying.

The news anchors have that trapped, panicked look. Just like the rest of us. Food may be scarce, but desperation is in abundance.

"Just the infirm and the elderly are dying," they told us in the beginning. *Just.* That's what everyone always says at first. As if us sick people were just hanging on to our mortality by a thread anyway, waiting for a good stiff breeze to knock us over the edge. As if this virus was doing society a favor by getting rid of us. Normal people everywhere sighed in relief and went back to their CrossFit and backyard barbeques and complaints about their nine-to-fives. And then it started picking them off like flies. Not just the grandmas and cancer patients. The man at the Indian takeout who knows your order and greets you by name. The PTA mom with all the cookies. Your wife. Your son.

"Cull the herd," Laura Ingram declares from the screen. She's referring to the pharmaceutical companies that have the audacity to keep producing non-*caelivirus* medicine. Her face is gaunt, her hair gray instead of bottle blonde. "It's for the greater good. Why waste resources on people who will die anyway?"

No one ever thinks they're the one getting culled. Watch the beginning coverage of the virus and yesterday's story back to back and you'd be shocked. But watch each video in the progression and it will start to feel almost rational.

PEOPLE UNDERESTIMATE THE HANGING-BY-A-THREAD crowd. We're the original Survivors' Club. The founding members. I've been sick long enough to know a life spent hanging by a thread just means I have a better grip.

Before and after my transplant, pumped full of anti-rejection drugs and immunosuppressants, I'd whiled away the months reading alone in my room. Away from the world and all its germs. I've been in quarantine long before most people, and I'll be here long after they're gone. Sick people won't straight up tell you, but I think most of us feel this way. Quarantine is the world as we're used to it. Everyone else is just visiting here. We've been down this road before, and damn if we don't know where all the potholes are.

"Those with respiratory issues won't survive this," a guest doctor on *Fox and Friends* said in the beginning.

I snorted. Like I haven't heard that one before.

IN RETROSPECT, I SHOULD have seen that letter coming from a mile away.

I plucked it out of the dropbox in my door two months ago.

The stylized letters "HC" inside of a heart stared back at me. My health insurance company's logo. I'd figured a thin envelope couldn't impart any life-changing information. Probably just a summary of benefits that month or a list of money spent on my medication.

Then I opened it.

The words jumped out at me. Like they wanted to leap off the page and strangle me themselves.

I sat there on my IKEA chair in my sun-soaked kitchen, the letter trembling in my hand. I stared at the wall. Painted yellow. An *HGTV Magazine* article at the beginning of quarantine had promised light colors would visually expand a room while creating the illusion of light.

HGTV lied. My apartment is five hundred square feet and no amount of lead-free specialty paint in *Here Comes the Sun* is going to change that.

I set the letter down on my red checkered tablecloth. I looked at the cracked blue teapot with the flowers on the side and thought, *So this is how it ends.*

I dislodged a dusty bottle of wine from the very back of the pantry. A cheap red, although it would go for much more now. I tilt my head back and let the liquid slide down my throat, barely tasting it. Three glasses in and that reliable tangle of neurons and synapses in my skull spit out some semblance of a plan, like it always does.

Then I drunk-dialed the insurance company.

I interrupted the automated system by repeating "Speak to a representative" over and over. An hour wait later and a cool female voice answered. I gave her my policy number, then asked about the letter. "There must be some mistake," I said with false confidence.

"There's no mistake. Your medication—pred...pred...

prednisone? And Cell...cept?"—she tripped over the names—
"are no longer approved for lung transplant patients. It's a new
government mandate. Drug companies are only offering *caelivirus* treatments now, unless you're over sixty-five."

"But I need them to survive," I said flatly.

"It's for the greater good." I heard the click of her pen over
the line.

"Yeah, here's the thing: I didn't sign up to be your
sacrificial lamb—"

"Sorry, we can't help you."

*The greater good! Can't you understand? The goddamn greater
good!*

"I'm a *lawyer*!" I yelled into the phone. *Click.*

I poured more wine to dampen this fresh wave of despair.
And despite my alcohol-induced blurred vision, I saw the
world more clearly than I ever had. I can stuff my kitchen to the
gills with food. I can sock away a nest egg that would birth an
ostrich. I can do everything not just right, but better than everyone else. But this is a game I was never meant to win.

One letter. Just one letter. That fortress I thought I'd built?
It's nothing but a straw house.

THE DRONE DELIVERY TO Mrs. Finch's house shakes me out of my
funk. It had been at least a month since I last heard from her.
She hadn't answered or returned my last few calls. I watched,
transfixed, as a nondescript white box tumbled into the
dropbox affixed to her window. I stared at that box for a long
time that day.

I set aside the mug of hot water I was pretending was coffee.
Then I shake my head as if to permanently dislodge the memory of that phone call.

In preparation for deliveries, the Sanitrucks were all over

the city this morning, spraying foamy white disinfectant over the buildings. The repurposed fire trucks hit the tallest buildings, like the ones in midtown Manhattan. For the rest of the day, clusters of white bubbles dripped onto the street, as if the entire city were really just toys in a giant baby's bubble bath.

My stomach clenches. Soon the drones will start buzzing by. That little box will land in Mrs. Finch's dropbox.

After Mrs. Finch's husband died of cancer ten years ago, she told me the pharmacy continued sending his immunosuppressant for nearly a year. CellCept—the same one I'm on, which my insurance company also canceled. Because Mrs. Finch couldn't bear to call and cancel, she just stacked them in the medicine cabinet. As if she'd wake up tomorrow and Mr. Finch would be sitting at the kitchen table, wanting a cup of black coffee to wash those pills down.

I know they're still there. Expired, but in all likelihood still effective. Certainly better than nothing. Mrs. Finch isn't the type to throw things out.

MRE deliveries from the government bring out the looters. The looters look ridiculous in their homemade hazmat suits, but that doesn't mean you shouldn't fear them. Garbage bags duct taped to their bodies. Goggles and scuba masks over their faces. I once saw a guy with a fishbowl over his head—no joke. The criminals of the past dressed in black, slunk out under the cover of night, fitted their gun barrels with silencers. It makes you wonder how Hollywood will cast bad guys in the future.

If there is a future.

I open my closet and push through shirts and old dresses until my hand touches the plastic of the hazmat suit my friend wore to visit me in the hospital when he came to visit after my transplant. He'd wanted to throw it away, but I kept it instead. "It's bad luck," I said. Every sick person knows as soon as you throw away your hospital gown or comfy socks, you're going to need them again.

I pull the hazmat suit on over my clothes. My hands shake. Nothing good could come of this. Everything could come of this.

I'VE ALWAYS BEEN GOOD at remembering statistics. Fifty percent of patients will survive five to ten years after a lung transplant. In every ten meters of air, there are approximately twenty *caelivirus* particles. In the twelve hours after the Sanitrucks make their rounds, this number decreases to two—meaning the odds of infection from opening a window briefly hover just around six percent. Six percent is not zero, but I'll take my chances.

I'M STANDING NEAR THE fire escape, window still closed, when the flashback slams into me. I double over, gasping for breath. Because this isn't the first time I've made the trip over to Mrs. Finch's.

Delivery day, last month. I'd climbed down the fire escape with trembling fingers. No front doors for me, with their ID scanners, armed guards, and series of airlock doors. The cool breeze had enveloped me, dangerous yet somehow comforting—a reminder of walks in the park and car rides with the window open. Mrs. Finch's fire escape creaked as I climbed it. A few minutes at her window with my screwdriver and I slip in, shutting the window quickly behind me in one fluid motion.

My heart pounded. I didn't bother to call out Mrs. Finch's name. Over the past six weeks, I'd watched her prized African violets wither into nothingness, her curtains hang still. Phone calls went straight to a full voicemail box. I'd never seen a dead body before. I think that scared me even more than the virus.

I pulled Mrs. Finch's curtains closed, then flipped on the light switch. Dirty dishes piled in the sink, the food petrified and rancid. A single teacup sat on the counter, a fly floating in the film that had formed over the top.

I was near the bathroom when I heard it. A whisper. Weak, barely audible, but unmistakable. I tiptoed back to the bedroom and opened the door.

A wave of musty air hit me. Even through the hazmat suit, the room reeked of mildew and urine. A lump under the blankets moved. I turned on the lamp on the bedside table. Mrs. Finch's hand was soft and dry. A wave of something like warmth crashed over me. Grief and longing with an undercurrent of joy, oddly enough. It was intense, so intense my eyes burned, and I've never been a crier. That's when I realized: I hadn't physically touched another person in over four years. Not a single soul.

I don't know how long I sat there, holding her hand and speaking in soft tones to her. Then I filled a bucket with warm water and soap. I washed her hair with shampoo, then peeled off her sweat-soaked nightgown. Mrs. Finch whimpered in pain, even though I was gentle. But because I'd always known Mrs. Finch to be someone who needs things to be clean, I kept going. Sure enough, she thanked me in the end with a voice that sounded like dead leaves on the sidewalk.

Even in her state, she knew exactly why I was there.

"The medicine cabinet," she whispered, even though I didn't ask. As if she wasn't the type to wash her dishes every night and fold her underwear into perfect little squares. A place for everything and everything in its place.

Eighty-nine but still sharp as a tack. This awareness pierced my heart like a needle. No mind-numbing drugs or dementia to guard Mrs. Finch from the truth. She knew she was almost gone.

"Monday," she whispered. "Once a month. The armchair. By the window. Leave me here. Buy yourself some time."

And that's when the fantasy started. I could hoist her onto my back and carry her to my place. Climb the fire escape with her. Feed her chicken broth and nurse her back to health. Or maybe I could move in with her. Pack up my laptop and some clothes, and the few MREs left in the pantry. Words spilled out of my mouth like water from a dam.

A ghost of a smile crossed Mrs. Finch's lips. I had to lean in to hear her. "That's nice, dear."

Her words sent reality crashing back like a piano dropped on my head. Even in her frail state, she was too heavy. We'd never make it across the alley and up the stairs. I could barely make it alone.

And if the authorities found out I was living in an apartment that wasn't mine and figured me for a looter? I shuddered.

I carried her to the armchair facing the window. I spread a blanket over her lap, along with a half-knitted scarf, knitting needles still attached. I watered her African violets, knowing no amount of love could save them. Then I sat beside Mrs. Finch. I held her hand through the night. Screw the looters. When her breath became shallow and her pulse faint, I stood. As the sun started to rise, I washed her dishes and wiped her counters. I stuffed the contents of the medicine cabinet into my backpack. I brushed the hair away from her face, swallowing the lump in my throat.

Tears burned my eyes as I zipped up my hazmat. I sobbed the whole trip down the fire escape, across the street, up my fire escape. I repeated the words over and over like a mantra to beat the weakness out of myself. *Don't touch your eyes. Don't you touch your eyes. Don't you dare touch your eyes.*

I stood by my window a long time as the sun rose. Chest

heaving, lungs burning. I didn't care if I looked like a target, like some poor sap who's finally cracked. Just before I turned to head to bed, Mrs. Finch lifted a frail hand as if in greeting. She propped it up against the back of the chair. That hand was still there in the morning. That's how I knew she was really gone.

I WAIT FOR MY hands to stop shaking. Then I swallow the rest of the water in my coffee mug, even though it's cold now. I look out at Mrs. Finch as the sun dips below the horizon, sucking the light from the sky. I pull the hood over my hazmat suit.

I think of the years leading up to my lung transplant. "Fighters keep swinging. Steppers keep stepping," my favorite nurse used to say as I lay in my hospital bed, my skin tinged blue from lack of oxygen. The first time she said it, I'd tried not to laugh. I couldn't even take one step. But over time, the words sunk in. They became the rhythm I moved through life to, the armor that grew around me like a second skin. Sometimes you can be so focused on your next step that that's all you know how to do anymore, and then you walk right past the reason you're stepping in the first place.

People still exist in the world who will reach out to catch others without ever thinking of the germs their extended hand might touch. I can be the strongest of the strong, tougher than tough, and still need other humans. We can build up tolerance to depravity, to scarcity, to cruelty, but all it takes is a second of kindness to bring us to our knees.

The sun is gone, leaving nothing but darkness pierced by neon lights. Mrs. Finch's key burns in my pocket. I spray the air inside with bleach as a precaution, then square my shoulders before resting a hand on the window latch. Chin up. Hands steady. Don't look down.

Which Doctor

Lane Chasek

"I DON'T THINK IT'S anything to be ashamed of," said Susan. She slid across the concrete bench and leaned in closer to Claire, so close that Claire could smell the artificial lilac of her lotion, the coffee from their breakfast that morning. Combined with the chlorine stench of the fountain in front of Federal Bank & Trust, Claire found Susan's presence nauseating.

"It can't be easy for your husband," said Claire. "Tom wouldn't be able to live with himself if his wife was...you know."

"A sicko?"

Claire was surprised at how easily Susan said the word. "Exactly. That doesn't bother you? Being sick like this?"

"I'm sick, but I get treatment." Susan pointed down at Claire's ankle. "A physiologist could help with that ankle. Give you a few pills, maybe snap it back into place."

"Snap? Snap out of what?"

Susan laughed. "*Physical* snapping, not mental snapping. You should read up on it, it's a fascinating field."

A conversation like this wasn't decent. At least, not publicly decent. The people eating macarons in front of the bakery across the street, the men unloading beer and liquor into the back of the Polish restaurant, the pedestrians streaming past their bench—there were so many potential eavesdroppers.

"It's pseudoscience, Susan."

"No, it's real science. It's an emerging field, is all."

"No, therapy is science. It was science to the ancient Greeks, the Romans, the Victorians. Physiology is a bunch of hippies and beatniks in drum circles," Claire declared.

A boy ran through the jets of water that shot out of the fountain's shallow basin, soaking himself, smiling triumphantly at no one, for no one. From the other end of the block, his mother screamed at him. The boy ignored her.

"They have physiologists who specialize in kids, too, you know," Susan said.

Claire couldn't believe this. What kind of parent would do that to their own child? She couldn't think of anything crueler than thinking your own child was a sicko and forcing them to see some quack who would prod and poke their tender body. The labeling, the diagnosing, the alien nature of it all.

Claire's ankle throbbed. She winced. The pain was a relentless reminder. Whether she wanted to admit it or not, she knew normal doctors were never going to help her with a problem like this, a problem that was more physical than mental. Maybe it wasn't stress- or trauma-related in any way. Maybe she really *was* a sicko.

"I think I might be a sicko," Claire whispered, feeling the weight of the word in her mouth.

"You don't have to whisper. Remember, if you're a sicko, then I'm a sicko, too."

"You talk about it like it's no big deal."

"It really isn't," Susan said. "People have been getting sick since forever, don't you know? We're just getting better at seeing who's sick. In fact, my physiologist tells me everybody's a little bit sick. Sometimes it's the joints, the lungs, a weak heart."

Claire shook her head. "I doubt that. Look, don't take this the wrong way, but if I weren't desperate, I wouldn't even be asking you about this. Do you know a physiologist I could see for my ankle?"

Susan pulled a tattered receipt and pen from her purse. She wrote something on the back of it, folded it over, and handed it to Claire. "This guy's good. Especially for first-timers," she said.

Tom, Claire's husband, told her the pain in her ankle was nothing to worry about.

"But what if it's something serious?" Claire asked.

Tom smirked at her. "Do you want me to take you to a *physiologist*? Are you getting sicko on me?"

Claire sighed, defeated. "No."

She sat at the foot of the bed, rubbing her swollen ankle. The past two years hadn't been easy on either of them. Tom's boss had threatened to fire him because his family's history of anxiety disorders was considered an "unacceptable risk factor," and the factory's insurance provider had chosen to cancel his coverage. Tom quit soon after, searching for a job that would actually provide the health insurance he, his wife, and their two teenaged sons, Montague and Vincent, would need.

"Did you talk to Dr. Zweikler about it?" Tom asked.

Claire winced. The flesh of her ankle was pink and puffy. She'd taken to rubbing it after every other treatment available had failed. Therapy sessions hadn't worked, ambient noise and meditation seminars had done nothing, and—most recently— aura-channeling had been a complete failure.

"You know I didn't talk to Dr. Zweikler," Claire said. "We can't afford any more doctor's visits. Not right now, anyway."

Tom stood in front of the mirror, carefully weaving his tie into a half-Windsor. Today marked yet another twelve-hour round of job interviews followed by an evening of waiting for callbacks that never came. His large belly strained against his white button-up shirt. It had been growing larger throughout the fifteen years of their marriage. Tom's weight had been a problem ever since he started work at the Pastrel factory, loading crates of air filters onto truckbeds for so long that when he would arrive home at six thirty, his back and knees burned with pain. Dr. Zweikler hypothesized that Tom's excess weight was his unconscious way of coping with his father abandoning him. Tom's father had left him and his mother when he was only three. The theory averred Tom's weight was the result of him unconsciously trying to assume a more feminine appearance as a way to oppose the masculinity represented by his absent father. To lose the weight, Zweikler said, Tom would first have to resolve the resentment he felt toward his father and father figures in general. Only then would the weight go away; only then would the pain cease.

"Will you be back before dinner this time?" Claire asked.

"I wouldn't count on it," he said. He didn't look back at her in the mirror. He threw on his suit jacket and exited the room, head down, ready to hole himself up in the web café until one in the morning. Maybe tonight would be the night he finally found a job offer in his inbox, but Claire knew better than to be too hopeful.

So THIS WAS A free clinic, Claire thought. She'd sat in the waiting room for hours, surrounded by young mothers with toddlers in their laps who needed a routine psychoanalysis, as well as young men with bullet and knife wounds who needed to talk about their aggressive tendencies before they inevitably bled to death. When she was called into Dr. Hansen's office, she was shocked by how young and handsome the recent med-school grad was.

"Tell me about your father," Dr. Hansen said.

Claire sat on a couch while Dr. Hansen sat on a leather sofa opposite her, scribbling notes and eyeing her from time to time. She wondered if Hansen knew Zweikler, and whether Zweikler would feel betrayed that she was seeing the young (and more affordable) Dr. Hansen. Psychologists, after all, were a tight-knit professional group. If a long-time patient defected to another practitioner, they were bound to speculate with one another, trying to determine who was broken, who was to blame: the doctor, the patient, the system.

"I haven't been able to really think about my father lately," Claire said. She tried to lie on the couch comfortably but couldn't. Her left shoulder began to ache, and her left ear began ringing.

"You don't think about your father?" Dr. Hansen sounded surprised. "What about your mother?"

"Could we please talk about my ankle?"

"We will." Dr. Hansen wrote something. He looked at her nervously. "When did you first learn to walk again?"

"I don't know. A year old? Around the same time as everyone else, I guess."

"Alright. And how long did it take you to become potty-trained?"

"Can we skip this?"

"Certainly." The doctor tore a page from his legal pad and threw it into the wastebasket beside his chair. His youth and inexperience were showing, despite the care he'd taken in grooming himself to look like a seasoned hotshot analyst. It was obvious he hadn't mastered regression or even the pensive tilt of his head he was supposed to give while asking obvious questions. He lacked a receding hairline also, Claire realized. In order to make up for this deficiency he'd slicked back his bangs and glued them to his scalp with copious amounts of hair gel in an attempt to make himself look older, more haggard and world-weary.

He drummed his fingers against his legal pad and asked, "Mind if we talk about what you do around the house? Do you feel complete as a homemaker?"

Claire had never given it any thought. She supposed she was happy enough being a mother, the one who cooked, cleaned, etc. As far as she could tell, the way she thought or felt had nothing to do with pain. At least, not her kind of pain.

"As complete as I can be," Claire said.

Dr. Hansen tapped his lower lip with his pinky, lowered his eyelids as he studied Claire. Though she knew it wasn't the proper thing to do, Claire always wanted to tell doctors what she thought they wanted to hear rather than what she wanted to say.

"My husband got laid off, but it doesn't bother me," Claire added. She would have said something about her ankle, but Dr. Hansen wouldn't want to hear that. Doctors couldn't treat bodily problems. Bodily problems were meant to be dealt with alone, while lying in bed, about to fall asleep, listening to the steady pulse of blood in your own ears.

Dr. Hansen continued studying Claire with narrowed eyes, either deep in thought or bored with hearing about her life. "We can move on if you'd like," Dr. Hansen said. He capped the pen he was writing with and produced a red crayon from his breast pocket. Bringing his face closer to his legal pad, he proceeded with a new slew of questions. Claire had no choice but to endure them, along with her ankle and shoulder and the ringing in her ear.

THE PAIN IN CLAIRE'S ankle increased as the days wore on. It hurt to walk, and unless she was leaning against a wall or chair, it felt as if her ankle would snap in two from her weight. She called Susan out of desperation, in search of an answer. Claire had to call that physician Susan recommended, but calling that doctor (if you could even call him a doctor) seemed like too great a leap. As soon as she called the physician, she'd be a sicko for life. Suffering silently was easier, and if she needed someone to talk to, she could always call on Susan.

The fountains were only a short walk away from Claire's apartment, about twenty minutes. It took longer for Susan (around forty minutes), but Claire enjoyed being able to have a bench to herself while she waited. It was a Tuesday afternoon, moderately sunny, not too hot. The only people out were mothers with small children who constantly ran through the streams that shot out of the brass grates in the fountain. The burst of each jet of water, the white spray it emitted, its rapid yet graceful arc as it made its way back to the fountain's algae-encrusted basin—all that motion and color helped divert her attention away from her ankle, which was now throbbing, swollen to the diameter of a grapefruit.

When Susan arrived and sat next to Claire, she wore black heels and a sun hat. She breathed heavily, wheezed, coughed violently. Her face was the color of a red plum.

"Sorry I kept you waiting," she said.

"It's no problem," Claire said. Susan was always apologizing for being late. That was something else that turned Tom and Claire's children off of Susan. Tom always said you couldn't trust people who apologize too much. Something gnawed at their conscience, he believed, some emotional wound left by a parent or child, something hurtful and secretive that needed uncovering.

Fan in hand, Susan hid her face behind it as she coughed again. Mothers turned to stare and directed their children away from the bench and the fountain, as if Susan's physical illness were obscene. Susan didn't seem to notice. And if she did, she didn't care.

Susan placed her purse in her lap and unclasped it. She produced an orange bottle of pills, emptied three small purple capsules into her palm, and swallowed them dry. Claire blushed, burning beneath the eyes of the people around her. The city was watching.

Susan's voice was strained and husky when she said, pointing down at Claire's ankle, "It's gotten worse." Claire nodded. Susan shook her head and asked, "Remember Jared Mathers?"

"That senator from Idaho?"

"That's the one."

Claire remembered. The Idaho gubernatorial race of 1994, Jared Mathers (R) versus Alex Corinth (D). Mathers boasted about his military service, Corinth reminded Idahoans of his years of service in the House of Representatives. According to both candidates' smear campaigns, Mathers and Corinth were both adulterers and neurotics, men with unsublimated Oedipal tendencies which would make both of them terrible governors. Typical rhetoric for a gubernatorial race. Most people in America (especially people who lived outside of Idaho) wouldn't have cared about this race if it hadn't been for the scandal that ensued. Mathers, it turned out, paid regular visits to a physiologist in Boise.

Up until this shameful discovery, it had been no secret that

Mathers was receiving treatment from injuries he'd received in the Vietnam War. As far as most Idahoans knew, Mathers received treatments for PTSD and general wartime trauma (as well as unsublimated Oedipal tendencies, but every politician gets treated for that eventually), but Corinth and his team of mudslingers revealed that the valiant, patriotic Vietnam vet had to have shrapnel removed from his back.

"We can't have a sicko in the capitol," Idaho (and America as a whole) declared. And that was the end of Mathers's dream of the governorship. Corinth, a Democrat (and a Jungian, no less), won in a landslide.

"I don't want to be a sicko," Claire said, practically in tears. "You know how people are."

Susan stroked Claire's back, played with a lock of hair near her friend's left ear. With Susan so near, Claire found herself wondering what Susan's relationship with her mother had looked like. She hated herself for thinking about something so crass, so vulgar, but she couldn't help it.

"Mathers is still alive," Susan said. She coughed, spat something on the sidewalk. "In fact, he's still a senator."

"Yes, the sicko senator."

"You know that number I gave you? That's Mathers's physician. And he's my physician, too. In fact, he gave me these." She rattled the orange bottle of pills in Claire's face.

"Dear god," Claire said.

"If he can pull shrapnel from a senator's back, he can help you," Susan said.

"Please, not so loud."

"Trust me, he's amazing. You'll think he's unhinged, but he's really a genius."

"I'm still not sure."

"You want the pain to go away, don't you?"

Claire nodded.

"All you need to do is call him," Susan said.

SHE GAVE IN AND called the physiologist. The next day, she saw a physiologist and his office for the first time.

The body-length coat he wore was as white and stainless as the rest of his office. A thin tube of black rubber with pieces of galvanized metal on either end hung around his neck. Rubber and metal seemed to dominate the office, except for the Packers poster that hung on the door. Rubber straps, small rubber hammers, and small metal picks and rods with black rubber handles hung from the walls like an antiseptic arsenal. The smell of old paper, coffee, and potpourri which she associated with doctors' offices was absent, replaced with an acidic, soapy smell.

She limped into the office and Dr. Wyatt immediately took hold of her arm.

"Here, try to stay off that foot," he said. Claire hopped on her good foot as Dr. Wyatt guided her to a piece of furniture that looked like a couch from a regular doctor's office, only different. It wasn't cushioned and inviting, and it was taller than she was used to. Instead of corduroy or plush, it was covered with orange, leathery fabric, with a long sheet of thin white paper draped over it. Dr. Wyatt helped her sit on it. The paper crinkled loudly beneath her.

Cradling his chin, Dr. Wyatt clucked his tongue and looked at Claire's ankle. He took a seat on a vinyl chair and lifted her foot carefully onto his knee. She was surprised to see that he wore blue jeans beneath his lab coat. He turned her foot slowly while making casual conversation with her.

"So you're a friend of Susan's?" he asked.

"I am. She said you could help me with my...condition."

"I wouldn't call this a condition. Just a minor injury. How long has your ankle been giving you problems?"

"A few weeks. It hurts to walk. It *really* hurts."

Dr. Wyatt hummed a march (or was it just the fighting song of the Green Bay Packers?) to himself and tapped his foot. He seemed to be thinking something over.

"Is this your first visit to a physiologist?"

"It is. Honestly, I never considered myself the sicko type."

Dr. Wyatt smiled at her, then narrowed his eyes.

"Sicko?"

"You know what I mean," Claire said.

"Yes, I know. It's just funny hearing new patients say it. Did you know 'sicko' isn't even a clinical term?"

Claire shook her head.

"Hold on a second. Does this hurt?" He pressed a finger against the ball of her foot. She shook her head. He continued prodding the rest of her foot, working his way closer and closer to the swelling. The closer he got, the more intense the pain.

Dr. Wyatt lowered her foot and opened a nearby cabinet. "It isn't a joint problem, that's for sure." He took a brown plastic bottle from the cabinet. Lifting her foot again, he uncapped the bottle and poured a cold, blue gel on her ankle. It stung at first, but then Dr. Wyatt began massaging the gel into her skin, chilling it and dispelling the pain, as if the pain had been a burning wick that Dr. Wyatt had easily blown out. She let out a sigh of relief and breathed deeply. She leaned forward to get a better look at her ankle. Dr. Wyatt's thumbs moved in circles over her skin. The blue gel soaked into her pores, leaving behind a shiny, oily layer where the swelling used to be.

He handed her an orange bottle of small capsules. They looked like breath mints.

"For the pain," Dr. Wyatt said. "One after breakfast, one after dinner."

Claire didn't know what to say other than "thank you."

She walked out of Dr. Wyatt's office, still limping but less noticeably than before. Just as she was about to leave, she remembered the issue of billing. She turned around and asked, "How much?"

Dr. Wyatt sat on a chair, leafing through a faded magazine with half-naked models on the cover. He smiled at her and shook his head. "No charge for the first visit," he said. "Just focus on getting better and see me next week, same time. We'll work things out from there. Sound good?"

Claire nodded.

"Good," Dr. Wyatt said. He smiled, revealing a row of yellowed teeth which, while not beautiful, were more comforting than any bleached psychoanalyst's smile she'd ever seen.

It was either Aristotle or Hippocrates who'd first proposed the concepts of the id, ego, and superego. Claire couldn't remember who exactly, but it was someone like that, one of those ancient Greeks. After that, the march of science and progress had produced psychoanalysis, marriage counseling, desensitization therapy, group therapy, logos therapy, forced encounter, etc. Before meeting Dr. Wyatt, it had all seemed so complete, so sufficient. If you felt bad, you scheduled a therapy session, talked about your life and your problems. People had been doing it for millennia.

But as soon as Freud began suggesting physical treatments for people's problems, like water submersion, electroshock therapy, medication—that's when things got confusing. These physician types claimed people could be "sick," with things called "glands" that didn't work properly, and muscles that needed to be rested and massaged. Claire had even heard rumors of new-age physicians called surgeons who cut people open and moved their internal organs around. She could barely stand to imagine it, but she supposed some people were desperate enough to try anything.

When she found Tom the following afternoon on the floor of their bedroom, hands clawing the carpet fibers, debilitated by pain, she didn't try to comfort him, didn't attempt an analysis or regression. Instead, she knelt by her husband, told him she knew someone, someone who could help.

"You'll think I'm crazy," she said, "but you need to trust me. It's nothing to be ashamed of."

Brainstorm

Travis Flatt

TRUE TO HIS NICKNAME, the Lightning Doc bursts like an Olympian thunderbolt into our hall. He swaggers, hips out, wearing an ugly cartoon grin across his ferret face. It's two in the morning, but his voice rings thunderous: "Is room 701 empty?"

The night nurses scatter to prepare the room. Many of these nurses are young. They're the earth supporting the tree. It's a shit shift. John, tonight's head nurse—a Caribbean man with bass-string thick nerves who sashays when walking like a sea elemental—disappears to conjure a custodian from a hidey-hole broom closet. He sends this mop-brandishing Viking forth, eyes bloodshot and weed-reeking. You've got half of the nurses and techs cringing at the Lightning Doc up here while this guy's off toking and exhaling into a vent somewhere. Small wonders.

Whenever the Lightning Doc deigns to appear on the Epilepsy Monitoring Unit, his presence is a tempest, and his word a tsunami. Now these dreary and dingy halls, which nightly sink into a sour stickiness of tepid tedium, energize. Like all night-shifters, these nurses are hour-watchers. Yet life on the EMU must be conductive, ready to ride the voltage of the self-electrocuting patients and their volatile overlord. A constant chorus of sobbing from the miserable, baffled postictal becomes background static ignored for sanity's sake.

A patient on this floor is allowed only one guest. Abandon all hope ye who checks in without family. The grown beg for their mothers like toddlers until they're finally tranquilized.

Until a moment ago, I was flirting with some new nurses. Now I dash back into the technician's booth. Who's coming to fill room 701? What's got the Lightning Doc so amped up? The mayor's been breathing down our neck. We need to cook. Nashville's thirsty for juice.

I scan the readout, papers newly processed downstairs in Admissions zipping through the hospital's system with a few clicks. Welcome, Amy Harmon, age eighteen, from Lebanon, our sister city down the interstate.

I glance at my hallway camera monitor and watch as she's rolled off the elevator, sitting serenely in her wheelchair, pushed by an admittance worker named Carla, a mid-fifties bruiser who reeks of cigarette smoke. You can smell Carla's smoke-ghost in an elevator car for hours. The kid, Amy, looks saintly, biblical. Her chestnut hair drapes in waves, curtaining her serene and downcast face. Even dispirited, her stunning, television-good looks shout both "class president" and "soccer captain." She's a marvel of symmetry. But then, prowling at the edges of her beauty, I see it: the fade.

The fade hasn't yet begun to creep in. It prowls around the campfire of her youthful glow. My myriad tech booth screens are color. Her gown is green, her skin is tanned, her hair sun-blond, her eyes tigereye brown-orange. After the Lightning

Doc orders we rip away her medications, she'll start to look as though she's broadcasted in black and white, sallow, shadowed, and scalded.

"Juan, reroute the system to downtown!"

The Lightning Doc has poked his head in the booth. I was too mesmerized watching them wheel in this doomed angel to notice the greasy little man slip into my booth.

"Juan? Juan!"

"Alright!" I begin yanking cords, flipping switches, and pushing levers. I feel the heat of his annoyance at my impudent answer. "Yessir."

He reads from a clipboard. "The girl has tonic-clonic, focal seizure. Adult-onset. They began this year."

So, in other words, big, bad boys that spread through her brain. The kid was probably in high school if they started this time of year. I tuck my chin and cross myself while the Lightning Doc smiles at his clipboard as if he's reading an extravagant menu. He's pleased by today's special.

I've switched around the cords—thick, ropey veins like guitar chords—on the booth's long, complex board. The board looks like a recording studio. It's all very Nashville. Everything's rerouted from the settings labeled "Brentwood" and "Old Hickory," channeled toward downtown.

I watch Head Nurse John help the kid up and onto her bed. She doesn't have a guest and is facing this alone.

"Go wire her up," the Lightning Doc says. I pick up my bag and head for my cart.

"Hello—I'm Juan," I say, rolling my cart into room 701. Amy Harmon returns my smile. She looks cold, shivering in her hospital gown. "I'm a tech on the floor."

She nods.

"This will only take a second; you're going to need to sit sideways on your bed. We can get you a heated blanket," I say.

She shakes her head. I've rolled the cart into the narrow space between the wall and her bed. The patient rooms are small, but at least they have their own bathroom. The technicians can watch the patients from ceiling-mounted cameras. Everything is recorded at all times.

"You've got a lot of hair," I say. I take out my rag and bottle of glue. I'm about to glue twenty EEG pads to this kid's scalp. If her family had read the paperwork, they'd have known we recommend buzzing off your hair before admittance. Patients and their families rarely read the whole brochure.

I put on latex gloves. "This part's a little rough, but it'll be quick. So, are you in school?"

I tend to chatter as I work.

She says she's going to UT Knoxville for a communications major. Her voice is soft; she sounds tired. First, I have to rub her scalp with a rag dipped in antiseptic. We're taught to do this hard, and the skin often turns pink. Amy tries to hide her wincing. Next, I squirt on dabs of glue—it has an acrid chemical smell like nail polish remover—and press on the EEG pads. To each pad is attached a wire. When I'm finished, Amy's become a Lisa Frank cyborg gorgon with a rainbow of wires snaking off her head. I'm glad the poor kid can't see herself. I make a pony tail of those with zip ties and they all run into a little black box. The box goes in a purse that lives on the patient's bed. They carry that purse if they stand up for the bathroom.

I flip on her room's EEG monitor. Amy is sitting slumped slightly forward, asleep. "Hey, Amy? Check this out."

She snaps to. I ask her to say, "A flea and a fly in a floo were stuck, so what could they do?"

She chuckles. "What?"

I repeat, slowly. "Say that and watch the screen." I point to her EEG monitor, which hangs in the corner of her room. A dozen wavy lines run across the screen. Back in the tech booth, I have more—one for each pad.

She tries to say the tongue-twister, drowsy. When she talks, a few lines grow rough and spiky.

"Cool, huh?" I say.

"Those are different parts of my brain?"

"Yeah. Tomorrow we'll show you what corresponds to what."

She yawns and says, "But you have to go to school to understand how it works." She starts to lay down, and I begin rolling the cart toward the door. I want to give the kid space.

"You want the light off?"

"Please. Are you a doctor?"

"No. I... I'm a tech—"

From the door of the darkened room, I can tell she's fallen asleep. I roll the cart out quietly. In the morning, when I take Mom to mass, I'll pray for this girl.

My Sunday shift starts at six p.m. I arrive fifteen minutes early. In the nurse station, John is eating something that smells loudly unpleasant from a Tupperware dish. Linda, the day-shift tech, who always sticks around to flirt with John, pokes at John's dinner with a plastic fork. She chews and wrinkles her nose simultaneously. They laugh.

The same nurses as yesterday are clocking in. They already look tired. As I pass between rooms 701 and 702, the blue siren goes off outside 701—Amy's room—and the two of the new nurses, looking nervous, dash in. Linda goes to the elevator and repeatedly hits the down button. From the nurse station, John shouts to me: "Go an' help them, Juan."

I've never seen anything like it. I recall those old illustrations of lockjaw patients. Amy's back is completely arched, and she's bent like a bow in the bed to the point where only her head and feet are touching the mattress. She's wet her gown, her lips are pulled back like a horse, and she's gritting her white teeth as if to shatter. The protocol is to ask the seizure patient questions and have them describe what they're feeling. That's if they can respond. This is all being recorded, video and audio. One of the two nurses—she's hardly older than Amy—bursts into tears. The other nurse thought to grab a syringe of valium at least, and she attempts to plug it into Amy's IV. She fumbles the syringe. It rolls under the bed. Amy is growing tauter and tauter; the lines on her EEG monitor aren't waves, they're chaos without space between the spikes, just blackness on screen.

Downtown, lightbulbs must be shattering.

Sliding between our useless bodies, John appears with a fresh syringe. When he pumps valium into the IV, Amy slumps in her bed, awake but stunned and gently crying. She apologizes for urinating on the sheets. Depending on how you approach them—it's best to give them space—postictal patients are either combative or apologetic. They're always confused.

I slip out of the room; I need to get to the tech booth.

Inside the booth, it smells like smoke. Tiny wisps rise off the board.

I start to grab a fire extinguisher, but remember the Lighting Doc, think of his ire, his hurling thunderbolts. I check the breakers. Some are shot.

The Lightning Doc bursts into the tech booth. "What the fuck is going on? The mayor just called. He said the Batman Building just caught on fire. There are trucks all over downtown!"

"701," I say.

He waves his bony hand in front of his weaselly face. "It smells like shit in here, Juan." He steps to the board and reads the EEG playback. "This was 701? Just now?"

"It almost killed her."

He just shrugs and starts making notes on his clipboard.

"I said it almost killed her, Dr. Ledbetter."

No one calls him "Lightning Doc" to his face. Ironically, he earned the nickname by being struck by lightning while jogging in Centennial Park. I don't know if it had anything to do with this place, but it makes me wonder. I get nervous when I hear thunder. I'm nervous around my appliances. I'd go to a therapist if I was allowed, if it wasn't for all of those nondisclosure agreements I signed.

One watches their tongue outside of the Lightning Doc's dominion. One doesn't speak of the thirst. My mother's stopped asking why my hands shake.

"We'll consider putting her back on Keppra," he says. He gives me a look of disgust and goes back to making notes. We're the same height, short men. There's a permanent blackhead in the middle of his pale forehead, like a bindi. He points the clipboard at me. "I'm calling Linda. She's in charge of 701 now. We probably overheated all the hospital's batteries. And the city's, too." He storms out of the booth, muttering, "God forbid we burn down the goddamn Batman Building."

I QUIT THE NEXT day. I moved out of my mom's house and found a cheap place in Cumberland Gardens.

After living for three years cringing at the sound of ambulance sirens and once breaking into a cold sweat when I saw EMTs flood my apartment complex to attend to some neighbor's disaster, I finally began to ease up.

I found pills that helped me sleep better. Mom and I kept going to mass, and I always prayed for Amy Harmon.

Four hours ago, I friend-requested Amy Harmon on Facebook. I must have lost my mind. Just now, she accepted. You know how when you accept a friend request on Facebook, it sends an automatic "Hello!" message in the Messenger app? Attached to her hello is an actual message she wrote. Amy says she's in college but having trouble with her memory. For some reason, she thanks me. She says she remembers me being kind and helping her?

I just left her there.

Three years of living like this, three years of doing community service, three years of going to church two or three times a week, spending thousands of dollars on therapy: none of it helped. I just left Amy Harmon there, and now she's thanking me.

Someone just knocked on my door. I consider turning the lights off, and then I realize that's silly. I can tell whoever it is is still outside, so I open the door. Standing in the hall is the Lightning Doc, grinning that hideous grin. Amy Harmon accepted my friend request seven minutes ago, and here he is, in a flash—the Lightning Doc.

"Juan, we need to talk."

Epilepsy Monitoring Units serve multiple purposes. The most common is to develop a new treatment plan for the patient. This is the case for epilepsy patients who aren't responding well to their medications or surgery.

What the EEGs are designed to accomplish is to locate a seizure focus. The EEG pads are a nonintrusive way of finding exactly where the seizures are coming from within the brain—that's called the focus. Unfortunately, it's not always one hundred percent effective. A brain is a complex machine. We don't fully understand it and possibly never will.

But we're talking most Epilepsy Monitoring Units, of course. This one operates for a different purpose. I'm not sure when the deal was made—the deal with the city, I mean. I imagine it was sometime shortly after the Lightning Doc invented the technology. He calls it "The Harness."

Seizures can be triggered in non-epileptics with electric shock therapy. And sleep deprivation. Most people know that.

EVERYONE ON STAFF PRETENDS not to recognize me—they have more sense than I did. I know them. I'm certain I know some of them. There's a black guy named John with a funny accent. I think we were friends before I got sick. My room is 701. My mom tells me that when she visits. She reminds me of my room number all the time as if I'm going to wander out and get lost.

Mom stays with me on Sundays.

"Juan, you're in 701," she says every Sunday when she leaves to go to mass.

Spore, Bud, Bloody Orchid

Jaye Viner

THE TORSO LOOKED LIKE a child's toy; it belonged to him in a way that I didn't any longer. The eggshell-white cavity wasn't any living person's skin tone, but it was packed full of brightly colored plastic organs he had often pulled out and used to illustrate the progress of my cancer. A blue liver, a red stomach, yellow intestines. These were the milestones that had built us, his guidance and my obedience, desperate for the survival he promised.

This doctor, *my* doctor, in his sterile coat, large warm hands fingering those organs as they'd fingered mine on the operating table—cutting in, extracting, rearranging—had delivered survival. He put all my organs back into the torso, minus tumors, a miraculous recovery. I shouldn't have needed to see him again.

"Nice to see you," he said. But not my name. He didn't include my name. Only four weeks cancer-free after years of treatment and he didn't know my name. I began to pull the toy organs out of the torso as I struggled to voice my problem.

"Are you sure you got it all?" I asked.

"We did." A sly smile of self-congratulation. He was oh so good at his job.

"But it can come back without notice, right? Gone one day, back the next?"

He blinked, a brief glitch in the polite doctor façade. I saw him do it before he actually did it, because part of me knew I was being unreasonable. "Transitioning back to regular life can be difficult," he said. "But I promise you're the healthiest you've ever been. Clean tests three times now." A false cheer. He did everything but check his watch.

"I feel there's something still in there. Maybe not cancer." I struggled to fit both plastic kidneys back into the torso and left one out as I moved on to the liver.

He did actually look at his watch. "I can recommend you a psychiatrist. But you have to make the choice to trust the science. You're saved."

But I didn't feel saved. In fact, I remembered being in this very room just four months earlier and him saying with belabored seriousness "there was nothing he could do." In his role of savior, guiding me through what had been a two-year journey with a giant fork between life and death always looming, he had given up. He'd asked me to prepare for the dark side of the fork. And I had.

I had prepared so well I didn't belong with the living anymore. Why couldn't he see it? Of all people, I thought he'd understand. Being that he clearly wasn't good with names, I knew he would need to leave the room to get the psychiatrist referral, so I said, "Yes, a psychiatrist might help." And while he was gone, I stowed that extra kidney in my purse. He'd never notice it was missing.

THE KIDNEY FOUND A new home on the dashboard of my Nissan Murano, which I used in my work driving passengers around the city, a taxi service without a union. Customers sometimes asked to hold it. Out of the context of its body, the kidney didn't look quite like a kidney. One customer thought it was a malformed bean from a child's kitchen set. Another thought it was a dog toy and was disappointed when it didn't squeak.

John, one of my regulars, was the only one who I offered a kernel of the truth.

"It's my oncologist's kidney."

"I wonder how he's handling the absence." John liked to wax philosophical about the nature of bodies. He thought our worship of the brain as the center of life heretical. The body, as a whole entity, directed our lives in ways we could never recognize. He knew my brain had nothing to do with what was wrong with me.

"My husband keeps making these meals that I can't eat," I said. "It's like I'm full all the time. Just like when I was on chemo. I don't understand the rationale behind eating."

"You could have orchids," said John.

In response to the questioning look I sent him through my rearview mirror, he waved his hand through the air, searching for words to explain the inexplicable. "Cancer wards are excessively cleaned. Only certain things can grow there. Orchid spores for instance, are a problem in operating rooms. Maybe you breathed them in while you were under."

I missed a turn while trying to pull together what he was talking about. Fungus had spores. Didn't orchids have something else? And in operating rooms? Really? My phone navigation chirped at me in digitized angst. I needed to redirect.

"You're saying I've inhaled orchid spores and that's why I feel full?" I laughed.

But John was serious. "Bodies near death make changes. Some wither, some welcome something new."

This at least rang true. I thumped the steering wheel with the heel of my palm. "That's exactly it, John. I was prepared to wither. He told me I was done, and I believed him. I'd said goodbye. I'd picked out my own goddam casket for fuck's sake. And this doctor. He looks at me like I'm bonkers."

"You don't look withered to me," said John. "If anything, I'd say you're glowing."

My phone chirped as I pulled up to his destination.

"Watch for lumps," said John with a wink as he climbed out.

THE NEXT MORNING, OVER a breakfast that rivaled those fancy hotel brunch buffets, my husband waved the newspaper at me. "Another person was killed last night," he said.

I'd had the same bite of pancake on my fork for over a minute, staring it down, telling it to come to my mouth. But it remained hovering over my plate dripping syrup. All my husband's hard work. Up before dawn. He was so determined to have our second life together.

"I really think you should stop driving after sunset," he said. "The suspect is a white male in his thirties. All the victims have been terminally ill."

"Then I'll be perfectly safe." I forced fork to mouth and shoved the pancake between my teeth. As I ground them together, I thought it would've been a beautiful thing to have been killed by a murderer. I knew exactly when I would've wanted it to happen. A week after my doctor told me I was going down the dark fork in the road. Before that I had believed in the process of survival. I had trusted my doctor and his plastic organs and his calm assurance it was all worth it.

I'd taken the hope of survival into me. It had sustained me through horrors untold as I'd been caught up in the life-saving jaws of the medical industrial complex. I had clung to it while humans trained to be robots looked at body parts like machine parts and played unending rounds of high-stakes dice to win against cancer. Somewhere in that week, I'd begun to see me the way the industry did. A thing to win or lose, not a life bound up in complexity and nuance and limits. A particular exhaustion drifted in to wear away the sharp edges of my selfness, revealed the porous edges of the limits to what a person could experience and continue to see themselves as alive.

My doctor deserved to lose more than his plastic kidney.

"What would you be doing right now if I was gone?" I asked my husband.

His face was hidden behind the newspaper, but I felt the sudden stillness of him. He'd stopped reading. I saw coverage of the serial killer on the front page. The woman had been killed in the same neighborhood where I'd dropped John off. Not just the same neighborhood. The same block.

My husband shook the newspaper, folded it not quite along its already formed creases. "I think we should take a vacation. How do you feel about Niagara? We could buy one of those gaudy RVs, endless road trips." He had tears in his eyes. I felt him holding out his hand, ready to pull me back to life as he knew it if only I'd accept his offer.

"I'd like to keep driving for a while yet."

I held my breath, waiting for him to jump up and rage, or just simply walk out, done with me. But this was the thing about my husband. After my oncologist had told us he was ceding the win to cancer I'd taught myself to let go, but my husband had taught himself to hang on.

THE NEXT TIME JOHN signed up for a drive, I stood outside the back door, blocking him from entering, as he approached my Murano.

"Are you killing those women?"

He stopped short, glanced around like someone could've overheard me. We were in a McDonald's parking lot choked with grease stink and exhaust from the cars in the drive-through. Scents I associated with death, though I didn't know why. Vascular pollutants. The thought came to me, right in the middle of me giving John my 'you'd better come clean' face. I felt the sliding sludge of them seeping into my veins, the fumes of grease and exhaust. Poison. Poison. Poison.

"Are you all right?" asked John.

My head swam like it was starved for air. I'd intended to be powerful, demanding, to make a foolproof case in favor of being John's next victim. Instead, I could barely gasp out, "I want you to kill me."

He watched as I struggled. In his gaze I saw a hint of my doctor's look, evaluating my chances just before he placed his bets. But the difference was the doctor saw sheets of calculations describing the odds. When John looked at me he was evaluating life.

"If you really wanted to die, it could happen right now," he said. "Stop struggling."

If I'd been able to laugh in that moment, I would have. He made it sound so simple, as though death after all this time was a choice I'd failed to make.

My hands reached out, clutching at empty air and then his shirt as he stepped into me and held me up.

"Help me," I rasped even though they were words I had learned to hate. I hated them for all the times they'd unwittingly revealed my desperation to that robot of a doctor who did know the madness of trying to follow his instructions to protect a surgery incision from bursting while also puking. While also struggling to make it to the toilet for the puking because every bone screamed in agony.

The madness of worrying about the mess that would be made if the mission to reach the toilet failed. My husband yet again cleaning up my filth, trying to use his not-medical expertise to evaluate if one pulled stitch and the bleeding that came with it was worthy of an ER, or adding a phone call to the shameful churning sea of so many past ER visits and phone calls and emergencies we saw as emergencies only to be told they were normal.

"Help me," I said again.

John put his arms around me, bundled me into the passenger seat of the Murano. He drove us through the city, out to the suburbs, past my neighborhood, out to the acres of preserved prairie that some insightful person had protected back in the 1970s when no one else was imagining the city would ever grow so large the wilderness around it would need protection. He bundled me out of the car, and we stumbled together down an uneven gravel path to a small deck for visitors to look out at what had existed in this place before humans.

The sun beamed down high overhead. It was the apex of summer. The time of year I most dreaded being outside, for the heat, the sweat, the lethargy. That had been pre-cancer me. The rules had changed. John let me go. I flopped down on the decking, spread myself out like a starfish beneath the sweltering radiation I'd been told my entire life would give me cancer. Ha! I could breathe. Here, even though the highway and housing developments encroached less than a mile away, the air was clean and sweet.

John sat down beside me and rolled up the sleeve of the driving jacket I wore because I kept the AC at max in the Murano. He ran his fingers along my arm. I realized my arm was not the arm I expected, a smooth line of skin-covered bone. Small lumps interrupted his movement. I yanked off my jacket and found larger lumps in the corner of my elbow and along my ribcage.

"Cancer," I breathed, flushed with hope. I could return to my doctor with legitimate things for him to test. He would see that I was right and he was wrong. I hadn't been saved. Just as quickly as I rose to this great hope, something sharp and heavy coalesced in the bottom of my gut and I began to crash down again. My husband would be devastated.

I CAME HOME TO tell him ready to be the strong one, calm, clinical, and as detached as my doctor was. But all my preparation turned out to be useless because my husband was already up in arms for another reason. I had to explain how our neighbor had seen a man driving my car, with me clearly in distress in the passenger seat, as we plowed through the four-way stop that turned into our subdivision.

"He's a client," I said.

"Are you all right?" he asked. I realized he'd thought I was being kidnapped, taken by the serial killer for a grisly death. This was how my husband would've seen suicide by John, grisly, an unspeakable horror that somehow surpassed the thousands of small atrocities that had already been committed against me in the name of beating cancer.

"I'm fine," I said, which was strangely true. My sun basking had left me dazed, high, like being on codeine but without the dread of the GI problems that inevitably followed. I held out my arm. "But I think something is growing again." I closed my eyes so I didn't have to watch his face crumble. I'd become so good at this retraction, protecting myself from the roller coaster. All I had to do was stand there, an unbreachable bastion of survival, and eventually he would pull himself together and we would resume plunking our four feet forward together again.

Except the need to be a bastion had passed.. I hadn't survived. All my best practices were wasted energy. And I needed that energy to feed whatever was growing in me. Cancer or orchid. I struggled to suppress what would've been a horrific laughter. Surely not orchids. But it was pleasant to think of cancer being a plant, something doing a natural thing, a lifecycle. Instead of this monolithic enemy to be defeated. I was done thinking of my body as an enemy camp.

So, I walked across the flagstones to the front door where my husband half crouched, slowly being crushed by the realization that all his striving, his chin-up determination that somehow we'd get through this, was for nothing. I pulled him up into my arms and held him until he'd wrung himself out and then I dared to look him in the eyes and tell him it would be okay. And then, because he clearly didn't believe me, I dared further. I made a plan for a future.

"I'd like to learn to garden," I said. "If you're going to be doing all this fancy cooking, we should have our own garden."

He still thought I was saying this just for him, because he knew I knew what he wanted most for me was to reattach, put some roots down into our life. He was too much in need of hope to challenge me, so he accepted my offering. Hand in hand, we took a couple shaky steps forward. I took the evening off driving and we toured around to all the garden stores spending egregious amounts of money we didn't quite have on green blooming things we had no idea how to keep alive.

IT WASN'T ENOUGH.

Each day that passed as I waited for my appointment with my doctor, I lived with a sour taste in my mouth, a falseness. I was still pretending I was alive, living by the old rules. A week passed. The lumps broke the skin along my ribs and revealed themselves as clusters of hard green nodes others might call buds. New lumps rose along my spine and under my armpits. I hid the buds from my husband. They were clearly not cancer and I didn't know how to explain, didn't want to go through the emotional chaos of uncertainty. Cancer was a dance with steps we knew.

For instance, we knew if we called the clinic every day some other patient's cancelled appointment could give me the chance of seeing the doctor sooner than my scheduled appointment. So instead of waiting several months—which would've been when our fall greens, the kale, mustard, and chard we'd planted in our new raised bed would've been nearly mature—I saw my doctor a week later. My husband came with me as he always had.

The doctor entered in a rush, already perfunctory, his mind skipping ahead to whatever came after me.

"Nice to see you," I said and left off his name. Our relationship had moved beyond personal niceties.

"Back again," he sighed. "I suppose you'd like to do some scans?"

"Nope."

I said this to get a reaction. But he didn't even look up. He sat adjacent to me at the little computer desk. A counter jutted out from the wall with a torso on it like a beheaded bodyguard. Was it protecting me or the doctor? I ignored my husband fidgeting at my side, wondering what the fuck I was saying. We'd clearly come for tests. I dug my fingers under the colon organ and flicked it off. I meant to catch it when it fell, but I missed and it clattered to the floor instead. My doctor continued studying the computer screen.

"I suppose we'll start with bloodwork. What symptoms are you having?"

"There are fucking lumps all over her," my husband burst out. Righteous masculine anger tended to get doctors' attention. The doctor turned, blinked at him and then at me, at my limp arm being held by my husband. I wore long sleeves because I'd woken that morning to find all the lumps along my arm had broken through to reveal themselves as buds. I was going to do a two-for-one show (husband and doctor) and hopefully mediate the chaos that would follow.

I rolled up my sleeve with striptease slowness, winking at the colon-less torso. It knew what was up. Probably it had seen this peep show a million times. It was the show where a woman reveals what was exceptional about her body for the eyes of men and they respond in all the wrong ways.

"Looks like you've got a touch of neurofibromatosis there," said my doctor. "Interesting. We see it most often in children, but," he shrugged, calculations clicked behind his vacuous eyes, "the tumors are usually benign. We'll do a biopsy and take some blood." He stood, shook my husband's hand even though my husband was staring at me, at my arm, mouth working and failing to form words. We'd spent two weeks together building and seeding a garden bed. He knew what was on my arm.

As soon as the doctor stepped out, I leaned over and retrieved the colon from the floor, stuffed it into my purse, and sat, staring at one of those suicide prevention landscape prints on the opposite wall, braced for impact.

My husband jumped up from his seat and ran the three feet to the opposite wall, shoved his hands up into his hair, his back to me as though that would erase what he'd just seen. "What the fuck is going on here?"

What words could I use to explain both desolation and rebirth? I needed him to understand something impossible, a truth I suspected would be more devastating than the actual return of cancer.

"It isn't possible to survive cancer." My voice came out as a toneless whisper. "You either die or you become something else."

A sob or hiccup rose up out of my husband.

"I want a life with you, but a different life."

"What does that mean?" he croaked.

"I don't know yet. But I think it could be good. It might even be beautiful."

He shook his head. "I don't—I just, this isn't possible. There are limits." He rushed out before I could ask him to clarify if he meant limits to what the human body could do or what he as a spouse could endure.

The nurse came for the blood and biopsy. Both familiar procedures, but this was the first time I'd gone through them without my husband. I watched the scalpel scrape along my skin and behead the buds on my forearm. No pain, not blood even, just a little pus. By far the easiest biopsy ever. But a thick bile rose up in my throat as I considered the possibility I might be venturing into this new life alone.

As she drew three vials of my syrupy ruby blood, I cursed the nurse. I cursed the plastic torso and the man who owned it, a living body of toy organs, who had so carelessly given me over to this new life I'd never asked for.

"THIS COULD BE A weapon," said John, swinging my doctor's stolen colon around in the Murano's back seat like a boomerang. It was an ugly, bulbous gray tube, bent to form a right angle not quite in the middle. Part of it was cut away to show the colon's lining, various pink bubblegum tones showing different diseases of the bowel.

"I'd prefer a knife. It'd go in easier."

"But this is cleaner," said John. "Could be a choking hazard."

"I'm done with clean."

John paused his swinging, turned sober. "I thought you were beginning to like your buds."

"I am. But that doesn't change the fact that he doesn't understand. He's just going to keep on using people so he can try to play God. He doesn't care what it costs."

"I think they teach cost-benefit in business school, not medical school." John chuckled, a dark private joke I half understood. Since I'd begun to suspect the nature of John's evening activities, I'd seen quite a bit more darkness in him. He was detached from the regular rules of the living in the same way I was. Probably he'd survived something unspeakable and emerged on the other side separate.

"Who are you doing tonight?" I asked.

"I don't know until I get there. They call to me. That's my curse, you could say. I didn't bloom, but I didn't die either. I can sense both those who are seeded to grow and those who will wither. I try to do what I can for the withering."

"Because no one should go through that, death by medicine."

John tapped the colon against the doorframe. "I'm not a

prophet. But I have this sense that you need to do something before you're going to have peace. That thing..." he paused, looked out the window at the passing city, "you'll be safe doing that thing. They won't catch you."

I was concentrating so much on his face in my mirror that I drove up onto the curb and thunked the front bumper into a yellow cement pole. We came to an abrupt stop. I knew the thing he was talking about it, a thing I knew but hadn't even told myself.

"How can you know I'll be safe?"

He tossed the colon into the front passenger seat. "Because you have different rules now. It isn't possible for people in the old world to look at you unless you want them to."

"And my husband? Will he see me?"

"Eventually. Growth is a slow process on all sides." John paused with his hand on the door handle. "You're not going to see me again. Whatever happens, don't forget to stretch for the sun and bloom well."

ON THE WAY HOME, I stopped to pick up milk even though I didn't drink milk. We were out. My husband would've asked but we weren't exactly speaking. I also picked up a set of Japanese knives. The super sharp kind that my husband had been ogling but couldn't bring himself to splurge on.

I found him waiting for me on the back porch, looking out on our yard that was now mostly rows of planters and mounds of dirt pockmarked with green shoots.

"I don't want to lose you," he said.

"I'm not going anywhere."

He nodded and tucked away the other things he might have said. The sun was setting. It was that violet hour of dusk when the air stilled and everything was perfect and the sky painted itself so many colors the mind emptied of all thoughts except how beautiful the natural world could be as it rotated through its cycles of birth, growth, death, and decay. Humans were so fixated on the first two, they struggled to see the beauty in the rest. New things came from death. They needed to be seen and loved.

I looked at my husband's face awash in the purple light of the dying sun and knew he wasn't going to fail me. So, I pulled up my shirt and revealed the three bloodred orchids that had bloomed along my ribcage. The first bounty of my new life.

WHILE WE WERE SITTING in that sunset, John was in a shootout with police. They called it a shootout, but really it was a misunderstanding about the kind of weapon he had. Maybe he wanted them to shoot him. Later, I would have to answer a lot of questions because he named me as the executor of his will. It's quite a thing to be an executor of a serial killer's will and not be a lawyer. Once they decided I was not an accomplice the rest was easy. He wanted his body to go into the ground and be part of growing things in a field, not a cemetery. This was slightly illegal, but I managed. By the time the police came knocking, I was an expert criminal.

The morning after John's death I went to my doctor's office for a follow-up appointment to discuss the results of my biopsy. The scheduling nurse sounded cryptic over the phone. They'd found something unusual, but she wouldn't say what. I brought the doctor's kidney and colon with me to return to him. My purse also held one of the new Japanese knives, which I would use to help make space for the lost organs in the doctor's torso. As I checked into the clinic, the receptionist noticed the orchid I cupped in my free hand, harvested from my ribs that morning, already beginning to wilt.

"So pretty," she said.

"It's for my doctor. See the spores? They don't always take. But he'll have the same chance I had to become something new."

She did an uncomfortable giggle thing. Uncertain if I was making a joke or perhaps revealing an affair. Both and neither were true.

I looked at her and made up my mind I was someone else, someone she couldn't see, which was true. When the nurse called me back to see the doctor, I got up and walked past her through the door as she kept calling and calling a dead woman's name.

Thunderheads and Burial Goods

Cormack Baldwin

USUALLY WHEN IT BEGAN raining inside, Jack had a simple answer. He would join whoever he was with in marveling at the strangeness of it, accuse the architects of faulty plumbing lines, and excuse himself before they could invite him to the refuge of another room. Occasionally he'd even point it out himself, just to tut about how the landlord should have let them know about this beforehand. If anyone noticed it stopped when he left the room, they never said anything. He'd gotten so good at it that he could nearly convince himself.

The lightning, though—that was harder to explain. It didn't help that he was trapped in something thick and tight as a spider-silk rope, cloying to his skin. Or that the entire world stung with the reproach of ozone and glint of teeth. He gasped, thrashing out against the ties that bound him to the unyielding ground.

With a boom of thunder and a rush of vertigo, Jack found

himself still in Soho, still in his flat, still alone, tangled in his rain-soaked sheets. The early morning sun turned ravaged wallpaper the color of watered-down beer. One bookshelf was now leaning on the other like a drunk. Most of its contents had been disgorged onto the floor, dangerously close to the paper-wrapped volumes of an upturned apple crate. A glance to the kitchen suggested it had mostly been spared, though a couple of tea bags were cold-brewing on the tile floor.

Jack grimaced as he pulled his brace out of a puddle. The fact that the thing hadn't rusted through by then was nothing short of a miracle. His fault, really, but he couldn't afford a new one, not to mention the dread even the thought of the white linoleum hospital dredged up. He suppressed a shudder at the sensation of cold metal against his thigh as he strapped it into position. The leather strap over his knee tore a millimeter more as he pulled it taut.

He extracted one crutch out from where he'd stashed it halfway under the mattress. That would be good enough to get him up and to the other crutch currently pinned against the slouching bookshelf. In between, he crouched to pick up scattered volumes. Some of the paperbacks had landed in puddles and were dissolving to cream-of-wheat mush on his floor, but the hardbacks had survived worse. Rings of discoloration suggested their high-water marks.

One last volume caught his eye. Perhaps a foot in front of Jack's second crutch sat a clothbound edition he didn't recognize. He could pass it off as his own poor memory were it not for the sense he'd just swallowed lead. For the second time that morning, a rush of cold ran through to Jack's fingers and manifested as a spattering of rain. The cover flipped open in a whip of wind.

Puer de Mort, read the front page.

Jack didn't speak French, but had anyone been there to witness the next minute, he would have had to excuse himself for it.

To say Jack Abelman had a curse was like saying he had polio, though as far as he could tell the two were unrelated. To *have* a curse suggested that one might peel it off, toss it in the bin, and be done with it. It had never occurred to Jack to even try. For as long as he could remember, he'd been followed by the peculiar. Harmless, mostly, like vases connected to the ocean (only a problem if you spilled it, which he had) or screaming toy soldiers. Dangerous, more often than he'd like. Journals that wrote in blood. The more violent haunted dolls, most of which had discovered that porcelain shards were exceedingly sharp.

An Almanac that turned the barest hint of an emotion into a raging storm. An Almanac whose paper shell he'd burned long ago. An Almanac that was too intertwined with him to remove.

At this rate, Jack had a good grasp on these things. Call it second sight, call it intuition, but really, just call it common sense. If a book appeared in your home without warning (check) or a listed author (check), and generally made you feel like you were watching someone etch your tombstone (check, check, check), it was probably cursed. He'd seen enough to know.

Which, of course, was why Jack was sitting with the latest offender on his kitchen table as he sipped a cup of tea from a stormproof tin mug. The potbellied stove in the corner of his flat was still crackling away, ready to send the book spiraling out of the chimney in particles of ash if need be. They hadn't reached that point, though. Destroying a book prematurely was akin to hanging a 'Vacancy' sign on whatever ethereal door the objects came through. Better the hoard of safe books he'd shoved into the bottom of an apple crate than gambling on not getting another Almanac. For all he knew, the sense he was looking into the face of death was the beginning and end of the book's powers.

Puer de Mort, the front cover whispered.

"I've got more than enough matches to eat you alive," he replied.

The contest couldn't continue forever, though, and Jack knew it. His shift began at eleven, and once he got there he would bundle the book up and tuck it under the counter to keep an eye on as he tended the pub. That, or leave a cursed object in a soaking, empty flat, whose other cursed contents were scattered across the floor in puddles of water and shreds of butcher paper. He needed a plan, but his mind proved empty except for the stark black cover, its silver binding like the hinges on a casket.

The chime of the travel clock made the decision for him. Good idea or not, he was bringing the thing to work. It wasn't like the pub lacked matchbooks, or trash bins, or anything else one might need to destroy an artifact of fear. Jack wrapped the book in a scarf, slid it into the inner pocket of his rain jacket, and slipped out the door.

Cheri's was not a famous pub by any stretch, but it did have a small crowd of people idling around it pretending to be interested in the "For Lease" signs in nearby windows while he fumbled for his keys. He spat a curse as the wrapped book fell to the ground with a *thump* and the snap of binding, punctuated by a hacking cough. "Just a moment, Mr. Anders," Jack muttered. He unlocked the front door with a click before grabbing the book. The customers followed him in like sheep after their shepherd. Mr. Anders hung back, letting out another volley of coughs.

The titular Cheri sat at the bar, counting coins. He shooed

her off the stool behind the counter and took her place. "I've had something of a morning," Jack warned her.

She raised her penciled-in eyebrows as she raised her voice to be heard above the hubbub behind them. "Should I fetch an umbrella?" she asked. Then her eyes fell to the worn black cloth peeking through the dirt-streaked scarf. She sucked her teeth in a gesture more eloquent than any words. "One of those."

He was about to confirm when one of the patrons, evidently fed up with the half-minute delay, wove a hand in front of Jack's face. "Hey!" The patron planted one fist on her hips and gestured with her free hand toward the door, where the others stood in a circle.

Jack shot her a glare. "A moment, please."

She huffed. "There's a dead man outside. You have a phone, don't you? Call the police!"

In the fog of his memory, Jack would later recall the events as a series of poorly arranged film cuts, akin in style and detail to the silent movies that went out of fashion when he was still a child. Frame 1, Cheri disappears into the back room to twist the dial on the phone until she gets the number she vowed never to call. Frame 2, Jack fights the urge to vomit as he pushes the crowd back from the body of Mr. Anders. Frame 3, the book clatters to the floor. The title card reads *BANG!* in time with the gunshot across the street. A singed hole remained where Frame 4 (someone screaming, someone else cursing, sirens wailing) should have been.

The reel began again with Jack suddenly aware that he was outside, talking remarkably calmly given the wide-eyed corpse of Mr. Anders at his feet, to a police officer who had once locked Jack up for a night on an indecency charge. "He had tuberculosis or something. Constantly coughing," he found himself saying.

"And that one?" asked the officer, gesturing across the

street to where another cop watched blood pool out of the hole in someone's chest. His eyes remained on Jack's crutches as he spoke, as if gauging whether the metal tips might have gouged out the wound. If it weren't for the pounding of his heart against cardboard and paper, Jack would have forced his eyes upwards.

"Not a clue, sorry." And he truly was sorry. Whether they found the gun or not, he knew he was clutching the murder weapon to his chest, fearing another tear of its leaf-thin pages would send someone else breathing their last.

"Shame. Suppose it is Soho," the officer concluded, as if death were native to Soho in the way that tigers were native to the jungle. "Thank you for your time."

Jack didn't return the sentiment. He watched Cheri flip the sign to 'Closed' before anyone even bought a drink. Guilt swam through the numbness in his gut like a fish through river sludge, its effects most clearly seen in the ripples of air around him. Rain prickled his skin as he walked back to his flat, his heart thrumming any time anyone got close enough to notice the bulge of the book tucked in his rain jacket. Telling himself it was safe from the moisture in Jack's pocket didn't stop the thrill of panic every time it rasped against the lining or threatened to topple to the cobblestones while his hands were too occupied with his crutches to catch it.

He shouldered through the doors to his building and half-dragged himself up the stairs to his doorstep. Any relief that he might have felt upon returning to his flat was disjointed by the sight of a small crowd down the hall. He had neither time nor energy to look further before the relief dissolved fully as the door opened to reveal what remained from that morning. The stove had long gone cold, leaving the puddles to stagnate on the floor. The table was no better. Had he put the book in one of the pools that morning? Had it been lashed by the rain? Fear crawled through him and released in another moan of wind through the cement hallway, carrying with it the murmurings of the crowd.

He was going to kill someone. He already had.

Cameras flashed at the end of the hall. "Found dead this morning. Murder, must be," the officer confirmed to the journalists circling his neighbor's door like vultures. Still, he didn't look Jack's way. He only shook his head. "How else do you explain it? Drowned in the middle of her flat. Nothing to do but bury her."

THE DIVINE MERCY FUNERAL Home was, in a word, quaint. Red brick and ivy, it didn't boast advertisements of "best services in London," or "enjoy it or your money back," nor even explanations of what services it might provide outside of what the name suggested. After twelve hours of staring down a murderous book, taking odd shots of scotch to try and calm his nerves, and waiting for night to fall, it was even comforting. Completing the image of bucolic innocence, the ground-story window was ajar.

The first part to breaking into a building that way was to pry the window open and toss his crutches in. Second, Jack pulled himself up and weaseled his upper half through. That was when he heard it—or perhaps he saw it first. The light in a distant room, casting yellow beams of light down the hallway. The voice, tentative yet not afraid, calling, "Hello?"

Rapid mathematics played out in Jack's panic-addled mind. Going back out would all but guarantee that he would lose his crutches without earning a casket in the deal. He wouldn't be able to escape if he backed out, though. He'd be caught the moment they looked out the window. In a move not unlike a rat he'd once watched force its way through a grate on the Underground, he planted his hands against the wall, sucked in his stomach, and squirmed. Pain ricocheted up and down him as he hit the floor with a dull *thump*.

"Is someone there?" the voice called again.

Well, Jack, about time you talk your way out of this one. It was a new scrape, that was for certain, but hardly the worst thing he'd gotten himself into and out of again. With the calm of a lamb admiring those beautiful knives on the abattoir wall, he grabbed his crutches from where they landed and levered himself upright.

The man with the torch was not what Jack was expecting, though he hadn't had a picture in mind beforehand. He was massive—tall, wide, and not quite fitting in his suit. He couldn't have been much older than Jack, if he was older at all. His face was smooth, round, and dark, framed by nearly white hair.

"Something must have scared you, mate," was the first thing Jack thought to say. To the man's puzzled expression, he gestured upward at the shock of white hair. "Seen a ghost? Heard they live around these parts."

"What are you *doing*?" was the first thing the man evidently thought to say. A much more reasonable response to the situation, really.

The truth was a fickle thing, in Jack's experience. Most people lived without wanting to know anything resembling the truth. It was best wasted on drunks who would write it all off as a misunderstanding in the morning. Still, he didn't have a better lie prepared. "I needed a casket. Have you got one?"

"What are you doing *here*?" the man corrected.

"I figured a funeral home would be the best place to find a casket." Rain tapped at the open window, making Jack glad he'd left the offending volume at home.

The man pinched the bridge of his nose and sighed. "Perhaps I was wrong to assume that respecting funeral homes wasn't a strictly Filipino custom."

Another Jack, somewhat less tipsy and in less desperate of straits, would have pitied the man. The Jack that stood there then teetered on the cliff of shame but wasn't in a position to indulge the notion of falling. Instead, he patted the man's arm in two clumsy swats. "No, I'm quite certain that one's universal. I'm just in a bit of a bind."

It took another few breaths before the man gathered himself enough continue in a customer service voice two octaves above his initial interrogation. "If it's for a loved one, we do offer reduced price options if you are unable to afford a standard burial. However, I would suggest we do that in the morning."

Jack shook his head. In for a penny, in for a pound. "Good to know, I suppose, but no. It's for a book. A book that induces the fear of death in its holder and kills someone nearby if damaged. I don't know how it works, nor do I care to. I figure if it's in a box six feet underground, it's really not my problem, is it?"

Silence returned. Jack wondered if the man had already called the police and was just waiting for them to cart him off. He couldn't blame him if he had. Then, like dawn breaking over the horizon, "Cursed, I imagine." The man turned and waved him down the hall. "Come along. Best to have this kind of talk over tea."

"You do know what I'm talking about, then?" Jack followed, caring less about the answer than the result.

In the pale reflection of the torchlight, Jack could see the corners of the man's grimace. "Unfortunately. Have you a name? If I'm to do you a favor, I'd like to know you as something other than 'casket fellow.'"

"Jack. Are you, I mean, I'm cursed—are you?" The kitchen,

as it turned out, was a gingham-clothed affair consisting of a table surrounded with dark wood chairs and a stove just large enough for a heavy iron kettle. A single bottle of milk in a melting ice bath, a silver carafe that looked like someone had scratched off the words "holy water," and an enameled lunch box were the only suggestions of actual food.

"Davide Bautista. I help the dead." With that, he set to filling the kettle from the carafe on the end of the table and setting the stove to light. "How do you know the book won't hurt anyone if it's buried?"

Jack took a spot at the end opposite the carafe. More questions burned under his tongue, but he was familiar enough with deflections to know pushing wouldn't get him any further. "I don't. But I figure it's safer there than with me—with *anyone*. No offense, but I'd prefer your business not get any more traffic because someone spilled coffee on the thing."

Davide waved away the thought. "None taken. We have a burial tomorrow morning. I wouldn't suggest leaving the book in the casket, because, well, with decay—"

Jack cut him off before his stomach could curdle further. "I can imagine. Suffice to say I don't want to leave it with the corpse of old Miss Havisham, regardless."

"Mrs. Bell, actually. However, the pit is already dug. I can show you the spot, and if you bury it underneath the current ground level it won't be disturbed during or after the burial. You wouldn't want to bury a full-size casket, though."

Really, he'd be happy to not have to bury anything at all, but that wasn't how life had turned out. "Not really, no. That does lead me to another question, though. Wood rots. Metal rusts. Do you have some way of making sure the, er, charge remains high and dry?"

Davide sighed as the kettle grumbled its assent. "No, that's not usually a concern." The rumble became a whistle, and he got up to pour steaming black tea into china mugs.

Porcelain, that was an idea, except it would probably shatter when six feet of West London mud was piled atop it. Soaking the thing in embalming fluid would do more harm than good. Stacking caskets like matryoshka dolls would help, though that would likely exceed any stranger's goodwill. He wasn't entirely sure how much caskets cost, but he imagined it was his weekly salary several times over.

"Milk and sugar?" Davide asked.

"Just milk," Jack replied. His eyes continued their roving exploration for proper burial materials after his brain had thrown up its hands. Glass had the same problem as porcelain. Stone would be best, where did you even get a stone box? Were urns stone? The only funeral he'd ever attended had been his mother's, and she'd been buried in a regular coffin. He'd always assumed urns were the size of a vase. The book might not fit in that—he'd need something closer to the size of a lunch box.

The lunch box. The feet of the chair screeched as Jack pushed himself back from the table and made his way to the counter just as Davide placed the cup in front of where Jack had sat. Up close, it was nearly the size of a briefcase. Tiny scratches marred the otherwise shining Bakelite surface, but that was the only sign that the thing had been around for more than the ten minutes Jack had been in the room. No dents, no tarnish. Just a powdery pink faux-marbled with white. He unlatched it and flipped open the lid. Empty except for crumbs. "What little old lady left this here?"

"It's mine, if you don't mind," Davide sniffed. "I've had it for a decade now and prefer you not mess with it."

Jack shook it, ignoring the hissing intake of air between Davide's teeth. "I think it'll do nicely."

"Nicely for what?"

The sun was rising over the skyline of the Divine Mercy Cemetery, and Jack wanted nothing more than to curl up in the grave and fall asleep in the cool soil. Dirt already coated his face and arms like a second skin. At this point the only thing keeping him awake was the cold of his sweat and rain-soaked shirt and the pain tearing through his legs as he fought to stay upright long enough for his braces to lock into position.

"They'll be coming out for the burial," Davide reminded him from above. As if they both hadn't been checking the time more often than the minute hand could change.

"That's fine." Jack stood back, leaning on his shovel to survey his lopsided work. A half-meter-high mound of loosened clay sat next to the fresh hole. After an hour of digging, it was just big enough to fit the box in Davide's arms, provided he maneuvered the padlocks to be on top. "Hand it down." Pastel pink peeked out between the steel chains, not a hint of black cloth to be seen. Perfect. He dropped to his good knee with a grunt and let the bad one follow in reluctant pursuit. The padlocks slid but didn't scratch the surface as he forced the box into the hole, moving it back and forth until something gave way with a *crack*.

His stomach dropped with a rush of freezing panic as his numb hands fumbled for the spiderweb of damage he was now certain was rubbing the book like thorns, toying with someone's flesh in tandem. Dirt-crusted nails slid over polished plastic, finding nothing except the crushed remains of a pebble, lodged in a microscopic dent.

Thunder rolled, and with a full-body tremor, cold air pulled itself into Jack's lungs. It took him a moment longer to steady himself. "Tell me if there's anyone coming."

With that eulogy came the task of undoing the work of the past hour, throwing back rocks he'd had to scrape out of clay to pull, patting down clumps of dirt he'd had to claw out with only the tip of the shovel. The earth took the box without protest, and the book disappeared without gunfire or the wheeze of a final breath. Soon all that remained was a small mound where flat ground had once been, and a lancing pain through Jack's body.

"Help me out, would you?" He reached up his free hand and let Davide pull him out of the grave, at least to the point that Jack could harpoon the shovel into the topsoil and haul himself onto level ground. For a moment he lay on his back, panting from both exhaustion and exhilaration as he looked up at Davide's concerned face, framed with white hair so far beyond his age. He'd kiss those frowning lips if he could. "We did it," Jack whispered, like speaking too loudly might make it untrue.

"I don't know if we've done anything at all," Davide said.

Jack reached out a hand and let Davide help him to his feet as the procession of black-clothed mourners began. "We've done enough."

Song of Bullfrogs, Cry of Geese

Nicola Griffith

I sat by the side of the road in the afternoon sun and watched the cranefly struggle. A breeze, hot and heavy as a tired dog's breath, coated the web and fly with dust. I shaded my eyes and squinted down the road. Empty. As usual. It was almost two years since I'd seen anything but Jud's truck on Peachtree.

Like last month, and the month before that, and the third day of every month since I'd been out here alone, I quashed the fear that maybe this time he wouldn't come. But he always did come, rolling up in the cloud of dust he'd collected on the twenty-mile drive from Atlanta.

I turned my attention back to the fly. It kept right on struggling. I wondered how it felt, fighting something that didn't resist but just drained the life from it. It would take a long time to die. Like humankind.

The fly had stopped fighting by the time I heard Jud's truck. I didn't get up and brush myself off, he'd be a few minutes yet;

sound travels a long way when there's nothing filling the air but bird song.

He had someone with him. I sighed. Usually, Jud would give me a ride back down to the apartment. Looked like I'd have to walk this time: the truck was only a two-seater. It pulled up and Jud and another man, about twenty-eight I'd guess, maybe a couple of years younger than me, swung open their doors.

"How are you, Molly?" He climbed down, economical as always with his movements.

"Same as usual, Jud. Glad to see you." I nodded at the supplies and the huge gasoline drums in the back of the truck. "A day later and the generator would've been sucking air."

He grinned. "You're welcome." His partner walked around the front of the truck. Jud gestured. "This is Henry." Henry nodded. Like Jud, like me, he wore shorts, sneakers, and T-shirt.

Jud didn't say why Henry was along for the ride but I could guess: a relapse could hit anybody, anytime, leave you too exhausted even to keep the gas pedal down. I hoped Henry was just Jud's insurance and not another piece in the chess game he and I played from time to time.

"Step up if you want a ride," Jud said.

I looked questioningly at Henry.

"I can climb up into the back," he said. I watched him haul himself over the tailgate and hunker down by a case of tuna. Showing off. He'd pay for the exertion later. I shrugged, his problem, and climbed up into the hot vinyl seat.

Jud handled the truck gently, turning into the apartment complex as carefully as though five hundred people still lived here. The engine noise startled the nuthatches nesting in the postal center into a flurry of feathers; they perched on the roof and watched us pull up ten yards in, at what had been the clubhouse. I remember when the brass Westwater Terraces sign had been shined up every week: only three years ago. Six months after I'd first moved in people had begun to slow down and die off, and the management had added a few things, like the ramps and generator, to try and keep those who were left. It felt like a lifetime ago. I was the only one still here.

"Tiger lilies are looking good," Jud said. They were, straggling big and busy and orange all around the clubhouse; a feast for birds and bees.

The gasoline drums were lashed down, to stop them moving around the flatbed during the drive to Duluth. Henry untied the first and trundled it forward on its casters until it rested by the tailgate.

Inside the clubhouse the dark was hot and moist; a roach whirred when I uncoiled the hose. Back out in the sun I blew through it to clear any other insects and spat into the dust. I put one end in the first drum.

I always hated the first suck but this time I was lucky and avoided a mouthful of gas. We didn't speak while the drums drained. It was an unseasonable May: over ninety degrees and humid as hell. Just standing was tiring.

"I don't mind walking the rest," I said to Henry.

"No need." He pulled himself back up into the flatbed. More slowly this time. I didn't bother wasting my energy telling him not to use up his trying to impress a woman who was not in the least bit interested.

Jud started up the truck then let it coast the twenty yards down the slope to the apartment building I was using. When he cut the engine, we just sat there, listening to it tick, unwilling to step down and start the hauling around of cases that would leave us aching and tired for a week. Jud and I had worked out a routine long ago: I would go and get the trolley; he would unbolt the tailgate and slide out the ramp; he'd lift cases onto the trolley; I'd trundle them into the apartment. About halfway through we'd stop for iced tea, then swap chores and finish up.

This time, when I went to get the trolley, it was Henry who rattled the bolts on the tailgate and manhandled the ramp down from the flatbed in a squeal of metal. I did my third of the lifting and carrying, but it felt all wrong.

When we were done and the cans of tuna and tomato and cat food, the sacks of flour and beans, the packets and cases and bottles and tins were all heaped in the middle of the living room floor and we'd bolted the tailgate back up, I invited them both into the cool apartment for iced tea. We sat. Henry wiped his face with a bandanna and sipped.

"That's good on a dusty throat, Ms. O'Connell."

"Molly."

He nodded acknowledgement. I felt Jud watching and waited for the inevitable. "Nice place you have here, Molly. Jud tells me you've stayed here on your own for almost three years." It was closer to two since Helen died, but I let that pass. "You ever had any accidents?"

"One or two, nothing I couldn't handle."

"Bet they gave you a scare. Imagine if you broke your leg or something: no phone, nobody for twenty miles around to help. A person could die out here." His tanned face looked earnest, concerned, and his eyes were very blue. I looked at Jud, who shrugged: he hadn't put him up to this.

"I'm safe enough," I said to Henry.

He caught my tone and didn't say anything more right away. He looked around again, searching for a neutral subject, nodded at the laptop. "You use that a lot?"

"Yes."

Jud decided to take pity on him. "Molly's writing a book.

About how all this happened, and what we know about the disease so far."

"Syndrome," I corrected.

Jud's mouth crooked in a half smile. "See how knowledge-able she is?" He drained his glass, hauled himself off the couch and refilled it in the kitchen. Henry and I did not speak until he got back to the couch.

In the past, Jud had tried everything: teasing me about being a misanthrope; trying to make me feel guilty about how the city had to waste valuable resources sending me supplies every month; raging at my selfishness. This time he just tilted his head to one side and looked sad.

"We need you, Molly."

I said nothing. We'd been through this before: he thought I might be able to find a way to cure the syndrome; I told him I hadn't much chance of succeeding where a decade of intense research had failed. I didn't blame him for trying—I was prob-ably one of the last immunologists alive—it's just that I didn't think I could do anything to help: I and the world's best had already beaten our heads bloody against that particular brick wall and gotten nowhere. I'd done everything I could, and I'd had a very good reason to try to achieve the impossible.

I had tried everything I knew, followed every avenue of enquiry, run down every lead. Working with support and good health, with international cooperation and resources, I got nowhere: my promising leads led to nothing, my time ran out, and Helen died. What did they think I could achieve now, on my own?

They'd told me, once, that they would take me into Atlanta forcibly. I said: fine, do that, see how far it gets you. Coercion might make me go through the motions, but that's all. Good research demanded commitment. Stalemate. But the way they saw it, I was their only hope, and maybe I would change my mind.

"Why do you stay?" Henry said into the silence.

I shrugged. "I like it here."

"No," Jud said slowly, "you stay because you still like to pretend that the rest of the world is getting on fine, that if you don't see that Atlanta is a ghost town you won't have to believe it, believe any of this is real."

"Maybe you're right," I said lightly, "but I'm still not leaving."

I stood and went to rinse my glass. If the people of Atlanta wanted to bring me food and precious gasoline in an attempt to keep me alive until I changed my mind, I wasn't going to feel guilty. I wasn't going to change my mind either. Humanity might be dying, but I saw no reason why we should struggle, just for the sake of struggling, when it would do no good. I am not a cranefly.

I WOKE UP BRIEFLY in the middle of the night to the soft sound of rain and the eerie chorus of bullfrogs. Even after two years I still slept curled up on one side of the bed; I still woke expecting to see her silhouette.

My arms and hips ached. I ran a hot bath and soaked for a while, until I got too hot, then went back to bed where I lay on my back and did qigong breathing. It helped. The song of bullfrogs steadied into a ratchety rhythm. I slept.

WHEN I WOKE THE sky was still red in the east. The bedroom window no longer opened so I padded stiffly through into the living room and slid open the door onto the deck. The air was cool enough for spring. I leaned on my elbows and looked out across the creek; the blank-eyed buildings on the other side of the gully were hidden by white swamp oaks that stretched their narrow trunks up into a sky the same powder blue as a bluebird's wing. To the right, sun gleamed on the lake. Birds sang, too many to identify. A cardinal flashed through the trees.

My world. I didn't want anything else. Jud was partially right: why should I want to live in Atlanta among people as sick as myself, listen to them groan when they woke up in the morning with stiff knees and stomach cramps, watch them walk slowly, like geriatrics, when I had all this? The birds weren't sick; the trees did not droop; every spring there were thousands of tadpoles in the pond. And none of them depended on me, none of them looked at me with hope in their eyes. Here, I was just me, just Molly, part of a world that offered no pain, no impossible challenge.

I went inside but left the door open to the air and birdsong. I moved jerkily, because my hips still hurt, and because I was angry with all those like Jud who wanted to fight and fight to their last breath. Humankind was dying. It didn't take a rocket scientist to figure that out: if women had so little strength that they died not long after childbirth, then the population would inevitably dwindle. Only five or six generations before humanity reached a vanishing point.

I wanted to enjoy what I could of it; I wanted to write this book so that those who were born, if they survived the guilt of their mothers' death, would at least understand their doom. We might not understand the passing of the dinosaurs, but we should understand our own.

After breakfast I put on some Bach harpsichord music and sat down at the laptop. I pulled up Chapter Three, full of grim statistics, and looked it over. Not today. I exited, called up Chapter One: How It All Began. I wrote about Helen.

We'd been living here at Westwater Terraces for two months. I remember the brutal heat of the August move. We swore that next time we had to carry desks and packing cases, we'd make sure it was in March, or October. Helen loved it here. I'd get home from the lab after a twenty-minute drive and she'd bring me iced tea and tell me all about how the fish in the lake—she called it the pond, too small for a lake, she said—were growing, or about the turtle she saw on her lunchtime walk and the way a squirrel had filled its mouth with nuts, and she'd ease away all the heat and snarl of a hard day's work and the *Mad Max* commute. The pond was her inspiration—all those wonderful studies of light and shadow that hang on people's walls—her comfort when a show went badly or a gallery refused to exhibit. I rarely bothered to walk by the pond myself, content to see it through her eyes.

Then she won the competition, and we flew to Bali—for the green and the sealight, she said—on the proceeds. I was grateful for those precious weeks we had in Bali.

When we got home, she was tired. The tiredness got worse. Then she began to hurt: her arms, her knees, her elbows. We assumed it was some kind of flu, and I pampered her for a while. But instead of getting better, she got worse: headaches, nausea, rashes on her face and arms. Moving too fast made her lower body go numb. When I realized she hadn't been around the pond for nine days, I knew she was very sick.

We went to the doctor who had diagnosed my gastro-enteritis last year. She suggested Helen had chronic fatigue syndrome. We did some reading. The diagnosis was a blow and a relief. The syndrome had many names—myalgic encephalomyelitis, chronic fatigue syndrome, post viral fatigue syndrome, chronic immune dysfunction—but no clear pattern, no cure. Doctors scratched their heads over it, but then said not to worry: it was self-limiting, and there had been no known deaths.

We saw four different doctors, who prescribed everything from amino-acid supplements to antibiotics to breathing and meditation. The uncertain leading the ignorant. Most agreed that she would be well again, somehow, in two or three years.

There were weeks when Helen could not get out of bed, or even feed herself. Then there were weeks when we argued, taking turns to alternately complain that she did too much, or not enough. In one three-month period, we did not make love once. Then Helen found out about a support group, and for a while we felt positive, on top of things.

Then people with CFS began to die.

No one knew why. They just got worse over a period of weeks until they were too weak to breathe. Then others became infected with a variation of the syndrome: the course of the disease was identical, but the process accelerated. Death usually occurred a month or so after the first symptom.

Helen died here, the day the Canada geese came. She was lying on the couch, one hand in mine, the other curled loosely around Jessica, who was purring by her hip. It was Jessica who heard the geese first. She stopped purring and lifted her head, ears pricked. Then I heard them too, honking to each other like they owned the world. They arrowed past, necks straining, wings going like the north wind and white cheeks orangy-yellow in the evening sun. Helen tried to sit up to look.

They circled the lake a couple of times before skimming in to land. Their wake was still slapping up against the bridge posts when Helen died. I sat there a long time, holding her hand, glad that she'd heard the geese.

They woke me at dawn the next day, honking and crying to each other through the trees on their way to wherever. I lay and listened to the silence they left behind, realized it would always be silent now: I would never hear Helen breathe beside me again. Jessica mewed and jumped up onto the bed; I stroked her, grateful for her mindless warmth and affection.

I came home tired from the funeral, with that bone-deep weariness that only comes from grief. Or so I thought. It took me almost a week to realize I was sick too.

The disease spread. No one knew the vector, because still no one was sure what the agent was: viral, bacterial, environmental, genetic? The spread was slow. There was plenty of time for planning by local and national bodies. It was around this time that we got the generator at the complex: the management were still thinking in terms of weathering the crisis, persuading occupants that it was safe for them to stay, that even if the city power failed, and the water systems, they'd be fine here.

There's something about the human race: as it slowly died, those who were left became more needy of each other. It seemed that we all became a little kinder, too. Everyone pulled inward, to the big cities where there was food, and power, and sewage systems. I stayed where I was. I figured I'd die soon, anyway, and I had this irrational urge to get to know the pond.

So I stayed, but I didn't die. And gradually it became clear that not everyone did. The latest count indicated that almost five percent of the world's population has survived. The deaths have been slow and inevitable enough that those of us who are still here have been able to train ourselves to do whatever it takes to stay alive. It wasn't so hard to keep things going: when the population is so small, it's surprising how many occupations become redundant. Insurance clerks now work in the power stations; company executives check sewage lines; police officers drive threshing machines. No one works more than four hours a day; we don't have the strength. None of us shows any signs of recovering. None but the most foolish still believe we will.

WESTWATER TERRACES IS BUILT around a small lake and creek. Behind the water, to the west, are deciduous woods; other trees on the complex are a mix of conifers and hardwoods: white pine and oak, birch and yellow poplar. The apartment buildings are connected by gravel paths; three white-painted bridges span a rivulet, the creek, and the western end of the lake.

I stood on the bridge over the rivulet, the one Helen and I had always called the Billy Goats Gruff bridge, and called for Jessica. Weeds and sycamore saplings pushed through the gravel path to my left; a dead oak straddled the path further up. Strong sun made the cat food in the dish by my feet smell unpleasantly.

The paint on the bridge was peeling. While I waited, I picked at it and wondered idly why paint always weathered in a pattern resembling a cross-section of epithelial cells, and why the wood always turned silvery gray.

Today I missed Jessica fiercely, missed the warmth of her on my lap and her fur tickling my nose when I tried to read. I hadn't seen her for over a week; sometimes the cat food I put out was eaten, sometimes it wasn't. A warbler landed on the bridge and cocked its head, close enough for me to see the gleam of its bright eye and the fine wrinkles on the joints of its feet.

I waited longer than usual, but she didn't come. I scrunched over the gravel feeling annoyed with myself for needing to hold another warm living creature.

Late morning was edging towards noon and the sun was hot on my shoulders. I was thirsty, too, but didn't want to go back to the beige walls of my apartment just yet.

The lake used to have three fountains. One still works, which

I regard as a minor miracle. A breeze pulled cool, moist air off the surface of the water and through my hair. A frog plopped out of sight, warned of my approach by the vibration of my footsteps. The ripple of its passing disturbed the duckweed and the water lilies. They were open to the light: white, pink, yellow. A bee hummed over the rich yellow anthers and I wondered if any ever got trapped when the lilies closed in the afternoon.

The bridge spanning the thinner, western end of the lake was roofed, a kind of watery gazebo reigned over by spiders. I crossed carefully, watchful of their webs. Helen used to call it running the gantlet; some of the webs stretched five feet in diameter, and very few were empty.

For me, the bridge was a divide between two worlds. The lake lay on the left, the east, a wide open expanse reflecting the blue sky, rippling with fountain water, surrounded by white pine and yellow iris. The right, the western end, was the pond: green and secret, shrouded by frogbit and lily pads. Stickleback and carp hung in the shadow of cattails and reeds, finning cool water over their scales.

There are almost a dozen ducks here, mallards mostly. And their ducklings. Careful of webs, I leaned on the rail to watch. The one with the right wing sticking up at a painful angle was paddling slowly toward a weeping willow on the left bank. Two of her three ducklings hurried after her. I wondered where the other one was.

It was getting too hot to be out.

Walking around the other side of the lake to get back to the roadway was hard work. The ground sloped steeply and the heat was getting fierce. Storms brought heavy rains in the summer and they were gradually washing away the dirt path, making it unsafe in places. The lake was twenty-five, maybe thirty, feet below me now and to my left, partially screened by the trees and undergrowth on the sloping bank. I heard a peep-ing noise from the water, just behind a clump of arrowhead. Maybe it was the missing duckling. I stepped near to the edge to get a closer look.

I felt the bucket-size clump of dirt give and slide from under my left foot, but my leg muscles, already tired from the heat and the climb, couldn't adapt to the sudden shift. My body weight dropped to one side with nothing to hold it but bone and liga-ment. I felt the ligament tear and pop and bones grind together. Then I fell, rolling and sliding down the slope, pain like a hot rock in my stomach.

I crashed into the knobbed bark of an oak; it took the skin off my back and shoulder. I saw the mossy rock clearly just before I hit it.

I WOKE TO HEAT thick enough to stand on. My mouth was very dry and my cheek hurt. My face was pressed against a tree root. I blinked and tried to sit up. The world swooped sickeningly. This time my face fell on grass. It felt better at first, not so hard.

I was hurt. Concussion at least. Something crawled down my cheek and into my ear. It took me a moment to realize it was a tear; it felt like someone else was crying, not me. I closed my eyes and began my testing with the left leg, moving it just an inch or so. More tears squeezed out from under my eyelids: the ankle and knee felt like they were being cut into with a rusty ripsaw. I moved my right leg. That was fine. My left arm seemed all in one piece, but moving the right hurt my ribs. I remembered hitting the tree. Probably just bruising.

I opened my eyes. The tree root my face had been resting on belonged to a smooth-barked birch. If I was sitting up I might be able to think.

I pulled my right leg under me and pulled myself forward with my left elbow. My moan startled a lizard sunning itself behind a leafy clump of purple loosestrife; its belly flashed blue as it skittered through the undergrowth and disappeared into a rotting tree stump. Sweat wormed over my scraped ribs, stinging. I dragged myself forward again.

I had to lift my head, bring my right elbow down to hip level and twist to roll over onto my back. The pain and the dizziness pulled thick, stringy nausea up over my skin. I thought I was going to pass out. After a moment, I sat up, shuffled back a couple of feet, and leaned against the tree.

The sun shone almost directly into my eyes. The floating sunlotus were open now, damselflies flashing metallic blues and greens against the rich yellow cups: must be about three o'clock in the afternoon. The air was still and quiet; the frogs silent and the birds sleepy. Fountain water pattered and splashed. I was very thirsty, and the air felt too hot and big in my lungs.

The slope stretched more than twenty feet upward to the path. I could do it if I moved in a zig-zag and used every tree for support, and if I started soon: I was dehydrated and every moment I spent out here in the sun made it worse. The water was about ten feet away, downslope, almost hidden by the tangle of ivy, undergrowth and dead wood.

I edged myself around the bole of the birch and shuffled backwards. The next closest tree was a white pine, about five feet away to the right. I had to stop four times before I got to within touching distance of the pine. I rested against its trunk, panting. The bark was rough and smelled of sun-warmed resin.

It was taking too long: at this rate, the sun would have leached away all my strength before I got even halfway up the slope. I had to risk moving faster. That meant standing up.

I wrapped my arms around the trunk and got myself onto

my right knee. The soil was cool and damp on my bare skin. I hauled myself up. The ridged trunk glided in and out of focus.

The next tree was close, only two feet directly upslope. Trying not to think how easy this would be if both legs worked, I took a deep breath and hopped.

The world came crashing down around my head.

I OPENED MY EYES. The pool was slicked with sunset, hot and dark and mysterious. Whirligigs and water boatmen dimpled the surface. My hand hung in the water. I pulled my face forward a few inches and lapped. Some went up my nose and dribbled down my chin, but enough went into my mouth to swallow a couple of times.

I drank again. It tasted odd, thin and green, but I could feel the good it was doing me. My cheeks felt hot and tight: sunburn. I dipped one side of my face in the water, then the other, then rested my forehead on my arm. Cicadas filled the evening with their chitinous song.

It looked like I'd been out four hours or more. No point beating myself over the head with my stupidity. The best thing I could do for myself right now was rest, wait for the coolth of night, rehydrate. Then think.

Swallows dipped and skimmed over the center of the lake, drinking in flight, snipping up unwary insects with wing-flicking grace. A cotton mouse nosed her way out from under a pile of leaves and scampered from the shelter of a log to a tree root. She sat up and gnawed on a seed.

I tried not to think about the green peppers ripening on the slope behind my apartment, of the fish in the freezer and fruit in the refrigerator.

About two feet away, a big spider sat on a lily pad, perfectly still but for one of its back legs that hung in the water, twitching. I thought maybe the leg was trapped by something, some hidden weed, but the rhythm was too deliberate; the spider was using the surface of the water as a drum. A mosquito fish came to investigate. It was tiny, no longer than a fingernail. The spider shot out its front legs and hauled the fish onto the lily pad, into its mouth.

The sunset had turned to purple and I could see stars. Tonight I couldn't recognize any of them; they looked cold and alien. It was cooling rapidly now, but I made no attempt to sit up.

My concussion and exhaustion had prompted a poor decision earlier: heading upslope was not the only way. If I could see a route along the lake shore that was relatively clear of undergrowth, I could walk or crawl around it until I reached the eastern end where the bank was only four or five feet high. That route would also bring me closer to the roadway that led to the apartment.

I blinked. I'd been asleep: the moon was up. This time, I could dip my hand into the water and bring it to my mouth to drink. I felt less like a wounded animal, more like a thinking, reasoning human being.

All around the pond, bullfrogs were singing. The moon was bright enough to reflect the flutter of trapped wings four feet from where I lay: perfectly still, a frog sat half hidden by cattails, a caddisfly in its mouth. The fly stopped struggling; they only lived a few hours anyway. Born without mouths, they reproduced then died. The frog's eyes glittered cold in the moonlight, watching me. Bullfrogs lived fifteen years.

They sang louder, following each other's lead, altering duration, pitch, and rhythm until the water boomed and echoed with their song. Tree frogs buzzed in the higher registers. I felt surrounded and menaced by sound.

Leaves rustled; a shadow eased through the undergrowth behind me. I turned my head slowly, faced two green eyes like headlights. Jessica. A friendly face.

"Jess. Here baby." She sniffed at my hip. I patted my chest, an invitation for her to snuggle. She froze. "Come on Jess. Come here baby." She sniffed my hand, and purred. I laughed. "Yes, you wild thing. It's me." Your friend.

She licked my hand. I lifted it to stroke her. She hissed. "It's me, Jess. Me." She regarded me with cold emerald eyes; in the moonlight, her teeth looked like old ivory.

A small creature, maybe the cotton mouse, scuttled somewhere close to the water. Jessica crouched, bellied forward.

I remembered how she had looked as a seven-week-old kitten, the way she had comforted me when Helen died.

Now I saw her as she had always been: a hunter, a wildcat who only licked my hand for the salt. I was not part of her world. I was not any part of anything's world. What I saw when I looked into the eyes of a frog or a mouse was nothing: not fear, not affection, not even contempt.

But I stayed. For Helen. To be part of the world Helen had loved. But staying here did not make me part of Helen's world: Helen was dead. Gone. She'd gone and left me with nothing. No one. It wasn't fair. I didn't want to be alone.

Why had she died and left me alone? I beat the dirt with my fist. Why? Why, Helen?

"Tell me why!"

My scream was raw, too hot, too human for this place. Tears rolled down my cheeks, big tears, big enough to reflect the world a new way. Helen was gone, and the geese were gone; I could stay here forever and she would never come back. I shouldn't be here.

The realization made me feel remote, very calm.

I sat up, ignoring the pain. Getting my T-shirt off was difficult; stretching for the branch two feet away, even worse. The T-shirt was already ripped; it made it easier for me to tear it into strips. I had to try several times before I could tie secure knots around the makeshift splint. Whenever the pain got too much, I rested.

An owl hooted, hunting.

I levered myself up onto knee and elbows, left leg stuck out behind me, stiff in its splint. Pain was just pain.

I dragged myself forward through a monochrome world: water sleek and black; trumpet honeysuckle leached lithium gray; moonlight lying like pools of mercury on leaves the color of graphite. Nature, thinking there was no one there to observe, let slide the greens and purples, the honey yellows, and showed her other face: flat, indifferent, anonymous.

I imagined making my pain as impersonal as nature's night face, putting it in a pouch at the small of my back, zipping the pouch shut. Out of sight, out of mind. Somewhere, I knew, there was a place where all the colors and scents of the day waited for morning, and then I would smell iris and pine resin, rich red dirt, and green pond scum. And feel the hot orange jags of pain. In the morning.

Right elbow, right knee, left elbow, drag. I focused on the tree forty yards away on the eastern bank, the tree I would use to haul myself upright and up onto the road. Right elbow, right knee, left elbow, drag.

Behind me, I heard the squeak of a small animal. The cotton mouse. Right elbow, right knee, left elbow, drag. The night stretched on.

The tree bark was rough on hands and arms already red and raw. No pain until morning. I pulled myself up the incline. The road felt marvelously smooth. I lay my cheek on the asphalt and breathed in the smell of dust and artificial things. Below, the pond glimmered, obsidian. The bullfrogs sang.

My ankle was not broken. I suspected that several ligaments were torn in my ankle and knee, but distalgesics and support bandages kept me able to manage until, eight days later, I could get around using a heavy branch as a cane. It was hard to hold the cane: the bandages wrapped around my hands and forearms were thick and clumsy.

I limped out to the deck and lowered myself into the hammock: the sky was thick with churning clouds. Usually, I loved watching the sheer power of a storm, the way it could boom and slash and drive over a hot and parched world, cooling and soaking. This time it was different. This time, when the wind tore through the stand of swamp oak, it seemed to me that it was killing things, flattening them, exposing them: turning the oak leaves silvery side up, ripping off branches, bending the trees almost to breaking point, pressing the grasses flat to the earth and snapping the heads off the marsh marigold. It was brutal.

I swung myself off the hammock. The show could go on without me. Inside, I made myself hot tea, put on Vivaldi—human music to drown the sound of the storm—and retired to the couch with a book, facing away from the glass doors. Let it do what it wanted. I refused to watch the rain swell the creek until it rose high enough to fill the burrows of voles and mice and drown their young.

My ankle and knee improved and I could walk slowly without the cane. I took the bandages off my arms. I did not go near the pond and walked only on the black artificial surfaces of the road.

Tonight was soft and warm; there was a quarter moon. I

walked over the Billy Goats Gruff bridge and listened to the frogs singing around the pond. I turned and walked up to the clubhouse. It took me a while to find the red switch handle. I threw it; the floodlight still worked.

I stood on the road overlooking the pond. Sodium light heaved greasily on the water next to the silver ripple of the moon. The water looked mysterious, unknowable, like an ancient harbor lit by naphtha flaming in a great bronze bowl.

I looked at it a long time. Helen was not here, she was in my heart. The pond belonged to the past.

I WAITED BY THE side of the road for Jud. There were more flowers, and it was just as hot and dusty, but this time there was no spiderweb, no cranefly. Just the birds singing, and me sitting on my suitcase. Three of Helen's paintings, wrapped in our sheets, leaned against the gate.

Jud was on his own. He coasted the truck to a stop and climbed down. I stood. He saw the suitcase.

"This mean what I think it means?"

"Yes."

And that's all we said. He always did know when to speak and when to keep quiet. He helped me push the case and the paintings up into the back, in among all the cans and bottles and sacks I wouldn't be needing.

"You want to drive?" he asked. I shook my head. We climbed up. I put the seat belt on; my life had suddenly become more precious. Jud noticed but said nothing. He made a U-turn and we set off back along the road to Atlanta.

I leaned my head against the window and watched the dog violets nodding at the side of the road. I had nearly died out here, believing struggling was for fools and craneflies. Perhaps those who struggled were fools, but they were fools with hope.

They were human. Helen was dead. I was not. I was sick, yes, but I still had intelligence, direction, purpose. And time. Something craneflies did not have. If I personally could not finish the research I intended, then those who came after me would. I could teach them what I learned; they would build on it. If I struggled and failed, that was not the end. I am not a cranefly.

The Things I Miss the Most

Nisi Shawl

THE TALK. THE SEX. Somebody to trust…

Before the Grigsby Process my life was like a series of ads being skipped. I blacked out a lot. Had lots of seizures. So many that sometimes my learning software obsolesced before I could complete a semester. At home I avoided clothes—they'd just get peed in or tangle me up and hurt me. I averaged four grand mals a month, but there were strings of lesser "events" too, which made me the perfect candidate, as the doctor explained to my moms when I reached fourteen. That and my resistance to the usual drugs, and my age.

"She's entering her second neuroplastic peak." Dr. Skilla had us all in his old examination room. It was stuffy and crowded.

Mammai nodded. She's Sicilian, so that meant "No." She didn't want me getting the Grigsby. Mombie put it into words for her, like she does: "Another gadget? I don't think so. How this gonna be different than VNS?"

Dr. Skilla pushed his blond bangs straight back and licked his lips. "Vagus Nerve Stimulation has a success rate of sixty percent at thirty-six months after implantation, and is especially effective with younger patients. Julia, though, is outside the optimal—"

"Cut to the chase." Mombie hates every minute spent in Private Space. She wanted to get away from the office and back on the Web. "If we'd a done the VNS first off insteada fartin around with drugs you wouldn't have to try no experiments like this Artificial Interthalamic Adhesion. Amirite?"

Skilla looked surprised. Probably that a woman fluent in AAVE and Leet could pronounce "interthalamic." Offended, too. "Surgery's only recommended for highly refractory cases. We had to be sure—had to exhaust all the pharmacological options prior to moving on to non-pharmacological therapies, and each formulation requires a period of several months to test its adequacy for the patient and register inconvenient side effects. There was no way to have known we'd reach this point. Fortunately, new developments make AIA a real possibility."

"I want to do it." I don't know why I said that. I mean, I had no idea then about Angelique.

Mombie looked stunned. "Chile—"

Mammai jumped in. On my side. "She want it, she have it." She shook her head yes.

And that was that. They argued, of course. Even in 2036 brain surgery was a big deal—sawing open someone's skull is no joke. But Mombie never denies Mammai what she wants, because she loves her. A thing I finally understand.

Apparently I stayed in a hospital the night before they put in my AIA. Apparently I was in there a couple of nights afterwards, too. I don't remember. That's how this stuff works.

OTOH, as Mombie would say, I remember plenty of incidents that never occurred.

For instance, my first meeting with Angelique. It was snowing, very rare these days. The white crystals clung to her dark hair, stuck to her striped and spotted furs. The sky churned with weather, gray on silver on dusk. In the shelter of a pine she stood alone, a cone of pinkish light falling toward her from the lamp across the street, her huge eyes dazzlingly beautiful. "Girl, why are you crying?" she asked me. Which made me laugh in recognition of the line referenced—I wasn't crying, actually. But *Peter Pan* is my favorite. It's a play about playing—something I would have needed friends to do.

According to what I found out later Angelique wasn't there. Oppositional Personas never are, per consensus reality. My ride home picked me up, and before it came I waited for it safe inside the community center, with all the other kids whose parents sent them there in the hope they'd form relationships with one another. But what I remember—what I believed before her death and in some sense still believe—is that she was waiting out there for me after choir practice and we walked home together and I was nine. Nine years old.

Five years ante surgery.

Angelique was my age. Always. How could she not be? As I'm told, she *was* me—the personality generated by the brain hemisphere that was split off during my callosotomy. In preparation for implanting the AIA, the major connection between my head's halves—the corpus callosum, it's called—was severed, along with a couple of other connections. Then the AIA was put in place, to funnel signals between the halves through there instead and filter out anything capable of causing a seizure.

Angelique had always been around, according to my restructured memories. Our initial meeting had felt fated—well, yes. Left, meet right. But in addition to an unreliable record of that first snow-hushed encounter, I had impressions of hearing of her earlier exploits, stories like flickering shadows or nonexistent flames: she was popular with other kids. Adults, too. She was a poet, a child prodigy—I'd read her work. It was published on several pages and I'd saved some of the most interesting pieces. Mine, I'm told, though I don't remember writing them.

Nine is too young for what we were. My retroactive recollections of the time before the operation include hand-clasps, wrestling holds, casually draped arms. Though we always seemed to be by ourselves, it wasn't till we turned fourteen—till the Grigsby—that our intimacy became more physical.

How could it? I know. Dreams aren't physical. And Angelique was very much like a waking dream.

Masturbation is such a sneaky-sounding word. Besides, we didn't just manipulate our—my—genitals. The softest brush of the back of her hand against my shoulder curled my toes.

Why didn't I notice immediately that she never operated the door controls? They opened and she came in, or more usually was already there. She left with or without me by simply being gone. She never used my setup's touch pad, either—I did all the searches she suggested and followed the links she sent in texts, and I made and found my own threads, too. By the time I noticed what was missing from it I had come up with my own version of Angelique's existence and believed both its contradicting sides. She was me. She was herself.

I knew I was right.

Seizureless weeks became seizureless months. The surgery's success seemed more and more self-evident, and gradually Mammai and Mombie grew accustomed to honoring the room lock I'd configured. I put on clothes most of the time, since it no longer felt so futile. And taking them off along with Angelique's felt so good.

I can't stop thinking about the last day. The last twenty-four hours we were together. I was seventeen. We were "studying." Angelique sat on my bed so lightly the covers barely wrinkled. Or maybe they didn't wrinkle at all.

At Mammai's ping I swiped off the lock and let her in. Her frizzy ponytail swung side to side as she scanned the room. "Where at is your Angelique?" she asked. I pointed. "Okay." She made a show of looking in the right direction, then turned back to me. Neither of my mothers ever pretended to talk to Angelique. "I leave this informational brochure for you to see later. When you are *alone*."

Which was whenever I wanted to be. Which was never.

The door opened again without me getting a ping. Mombie leaned in. "You havin problems with your studies? With that analogy question? It might make more sense if you get out an mix with real people your own age. Now you ain't all the time naked and you takin an interest in how you look." Pressure to relate to my supposed peers had increased with my neurotyp-icalness. "You be gettin better grades when you listen to how we want you to do. Don't hafta rely on that clunky old AIA no more, accordin to what we hear."

If I acted nice they left faster. "Okay. I'll watch the brochure. But first I need to see if the Miss Splooge patterns fit better than Dressy-Dress. They have wider colors." There. Nothing mono-syllabic about that answer.

Angelique sucked her puckered lips to make big fake kiss-ing noises. I scowled at her, then grinned to show I wasn't genuinely mad. She smiled her gorgeous smile, like a fat-bot-tomed cupid's bow.

Sure enough, Mammai joined Mombie at the room's threshold. But she wasn't quite ready to give up the inquisition. "How much higher are their price—"

"Doesn't matter," I interrupted. "Thirty-day approval period." Then I went into a long-winded enough of an explanation to drive them completely off and we were by ourselves at last. I set my tablet down on my carnation-molding nightstand and reached for Angelique's plump upper arm.

She flashed her palm at me in warning. "Stop. Are you sure they're gone?" Impatiently I picked the tablet back up and opened a surveillance window to show Mombie's back retreating from my door—though nearer than it should be.

"You think they don't know we fuck?" I asked. Mombie left the window's frame. Mammai's head replaced her.

"I think they'd rather they didn't have to. What's it cost to humor them?"

Precious seconds passed. The window cleared. The hairs at my neck's nape stirred and lifted in Angelique's damp breath. Then her lips pressed them flat, her teeth nipped the skin beneath, and as I turned and clutched her to me her tongue slicked half a circle around my throat. Instead of completing it, she lapped the tender triangle under my jaw and chin. I tilted my head up to feed her, then down to devour her mouth.

I held her. I held the world. Now I'm empty.

Such pleasure that night. After we tired, we slept. In the morning we woke curled together. Everything as usual. I wouldn't change that if I could.

I made tea, eggs, and toast in the kitchen and brought them in on a tray. Breakfast in bed. I can't recall—ever—her eating or drinking anything, but we talked and eventually it was all gone.

Our top topic was music. Angelique turned me on to jazz.

Not that fake-hallelujah stuff they play in churches that's supposed to make you join in. The real thing.

She got me to buy a keyboard for my tablet. "Here and here and here." She arched my fingers—too long, we'd decided, for a sax or guitar interface—and poised their tips on the ivory-colored oblongs.

"That's still a C minor?"

"The F note makes it a C sus 4. Same if it was major. Now add a low A and double the F in that lower octave."

The chord rang like sleigh bells, crisp and metallic. "What *is* it?"

Angelique laughed. "You want a name? Call it what you want. Murgatroyd. Throckmorton."

Our second choice of topic was star worship. She went for old people like Gonzalez and Hudson. They made me nervous, tottering around their modified circuits, always on the verge of collapsing, it seemed, despite the guardrails and nets and cushions surrounding the seniors' courses. I crammed them into the tablet's smallest window and projected Audie T and Scrapple from the Apple and Martha Vineyard on the wall screen. Audie jangled when she walked or jogged or skipped or jumped over obstacles, with the musical clash of her twentieth century-style bling. Martha wore quilted skirts like ruffs, multicolored tutus that rendered her leaps for marginal targets tougher to execute but fun to watch. She twirled excitedly while waiting her turn to run the course. Scrapple painted his body with a variety of patterns and always fussed at perceived attempts to mess them up. This morning he was threatening Audie with dismemberment for allegedly smearing his leopard markings.

"You know they make that shit up," Angelique said.

"'That shit'?" I repeated, snarking it.

"It's all an act to attract sponsors."

"Works, doesn't it?"

"So would authenticity."

Sometimes our talks became arguments. I hated them then. Love them now. Or anyway, I long to have them back.

The third most popular topic rotated a bit, usually between my health, my moms' increasing insistence on a non-Angelique social life, and plans for the future. All related. I had an appointment at the hospital in the afternoon, so perversely we avoided talking about anything to do with the improvement in my condition. I didn't tell her what the brochure had shown me when I watched it in the kitchen that morning. But if she was me, she must have known. Must have.

When our argument over who in the game to cheer for turned stale, I switched to wondering out loud what my moms found deficient about her. I fixated on how even the wind pushed things around but Angelique didn't: leaves and branches tossing in the breeze. Visible effects of things invisible to see. If we could change that, they'd cease their objections, right?

"Tilt it back," I told her, pointing at my Eames lounger. Obligingly, she settled onto the teal mohair cushion covers. But the seat's incline stayed stubbornly at forty degrees until, encouraged by Angelique's pats, I joined her on its edge and used my long legs to push us out of true.

"It's observer interference," I said, letting the chair's legs settle down again. This was the one serious thing we seriously fought over: what made her real. Sometimes we changed sides, though neither of us ever would give in.

"You mean, I'm here because you see me? Hear me?" She pinched my nose lightly. "Feel me?"

"Mmm-hmm." I nuzzled the fold of her armpit. "Smell you. Taste you."

"So if you were everywhere at once, I would be everywhere at once too."

"And if I die—*when* I die—you'll disappear." The logical conclusion. The one that made me cringe and change.

"Die?" Laughing bravely, fakely, she shook an admonishing finger in my face. "No! Nononono! You're rich—you *can't* die!" She snaked one arm between me and the scoop of the seatback, wrapped the other around my sweatered curves to meet it and hold me tight. I lost sight of her face. Laughter or sobs now? "Swear you'll never die! Swear we'll live *forever*!"

I swore. According to what I've been told, it was a promise asked of and given to myself.

My minder chimed for school. I minimized the game's feed and opened the latest module: historical precedents for restricting political representation. Recorded lecture, then an essay prompt, then access to a forum. Angelique helped with the essay and gave me feedback on my forum posts before I sent them in. "Too involved," she complained when I tried arguing that nonhuman intelligences like sharks and foxes deserved a voice in government too, now the pendulum was reversing. "That's, what, three points in one paragraph?"

"But they're true!" I protested.

"Doesn't matter. Copy and delete." Trailing her smooth fingers along the part in my hair. "Send the first sentence; save the rest to use later."

She was right. I got twelve replies, and a lively conversation in which I not only brought forth my other assertions but heard new proof of them. Who knew snails were so devious? Before we finished answering all the threads my minder chimed again. "Not another module," I groaned. No. It was my hospital appointment already. Annual follow-up on the success of my Grigsby. And the choice the brochure presented.

Angelique and I chose my outfit: an orange-and-violet pol-ka-dot tent dress and spangled silver tights. Kind of a circus theme. Miss Splooge's specialty. I've kept it, but I don't wear it anymore.

"Your Angelique comin along?" Mombie asked when we found her waiting out on the porch for our ride. "I booked for four, in case." A brown Placid pulled around the cul-de-sac's corner as she spoke.

"Yeah. Where's Mammai?"

"Here I am." She stepped out through the front door and we went down the steps and got in the Placid. I reminded Mammai to leave room for Angelique in the middle of the back seat. She had made a joke out of sitting on Mammai's lap that first trip to see Dr. Skilla, but of course I wasn't fooled.

Mombie and the contingency driver talked about the game I guess—I don't recall. I was splicing both Angelique's hands to mine, twisting to face her and knotting our fingers tight. Anxious.

Skilla had a new office on the sixth floor. We got out of our ride on the third. "Stairs this way," Mombie said. "Use it or lose it. Cmon."

Angelique passed me on the way up but waited on the last landing. Mammai opened the fire door for us. Then we had to find the elevators anyway, to check the directory.

The new examination room was part of a corner suite of epileptologists who shared a single reception desk. Seconds after sitting down in a carpeted lounge sort of area we were admitted. A nurse unnecessarily took my height, weight, temperature, pulse, and blood pressure, and used—I am not making this up—a little rubber mallet to tap my knee and test the speed of my reflexes. Then he left us to ourselves long enough that Mombie stood up and scouted the room for inactivated Web access points. Would she really dare open one? We were the only people around at the moment, but potentially exposing other patients entering what was supposed to be Private Space could mean a big fine. Angelique and I watched her anxiously.

At last Skilla showed. Mombie subsided. Paging through my file via his proprietary display, the doctor hummed a happy-sounding tune. "Excellent!" He looked away from the blank wall where he'd been projecting. "Nearly four years without an event. I think it's safe to say you're cured!"

Mammai smiled a small, tentative smile. But Mombie frowned. "That it? How we spozed to handle that other thing we brung up?"

"Yes, well, when we turn off the AIA the situation with the Oppositional will resolve itself."

I edged closer to Angelique on the love seat. "What do you mean, 'when' we turn it off?"

"As per the brochure, removal's unnecessary. And far too invasive. The organic adhesion that's built up mimics the AIA's structure fairly strictly, and in some cases the two are indistinguishable. Much easier to simply flip off the bridging current and leave the disabled hardware in place."

"You—you already decided on doing this?" Mammai only shook her head in agreement; she didn't talk much around strangers.

"It's in the literature I sent Ms. Klaver."

Mombie cut her eyes away from mine. Anger fought a thrill of uneasiness. "We ast was there a risk of your seizures startin up again. Tell her."

"No risk. The natural adhesion has essentially taken over the AIA's function. The Grigsby Process *is* a bit experimental, even today," he admitted. "But if there's a recurrence we can turn your AIA back on. Easily."

A soft weight against my side: Angelique's warm, sweet-scented flesh. I couldn't lose her. I wouldn't.

Nothing in the brochure had hinted at it.

Mombie, though—"That other thing we brung up"? Which the doctor blandly assured her would be resolved—which involved my Oppositional—that sounded potentially problematic. "What if you don't turn the AIA off? If I don't authorize it?" I asked. "What if I want to keep things how they are?"

A momentary silence. Dr. Skilla seemed puzzled. "Why?" he asked. "I've never had a patient refuse at this stage—wait!" He leaned toward the wall again, thumbing virtual pages. "Ms. Platto reported that you've become attached to your Oppositional, even named it—'Angelique,' right?—and that it seems to impede your social progress. Don't let an unfortunate side effect dictate your behavior."

Dictate? My Angelique?

"Besides," he added, "technically, for now, you're a minor."

Mammai sat forward and laid a spidery hand on my sleeve. "It is for your good." Mammai's words were valuable in their scarcity.

Mombie faced me full-on at last. "You gotta trust us. Everything gonna be all right."

Everything would be all right. The situation would "resolve."

I looked at Angelique. Her eyes were wide. She was scared. Like me. But according to her argument, she was real, with or without me. Which I believed when she didn't. And the natural adhesion had already taken over from the AIA. And they could turn it back on easily. That would surely restore her. Surely.

"Okay."

The switch was internal; they used a thing like a light-up tiara to move it. I put on the tiara. Felt nothing. I took it off and Angelique was gone.

I put the tiara back on and made them make the AIA work again. And again. And again.

She stayed gone. Gone for good.

Dr. Skilla and his techs say there's no reason why. None they know. It's so experimental. Give it time.

How many years.

Once in a while, yeah, I see her out of the corner of my eye, catch a glimpse of that adorable ghost. A lie.

The sex; the talk.

Somebody to trust.

Gone Astray

The Sorrow Stealer

A.J. Cunder

THEY SAY IF YOU pray hard enough, I'll come to steal your sorrows. While you sleep, I'll slip like smoke through a window cracked open. Like a whisper through a door ajar, a draft through a chimney or a mousehole. Always for a price. Payment must be made. I won't take grief for free.

Those rumors and whispers, those legends of the Sorrow Stealer, you once refused to believe. But soon you'll know they're right.

As my shadow slides across your bedroom walls, I riffle through your memories. Perhaps I'll take one in exchange as I browse your thoughts and dreams—a dinner with your daughter when she still looked up and smiled; a first kiss from your husband, when love began to blossom; your first time swimming, first time skiing, first sunset on the beach. Each memory a portal, a window to the soul, a hint at what joy might be, what hides behind your half-remembered smiles—something I can never touch, no matter how hard I try, how deep I prod and pry.

Or perhaps I'll take a trinket, a ring rose gold and tarnished that slipped beneath your bureau, last worn years past, before they called you *widow*. Or a dog tag forgotten, from a pet long passed and buried; an acorn found and kept when you were small, hiking with your father, sheltered in a jar of glass, precarious on the mantle. All symbols of these moments that once turned your lips up high, something I can never have, a heart air-light and free. Before your sorrows came. Before you begged for me.

Now, as grief for loved ones lingers, as heartache binds you tight, a relationship so promising turned sour overnight, I dig my fingers deep, I plunge them in and squeeze. And all your sorrows fill me, like ink pouring from a well. For this, for sadness so thick it stains, a few years of your life I'll demand as my reward. It isn't joy, it isn't peace, but it's payment all the same.

And in the morning, you'll wake and smile, refreshed and carefree for a time. You'll know your prayers were answered, not caring for the cost. I'll bear your burdens for you, as my spirit wanders, attending mournful sighs, until you call again—

But wait, what's this? In a room beside your own, a girl of ten jolts up in bed. She looks at me with knowing eyes, an uncanny glow about her—no mortal sight can pierce my shroud, no creature of this realm should see me. Golden curls hang down in ringlets, a rosy face's frame.

"Sorrow Stealer," she greets me with a grin. "I've waited for you oh so long—and now at last you've come."

But why, girl? I ask as I swirl like vapor in this dimension, waiting for some trap to spring, some danger lying low. *I sense no sorrow in you.*

"That's because I have no sorrow, no troubles, grief, or woe. Like you, I come from another world, born of magic, hills, and barrows. A changeling child, here to learn and grow. To pilfer joy and laughter as fuel for fairy spells. But one thing I cannot understand among these humans and their haunted smiles is what their sadness feels like, their pain, their hurt, their sting when life turns bitter. I cannot touch it, cannot grasp it, cannot take it as you can. Maybe you can help me?" She bats her eyes and pleads. "Can you share the sorrows of this world, the sadness you've stolen?"

I hesitate. I wonder to myself, what's the catch? Could I even gift what I had taken, that clenching, binding numbness that forms my very essence?

Never have I done such a thing. I know not if I can. But if I do, a price I must demand from you.

"What would you have?" she asks, spreading wide her arms. "An ounce of moonbeam to light your darkest path? Perhaps an ell of stardust, the key to realms immortal? Or the bottled breath of pixie, to relive any memory?"

What do I want, my deepest, truest desire? I can ask of her nigh anything. Her magic would oblige.

Joy, I say. *Genuine and true. No memory, no imitation, no empty hollow years. Share with me the joy you've stolen from these humans, your companions. And then you'll taste what I have tasted these countless, endless ages.*

She chews her lip a moment, eyes darting to and fro. "Okay," she says, "a bargain struck, we'll do this here and now." Holding out her hand, her fingers stretched and eerie, she summons forth a spark of eldritch light, blue glow coalescing.

My fingers likewise reach, my core condensed, contracting. I pull up from the depths a strain of ancient pain, unraveled from my beginning—the first sorrow of humanity, so very long ago. Intellect evolved, spirits tarnished in a fall, and my shade sprang up in a garden. I offer it to this fairy girl who pauses before nodding. Our fingers touch. Dimensions merge, and I gasp in newfound breath. What is this charm that shatters my heart and builds it stronger anew? A sea of stars unfolds before me, reaching without end. In the infinite, the cosmic, the eternal, I *am*. A pinprick, a point, a creature who creates alongside countless others the tapestry of time. Who belongs, who *exists*, worthwhile and with purpose, a part to play in this universe, however large or small.

The changeling shudders, hugs herself, knees drawn up to her chest. Then she looks to me, her eyes wide gleaming saucers. "Return to me the perfect joy I've given!"

'Twas not our agreement. I'm itching to be off.

"But I realize now," she continues, "without that joy, I'm weakened. I thought, perhaps, pain might work, abundant in this world, a better fuel for magic. Surely, you as well must be diminished without your truest sorrow."

I have sorrows enough. For a while, at least, I'll last.

And in that time, a new plan forming, I know what I will do.

The changeling pounds her fist and cries. Strands of hair criss-cross her brow, like a spider's web entangled. I let her wallow in her sorrow, but before I leave, I pause. I find your room and whisper softly as you sleep, some surety of purpose, a certainty spoken, *no matter the sadness, you matter, a part of this infinite world. This universe created you; in its palm it holds you. It formed you, shaped you, breathed life into your bones. And while happiness and sorrow may compete in ebbs and flows, this truest joy you'll always know.* I leave a piece of what I was given, a peace that will endure—instead of simply taking sorrow, now I can supplant it. A germ of hope sown in the darkness, a reminder of goodness and grace, for each supplicant I visit, each grief-stricken cry, each anguished plea that summons me to steal their sorrow away.

It will weaken me, in the end, as these anchors of comfort

take root. But now this joy has plenished me, I know I can't contain it. Already it dilutes the sadness that sustains me. Soon I'll be like darkness clutching dawn, morning's fog banished in the sunlight. Before I depart, I watch your lines of worry fading, your once-clenched hands relaxing, your heartbeat calm and steady. I push the jar with its acorn away from the mantle's edge, polish the ring and place it beside your bed, dust off the dog tag forgotten. Perhaps the fairy girl will see these too, through her mourning thick and heavy, or find mementos of her own. Perhaps one day she'll call for me and bargain once again. Until then, with newfound purpose, I hearken to my next solicitor and slip out upon a breeze.

The Weight of Grief

Simon Quinn

GRIEF RUMMAGED THROUGH MY soul, picked apart my thoughts, and filled my bones to the brim with granite. People tell you "sorry for your loss" as if the Band-Aid words will fix the gaping hole that's been ripped right through your chest and filled with ice. But the words don't. They can't. Nothing will ever be the same ever again because the only person who's ever matched my soul piece for piece is gone. We'd only been together three years, married for one, and already I'd lost him to a snake bite the paramedics didn't get to in time. He's gone and he's never coming back and I am pinned to the bottom of an invisible river that keeps trying to smooth my edges into nothing.

His family told me to cremate him. The man I love, supposed to be reduced to ashes next Tuesday. The letters of his name pressed into the bronze bottom of the simple urn they paid for. It was too expensive to bury him and he wouldn't have wanted to be trapped in a box for the rest of eternity. He was claustrophobic.

But an urn was still a container. Smaller than a casket, and sure, there would be less of him to keep, but it's still a container. Surely he wouldn't have liked that either.

Whoever controlled the universe had a sick sense of humor and the ice in my chest plunged deeper toward the impossible zero kelvin. Why would they make me say goodbye so soon? Why did I have to accept it?

"Hey, we're closing. I'm gonna have to ask you to leave," a young woman said.

The café's bright blue walls were sporadically covered with potted plants, paintings from local artists, and large windows that were letting in the cherry-red and fiery orange light of the sunset. My table for two was pressed against the wall and the deep brown top held the rings of long-forgotten iced coffees and teas. Coffees and teas that I'd shared every Sunday with Ezra before the world took him away from me.

"Right. Sorry." I nodded at her as I gathered up my granite bones and stood to leave. Sunday drinks would never be the same again. The faint notes of outdated pop music followed me out the door before cutting off along with the tinkling sound of bells that jingled when the door swung shut behind me.

There wasn't anything left to do except go home and try to fall asleep in an apartment that wasn't supposed to be empty. The sheets in the bedroom still held the faint scent of his cedar-rosemary bodywash because I didn't have the heart to wash it out of them. It's all I had left of him to come home to. But both previous nights, I'd leaked tears onto his pillowcase for twenty minutes before moving to the couch because the bed wasn't supposed to be that big.

The headlights of my car flashed as I pressed the key fob to unlock it. Lost in my grief I almost didn't notice the flyer stuck under my windshield wiper. The black and pink paper fluttered as I picked it up and for the first time since I'd heard the news I could feel my heartbeat again. The simple *thunk babump* of hope restarting. The hope of a future back in my hands and the hope of getting to feel the soft skin of his fingers against my jaw as his deep voice rumbles my name, *Oliver*, a breath away from my lips.

The hope that my music wouldn't be lost forever. He was my muse and the world was silent without him.

> *Dear Oliver,*
>
> *I can't bring back your warmth. I can't bring back your music notes. But I might know someone that can help you not have to say goodbye. Someone who can give you the life you thought you were going to get to have.*
>
> *If you look for the rose that blooms in the darkness and follow the crack behind it down as far as you can go, you'll reach a painting on the concrete. A painting of yellow flowers growing from a grave will greet you. Press on the petals of the one closest to the headstone and be prepared for questions. You're not the only one who misses someone, so you have to convince them to help you if you wish to not be alone anymore.*
>
> *Hallie and Percy are kind, but they keep to themselves. Necromancers aren't ones for good company.*
>
> *Sincerely,*
>
> *A Friend*

Necromancy. Forbidden magic, sure. But it would mean Ezra back. Sunday-afternoon drinks. Sleeping in our bed and the tangle of his fingers in my hair as we watched our favorite shows.

It would mean I could sing again.

I could play the guitar again if it meant I could see him smile at me in that soft simple way of his when I played for him. That smile that lifted the left corner of his lips ever so slightly higher than the right and put love in his eyes as he listened.

If necromancy meant I could have that back, then I would risk any repercussions.

"THE ROSE THAT BLOOMS in the darkness," I murmured to myself as I reread the letter. What could that *mean*? We—I lived in a desert. Roses didn't bloom here. Unless…necromancy was a forbidden magic. Also forbidden: infused alcohol.

Magic interacted with alcohol in strange ways. Sometimes it made the partaker bubblier, but for others it had adverse effects. Some people grew thorns from their throats, others passed out for too long. Sometimes gravity turned off, or so much else. It was unpredictable. Extraordinary. Hidden but not impossible to find.

And for the people who wanted to find it, the most popular bar was under a blazing pink neon sign of a rose that turned on at midnight. Ezra and I had gone once, but we didn't stay long. The frenzied energy was too much for us and since it was forbidden magic, no paramedics could be called once people started to collapse.

I started my car and tried to find where I remembered going. The memory came back easily enough.

"ARE YOU GONNA WEAR your fishnets?" Ezra's teasing chuckle came from the bathroom where he was putting on eyeliner.

I grinned despite him not being able to see me. "Of course, who do you think I am?"

"I love you for a reason, and it's certainly not for your fishnets."

I rolled my eyes at the mirror where my reflection rolled his eyes back. I stood in my black fishnet tights underneath sparkly black booty shorts and my sheer purple top that showed my top surgery scars off nicely. My reddish-brown curly hair brushed over my ears and the freckles that lay scattered across my nose were partly covered by thin wire circle frames that emphasized my big brown eyes.

Ezra appeared behind me in the mirror. His hands cupping my shoulders as he whispered in my ear, "I can't believe you've convinced me to break the law with you."

I laughed, and he rested his chin on my shoulder. His sword earrings tickled my neck on one side and my shoulder on the other. He had done dramatic eyeliner and dressed in ripped black skinny jeans and a red crop top with a collection of music notes on the front. His blond hair tickled my neck when he tilted his head to press it against mine. "Well, whatever happens, at least it'll make for a good memory."

AND NOW ALL I was left with was that memory. Along with many other memories of course, but that one was already fading. The exact shade of brown his eyes used to be getting mixed up with the browns of the tables in the coffee shop and the bookshelves that lined our—my—walls.

I drove in silence until reaching the other side of the city. Parking in front of a music store, I waited until the clock turned to midnight so the rose would be in bloom.

Midnight crept up slow enough to count the stars appearing one by one in the sky above. The stars had always mattered to Ezra. He had memorized most of the constellations in the northern hemisphere and on any night the sky was clear enough, he would look up, grab my arm, and point out his favorites. I mostly just gazed at him. He was my own constellation on earth. Maybe I should have learned the stars for him instead of writing songs for and about him. I'd always loved music and Ezra became my muse. Losing him meant losing my music too.

Finally, the time was right, and as I stepped out among the scream of the cicadas I couldn't help taking a deep breath. I loved the taste of night air on my tongue.

The rose wasn't hard to find since I knew where I was going, but the crack took some searching. Finally I saw it, just wide enough for my slim frame to fit through the bricks. I couldn't tell if it was a type of alley, or if the "friend" that had left the paper on my windshield had also cracked the bricks for my journey.

The moment I shoved my way through the cracks, small purpl lights flickered on to guide me down stairs that wound and winded farther than I thought possible. I couldn't tell if I was at a basement level underground or if something shifted my perception, but time dragged slower than it should have before I reached the painting of yellow flowers. The concrete stairs that went down and down and down met brick walls that towered above my head as far as I could see. Small lightbulbs lit the path every few feet and cast deep shadows in their wake. Once I reached the bottom, the staircase opened up to a dingy corridor blocked by a concrete wall with the painting splashed across it. I pressed the petals as instructed and rumblings started underneath my feet. I stepped back a second before the wall the painting was on moved upward, opening to what looked like an empty courtroom that wasn't designed by someone who'd ever been in a proper courtroom. Everything was carved out of some kind of black stone. The section for jury members off to the left, a podium near the back wall under a massive clock where I assumed a judge would stand, and a lonely little chair in the center of the room facing the podium.

I stepped over the threshold of the corridor, under the wall that had lifted, and two women walked out of a door I hadn't noticed. They both went to stand behind the podium. I swallowed thickly. I'd really jumped into this whole mess without a plan. Without fact-checking. I didn't know who had left the letter, or if the someone who had signed it "friend" was setting me up for murder. But I was there. And if being there got my Ezra back, then it was worth it. I wasn't sure if the lonely chair was for me, but I went to stand behind it.

"Name?" the woman on the left asked. Her black hair draped around her shoulders like a shroud; her purple dress swirled around her thin frame in a mesmerizing manner.

"Oliver Cadence," I whispered, not able to form words any louder.

"Why are you here, Oliver Cadence?" Her voice held no malice, no anything. Maybe curiosity, but mostly it was empty. Like she was used to people appearing in her courtroom and telling them no.

"I'm here to get my husband back. I got a letter saying you could bring him back to me." I hadn't talked this much in days and my voice cracked at the idea of being able to hold him in my arms again.

"Why should we help you?" This time the woman on the right spoke. She was a redhead with flowers woven through the braid that rested on her head. Her round frame was swathed in pink silk that bunched in rosettes near her knees.

What was I supposed to say? That I couldn't go on without him? That he was the love of my life and without him I was empty? That life didn't have music without his light brightening my days? "Isn't the fact that I love him so much I considered coming here enough?"

"Many people come down." The one in the purple dress said as the lady in pink silk nodded.

"Oh." I swallowed. "Um, may I have your names?"

The dark haired one shared a glance with her companion before pointing to herself and going, "Hallie."

"Percy."

"So why should we help you? What can you give us in payment?" Hallie asked.

"I can sing for you? For payment?" I didn't know where the words came from. I hadn't even been able to listen to music without him, but I was offering to sing to strangers? I would do anything to get him back.

"Then sing. It'll help us decide." Percy pulled out two chairs from the empty jury section and she and Hallie sat down to listen.

So I sang. It was all I had. I reached down to the place where notes blossomed in my chest and I sang about our wedding day. I sang about his smile as he kissed me. I sang about his constellations. And I sang about my grief. The words came from somewhere outside of me as I poured out the ice that ran through me, the granite in my bones, and the Band-Aid words that didn't do anything to fix it. By the end tears streamed down my cheeks and the women had matching streaks down their faces as well.

Once I finished I couldn't stop shivering. Memories of Ezra kept me warm, but I'd just delved into the ice and not even the ghost of his smile could cut through it. I waited for their verdict as the necromancers found handkerchiefs to wipe their tears, and cleared their throats, and looked at each other before leaning close to talk. All I could do was wait.

So I waited.

After a bit I sat down in the chair. It was surprisingly comfortable and I sank into its invisible cushions.

And I waited.

The clock ticked above them. I got out my phone but it wouldn't turn on and my watch was dead. So I stared at the clock and bounced my legs.

Soon an hour passed.

A second hour.

I got up and walked in small circles to stretch my legs. The wait was getting to me and I was losing confidence by the minute.

In the middle of the third hour they stood up and watched me.

"If we do this for you, there are conditions." Hallie spoke.

"Can you trust enough?" Percy asked.

I nodded. "Anything to have him back. Anything."

Hallie looked at Percy once again, sucked in a breath, and looked back at me. "If you walk back all the way up with no looking back, no talking, and no reaching for a hand, we'll bring him back for you. But you have to trust that he's behind you every step of the way. You have to believe and you have to make it all the way out. Both of you. Before you can turn around, wait fifteen minutes. If you fail he's dead forever."

Forever. The word hung heavy over my head, but the hope of the promises made me lighter. I could do it. I could make it. "Just tell me how to get him back."

"You leave. He'll follow. Trust." Percy smiled, but that was that. An invisible force pushed me back to the bottom of the stairs. A single deep breath later and I was on my way.

Anything to have Ezra back. Anything.

So I went up. And up. And up.

And I couldn't hear footsteps. I couldn't hear winded breathing other than mine. My chest heaved as I trudged up those stairs. My legs started to cramp and I knew I still had so far to go.

But anything for him.

Doubt started to trickle in. I had no reason to believe Ezra was really behind me. Maybe Hallie and Percy tricked me. They took my song and sent me back with no Ezra to hold me close. They didn't want me to have him back. I still didn't know how I'd explain his presence. I only knew I needed him.

I shook my head. They had no reason to lie. They had cried during my song. Surely they wouldn't just make me sit there while they discussed their plans for next Tuesday. They had to have been debating my getting Ezra back. And they'd said I could have him if we just made it back up. If I just made it back up these stairs.

I could make it for him.

The sunrise greeted my tearstained face after another hour of trudging up steps and squeezing through the cracks in the brick. The cold dawn air stung against the dried tear tracks on my cheeks, but that sunrise meant he'd made it back with me. I could have him back. I got him back.

But I forgot about waiting fifteen minutes.

So when I turned around at the first sight of that glorious sunrise, my husband's gorgeous face twisted in anguish as he evaporated right before my eyes, taking every color of the world with him. Everything went silent again. My heartbeat, which had been so loud in the staircase, vanished. My veins filled back up with granite and ice, and the added weight brought me to my knees.

What was the point of living if Ezra wasn't with me?

The Song of the Forest

Mika Grimmer

As I TRACE THE stitches of well-worn embroidery with my thumb, I can still hear echoes of my mother's words from so very long ago. She warned me not to venture into the forest that skirted the edge of our village. She'd thought a healthy fear of the woods, which held any manner of creatures waiting to snatch up any child foolish enough to wander into them alone, would have been enough to dampen my curiosity. But as such warnings often do, her words only honed the curiosity already alive within me.

It was the midsummer festival when I finally entered the forest alone. That morning I picked out my favorite dress with pink flowers and intertwining vines wrapped around the hem and neckline Mother made for me. Even then, I could feel the love she poured into every stitch.

A riot of sounds and colors filled the village square as laughter of our neighbors mingled with the songs of the minstrels and flowed all around us. However, while I sat at my mother's side, I heard another song. One that only I could hear of growing things and mysteries laid buried in my heart.

I slipped from the trestle table and wove through the commotion in the village square, following the distant melody to the edge of the forest, then passed under the trees. The music grew louder with each step I took. The boughs of the trees skated across my shoulder as I sped down a game trail, each step carrying me deeper into the unknown.

The path shifted downward, and as I rushed forward, twigs snapped beneath my feet and I kicked up blooms of mineral-scented dust. I no longer had any control of where my feet landed when a chance root caught my foot, and I tumbled end over end. The world spun in a blur of green and brown all around me. I closed my eyes, until mercifully, I collided with something distinctly solid, warm, and furry.

I rubbed my eyes with my fists, blinking hard, and when my vision cleared, my eyes alighted on an enormous gray wolf grinning down at me.

I scrambled to my feet. "Hello, mister wolf." My voice shook only a little.

He stood, tail wagging slowly from side to side, then turned to follow the path deeper into the forest. After a few paces, he turned to look at me.

"You want me to follow you?"

He let out a soft bark before he continued down the trail.

I hesitated, looking back up at the hill and toward my village. At least, I thought I was looking in the right direction. I wasn't entirely sure as the thick pine foliage obscured any vestige of the redbrick buildings festooned in chains of paper flowers for the midsummer festivities. Even as I thought of home, the gentle music that first drew me here tugged at my mind. I took a deep breath and trailed behind the wolf.

Together we wended our way through a labyrinth of game trails until the thick trees gave way to a verdant glade teeming with life. A squat stone hut with a thatched roof the color of honey stood at the far edge of the clearing where a woman, bent-back and dressed all in black, knelt at the edge of an herb garden. When we neared I saw that despite her stooped back and gnarled hands, she only had a few strands of gray intertwined in the warm auburn braids that snaked around her head like a crown. She arched an eyebrow as she turned to face us.

"Why have you come to me?" She asked, pushing herself up from the ground.

I was unsure of what to say, so I told her the truth. "I didn't come to you. I came into the forest to find out where the music was coming from when I met the wolf."

The woman's chuckle surprised me.

"He is no wolf," she said, scratching him at the nape of his neck.

"He's not?"

"No, my dear. He's my familiar. Child, what is your name?"

"Martje." I stood a little taller, finding courage in the name I shared with my mother's mother.

The woman nodded. "Well then, Martje, I'll tell you why you are here. You're here because the forest sang to you, as it does to every witch, in their own time."

A witch? How could that be? My mother never told me of any woman in our family that'd taken on that heavy mantle of responsibility before. "But I can't be a witch," I said at last.

Her cheeks pulled back in a smile and it was as if the earth had split open to show the very roots of trees. It would have been frightening on someone else's face, but on hers it was good. It was natural. It was as if the forest itself was welcoming me into some secret it held just for me.

"Martje, dear, come inside with me and let me show you."

"Show me what?"

"Your future."

Maybe I should have turned away at that moment and run home. But when the familiar padded his way into the cottage, I knew no fear as I followed behind him. And besides, I wanted to see what she would show me.

The single-room cottage was homely and warm. Each corner held a new fascination. On one wall, dusty bottles of every color imaginable lined shelves that spanned from floor to ceiling. Teetering stacks of leather-bound tomes littered every flat surface of the room, and my fingers itched to page through each of them in turn.

The witch took a silver basin from the fireplace mantel and placed it on the table. "Take this," she said, handing me a ladle. "And fill this basin from the barrel of rainwater just outside the door."

I hesitated for a moment, but I did as I was bid.

"Good, now stand before the basin and do as I do." The crone touched the surface of the water. Silver ripples danced away from the contact. She drew her finger in a circle three times.

Again, I did as I was bid, and when I lifted my finger from the water, shapes began to shift and shimmer just beneath the surface.

"What do you see, child?"

At first the images moved too quickly for me to understand, but at last they slowed and came into focus, as if I were watching a play unfold beneath the water. "It's me!" I exclaimed. "But I'm older, I think. I'm grinding up the leaves of strange plants."

"You will learn in good time," she said.

The next image floated the surface. "There's a crow with a

broken wing is perched on my lap. His name is Senan. How do I know that?"

"Don't look away from the basin yet, child," she urged.

The image shifted again and I saw an old woman sitting in a chair by the fire. She held a scrap of faded cloth between her fingers, tracing the embroidery with her fingertips. Light spills into the room as the door swings open, framing the shape of another young girl.

When I look up, there she is. Her dark hair hangs by her face in tangled plaits and her dress is matted with mud.

"Why have you come to my home?" I ask, tucking the well-worn fabric into a skirt pocket.

"I followed this crow through the forest. Is he yours?"

Senan hops to his perch from the child's shoulder and fluffs up his feathers.

"Our bond goes both ways. He's my familiar."

The girl nods as if it all makes sense to her.

"Now tell me true, child, why did you enter the forest?"

She stands a little straighter and says, "I heard singing coming from the forest."

Delbrot, Peace Warrior!

Holly Saiki

THE HEAVILY MUSCLED WARRIOR known as Gongor lumbered through the forest with the grace of a stampeding buffalo herd, his ax and shield strapped tightly on his back. "Come back here, you vile coward," he howled. He wore an ornate breastplate and helmet, the metal dented and scratched throughout his years of adventuring. Rivulets of sweat poured down Gongor's face as he pushed his body to its physical limit, the cracks in his heavily dented shield growing bigger every time it slammed against his breastplate. "Could the stories uttered about the Shadow-Bound Lich be nothing but base lies?"

"The stories are exaggerated misinterpretations!" Delbrot, the Shadow-Bound Lich was an undead creature whose soul dwelt in a phylactery. A robe of living darkness draped over his fleshless form, the ends floating in the air. Delbrot levitated a foot above the ground, running across empty space to avoid tripping on a stray root. The hem of his outfit ended halfway above his feet to help expand the range of movement of his legs as he dashed away. A ruby-studded gold brace-let appeared every time he pumped his arms to aid his legs in sprinting. The sleeves of his robe moved like the tides of an abyssal ocean of shadows to expose the precious treasure every few seconds. "I don't go killing everybody who screwed me over."

"I don't care what you do in your spare time." Gongor's attempts to shout ended in a bout of ragged wheezing. "I want the bracelet back, you thief!"

"You stole it from me first," Delbrot shouted, wishing he had eyes to roll in disgust. The best he could do was shine the orbs of light floating in his eye sockets brightly. "It was my mother's favorite."

"Liar!" Gongor waved his ax in the air in sharp strokes. "It's a bracelet made to brainwash your helpless victims into think-ing you're a living being rather than the rotten, dusty corpse you truly are."

Not this demonizing "All liches are evil monsters!" business again! An eerie sigh—enhanced by the necrotic magic animat-ing his cadaver—escaped through Delbrot's teeth, heavy with bone-tired resignation. If not for Gongor's ax and his impa-tience, Delbrot could easily explain about his skill in Illusion Magic, relying on his willpower to use it instead of magi-cal items. But he knew the bloodthirsty adventurer wouldn't believe him. *Even though I don't have a drop of blood in my veins since I'm a lich,* he grimly thought.

Delbrot's reasons for wearing his mother's bracelet were a combination of practical and sentimental ones. It was a phylac-tery holding his soul, a cruel jest made by the necromancer who murdered his mother and transformed him into an undead monster. Whoever held the lich's soul jar would not only be able to destroy the creature but command them to violate the moral codes they held dear. *Like murdering innocent beings,* Delbrot thought with utter revulsion.

Delbrot shivered as he dwelled on the memories of his slow, agonizing murder and painful rebirth as a lich. The psychological coldness radiating through his skeletal frame was stronger than the physical chills he had when he was a sickly living boy. The necromancer had forced him to brutally murder his fellow villagers and turn them into mindless zombies. No, he wouldn't go through the horror of being forced to commit terrible deeds because somebody controlled his soul jar. Delbrot would rather smash his mother's bracelet than become the slave of a cruel sorcerer again.

A lush brown-and-green blur appeared on the horizon. The light in Delbrot's eye sockets shone with rising hope as the details of the shape revealed itself. It transformed into a forest filled with huge pine trees. Birds flew when the branches were disturbed by Gongor's pounding footsteps. Delbrot casted a cantrip, a minor magic trick, to bring back to life his dead sense of smell for a few fleeting moments. The strong smell of pine wafted into his nose cavities.

Delbrot realized the forest hadn't slowed his pursuer. Gongor had gained a few crucial steps toward his prey. *I hope Bramblewood is home,* Delbrot thought. Gongor's eyes gleamed with the lust of the hunt.

Delbrot gritted his teeth in raw fear, holding tight to the bracelet with skeletal fingers. The lights in his eye sockets blinked frantically like a candle flame fluttering in a breeze.

Please, please let Bramblewood be there, Delbrot thought, glad he didn't sweat anymore. He also was thankful he didn't need to worry about sore muscles or physical fatigue as well. He jumped over a gigantic moss-covered log, using some of his magic to expand the distance between him and Gongor.

Hey Bramblewood! Delbrot said telepathically as he climbed over a fallen gigantic pine tree, rich, green moss spreading over its surface. *Are you there? It's your old buddy.*

Hi Delbrot, a deep voice said, ringing in Delbrot's mind like a dozen joyous brass bells. *What seems to be the problem?*

Delbrot felt a gushing torrent of ecstatic hope drown the malicious demon of despair infecting his soul, along with some guilt for once again dragging his friend into his personal problems. With a quick twist of his head, he saw Gongor struggling to climb over the fallen tree, his armor weighting him down. Delbrot gained a spring in his step as a spark of relief blossomed in his soul.

There's another fool chasing me again, Delbrot replied, his telepathic message sounding more like a plaintive whine than a mature plea.

Let me guess. This one tried stealing your bracelet? Bramblewood said, the tone of his voice causal, like this was a regular problem.

Yes, Delbrot said, a loud sigh echoing through the psychic corridors of his brain. *Once again, I must deal with a violent thug who treats life so cavalierly.*

Well, you are an undead creature, Bramblewood replied, his voice sympathetic. *Most of the living usually do not know liches can be friendly, gentle creatures willing to negotiate for vital magical requests.* The sound of an ax furiously chopping into a tree, followed by Gongor screeching like a cat forcibly dunked into a tub filled with ice-cold water, harshly reminded them of Delbrot's pursuer. Bramblewood's deep, exasperated sigh moved through Delbrot's brain and into his skeletal frame. *I am not a bellicose being by nature, but it is obvious the adventurer is not going to listen to reason. Unfortunately, you may have to kill him to put an end to all of this.*

I used to be human once. It isn't right to kill somebody because they stole something from me, Delbrot said, an overwhelming sense of shame welling up from within. *Just because I'm an undead corpse doesn't mean I can't have the same values I had when I had a pulse.*

A loud, irritated groan echoed through Delbrot's mind as Bramblewood let out his frustration, the former making a rictus grin of quiet amusement. Delbrot wished he still had the ability to smile. There was a moment of silence before Bramblewood made the telepathic sound of a throat clearing to indicate he was going to talk again.

Fine, fine, he said. *Do you remember how to get to my home, the oak tree in the middle of the forest? Head over and I will handle this.*

Thank you! Delbrot replied, tremendous, ecstatic relief echoing through his soul. Bramblewood gave a small chuckle before cutting off the telepathic bond, his mirth softly fading away like the end of a sublime ballad.

Delbrot, his morale increased dramatically, used his magic to run as fast as he could. Undead creatures didn't have to worry about endurance the way the living did.

When he saw the huge tree smack-dab in the middle of the forest, Delbrot used his remaining willpower not to let out a huge scream of joy. He didn't want to inadvertently reveal his location to Gongor. Arms pumping frantically, Delbrot used all his magical energy to head to his destined location, nearly colliding with the trunk. His feet made an impression in the dirt as Delbrot roughly landed on the ground. His eldritch nature helped him to effortlessly maintain his balance.

Hey, careful there, mighty lich. Bramblewood's voice boomed merrily in his mind. *You do not want to accidently nick my home with your bony frame.*

Ha, ha, very funny, Delbrot telepathically said, his left hand pressed hard against Bramblewood's tree. A squirrel darting away from the tree the moment they sensed the lich's unnatural aura, scattering to ones where only the living dwelled. A burst of irrational guilt hit Delbrot's chest, making him curse his undead state.

I feel for you, but we really need to focus on the situation at hand, Bramblewood said, his tone sympathetic. *The "mighty warrior" is heading toward us, waving his ax in the air and speaking melodramatic buffoonery. Why do not I move one of the roots of my home and trip him up? If we are lucky, he will fall right on his ax and die.*

"Let me see if I can reason with him one more time," Delbrot said, his shadowy robe molding itself to his shoulders, enhancing the outline of the joints as they slumped in exasperation.

Okay, but I still say it is a hopeless cause, Bramblewood replied. *Good luck anyway.*

"Thank you," Delbrot said, turning around to face his opponent. The lights in his eye sockets transformed into a bluish-white color. His hands clenched into fists to look more intimidating than he felt.

Gongor saw his target standing still and abruptly stopped. His slamming his shield down to announce his presence dug up big clods of grass and dirt in all directions. An earthworm, its trajectory so rudely altered, quickly crawled back into the pile of earth. Gongor's arms waved frantically in the air as he struggled to get his bearings. Delbrot summoned all his willpower not to laugh as his opponent wobbled from side to side. He really didn't want to anger Gongor any more than he already had.

When Gongor finally regained his balance, he glared straight at Delbrot, the latter feeling his soul curdle as he gazed into his opponent's eyes. Gongor's hatred and rage were so intense, Delbrot was glad the man didn't have the ability to set things on fire. The adventurer would've very foolishly destroyed the thing he was chasing the lich for. Delbrot summoned as much courage as he could. He may have had a nearly indestructible undead body, but his skeletal frame trembled at the thought of Gongor destroying his phylactery through sheer dumb luck.

"Hi Gongor," Delbrot said, ruing the fact he didn't have lips to help express his friendly nature. Hopefully, his light, steady tone would lull the adventurer into a more peaceful mood. "You know, doesn't this seem rather silly, going through all this trouble for a little bracelet? If you really want some treasure, I could whip up something in my laboratory. Nobody needs to die."

Gongor stared in shock at the lich. His brow furrowed, lifting his ax as he stepped forward.

"Vile creature, how dare you try to trick me with honeyed words?" He waved his ax menacingly at Delbrot, "I am immune to your filthy blandishments. Now prepare to face your well-deserved doom!"

"I was hoping to end things peacefully," Delbrot said, his shoulders slumping in exasperation at Gongor's willful stupidity. "Okay, Bramblewood, you can come out now, but remember what I said."

"All right, I will not roast him to a crisp," the deep, thundering voice said, coming from the tree behind Delbrot. The sound frightened the nearby woodland creatures into fleeing farther into the depths of the forest. A loud rustling caused by the panicked flight of some birds shook the branches, causing some crisp mahogany leaves to fall on Delbrot's head and shoulders. "But it does not mean I will not give him the fright of his life."

The tree's surface swelled into a hill-shaped bump—like a grand castle rising out of the sea. The protuberance transformed into an elderly dragon's head. Bramblewood's scales were a deep, rich brown, the same color as the tree he dwelled in. Patches of dark green moss scattered across his face, giving the illusion he was made of the same substance as the place he called his home. Skinny, tan whiskers, one pair on each side of his snout, dangled when a gentle breeze blew against his face.

"Is this the little pipsqueak who stole a precious item and threatened to kill one of my dearest friends?" Bramblewood said, staring directly at the adventurer. Gongor's arms trembled as he hesitantly shook his ax at the dragon, his arrogant complacency crumbling before the presence of the mighty wyrm.

"Yes, foul creature, my name is Gongor, slayer of the Penumbra Witch of the Stars and conqueror of the Endless Dungeon of Agonizing Blades." He trembled, his terror loosening his grip on his ax. "Stand aside if you know what is good for you. I need to rid the world of an unnatural blight on humanity."

Bramblewood closed his eyes and laughed out loud, his delight echoing through the woods. Whatever animals were remaining now decided to flee. The rustling of the branches echoed the forest.

"You would certainly change your mind about Delbrot if you actually spent time with him," the wood dragon gently told the adventurer. "This lich would not be able to hurt a fly, let alone a foolish warrior."

Gongor stood still for a moment, studying the lich like a fascinating work of art. Then his face flushed a dark red. "You dare mock one of the greatest adventurers to walk the land of Solstice?"

"Stealing a person's precious heirloom and chasing the poor guy down when he takes it back are not what I call heroic. Unless the standards for heroism have lowered." Bramblewood rolled his eyes as he smirked at Gongor, the latter gaping at the dragon in complete silence, uncertain how to respond to his insult. Delbrot fiddled his fingers, a soft rattling sound as his bone digits rubbed against each other, waiting for the inevitable battle.

Gongor gave out a bellowing roar, causing Delbrot's skeleton body to freeze in stark terror. The lich watched as Gongor
raised his ax and dashed toward him. Bramblewood leaned
back, his cheeks swelling. Then he opened his mouth, spewing
an emerald-green mist straight at the adventurer.

Gongor abruptly stopped and tried to change his path, but
the mist swallowed him whole before he got the chance. The
ax fell to the ground with a dull thud, leaving a dent in the soft
earth. Gongor tried desperately to disburse the cloud by frantically waving his arms.

After a few desperate moments, Gongor's face became
slack. His arms hung limply at his sides as the mist's narcotic
properties overwhelmed him. His face drooped, the angry red
flush fading to a soft pink color as the fiery rage drained out of
him. Gongor's eyes glazed over with a dreamy, vague look, his
body moving like a grain of wheat blown by a strong gust of
wind.

Delbrot struggled with the urge to move away from
Bramblewood's tree and help Gongor. Despite the fact the
adventurer wished nothing but harm toward him, Delbrot
didn't want anybody to suffer.

Gongor locked eyes with Bramblewood while he regained
his balance, causing Delbrot's skeletal frame to tingle with
nervous energy. He took a defensive posture as hard as the
substance of his fleshless bones, not wanting to take the chance
of the warrior launching a surprise attack. Delbrot kept his
guarded pose, a tiny spark of hope growing in his soul.

"Hey, man." Gongor slurred the words as if he had drunk
several glasses of grog at once. "Do you know there's a swarm
of colorful fish moving around your head?" He broke into a
huge grin.

"Huh?" Delbrot said.

"The fish," Gongor replied. "If you don't want them bothering you, you should swat them away. Although I hate to think what sort of mess it's going to make."

"Um, thanks." Delbrot raised one skeletal hand to humor him. "If you're seeing fantastical creatures right now, then you better get home. I'd hate for you to get eaten by a monster in your condition."

"Hey, you're right!" Gongor's eyes opened as wide as dinner plates. "Thanks for helping me out. I don't know what I'd do by myself."

Probably slaughter anybody who looks the least bit "creepy" to you, Delbrot thought. *How I wish this was Gongor's true personality instead of the horrid berserker I dealt with.*

"Think nothing of it," Delbrot replied, waving his hand to show Gongor his gratitude. A pair of warm yellow orbs of light shined brightly in the lich's eye sockets. "I'd do the same for anybody else who was dosed with a huge amount of mind-warping gas." Delbrot tilted his head to glance at Bramblewood. The dragon responded by moving the tree's branches up and down, as a substitute for a shrug.

"Cool, you're a really great guy," Gongor said, turning around to leave. He gave one last glance at the two mystical beings, raising his hand in the air and waving it energetically. "Farewell! I hope the rest of your day is great."

The pair watched the drugged adventurer bound away across the grass, unwittingly disturbing some of the woodland animals' hiding places as he whistled an off-tune melody. They fled away from the drugged Gongor, not wanting to get crushed underneath his boots.

"It is a shame they are scared of him," Bramblewood said. "It would have been so cute to see adorable fuzzy creatures flock around a huge, brawny warrior like he was a fae princess."

Delbrot burst out into noisy laughter, holding his rib bones as he tried to prevent his mirth from toppling him over. The struggle lasted for two minutes until the lich fell right on his bony rump near the trunk of Bramblewood's home. Still chortling, Delbrot rolled on the ground, getting a few pieces of grass on his long, black robes. His energetic movements caused his hood to fall to his shoulders, unveiling the shocking revelation his skull didn't have any bizarre physical details to make it stick out of the ordinary. It was an ordinary cranium just like everybody else's. Minus the skin, of course.

"Hey, Delbrot," Bramblewood said, the bark cracking as he moved his head, "You better put your hood back on, unless you want to scare the forest creatures one more time." While the lich fixed his hood, covering his fleshless skull, Bramblewood's head sank back into the surface of the tree. The ancient wood then created a carving of an elegant double door, giving off a luminous grow to signal its completion. Delbrot walked up to the tree and pushed the doors open, his hood snugly draped over his skull.

The entrance faded back into the wood once Delbrot was fully inside the tree. Bramblewood used his magic to mask his friend's eerie aura to fool the woodland creatures into thinking the lich was gone. Silence pervaded the forest for a few moments before the birds began chirping. Some squirrels darted through the grass, while the rest of the animals went back to their usual routines.

Delbrot spent a week coming up with a plan to trick the adventurer into believing he killed the Shadow-Bound Lich. He would lure Gongor to an abandoned castle and have his duplicate fight the adventurer. After a light scuffle, the duplicate would maneuver Gongor into "accidentally" destroying a fabrication of his phylactery, causing the fake Delbrot to crumble to dust. With both the lich and the precious treasure Gongor coveted destroyed, he would have no choice but to shift his attentions towards another target. Delbrot wouldn't have to wait until the adventurer died to feel safe traversing through the land of Solstice.

Bramblewood pulled in some favors from his fellow dragons to provide the materials needed to create an authentic replica of Delbrot's mother's bracelet, while Delbrot used his necromantic energies to create a double. He left Bramblewood's home with his doppelganger walking behind him.

It's tough to be a good-hearted lich at times, he thought, gazing at his mother's bracelet, which sparkled when the sunlight touched its surface.

Everyone's a Critic

Andrew Giffin

PRINCE ERYN KNEW HE had mispronounced the spell when he realized he was a fictional character.

Scattered around his father's throne room was a tableau of kinsfolk, their gaze waiting on him. Ravenlords from the Sunken Marsh, Owllords from the Shadowed Woods, Vulturelords from the Shimmering Wastes, Pelicanlords from the Archipelago, and Ostrichlords from the Great Serengeti had all sent their greatest warriors and their wisest seers to take part in the group ritual.

They all stared at Eryn, seeking to confirm the ritual's success in driving back the Curtain of Darkness and her Veiled Hordes. Instead, the staggering awareness of his fictional nature stupefied him.

"Well, did it work, young prince?" asked the Ravenlord seer, her wizened features searching his face.

"I, uh...what's happening?" Eryn asked.

The kinsfolk exchanged worried glances. His father

intervened, extending his arms to address the circle. "My lords, give the boy a moment. The ritual has clearly taken a toll on his mind." He turned to his court wizard. "Cyrus, help him recover, please."

The wizard jumped from his seat and rushed to the prince. "Are you alright, Prince Eryn?" he asked, his voice hushed.

Eryn blinked at the wizard's long flowing beard and wild eyes. "You knew, didn't you? You knew none of this was real?"

A murmur spread through the throne room at the prince's accusation.

Cyrus glanced around the circle, putting a hand on Eryn's back. "Yes, of course I did. Let's discuss this elsewhere." Cyrus moved to guide him out of the room, his hand still on the prince's shoulder.

"No, you said I had to be the circle center because I'm—" he paused and leaned toward the wizard, the room leaning in with him. "Because I'm a virgin," he whispered. "But all along that didn't matter."

"Prince Eryn, I had no choice. You now know, as I do, that we aren't the ones who decide our actions. He does." Cyrus pointed up.

Eryn lifted his gaze and saw me for the first time. "What in the...who the hell are you supposed to be?" he asked, incredulous. The kinsfolk looked from the prince to the domed ceiling, puzzled. Eryn stared up at me. "You're the one who's responsible for all this?"

Yes, I am.

"And why did you make me aware of the nature of my world? Why do this to me?"

I shrugged. *I had an opening line that I liked.*

"So, the only reason I'm alive is because you thought of a sentence you liked?"

I guess so, yeah.

Eryn dropped to the floor. "What's going to happen to us?"

I dunno, I haven't planned that far ahead yet. I'll figure it out as I write.

He put his head in his hands. "Oh, gods."

"Uh, are we sure the boy's alright?" the Pelicanlord seer said.

The king cleared his throat awkwardly and stepped closer. "Yes, of course. Cyrus—" he leaned closer. "Who is Eryn talking to?"

"No one, your majesty." Cyrus shot me a dirty look. "No. One."

Eryn ceased his anguished moans, distracted by heavy footsteps on the marble floor. He turned to discover a large marble statue against the wall, a genderless bodybuilder whose crude, smiley-face head scraped the ceiling.

Eryn's eyes narrowed. "Has that statue always been there?"

Before anyone could respond, the statue bent to one knee. Extending its absolutely shredded arm, the statue curled their finger against their thumb and flicked Cyrus the wizard.

The enchanter flew through the dome, his scream trailing through a Cyrus-shaped hole in the throne room ceiling. The kinsfolk stared in shock as the statue straightened, dusted its hands together, and returned to its initial pose.

"My lords, this is the work of the Curtain of Darkness. Her evil magic infiltrated our circle. Any of us could be in her thrall!" the Ostrichlord seer shouted as he stepped away from the circle. Uproarious cries spread through the rest of the kinsfolk, the warriors' hands moving to their respective weapons.

"Will you idiots please shut up?" Eryn moaned. He removed his hands from his face to find the kinsfolk staring at him again, the warriors pointing weapons at him in accusation.

"The prince! The prince has been compromised!" the Owllord seer cried.

"My lords, be reasonable." The king's voice rose as the warriors approached the still-seated prince. "The prince is obviously struggling with exposure to powerful magic!"

Eryn stood, looking up at me and holding his hand out to the warriors. "Can't you do something about this?"

Oh, sure. Let me get rid of all the oxygen, that should do it.

"What?!" Eryn yelled as the assembled kinsfolk fell to their knees, their hands clutching at their throats as they gasped for air. Eryn grasped at his throat, as well.

Eryn, you don't need to breathe.

The prince straightened, testing this. He opened his mouth to speak, but no sound came out.

Come on, you don't need air to talk, either. Real-world physics have no bearing on you. Isn't that obvious by now?

"Well, I may not need to breathe, but they still think they do. Can you *not* kill them all?"

Fine, fine. They can have the air back.

Oxygen rushed back into the room. The kinsfolk gasped collectively.

Everyone but Eryn stand up and take three steps back.

They did.

Good. Now stay there.

The others mindlessly complied with my orders, mindlessly staring ahead. Eryn approached his father, waving a hand in front of the king's face. There was no reaction.

"This is so weird." Eryn turned to look at me. "So you control all this, right?"

That's right.

"You write a few words and whatever you say happens, happens."

Correct.

"So, can you write that we defeated the Curtain of Darkness? The spell worked, we lived happily ever after?"

Where would be the story in that? I need to write something satisfying, not some easy victory.

Eryn spun around, indicating the frozen kinsfolk. "This is satisfying to you?"

Well, no. Admittedly things have gone off the rails a bit. But that's kind of your fault, isn't it?

"My fault?"

Yeah, you were the one who screwed up the spell.

Eryn threw his hands in the air. "Are you serious? You wrote this! You're writing all this! The only reason I exist is because you liked a sentence! How can you say it's my fault?"

I dunno, just trying to inject some conflict here, I guess.

"This is ridiculous. You don't have any idea what you're doing." He shook his head and turned away.

Where are you going?

"I don't know, to find Cyrus, I guess."

Oh, he's probably dead.

Eryn whirled around again. "Probably dead?"

Well, yeah, I flung him through a wall to who-knows-where. Who could survive that?

"How do you not know if he's alive or dead? He's your character!"

Yeah, that's not really how this works. I'm only concerned with what's happening now. I'll figure out what happened to Cyrus later.

"Unbelievable. I've known Cyrus all my life. He was my teacher, my mentor. And you're completely unconcerned with his fate?"

Well, yeah. He already served his purpose in the story.

"And what about my purpose?"

You're serving it right now.

"By arguing with you?"

Yeah.

"Then I'll just stop. Kind of hard to have a story if your main character won't do anything, right?"

Uh...that's not really up to you.

Eryn sat down.

Hey, get up.

"No."

I said get up.

Eryn stayed on the floor.

Okay, fine.

An anvil fell from the sky and landed on Eryn. He died. No, wait, he didn't. It hurt him a lot but he's not going to die from any of this. Eryn's face twitched.

Had enough? No?

A piano fell on him, Eryn's head breaking through the soundboard, broken strings scratching his face. He looked up at me and smiled, piano keys falling from his mouth as if they were his teeth.

There, see? I made you do that.

Eryn flipped me the bird.

Where did you even learn that? Alright, you little jerk. You wanna get anachronistic? How's this?

A comically large safe fell on him. A bright blue monkey ran into the room, spinning the combination lock and swinging the door open. The monkey bared his teeth and leaped at Eryn. Their limbs intertwined as they fought, moving around the throne room as a cloud of dust obscured their actions. The monkey screamed, scampering away and out of existence forever.

Eryn stood, shaking like a dog after a bath. He marched back to the center of the circle of frozen kinsfolk. "This is what you're spending your time doing? Aren't writers supposed to be artists? Shouldn't you be saying something about life, the human condition, the nature of existence? Instead, you're entertaining yourself with this *Looney Tunes* bullshit."

I know for a fact you've never seen Looney Tunes.

Eryn scoffed.

Not every story needs to be capital-A Art. Sometimes they can just be silly. Also, weren't you the one asking me for a quick resolution with the Curtain of Darkness? Where's the art in that?

"I think it's a little too late to hope for art here. You could at least solve my problems."

Fine, you want a quick resolution? Let's see how satisfied that leaves you. Forget all of this. Let's reset.

Prince Eryn stood in the circle of kinsfolk after reciting the words Cyrus had taught him.

"Did it work?" the Vulturelord seer asked.

"Let us observe," Cyrus said. He waved his hands, enlarging his Ponderous Orb to the size of a shadow puppet's screen. It flickered to life, showing the Curtain of Darkness with her Veiled Horde, bearing down on the borders of the kingdom. A bolt of lightning struck her, knocking her from her horse. The entire horde stopped in their tracks before exploding.

"Aw man, I'm totally dead," the Curtain of Darkness said right before she exploded, too.

Prince Eryn glanced from his hands, covered in runes for the ritual, to the now-empty Orb. "Huh." He turned to face his father, Cyrus, and the kinsfolk. "Is it just me, or did that seem a little too easy?"

Yes, it did.

A Guardsman Remembers

Danielle Ranucci

BIRDS FLEW ABOVE OUR shanty, but it was all nonsense anyway 'cause I'd never been sure what I lived for. I couldn't think like that now. Ikarsia's capital city of Ekket Kan could promise us whatever it wanted, but it wouldn't stop my starving daughter Soraya from wanting to go there and shout at our king. Over how much they taxed us in Ojak, she was telling me, but I was her father and I knew her better. It had nothing to do with taxes and everything to do with the grief she didn't want to mention.

But I didn't want to talk about it either. So I eased myself onto the soft sand floor and said, "Soraya, it'll be foolish to go off on your own." Then I took a breath to tell her she couldn't possibly negotiate with that gray-towered city. If negotiation was possible, the Ojakians wouldn't've had to rebel all those thirty-one years back, lose, and get annexed.

Her green eyes went fiercer than they'd been in a long time. "Don't say I don't understand," she said.

That too. She was just a sandy-curled, sixteen-yeared kid repeating what she heard from the Ojakians she gallivanted with at night. "How can you understand?" I asked. "You're so young—"

"Maybe I'd understand better if I didn't have to stay here 'cause you're lonely after letting Mother die!" she retorted.

My throat burned. So she'd finally said it after all. Even so, I couldn't give up on her. I opened my mouth to try to force out an answer, to make her stop believing in her damn fool plans and everything her friends claimed, only nothing came out.

Soraya blinked. Pain chased the fierceness from her eyes. "I'm sorry," she said. "I shouldn't have blamed you."

I looked down and traced bewildered zigzags into the sand. "It's fine," I muttered. "I forgive you."

But that night, staring at the stars through a tear in the thin cloth roof, I couldn't stop thinking. My wife Marillion had died giving birth to Soraya, and I couldn't save her. Why *wouldn't* I try to keep my daughter out of trouble now? Soraya wanted to make her own way in the world. Wasn't she right to want that? I inhaled the thick summer air, hummed a dirge, then broke off. Maybe she was. Well…stars shifted through the sky. If she was, what did it mean for me?

Most of the night passed without sleep.

Finally, I dreamed about the folktale, the one where the archer ties his kid to an arrow-shaft and shoots him through the sky so the boy can experience flight, but the arrow hurtles down into the sea, drowns the screaming child, and leaves his father filled with wild grief.

I woke up when the boy drowned. I trembled for a long time. Then I rose and gazed at Soraya asleep on the other side of the shanty. She breathed soft, and the dawn light fell just so that I could make out her smile.

Damn that dawn light. After what she'd mentioned yesterday, she'd make her own way no matter what I did. But seeing
her like that, it was so...

Stop that. If I didn't let her go, she'd never be able to look at
me again.

I sighed. I shoved some supplies into a bundle. Then I
took my weapons and hurried out through our shanty's flap. I
trekked south, away from home, not letting myself see anything
but the red sand passing beneath my boots. I wished I'd kissed
Soraya goodbye before leaving her, but I wouldn't return just to
do that. I might not want to leave again. I couldn't possibly be a
good father to her then.

The desert turned into pale blue rock, and I looked up. I'd
reached the mountain range separating Ojak from Ekket Kan.

Wind bit my face. The sun rose above the mountain peaks.
I wanted to forget my daughter existed. I wanted to forget her
smile. Her laughter. That time she'd had a horrible fever. She'd
been twelve. When she had finally emerged from her delirium, she'd discovered me sitting up with her and her eyes had
flashed with merriment. I'd been clutching a candle, and she
had touched its flame for some fool reason. No matter how
many times I'd tried to understand it, she'd refused to explain.
It'd just been the way things were with my wonderful girl.

Wind tore at my face. I shivered and kept walking through
the sunlit mountains. I told myself again it would be better for
Soraya alone, till I almost believed it was true.

One afternoon, I arrived at Ekket Kan. Two massive walls
surrounded it. One contained the Outer City and one protected
the Inner City. The Outer City reminded me of home. A one-
armed man even sold drevisk lizard meat, the fiery-sweet kind
I'd always begged my guardian Levta Greif to make. I had

nothing, but this silly grin sprang to my face and I wound up spending my nothing to buy some. Not that I regretted it.

Meanwhile, sharp-smelling orange trees flanked the Inner City's people-choked cobblestone streets, windows glared down at me in the burning sunlight, and the massive, gray-spired palace brooded over the horizon like a broken-hearted man.

There wasn't anything more worth knowing about Ekket Kan except that they sought guards, and I outfought enough folks in their sparring trials for the Ekketians to ignore my Ojakian origins and hire me.

So, there I sat in the hellishly crowded, lamplit barracks at a rickety pinewood table across from two other recruits. Inochar and Emnor, sister and brother, both about twenty years old. Ekket Kan was filled with their like: taut jawlines, raised cheekbones, and black or blond hair; black for Inochar and blond for Emnor. That was all someone needed to tell them apart.

"Ojak!" Inochar exclaimed when I told her where I was from.

"So?" I asked.

Inochar looked toward Emnor. In the firelight he seemed to be scowling at me, but I could've just been imagining it.

"What's wrong with Ojak?" I insisted.

An uncertain silence.

"Cycles reenact themselves," Emnor finally prattled.

Nonsense. "Maybe I'd understand better if it weren't for the fact they let me into the guard."

Yeah. Emnor's gaze was definitely a glare. Well, I stared back till he glanced toward a guard playing a lively jig on her green concertina. To hell with Emnor. What mattered was waiting to receive instructions for the first night of our watch.

"Who are your parents?" Inochar asked.

I always liked telling people I never met my father and that, as my mother was liberating Ikarsia from evil, I tumbled out of her womb and landed safe beneath a dilapidated wooden fence in Ojak. Ignore that, and let's be honest. My mother never liberated anyone from evil. She abandoned me under that damn fence, and I never found out why.

Even Levta Greif hadn't known why a mother would forsake her son. All she could tell from my looks was that one of my parents must've been an Ekketian stationed in Ojak right after the rebellion. The other must've been an Ojakian, and according to Levta, it shouldn't matter that I couldn't discover who they were. *She'd* been the one who'd raised me after all. Forget those other parents.

Of course Levta wouldn't've understood my yearning. Raising me had meant she could live a happy life after losing her own son. Maybe she even wanted to believe he'd never died.

For me, not knowing my parents had meant I'd spent every day sneaking off to spy on the guards at the nearby Ekketian outpost and pretending the one that looked most like me was my father. Once, I'd even flung a stone through the window, hoping he'd recognize me and keep the other guards from attacking me.

"Stop! That's my son!" he'd shout, placing a protective hand on my arm.

He'd actually beaten my face apart. And when I'd woken up in the desert, bloodied and aching, was it any surprise I'd started wondering why anything even mattered?

Not like I'd tell that to Inochar now.

"I'm part Ekketian," I said instead.

She leaned forward and scrutinized me. "Really?"

"Yeah."

"I'd never guess!"

Emnor remained silent. Even so, his scowl told me he still somehow must've blamed me personally for the Ojakian revolt. Then he asked something about the desert and gazed at the table like he hadn't asked anything at all.

That was fine, I decided. I'd rather listen to the concertina anyway.

SOON, A HELLISHLY TALL man came over to our table and introduced himself as Trejin. He led us outside and up a rough staircase to the Outer City wall. Every night, from sunset till dawn, we were supposed to stand way up high on the eastern gates' crenellated ramparts and watch the darkness beyond. If enemies came, we had to sound this massive brass alarm bell for reinforcements. If negotiators came, we had to avoid attacking them. If no one came, we still had to stand up there like bastards, just in case anyone suddenly felt like showing up.

The absolute best part of my job was the uniform. In Ojak, I'd always been "Karadore, the widowed hunter with the head-strong child." In Ekket Kan, I was "Karadore, the immaculately dressed guard." It was nice to be seen that way. It made me think I could start over.

Of course, I didn't tell the other guards this. Emnor and Inochar smoked these sour-smelling clay pipes and gossiped. Foolish, but understandable. They'd never lost their loved ones. They even told me the worst day of their lives was when they had to move to another house 'cause their parents were pro-moted. I nodded and tried to return to my post, but they carried on about how they really knew life. They had experienced *pro-found suffering*, see.

They didn't know life. The only way to truly know life was to know death.

Emnor and Inochar almost made me wish I'd never joined the guard, except Trejin was different. He had a kind face and wise cerulean eyes, and his graying hair made him resemble an older version of me. I avoided him at first 'cause of it. Then, one fool night, I found myself standing beside him. He was straightening a torch, and I was helping him by swatting away a cloud of buzzing insects.

Oh Karadore, you bastard.

Worse, I found myself asking, "How long've you been a guard?"

"Thirty-two years," he said.

I was doomed to reply. "Anything interesting happen?" I asked.

He leaned against the parapet and wiped sweat from his neck. "On my second night, I turned nineteen and watched my fellow guards get slain."

Damn. He, for one, knew what life was about.

"It was the start of the Ojakian revolt," he added.

I looked away, my face burning.

"What's wrong?" he asked.

"Nothing." Then, since there wasn't any reason to be ashamed, "I'm from Ojak."

He didn't respond. I wished I hadn't ever spoken to him, but it was too late, wasn't it? I took a deep breath and looked into his grief-filled eyes. "Please don't blame me for the death of your friends," I said.

The grief softened on his face. "I would never think of it, Karadore."

I blinked. "Well, I never thought you would."

He smiled. I grinned back. And that was how our friendship began.

TREJIN WAS HELLISHLY PROUD our gilded eastern gates were the most used in Ekket Kan. I was interested in the folks using them. Were they happy with themselves? Or were they pretending?

I'd met many Ikarsians that were hell-damned good at lying to themselves. And see, people like that can never be happy.

After sunset, Inochar and I closed the gates using a heavy brass lever that groaned like my daughter whenever I kidded her. Sometimes, a husky-throated drunk sang hauntingly of death and forgetting. Trejin and I would place bets on what he'd sing next. Trejin was sure the drunk was pining for some two-timing lover, but I reckoned right away he was just sore about being tricked into leaving his old home, so Trejin always guessed the wrong songs and I always guessed the right ones.

Eventually the man'd pass out, and no matter how much Trejin insisted that I keep my winnings, I'd always stuff the jewel-encrusted Gimmuts back into his hand. It never stopped impressing him, see.

The night wore on. Emnor and Inochar would keep busy by walking back and forth along the parapet. No matter how hard I tried not to, I'd always fall asleep standing, only to jerk awake and find Trejin snickering at me.

"How do you stay awake?" I asked one chilly autumn night.

He held up an intricate puzzle box that looked like a giant mahogany knot.

"Where's it from?"

He smiled and said it was from his father, who'd been a carver in the Outer City. He'd gave it to Trejin to congratulate him for being the first in the family to make a living in the Inner City.

"Does it really keep you awake?" I asked.

"No. The hours are too long."

I watched him awhile through the fog of my breath. "Has anyone tried negotiating for shorter shifts?"

He nodded. "We just have to accept our duty and carry it out honorably."

"What a duty it is." I yawned, then made myself stand up straighter.

"Boredom's good," Trejin said, also yawned, then shot me an amused look. "It's better than marriage, anyways."

I stiffened. "Why the hell's that?"

"No one stays together. My parents didn't have enough money, I hated my own wife, and so on." He shrugged. "Never mind. My point is, just keep your balance."

Fair enough.

"So, why'd you join the guard?" I asked.

He hesitated. "Revenge."

"What?" Trejin was less spiteful than a breakfast pastry.

He looked at his puzzle box for a time. "You're an honorable man, Karadore," he finally said. "That's what truly matters."

I nodded. It meant something, coming from him.

A long while passed. Emnor and Inochar walked by us, gossiping about their powerful uncle Agnar getting someone executed for defiance. Trejin frowned, then yawned again. Below us slumbered the drunk.

"About revenge...guess part of me thinks maybe if I keep enough people safe I could've...could've kept 'em together after all," Trejin mumbled.

He was dozing off, I realized. I shook his shoulder. "Keep your balance!"

He started. I snorted. We stared into the darkness.

It had rained the night before. Beneath the cloudless sky, shadows glimmered like candlelight.

WELL MAYBE TREJIN WAS wrong about boredom. On the ramparts, staring into that darkness, I had time to think, and I was great at thinking of everything I didn't want to. Thankfully, I could also distract myself.

Like one evening in winter, I got out of worrying about Soraya by thinking about my parents. If one of them had been an Ekketian in Ojak, they would've been part of the guard. Maybe they'd moved back here. I wrapped my cloak tighter around me and imagined finding them. They'd gaze at me in surprise. Then they'd laugh and draw me into a fierce embrace, and we'd cry into each other's shoulders. Foolish, I knew, but still wonderful.

"Did you meet any guard members based in Ojak after the rebellion?" I asked Trejin.

Yes, he'd befriended the entire cadre, but they'd all perished. One's head had been bitten off by a massive yellow serpent, another had stabbed himself, and so on.

"Why do you want to know?" he asked.

My throat burned. "No reason," I muttered. And that was the end of that.

But it wasn't the end of my troubling thoughts. After my wife Marillion had died, I couldn't stop wondering what I lived for. When I'd raised Soraya, I had thought I lived for her, but it had been so easy to leave her. If I lived for her, I shouldn't've been able to do that.

Then again, it had seemed easy to watch Marillion die. I hadn't cried, or even felt sadness for a long time afterward. Maybe being left under that fence had stopped me from expressing sorrow or stunted my ability to reckon with it.

In the long hours before dawn I had time for grief. Or not grief exactly. Instead, it was more like an unease, or a sense of impending awfulness, and I dreaded it reaching me. Then I got to the point where my throat thickened, so I guess it was a form of grief after all, even though I never let myself cry. I got restless instead, and grief gave way to a dull throbbing in my head.

It was like that tale, where the old soldier goes home to

his family after the war. He learns his wife passed away years before, so he returns to the army and insists on standing guard for weeks without rest, out of anger and guilt. To punish himself for not reaching home before she died.

I used to think of that man a lot after Marillion's death. I used to imagine talking with him.

"How has it been for you?" I would've liked to ask him. "Have you found peace? Can you ever, with all your guilt?"

I don't know what he would've answered. Maybe he'd also tried being a good father, and maybe he'd also forsaken a daughter. Maybe he also fell asleep on watch, and maybe he also woke up, weighed down by his grief and anger and guilt.

Maybe I felt some of that, standing on the ramparts. Maybe I did. If my mother had left me and I'd let Marillion die and I'd abandoned Soraya, why shouldn't I feel any of that? But that painful throbbing filled my head, and the only way to make it go away was to cry or think of other things.

Only I couldn't think of other things, not anymore. So I thought of my mother who hadn't loved me, and I thought of Marillion, who had, and I thought of Soraya, who I wished I'd loved more.

Foolish now, right?

One warm night in spring the stars wheeled through the sky, just like they did back home, and I couldn't think of anything but my daughter's sand-colored curls and how she must despise me for leaving her before she could leave me. It set my head spinning so fast I burst out to Trejin about it all and ended up asking him why he thought we lived.

He sighed and said he'd thought about it some but wished he hadn't.

"Why not?" I asked, just to have something to say.

"Maybe people would rather focus on other things," he

said. "If you wonder honestly about it, maybe you start believing there's no reason. How are you to answer that?"

A sickening emptiness swelled within me, but I forced myself to laugh. "You must've thought about it a lot more than 'some.'"

Trejin fiddled at his puzzle box. "When you let everyone else get massacred and stare into nothingness every night afterward, you tend to think a lot."

I nodded, then squeezed my burning eyes shut and did not cry.

"Karadore?" Trejin sounded worried.

"I'm fine," I lied.

THAT NIGHT, I STAYED awake long enough to see the day. First, dawn light. Then the sun's blazing rays splayed out across the emerald fields below.

Once, my daughter had asked me, "Why does the sun keep rising?"

I'd shrugged, grinned, and wrapped my arm around her shoulders. "To help you find your way home when you stay out too late."

I'd been joking then, but as I stood on those ramparts and watched that sun rise, I realized I'd forgot how vast it was beyond Ekket Kan. And I thought of all those people that traveled here from across Ikarsia. Maybe the worst thing that happened in some of their lives was the day their favorite pair of boots no longer fit their feet. Maybe they didn't know much of death or guilt, but I thought of how much life there must've been in them put together, all the homes and families and friends and memories of laughter. I figured that somehow, there still must have been a lot of life within folks after all.

My grief faded then. I gazed again at the golden rays of the rising sun and felt its warmth upon my face and thought how wonderful it was.

And I smiled.

WIND BLEW. A GLITTERING speck emerged in the distance. I called the others over. Maybe it would be interesting.

The speck turned into a man that demanded to be let in.

"Enemies are approaching!" His voice broke in something like fear.

I raised my eyebrows at him. "What *kind* of enemie—"

"Ojakians!" he shot back.

Wind bit my face.

Far away, a crowd appeared. Lightning seemed to crackle within their armor's metal plates, and their torches illuminated the red and blue Ojakian emblems on their standards.

"Open the gates." Trejin's voice was taut.

Inochar came over and helped me heave them open. The stranger stumbled through. Emnor crossed over to Trejin. The two of them rang the alarm bell, and its colossal knell rattled my teeth and made my skull ache.

"Go below, Karadore!" Emnor called. "You can't possibly fight your own kind!"

"I can for the good of Ekket Kan," I retorted, and drew my bow to convince us both. Its smooth wood felt comforting.

Wind stung my eyes, and someone shouted from the crowd. I peered over the parapet. A buckling in my chest, I looked away and vowed to keep looking away so I could pretend it was someone else. Then Inochar shot an arrow that grazed her shoulder.

"Stop!" I yelled. "That's my daughter!"

Soraya marched ahead of the rest, unarmed, and in the

blazing light of sunrise, I saw her green eyes and the fierceness within them.

Inochar drew another arrow. "Emnor told you to go below!"

Wind tore through my throat. "Do you expect me to let you slaughter her?"

Inochar fidgeted with her arrow. It was long and sharp and adorned with cruel, serrated barbs. I counted ten of them on its steely head before nausea made me look away, toward Soraya. *Please, please look at me my child—no, don't, don't look at me after all, don't. I won't be able to stand it.* And she halted and saw me and said she wanted to negotiate with the king.

Maybe she smiled. I wasn't sure.

Trejin touched my arm. "Karadore, you say that's your daughter—" but Emnor hurried over and shoved between us before I could answer.

I crashed to the parapet floor. Trejin nearly stumbled off the wall. Emnor notched his bow, and I struggled back to my feet. "Don't shoot her, damn you!"

Inochar aimed her own arrow at Soraya and hesitated. Terror strangled me and I sprang forward and smacked the bow out of her hands. The weapon twisted through the air, over the edge of the parapet, and into the crowd.

In the silence, the air smelled like smoke. Then Emnor released his bowstring. His arrow hurtled down, down, down into the blazing sunlight, and toward my daughter's throat. I screamed, as all ten of those steely barbs slashed through her neck, as all ten of them burst out the other side, as the bloody arrowhead impaled itself in the ground behind her, as she collapsed beside it, and as the arrow-shaft stood and gazed down at her motionless body, trembling a little over what it had done.

For some reason my daughter didn't move. *Clever girl,* I thought. She was waiting to rise till after that arrow stopped vibrating. I bit back a smile and waited, too. But Soraya didn't rise even then. She didn't rise, she would never rise, and then a shudder jolted through me, 'cause she was dead.

My eyes seared and blurred. I was shaking. Why couldn't I stop shaking?

"Damn it, Emnor, how does killing her make you look?" Inochar was asking.

Emnor shot her a panicked look. "Agnar'll fix it," he said.

I was crying, I realized. I was crying, and Soraya was dead.

"No one needs to know," Emnor was saying.

No one needed to know? Fire roared through me, and I rushed at him. *Why not smash his goddamn head apart?* But the Ojakians bellowed and the bell keened and more cadres of guards were arriving to defend Ekket Kan, and before I could reach Emnor, someone else had caught my shoulder with an unsteady hand and was marching me down the staircase.

The person mumbled that there was nothing for it but to report me to the king and that I shouldn't have interfered with Inochar's shot because I would probably be executed after they suppressed the revolt, but I didn't give a damn about that, I didn't, I didn't—

THREE WEEKS HAD PASSED since Soraya died. I hummed dirges out my prison cell's window all the while.

My jailer was a young guard named Mitherys. He'd seemed friendly enough whenever we'd crossed paths in the barracks, but now he called me a traitor every chance he could. He made a point of serving me moldy bread and going off on these long-winded stories about how grateful the cook was to him for getting rid of her unwanted stock.

I ignored him. Bastard was just sore over being left to rot with me while the other guards suppressed the rebellion.

Then one day on bringing my food, Mitherys said he'd helped secretly bury Soraya beneath the southern gates. My chest panged, and before I could stop myself, I was pleading with him to tell me about her grave. He met my gaze, and I thought I saw concern flash through his eyes. Then he shot me a scornful glare and spat at me that there was no grave, that nobody else would ever mourn her. I could tell myself whatever I wanted, but that was the truth.

I almost hurled the food at him. I swallowed it instead. I didn't know why. I was going to die anyway.

A day later, Trejin visited. He stood outside my cell and watched me. His hair looked grayer than in the past. A fresh wound sliced through his chin. A faint furrow on his brow gave his face a troubled expression.

I sprang up. "Trejin, what happened?"

The prison was near the kitchens. In the morning silence, the chilly air smelled of apple turnovers.

"We suppressed the revolt," Trejin said at last. "Emnor broke his leg, but otherwise he and Inochar are alright."

A goddamn leg. What was that in the face of death? Absolutely nothing.

I started in on some stupid folktale. Didn't know why.

"Once there was a merchant that—" I broke off. I couldn't go on.

He frowned. "How do you mean?" he asked.

I shook my head. "What'll happen to me?" I finally got out. Maybe it wouldn't be death.

Trejin sighed. "You are to be executed in five days for treason," he muttered.

"'Cause of your report?" I asked.

He looked at his hands. They were shaking, I saw. "I couldn't do anything about it, Karadore. I tried my hardest. You shouldn't have to die for protecting your loved ones, but the king only said I could grant your last requests."

Well.

I found myself grinning. "If you really believed that, why did you turn me in to begin with?"

Trejin crossed his arms. "I had no choice."

My grin vanished. "Yes you did. The Ojakians wanted to negotiate and Emnor and Inochar didn't let them. I tried to."

He didn't meet my gaze. "Interfering with Inochar's shot is still considered treason."

I glared at him. "And Emnor shooting a negotiator isn't?"

Trejin's jaw clenched and he didn't speak for a while. He seemed bewildered, maybe by me, maybe by Ekket Kan, or maybe by himself. Hell, he should be.

Then he uncrossed his arms, tentative. "But your abandoned daughter led what became a revolt," he said, "so preemptive action was justified."

I shook my head. "She wasn't even armed!"

Trejin fidgeted with his sword scabbard's gold locket. "Never mind," he mumbled. "It wasn't right of me to say that about her. I—I'm sorr—"

"You're one to talk, anyway," I went on. "Tell me, why's your letting others get massacred not considered treason while my trying to save someone is?"

He breathed in sharply. He obviously couldn't answer something like that, so I guessed for him.

"If Emnor and Inochar saw you hadn't turned me in after what they did, they would've tried covering it up by ordering your execution," I said. "Can't be a good guard for your parents then, right? So better me than you?"

A part of me had hoped Trejin would say I was mad, but he bit his lip, and I knew I was right.

I smacked the bars. "Damn you!"

He flinched. I left him standing there like a bastard and slumped against my cell's far wall and glared at the dark muddy ground and waited for him to leave so I could get executed and he could live the rest of his life lying to himself.

He didn't leave. "Karadore, I'm so sorry."

I hummed dirges and traced nonsensical zigzags into the mud and did not cry.

A while passed.

"I still need to grant your last requests."

Damn him.

"You can ask for anything."

My fist ached.

His voice became hoarse. "You could even request my death."

I looked up. "What?"

Trejin took a deep breath, then drew his sword and held its edge to his throat. "At least you'd get justice for what I did to you."

The bastard was serious, I realized.

I'd like to say I rose and shouted at him not to do it, but I nodded instead.

I nodded.

Trejin's knuckles tightened around the sword-hilt and his muscles tensed so he could jerk the blade through his throat, and only when I saw thick drops of scarlet blood rolling down his neck did I finally leap up and shout, "No!"

He froze, and we stared at each other. We were both crying, and a long while passed before I could speak again.

"No, Trejin, don't die," I mumbled. "That won't mean anything."

He let out his breath and sheathed his blood-edged sword.

He seemed vaguely astonished.

I dried my eyes and watched the blood on his neck and wondered why I wanted him to live when I was going to die anyway.

"What's in your puzzle box?" I asked.

His voice was still hoarse. "Nothing."

"Then why do you work at it?"

He shrugged. "Why does the sun keep rising?"

My throat burned at that.

His brow furrowed. "Karadore, what's wrong?"

I stared at the bars between us. *Nothing's wrong,* I wanted to say. "They—they buried my daughter secretly."

"I know," he said. "I was there."

Why did I even tell him these things?

"Her face was happy. I wanted you to know."

He was lying. Soraya wouldn't've been happy when she'd seen me. Even so, I found myself hoping, 'cause maybe…

"Where'd they bury her?" I asked.

"Under the southern gates."

"You're right," I said. "But—"

Mitherys appeared. He saluted Trejin with his ax-head. Trejin said something to him, I didn't know what; I was thinking of when I'd seen Soraya before she'd died.

When she'd met my eyes, she hadn't gotten angry like I had dreaded. My wonderful girl must've smiled instead.

She had smiled.

I swallowed.

"Karadore." Mitherys was gone, I realized. Trejin was asking me if I had any requests.

"Nothing you can help," I said. "Just that I wish I had wanted more out of life."

"How do you mean?"

I shook my head. Soraya had forgiven me. How could I explain something like that? I couldn't.

I tried anyway. "Ever see folks near death? They're like kids again, curious about everything. Like once, Soraya came out of delirium and touched a candle-flame as if she didn't know it'd burn her. But she must've known. Maybe she didn't care." I took a deep breath. "Maybe she just wanted to live."

Trejin's eyes went bright. "I...I think I understand what you mean. After the massacre..." He wiped the remaining blood from his neck. "But you're right. I can't help you with that."

Of course not. "It's enough to just understand."

Then, because some sorrows nobody can understand, I went back to sit against the far wall.

"Do you have other requests?" Trejin asked.

I took a shaky breath. "A marker for my grave. And Soraya's. It'll make you a traitor too, but there's life beyond Ekket Kan, you see."

He nodded. "You have my word. What else?"

Afternoon light tumbled into my cell. The sweetness left the air, replaced by the rich scent of beef-and-cabbage stew. In the corridor outside, someone started up a lively jig on a concertina, played a wrong note, then let the song fall silent.

"Nothing," I said, thinking again of Soraya's smile.

Suffer the Silence

Ellis Bray

IT CAN'T REALLY BE called a forest; it's more like a city park gone
feral. Not that it matters, I guess. It's still the only place where
my brain goes quiet and the voice vanishes and I can just *be*.
This little creek runs through the middle of the park where I can
lose hours in the silence, and so I do.

Even with winter lurking in the shadows of its trees, while
I white-knuckle my way through suddenly stopping my psych
meds—a big no-no, according to the experts, all of whom have
reliable income and decent health insurance—this clearing and
its creek have saved me in every conceivable way: body, mind,
soul. The only way I know to return the favor is by coming back
and existing here. It's our unspoken pact: I give them a purpose, they give me a place to work through the worst of the
fevers and chills and cramps and panic and sudden propaga-
tion of hateful, nasty, evil voices.

The relationship is a bit one-sided, I'll be honest.

Anyway, this small bit of city park offers me the most peace while demanding the least repayment, and I'm not going ask too many questions. I'm just going to sit here at the water's edge and drink in the isolation.

Or I would, except for some fuckin' reason, someone brought their kid, a baby, to *my* creek, and it won't stop crying. Just that high-pitched, constant wailing, like a siren, going on and on and on and

"Have you seen my baby?" an anxious female voice behind me asks.

The urge to turn around and see who's talking...God, it makes my skin itch. Instead, I focus on the creek. It's not my usual voice, but that doesn't mean it's real.

Keeping half an ear cocked for footsteps behind me, I glare at the stones beneath the surface of the water and start running through my mental checklist.

One: this spot is in a city park; anyone can come here.

Two: it's still daylight, so the park is still open.

Three: it's November and cold; I don't know much about babies, but if it's cold enough to hurt me—and it is—a baby probably doesn't stand a chance.

Four: no one ever comes to this creek

(except whoever brought the baby)

and no one ever bothers me

(except for this lady)

so chances are she's not real.

Baby's probably not, either.

"Have you seen him?" she says again. "My baby. I lost my baby."

It's weird, though, her continuity. People like her usually vanish once I'm done with my analysis.

I turn around now, scooting awkwardly on my ass, and she's standing there, looming over me, solid as the trees, wearing a white dress that is way too damn thin for the late autumn air. She doesn't seem bothered by the cold, doesn't seem to notice the icy wind rolling dead leaves across the ground.

The same wind that grabs my hair and shoves its frigid fingers under my collar, until my ears are hidden by my shoulders and I look as misshapen as I feel. The shivering that starts at the base of my spine, though, has nothing to do with the weather.

Keeping my eyes on her—if she's real, she's a complete stranger to me; if she's not real, I want to know when she's gone—I touch the trunk of the nearest tree and try one last time to figure out where I am in relation to reality. It's a trick the psych nurses taught me, way back when I was first diagnosed and we couldn't figure out which drugs I needed. Use your senses, all of them, and focus on the objective and the subjective, in that order.

Rough bark under my fingers, cold dirt under my ass. Sunlight, low and orange, slicing through the last of the leaves, landing on her skin, making her glow. The wet scent of mulch on the wind. The anemic tang making my stomach churn, a side effect of compulsively biting my lips. The creek babbling as it runs over the enormous, ankle-breaking rocks, almost—but not quite—drowning out the interminable high-pitched screaming of the...

"Baby?" I say, voice cracking.

"My baby," she repeats frantically.

She's scared, I realize.

"Don't you hear him?" I ask, nodding my head upstream, towards the hysterical wailing. I don't like kids, but even I'm starting to get worried. That kind of crying doesn't sound healthy.

She glances in that direction but there's no recognition in those colorless eyes. Maybe she can't hear him.

Maybe he's not real.

But then she takes a step closer to me and something deep behind my sternum wakes up, starts beating hard against my ribcage, trying to escape. Not jealousy, but a very particular kind of anxiety, the kind I learned real quick to pay attention to once I started sleeping outside. And I'll pay attention here, too, once I figure out what it is.

"Can you help me find him?" she repeats.

The sense of "unnatural" is stronger now, and growing, enough to make me try to wake up my sleeping legs and stand, meet her at eye level. Everything about her is like one of those kids' puzzles: *Circle the items that are out of place.* Except instead of a banana in the sock drawer, it's something about her eyes or her hair, something about how she says the words rather than the words themselves. It's so close I can almost touch it, whatever the hell's wrong with her, and the whole situation is more infuriating for missing something so obvious.

"Your kid's over there," I say, pointing again, where the baby can still be heard, although he sounds weaker. Hoarse. Tired. "Go get him. Leave me alone."

"I need your help," she says again, taking another step closer, holding her hand out, begging. "I can't leave without him."

Christ, maybe she's even sicker than me, and that's the thought that finally gets my feet awake and underneath me, gets my nerves singing.

"Sorry, I have a—a thing." I take a step back. "Important thing. Thing I can't miss."

"I *won't* leave without him." It's only a shift of one word, but with that word, her tone and her face and everything else changes, too, from desperate (I think) to furious (pretty sure), a familiar slide from control into madness

(not supposed to say that speak a name give a power and

besides it's unkind and maybe untrue you're better than this be
better than this)

(if the shoe fits)

(you're on your last pair choose your words carefully)

is terrifying to watch.

So yeah, I can sympathize with her

(empathize?)

(what's the difference?)

but that doesn't mean I want that particular transforma-
tion directed at me. I remember how destructive it can be, the
blinding rage when you finally understand just how far the
punishment outstrips the fuckup.

You miss a refill and wind up homeless.

You get distracted and misplace your baby.

Small mistakes, in the grand scheme of things.

"I don't know what to tell you, lady," I say, and I grab my
backpack, which has my whole life in it, ready to travel. "I'm
sorry. I gotta—"

"Please. Just *help* me." And she comes forward—

(so fast so much faster than she should have been able to
move and something about how she moves something about
the wind something about my senses my *senses* something
that shouldn't)

—and grabs my wrist.

You ever stick your hand in dry ice? Terrible idea—ice
burns are no joke. I did it once, because my voice told me he'd
go away forever if I did it, if I just hurt myself enough to make
him want to leave, back before I knew he wasn't supposed to
be there, back before I knew there were other ways to make him
go away. So I did, and I ended up in the hospital. First for the
burns, then for the schizophrenia, and, I don't know, shit just
kind of spiraled from there—

Her hand is colder than that. The burn is instant and deep and grinding, freezing marrow and cracking bones. And I can't help it. I scream and pull my hand back. She lets go and I can see her fingers, outlined in blisters on my skin, and the burning pain is *real* in the way that so much else isn't, clawing its way deeper into my body even when I'm not looking at it, and she's so close, she's *so close*, and now I know the pounding, shrieking thing in my chest is terror, trying to rip my ribs apart to use as weapons against a threat I didn't recognize.

The wind is blowing the leaves and my hair and cutting straight through every layer of clothing I have on, but she's completely unaffected. Her hair doesn't move. Her dress doesn't flutter. Her eyes

(hungry eyes, hunting eyes)

don't follow the leaves or the dust or the—Jesus, is that *snow?*—glittering in the orange light across her field of vision. She doesn't shiver like I'm shivering or seem at all bothered by how *cold* it is.

If it weren't for the burns—still shrieking along my nerve endings, bubbling through my skin from the corner of my eye—I'd think she was just a new voice made corporeal.

If it weren't for the burns.

"Your baby," I say, gritting my teeth and cradling my arm.

"My baby," she says, stepping closer again. I can feel the cold coming off her. It's not the wind at all. It's not the season or the setting sun or the spray of the water behind me.

It's her.

It's all her.

"He's...up...there." I shrug my shoulder upstream, even though I can't hear him crying anymore. I just want to back away from her, from this clearing, from this whole fucked-up

situation, but the water is right behind me, and I'm so cold. I'm
so, so cold.

"You will help me," she hisses
as she pushes me backwards
into
the
creek.

The whiplash of burning ice and stinging wet is all that
keeps me conscious, keeps me from freezing in terror. The skin
on my chest is raw and blistering where she touched me, even
through my shirt, and the wind is picking up, and really, how
hard would it be to just stop fighting?

(Easiest thing in the world)

I force myself to sit up and ignore everything my body
is telling me: cold and pain and fear and danger. From this
angle—me in the water, her above me on the bank—she looks
less than human. It's not the way she's unaffected by the wind,
or the way she just keeps repeating the same phrase over and
over. Shit, it's not even the burns on my arm and my chest, the
outline of her touch searing its way inexorably to my core.

It's how her skin is thinning. The lower the sun gets, the
more her skin seems to just…wither away. Like ashes, curling
away from wood. I've had visions like this in the past, but nothing that caused me real, physical harm.

And the redder and colder the light gets, the more crowded
my quiet clearing becomes. The wind carries whispers along
with the snow now, but I can't tell the words apart. And beyond
the woman, in the woods, something massive has arrived and
started pacing, a shadow just a shade darker than the others.
Each footfall rattles the rocks beneath me, up into my bones,
till I can't tell where its steps stop and my shivering begins. I

don't want to look away from the woman, don't want to try to see what's stomping behind her or who's whispering and what they're saying, because she's watching me, and every instinct I have says she's the most likely threat to end up on my autopsy report.

If I'm wrong, it won't matter. If I'm right, well, that'll be interesting, too.

"The gates are open," she growls through disintegrating lips, "and I cannot go through them alone. *Where is my baby?*"

"He's up there!" I shout, pointing to where the baby, incredibly, has started crying again. The sound brings heat with it; I don't know how to explain it any better than that. He's shrieking, which gets me back on my feet, which makes him cry even louder, which gets me more agitated

(but on his behalf, now, because how could something so small be so resilient when even his own *mother* was acting like this)

and on and on it goes, each of us building on the other, a positive feedback loop of sound and fury. "What kind of mother can't hear her own fucking baby? He's—*right*—*there!*"

And it stops. All of it. The only thing that moves is the creek, bubbling its way down from the mountains on its way to the ocean. Along its surface, as still as the rest of the world, floats a small doll-shaped thing, its fragile frame bumping every rock with a muted thud, echoing whatever was pacing in the trees.

The forest and everything in it, natural and not, stops to watch the tiny shape, and silence—the blessed, unremitting silence I've been looking for—falls at last.

The doll brushes against my leg before continuing its journey downstream. I don't touch him, don't try to pick him up or comfort him. His quietus is as profound as the world surrounding him, and I have no right to disrupt it. He drifts, unhindered and unhurried, around the bend and out of sight.

I turn back to the woman and find her gone. The clearing is empty, the shadow vanished. The bare trees crowd me now, empty of whispers, but no less threatening for it. Yes, I could pass through them, and in a few minutes I will, but it will cost me. My days of using the clearing and its creek as a place of respite are gone, taken by the woman and the shadow and the child.

I climb out of the water and sit back down beneath my tree (*my* tree).

The sun is gone, and everything is glittering gray light, but I'm not cold. The burns continue to bite and burrow, but in a vague, background sort of way. The voice that lives in my head is silent. Peace—warm and cottony and, most importantly, quiet—has arrived at last.

I'll need to get up soon, get moving, get help. In a minute, though.

In a minute.

Ziabetes

Lily Jurich

I CROUCHED BEHIND THE counter of the long-abandoned Bartell's, trying to keep my breath as quiet as possible. The three Undead I could see between me and the door were trapping me, and Arwyn was too far outside to call for backup. She was supposed to be watching the entrance while I grabbed supplies.

My heartbeat was deafening in my head. I could be swarmed in seconds; anything too loud would give away my position, even just a shaky breath or a twig snapping.

Their migration wasn't supposed to start for another month; that was the whole point of the supply run. Why had they already started? The scientists just recently developed ways of tracking them. How had no one at base noticed a change in pattern?

I couldn't book it for the door with the Undead still there, and I wasn't nearly fast enough to outrun them. I looked around for a distraction to divert their attention. I had a small pistol on me, but not nearly enough bullets for all of them. It didn't matter. It'd be too loud anyway.

Some miscellaneous junk remained behind the counter. Extra cash, lotto tickets, coupons. Anything that could be used for survival had already been taken the last time I came through here.

I saw an empty glass bottle of Coke a few feet away from me. If I threw it far enough, I could have just enough time to make a run for it.

My legs were killing me, as I was still crouching. I couldn't move very easily, though. It would be a bit of a hassle going for the bottle, but I didn't have any other options.

I tried to grab it by shifting my weight from one foot to the other, but it was just out of reach. I carefully maneuvered forward, my eyes on the bottle to make sure I didn't fuck up. I almost had it, only a little bit farther.

My foot crunched on something. It sounded like glass. I froze. It had only made a slight sound, but their hearing was piercingly sharp. I listened for any of the Undead coming to inspect the sound. I stayed frozen for well over a minute, too scared another sound might set them off.

Then I carefully lifted my foot and brushed away the glass. Painfully aware of where I placed my foot, I tried to reach for the bottle again.

Before I even touched it, the pod on my arm beeped. Never before had it been such a horrifying sound.

Fuck fuck fuck.

I forgot it was almost time to change the site. *God,* I'm an idiot—I forgot to check it before I left base. I was too busy scrambling to get out for the supply run.

I immediately covered my pod with my hand to muffle the

sound, but it was too little too late. The nearest three Undead ran straight toward the counter. I shot the closest one, which tripped up the one behind it, then I vaulted over the counter to dodge the third.

The others in the store were running at me, and I didn't even bother trying to slow them down. I blazed out the exit, trying my best to avoid the others coming in to inspect the sounds.

I took one of the pre-scouted escape routes as I ran behind the building through a small alleyway. I vaulted onto a ladder; not that it gave me much of a lead. As I started to climb, the closest of them clawed at my ankles. My boots were sturdy enough that they wouldn't be able to get to my skin. I kicked them off anyway. I didn't want them pulling me back down.

I finally reached the roof and collapsed on my back. I could feel my heart beating in my head and my hands were slightly shaking. I had to take a few deep breaths to steady myself.

The Undead's fine motor control was practically nonexistent, so luckily they couldn't climb ladders. I was safe up here.

My pod alarmed the inevitable second set of beeps, but it didn't matter anymore. Once it finished I decided I needed to try to scout for Arwyn. Where was she?

I peeked my head over the edge of the roof. The Undead were so packed in the street that if she was down there, I could not see her.

She's probably dead.

It was bad. Really bad. I might have to camp out on the roof. I had supplies in my bag, but most of these were supposed to be for stocking. It didn't matter. Plus, if my pod was ending I wouldn't have much time anyway. I checked my meter for how much insulin I had left: eight units. That would last about two hours if I didn't eat anything.

Camping out on the roof wasn't an option. I needed to call

in to base, let them know what was happening. I switched my radio on.

"This is Sophie, calling in from District 3, over."

It seemed like an eternity before I finally heard the crackling of the line.

"This is Will from base."

Okay, good, I know Will. He can help.

I interrupted whatever he was going to say next.

"The horde is here early. I'm surrounded on all sides and I don't know where Arwyn is," I said in a single breath, skipping normal radio formalities.

Saying all that out loud forced me to acknowledge the horrific reality of my situation. I took a few deep breaths to calm down. I needed to focus.

He paused before he responded. "Okay, I'm going to talk with the sergeant. Stay where you are. Over and out."

The radio went silent.

I couldn't just sit and do nothing while waiting for someone else to save me. I wasn't some damsel in distress. Well, I *was* in distress. Could I be considered a damsel?

This isn't the time for fucking jokes, Sophie.

I searched around my bag for my binoculars before I realized they were with Arwyn. She had been scouting on the way down while I drove. We should've brought two pairs.

Our car was parked a mile away so we wouldn't attract more of the Undead. What good that did.

Suddenly, an arrow stuck into the wall beside me. Unless one of the Undead had magically learned to shoot, it had to be Arwyn. I looked toward the direction it had come from and saw a figure crouching in a small cluster of bushes. She was well hidden, but I could still tell it was her.

Thank god she's alive.

I looked for a way to get to her, but the Undead blocked every possible path. But she would be able to see my hands with the binoculars.

"Do you have a plan?" I signed over to her.

I couldn't see well enough if she was signing, but she was definitely shaking her head.

Everyone, at our base at least, knew ASL. The Undead were more sensitive to sound and not great on eyesight, so ASL and visual communications were preferable to verbal. Too bad most of the modern technology for diabetes relied on auditory alerts. We had a few people working on silent technology back at base, but nothing had come of it yet.

We needed to come up with something soon. Arwyn's hiding spot could be too-easily stumbled upon by one of the Undead. I was running out of insulin. The clock was ticking.

Auditory alerts, that's it!

If I emptied out my insulin, my pod would make that annoying, ongoing screech. If I triggered it and threw it far enough away, it could draw them away from Arwyn and me. I would start to spike, but I was going to run out of insulin either way.

I turned on my pod. Seven units. I couldn't just dump seven units into me and plummet my blood sugar, so I took my pod off first. Set it to give me ten units, just to make sure it would go off.

I got up and waved my arms to get Arwyn's attention. Once I could see she was looking at me, I signed, "Get ready to run."

It wasn't very descriptive but it got the point across. I packed everything else tight in my bag to make sure nothing would fall out.

I had my knife in one hand and Arwyn's arrow in the other. I planned on giving it back to her when we finally met up again. Arrows weren't cheap. Well, neither was insulin, but there I was shitting that away.

I anxiously waited for the insulin to go out, the tiny drop-
lets forming at the end of the needle and dripping down it. I
couldn't take my eyes off the meter; 3 units delivered, 3.1 units
delivered, 3.2 units delivered.

When 6.5 units had been delivered, I got ready to throw the
pod. I saw a perfect opening, an abandoned truck in the street. It
would take the Undead not long to get on top of it and destroy
the pod, silencing it. Any more time we could get, I would take.

If I threw the pod at the sign above the truck, it could bounce
off and land on it. *If* I threw it at the right angle. A small click
sounded before the indefinite tone started. It startled me a bit,
even though I should've been ready for it. I took a deep breath
and threw the pod at the sign. It hit, bounced, and landed in
the truck bed. That was somewhat of a surprise. My aim is normally really shitty. No matter.

I sprinted to the back of the roof where the ladder was. I got
down right as Arwyn reached me. We both ran toward the car.

"That was your plan?" Arwyn hissed through rapid breaths.

"Better than *your* nonexistent one."

She grunted in response.

A few of the Undead kept on us, ones that either didn't hear
my pod or didn't care. We slowed down to clear them; I shot the
ones closest to me while Arwyn used another arrow to stab hers.
She had a knife on her; the arrow was unnecessarily extravagant.

We quickly got back to running.

"Here's the arrow you almost shot me with," I said, handing her the arrow she almost shot me with.

"I did not almost shoot you! I'm too skilled for that." She
begrudgingly accepted the arrow.

"Not skilled enough to warn me in time, apparently." Rude,
I know, but I was pissed. We could've died. We still could.

"That's not my fault, I had to go pee."

"Pfft, that's why you went over to the bushes? What, were you crouching in your own piss puddle?"

"That's gross, Sophie."

"You're gross."

She sighed. "One would think surviving the literal apocalypse might mature a person, yet here you are."

The radio in my backpack started talking to me again.

"The general wants you to stay there. We're sending help," Will said, slightly muffled by the leather.

Okay, that was total BS. He wasn't sending anyone. The rules have always been strict on not leaving base when a horde is present. Were they planning on leaving us for dead?

Arwyn picked up the same thing. "There's no way."

"Apparently, there is. Let's just get to base and we can figure it out then."

We were finally far enough away that we could walk towards the car instead of running. None of the Undead seemed to have noticed or followed us after those first few. It was a bit of a walk, but it wasn't too bad. We got to the car after about half an hour, as we had to quietly sneak around a few stragglers. The horde was generally behind us.

"That was...fun," I sighed, closing the car door.

"Let's just get the hell out of here."

I turned the key in the ignition. It spit out a low, rumbling cough, sputtered a bit, and died.

"Fuck."

The Warp and Weft of a Norse Villainess

El Park

THE GODDESS IDUN SWIRLS onward, her crystal wake settling in drifts as we reach together for the cloth on our life loom. The goddess had come, as is her duty and her right, to smear the looms of the Aesir Gods with the fruit of immortality. Alas, arriving as she did from the Land of Ice and Mist, she brought with her a cold so keen it chilled the earth below the Tree of Life to a crackle.

We live beneath her, Yggdrasil, the Tree of Life, deep in her soil. I say "live," but one would not call what we do living. Our duty is to fashion the unsullied souls of mortals, who in turn believe our purpose is to manipulate their fates. For thousands of years we have sculpted them, and the men and women thus shaped never noticed that their fates are all the same. They are born, they live, and they die. It is hubris to think that dull human fates give purpose to the Sisters Three. Our toil with their threads of mortality is no more than the efforts of farmers with their seeds. Does the fate of each grain matter to the farmer? Not at all. Only the crop as a whole is of significance.

We Sisters are long accustomed to the distinctive pertur-bations of our visiting gods: Thor's overturned looms, Hodr's clammy darkness, and the icy backwash of Idun's visitations. Verdandi pushes through the frost to caress our own lifecloth with one hand while tossing the shuttle back and forth with others. Urd joins her to brush the fabric of our lives free of the glittering ice gems. Together, the three of us pat the weave of our past deeds, then sweep our fingers along the receding warp to calculate the span of time left to us in this realm. Mere centuries remain of our service to Yggdrasil, with millennia of duty now behind us. Our end approaches. I am tired and eager to complete the task, to retire when the Gods meet their end at Ragnarök.

My sister Urd's many hands spin the threads that become mortal lives. This is true. My sister Verdandi weaves the tap-estries of brief journeys on this earth. This also is true. It is furthermore true that I, Skuld, cut their threads when they must relinquish blood, bone, and muscle to cross to the Land of Ice and Mist. All true. Nonetheless, our sacred purpose is not their dreary fates. We nourish the Tree of Life with the virtue of their souls.

One of my legion hands wanders among the looms, seeking respite from the surrounding chill and bustle in the purity of an unfinished tapestry. While its fingers alight, my other hands continue their grim duties. Nothing distinguishes the woven life it lands upon, chosen only for its warmth.

A life story emerges under my touch, that of a woman born far from our vocation in a district teeming with people and industry. I struggle to identify the city—one of so many I prowl—then the answer comes to me, and I enter her life.

Irma Levy is born in the New York of 1921 to parents who fled religious persecution. I stroke her conformation to pattern. Her early education in crowded schools, as is expected of immigrant children, then its furtherance in a local college, as is expected of her culture. She marries and has four children, as is expected of the women of this era, then moves out of the city and volunteers in the community, as is expected of the social class she ascends to. This soothes my harried heart, this life woven to a template of virtuous discharge of duty.

I say that we live beneath Yggdrasil and we do, underground, in her soil. *Of* her soil. Mortals say we have but one eye among us; they err. We have none. Instead, our creeping tresses penetrate the earth, rubbing and coiling about each other and the roots of the Tree, intimately entwined throughout the globe entire. What need have we sisters for eyes when Yggdrasil reveals her requirements through pulse, pull, and touch?

Rolling tremors break my contemplation of Irma Levy, announcing the arrival of the god Loki. I arrange myself in a pose of eager expectancy, for it would not do to anger a god with my preoccupation. They require absolute attention.

Loki has come, not to plead for the death of a mortal, but to save his own clever self. I turn to his life-loom, and yes, Idun has not touched it with the fruit. For this day his skull is promised to the dwarf Brokkur in settlement of a game of chance. I reach for a blade, but Loki stays my hand with his polished marble fingers, the smooth ones used to arouse awe in his conquests. They have no effect on a Sister.

"Not this day," he says, voice fluttering.

Unbidden, an image of Loki's handsome severed head comes to me, held aloft by its flaming hair in Brokkur's grip.

"Not this day," I reply, though the image lingers.

He drops my hand and departs without a word of thanks,

his splintered laughter drilling through the soil in glass-like shards, despoiling Verdandi's weaving and thrusting us off-balance as we duck and parry the solid Aesir daggers. Anchoring myself, I clench my teeth and knot the tenuous threads to hold his life in place awhile longer. My knot is ungainly and may trouble him.

As I reach for another life cloth, by chance my hand brushes the underside of Irma Levy's. I am struck by a subtle variation in its texture, a bulge underneath the early 1940s, when she leaves home to study for a doctorate in the natural science called geology. This is not part of the template for virtuous women of this age; doctorates are not for them. My solace-seeking is disrupted, and I skim further along the belly of the weave for indications that the pattern will reassert itself.

It does not. I find another bulge under her wedding ceremony in 1948, when she weds outside of her religious tradition. A man named Hanson. Oh, her family is dismayed. Her duty is to birth more Jews to replace those lost. There is wailing and hurling of pottery.

As I feel further beneath the fabric, I find that she does not raise the children in her faith.

The work on Irma's tapestry is in impeccable conformity to the pattern, smooth and orderly. But all along the underbelly, I notice the irregularities. I sit back with stilled hands, perplexed at the impiety of it.

The tug of Verdandi's distress reaches me through our hair. Loki's scraps of keen-edged mirth have spattered and gored her work, and I stretch to aid in the removal of his debris. I ponder this sister. Why did she permit a mortal woman to wander so far from her template? The templates are patterns for dutiful lives, designed to foster the virtue that nourishes the Tree. They accommodate mild variation, yes, but as warriors must always seek advantage and farmers must ever improve their yield, so must Jews raise their children in the faith.

With Verdandi settled to her task of repairing the god's damage, my hand moves of its own will to Irma's thread. I find another discrepancy decades later, when Irma subverts her duties to profess her geology at a citadel of learning. First, she marries and raises gentile children, then she neglects her womanly obligations in order to work in the sphere of men. This life is unnatural; it must give Irma spiritual pain. Does Verdandi not grasp this? The Sisters Three may not care for the fates of individuals, but neither are we monsters.

A scent of meaty sweat permeates the soil, auguring the arrival of yet another Aesir intrusion. Thor thrusts into our midst in his massive goat cart, brandishing his great hammer. Blind to our activity and my distraction, he overturns looms and scatters spindles. He seizes all my hands in his immense fist, barking that I have prolonged the worthless life of the trickster god and demanding to know the exact moment of Loki's death. I tell him only that Thor will survive Loki until Ice Eaters topple the gods at Ragnarök. He snarls. I cluck in semblance of sympathy.

At last he departs, and alongside my sisters, I sigh at the damage he has wrought. Verdandi's locks pull at us as she struggles to restore loom after loom. I turn away from her to resume my cutting. Urd's stillness signals her disapproval of me, then she assists Verdandi herself.

Later, the drone of Urd's humming lulls me into stillness. Verdandi weaves beside her, composed and serene. Her hands create a beneficial hum as they dance through the thick soil, giving no indication of her impious interference in the life of Irma Levy Hanson. I recall that Verdandi does indeed weave blasphemous lives, creating them in each generation as cautionary lessons. The miseries she inflicts on those who shirk their duties act as severe warnings for others who may thirst to deviate. I collect myself. This must be her purpose with Irma's life.

I startle, accidentally snipping short a life in Rome; a sixty-year-old gardener is taken by stroke, her trowel left half buried among the roses. In all the ages of our endeavors, I have touched only the upper surfaces of Verdandi's weavings until today, by merest chance, I touched the underbelly of this one. What if this deviance has been lurking underneath all along?

I reach for a nearby tapestry to probe underneath for the warts of transgression. I find them and withdraw my hands one by one from other obligations to stroke further. Not all tapestries are as heretical as Irma's, and some are unblemished, in perfect harmony with their templates. But the blasphemous lives do exist, and they are not few. There are far more than sufficient for instruction.

I begin to sense a pattern. It is the vulnerable whom she desecrates—those who suffer at the hands of their fellow mortals. Their lives are already burdened, yet she has increased their affliction with these misdeeds. Verdandi *must* be cognizant of the cruelty she has fashioned.

For shame, my sister, for shame!

I gasp at my own harsh thought, this indictment of Verdandi. My hands are shaking, but I compel my hair to quietude. It is unthinkable for Urd or Verdandi to know of my bitter suspicions. The Sisters Three do not quarrel. When Thor, blustering god of war; or Loki, impish trickster; or sullen Idun, goddess of immortality, petitions us to alter the fates of mortals, we acquiesce with tranquility. The gods provoke us often; they are nothing if not meddlesome. But each time, we obey, restoring the harmony and balance of our work when they depart, never pointing sulky fingers at one another.

I am drawn again to Irma's tapestry. I watch as her pace slows in her sixth decade and her body begins to fail. Her back aches, her digestion wavers, and she tires easily, but these are mere inconveniences. She remains cheerful, satisfied; she carries no burden. How curious that she should not suffer from my sister's cruelty and blasphemy. I nurture little hope retribution will yet come for Irma.

And what of Verdandi's obligation to the Tree? Surely this life will not yield a healthful soul for Yggdrasil. As if sensing my question, a twitching whisper reaches us from far-flung strands, and we halt our labors. Yggdrasil calls to us with a sacred message.

But no, it does not concern Verdandi's wrongdoing.

Yggdrasil hungers for more souls.

At once Urd's hands fly to her spindles and wheels. Birth rates climb, spurring Verdandi's nimble fingers to greater swiftness. Her tapestries grow hastily, adhering to the templates, or so it seems. I, too, speed my blades in service to our increased obligations. Our movements are hindered by the earth packed in tight around us. No matter. This is not a time for ease but for fleetness. The Tree of Life needs nourishment.

I hunt for the least sign that Yggdrasil knows of my sister's rebellion, but the Tree reveals nothing, no displeasure in her bearing nor damage to her health from the unruly lives my sister weaves. She consumes all mortal souls, the virtuous and the vile, with equal relish. I sense only the Tree's divine ecstasy as, across the globe, she gorges.

The discovery confounds me. Our duty is our virtue and our virtue is our duty. Urd spins. Verdandi weaves. I cut. Is *our* virtue, like Irma's, of no consequence to Yggdrasil? I suppress a shudder and force my hands back to their allotted tasks.

Much of my work was set in motion long ago. I cannot

adjust the pace of the earth's warming that will cause so many threads to be severed; the typhoons, droughts, and deluges have already begun. They will not be enough, however, to stem this new birth-tide of mortals, thus I must select other methods for their dooms. I consider my options as one hand inches back to Irma's tapestry.

While we have been toiling to multiply mortal fodder, Irma has aged ten years. I feel along her warp to mark that she is now, like us, beyond midlife. She has retired from her profession yet keeps her attachment to rock and mineral through the practice of sculpture. She chooses her stones carefully, holding each one for hours as she listens for the shape she will chisel from within. The grace in her trances, the confidence in her hold upon her tools, and the prayer in the patient way she polishes her statues reverberate with the sacred act of creation.

She is blessed!

An unfamiliar stab of envy pierces my liver. I, Skuld, have labored with virtue and diligence for all the ages of mankind and have never been so blessed. In what manner shall I slaughter this man, that family, those millions? These are my wretched "creative" choices. My acts of creation are foredoomed, each knit through with destruction and death.

My hair tugs in a thousand directions, and at first, I think it the result of my own distress. But no, again it is Yggdrasil. She craves yet more souls.

Urd accelerates to dervish pace. Infants are delivered in droves all over Africa, Asias Minor and Major, and the New World. Verdandi's composure falters, sweat courses from her body, creating a thick, muddy slurry which clings to her fingers and soils her threads. Her labors show no artistry; these children endure lives of nearly identical pattern—not enough food, too much disease, moments of joy amid hours of pain and toil.

I rake my memory for tools I've used in the past: locusts, cattle disease, the slaying of the firstborn. None of these will suit.

Thor, Loki, and Idun appear in quick succession asking for the shortening of this life, the lengthening of that, hardship for an urchin who dared sneeze near a God, immortality for a beauty who grovels to another. Thor rides his pointless goat-cart over our tools, shattering some and warping others. I do as they bid, spitting needles of disdain behind their backs, ignoring Urd's bewildered tugs of censure.

I cannot keep away from Irma. In the span of time that passes while we cringe from the Gods, she ages another twenty years. I finger the weft of her life tapestry and behold the wondrous works of art she sculpts and the toll this labor takes upon her body. Now wizened, encased in a wheelchair, her neck and hands twisted and rigid, she lives tended by strangers in a home for the very aged, her children descending for brief visits before fleeing to their own preoccupations. Is this the retribution for her sins, this pain, this life alone, trapped in her chair and subject to the whims of her attendants? A meager flame of hope rekindles in my breast.

But Irma laughs and the flicker extinguishes. She laughs while spinning tales of her youth for her attendants. I listen and rankle. I feel the weave of her life as she speaks. The acts of bravery and exploration she relates are not woven there. She did not jump out of airplanes to rescue refugees in her young womanhood. She did not discover oil in the far north. Her untruths are disgraceful.

I glower while Irma sighs with pleasure. Once again she escapes the confinement of her prescribed life, this time using the only resource left to her: her wits. As she nears her end, when rightfully she should descend into gloom and pain, her creativity continues. She truly glows with bliss.

This woman, this Irma Levy Hanson, has strayed beyond her station and duties, performing irreverent acts time and again. Even now, she ventures further from her template with bursts of selfish lies. Never has she repented of these transgressions. To the very end, she has dedicated herself to her own ambitions and not to the virtuous nourishment of Yggdrasil, the Tree of Life itself. And for that, Verdandi has spared her from suffering and the Tree feasts on regardless, taking no note of polluted souls like Irma's.

Irma has flourished, creating knowledge and life and love and art. And I? What have I created? The entitlement of those foolish gods and death, death, and more death!

Fie!

If all that I may create is death, then so be it! I will create it on a scale not seen since the age that ended with Baldur's passage to the Land of Ice and Mist. I will bring a scathing pestilence to spread swiftly across the lives Urd spins and Verdandi weaves into filth. I will annihilate those the gods have asked me to spare. The wars of Thor will be as trifles to my devastation. Verdandi's rebellion will be crushed under the onslaught of my plagues, and Yggdrasil herself will choke on the swollen harvest from my reddened knives!

The power of the Ice Eaters awakens in my marrow and I lunge for every blade forged by gods or dwarves. Chaos flows in my countless limbs as my fists close around the blades. I convulse, fervor coursing through my veins and hair, smiting my sisters with its force. I push another wave of exaltation over Verdandi and laugh colossal boulders of ruin upon her.

I pull the elements of the pestilence to me and pack them tight. My arms, long used to cutting, strain to imprison the contagion. Then, with cold rage thrilling through me, I cast the plague loose upon the mortal world. I slice through yielding threads, the slim ones of lives nearing their natural end, and others caught nearby. I ensure that Irma Levy Hanson is among the first severed. My strength does not falter as I launch plague after plague, each a more monstrous variation of the last.

A summons from Yggdrasil. Imperative. All the Aesir are called to respond, but I will not. Skuld stays her course, as she always has. I slice through lives and laugh my boulders. Verdandi, who has labored through tsunamis of mud, dust, ice, and clay, can move only her hair, her hands trapped in mountains of my rock.

The earth throbs with footfalls as the marching pantheon nears, and my encrusted grin widens. This I know with every swipe of fisted blade, with every wisp of writhing hair, with every fiber on my life loom: I, Skuld, was created for this devastation. And for what will come after.

Wild Space

A Broke Young Martian atop His Scooter

K.G. Delmare

I'D GONE AND LOST my great-grandfather's ring in the dreadful swirl of the Martian dust, and I still had an order to deliver. Work did not submit to my personal needs. ExPost penalized me quite readily for any professional slights, real or perceived, and I was not a man made for risk-taking. But when the scuffed little thing slipped off of my finger as I jostled boxes around in my temperature-controlled, ExPost-issued carrying case, I defied my own wisdom and stopped working.

The injury of guilt hit me first. I just couldn't shake the omniscient shadow of my dear, brave ancestor, boarding the crowded laborers' rocket, taking him from the derelict surface of an unstable Earth to a life toiling on the massive buildings dotting the Martian landscape, all with that one golden ring as his one glorious possession from home.

I scoured the dirt, frantic in my need to not leave it behind in one of the wide, coppery stretches of landscape between my apartment complex and the neighborhoods that enlisted my services. Finally, just when I thought my pulse could sprint through my veins no faster, I saw a distinct glint in the silt. I grabbed at it, hurriedly slipping the ring back onto my finger and saddling up in my StarScoot, hoping against hope I wouldn't rack up another late delivery deduction.

Though I'd long held on to the ring like it was an inextricable part of me—more like an organ than an accessory—I could never quite escape the feeling that those ancestors of mine had no pride for me. Their labor had built my world. They were the deft hands I'd learned of at the tiny schoolhouse.

Generations later, however, I had foregone the legacy to pursue a more modern career. The pay had been meager in choice, but ExPost had seduced me easily with promises of a flexible schedule without hardened travail. It was the great and noble path that had gotten me racing down the dirt in my secondhand StarScoot, tensed with determination to get my pizzas to Cerise Heights in time.

The party was downright raucous by the time I arrived. I could hear the music from the frosty outdoors, tempting in its ecstatic quality. The house I had been sent to was towering and glittery, with tall pillars out front and a hand-carved door with texture meant to mimic wood. Or stone. One of those old Earthly materials. It was designed in the typical style of upper -class Martian architecture with faux gold and silver trims. That is to say, it was pretty tacky.

When I rang the bell, jittery from the cold, a young man answered the door, with carefully coiffed blond hair and a generous supply of jewels adorning his neck, wrists, and anywhere that would have them. I was starkly aware of how odd I must look next to him—with my cheap ExPost oxygen mask and company-issued translator on my lapel.

He smiled at the pizzas, not me, and turned to bark out to his compatriots, "ExPost guy is here!"

To my great shock and distaste, he then swiped the case from my hands and passed it off into the bowels of the large house. I watched in stunned silence as the package changed hands many times over, fading off into the depths of the mansion to places blocked by the congestion of partygoers until my eyes could no longer follow its trajectory.

"I'm sorry," I said, more sheepish than I would have preferred, "but I'm gonna need that back." Several reasons existed for why I could not go back without my case, the least of which being that each ExPost contractor put down a hefty deposit on our valuable hardware.

The man was unfazed, breezy, his eyes refusing to land on me.

"We'll get it back," he said, and then he leaned against the doorframe and picked up a chat he had evidently been having with a woman beside him. I was left to stand rather awkwardly, my hands empty and wanting for the safe return of my case.

Soon enough, however, the case was within sight, being carried by a woman with glittery golden clips in her long, thick hair. She hauled it over to the man at the door, who then finally turned back to me, straps in hand.

"See, man? All it takes is a little patience."

I knew talking back to a customer was out of the question, so I opted to just take my case and make an exit. I heaved the cargo onto the back of my worn out old StarScoot, suddenly enlightened to the bag's weight after a long day of deliveries, and headed off back in the direction of my apartment.

Whenever I had to do a delivery in Cerise Heights—which was quite often—I tended to take the scenic route home. My StarScoot would putter along the coppery dirt in front of these manicured homes, and I would indulge in the unattainable dream that every ExPost delivery person probably had but would never achieve: to escape.

Our kind had only lived on Mars for a few generations by the time I came along. Most of us were still back home on Earth, languishing in a wrecked environment and trying to make do. Mars was a land for the progeny of billionaires, trillionaires, and their ilk beyond. They were happy to be alone, in their own paradise. But they were also not builders by trade. The solution was easy. Scoop up the broke and assiduous with promises of a passable schoolhouse for their children and a home without swollen seas gobbling up their world, all for the small price of building the new world from its bones. From their blood and exertion, I was eventually born.

I meandered my way back to my housing district, just twenty minutes from Cerise. It was close enough to easily commute to, but far enough to not bother the wealthier residents with the unsightly view of our uniform complex of bland-looking buildings.

As my StarScoot puttered its way into the parking lot, I couldn't help but notice the unusual drag. I dismounted and circled my vehicle, trying to discern the problem. It looked exactly as it always did, as dilapidated and aged as ever.

With no time to ponder, I picked up the case from the back end and quickly realized where the extra weight was coming from. In my haste to get away from the party, I hadn't noticed that something had been left behind, no doubt a pizza or some faux chicken. I undid the Velcro and peeked. The answer betrayed my suspicions. I held a book in my hands.

If one wanted to find someone with fat pockets, they would be smart to look for someone who owned books. Even our paltry schoolhouses were outfitted with factory-made screen readers. Supposedly whole buildings were packed with books on Earth, but that hadn't been our home for generations. That meant no books, no paper, nothing of the sort—not for us, of course. And one was in my possession.

Upon full recognition of the sight before me and all of its implications, I quickly shut the bag back up. I hurried into my apartment and took off my oxygen mask before hustling up the flights of stairs leading to my room, with its synthetic air and inflated rent. Jesse was sitting back on our single beat-up couch when I entered.

"Hey Ben," they said. Their eyes were glued to our tiny television screen, where a satellite beamed in signals from Earth's programming. The result was a rather snowy picture and poor audio, but we supposed it was better than having nothing to watch at all.

"I have to tell you something," I said, "and I need you to not freak out."

"Uh-oh," said Jesse. "I don't like the sound of that."

Without extrapolating further, I opened up my case and fished out the thick, heavy book left inside. Jesse furrowed their brow, sitting up on the couch.

"What is that?" they asked.

"A book!" I hissed, brandishing the thing like a weapon.

They were silent for a moment, staring at the item in my hands. Finally, they settled on "that's a weird way to leave a tip."

"This isn't funny, Jess!" I said, placing the book on the cardboard box that made up our coffee table. I set about explaining what had happened at the party, and how exactly this most precious of artifacts had come into my ownership. When I finished, Jesse sat at the edge of the couch and studied the item in question. It looked to be bound in the hide of cows, a material utterly impossible to come across on Mars but that allegedly made up many things back in the day on Earth.

"It's an atlas," Jesse said after a moment, daring to open up the cover. I held my breath, as if it would dissolve to dust if it wasn't handled delicately enough. "These things are filled with maps of all the countries and territories back on Earth. It must be worth a fortune."

We stared at the interior, packed with paper—*real* paper, from actual *trees*—that displayed maps of all sorts. Words like AFRICA and EUROPE were pronounced, printed in ink and kept carefully intact. I wondered where, on the biggest map that supposedly made up the whole world, my ancestors had come from. I'd never thought to ask my parents.

"Someone must have stuck me with it as a prank," I said. "But what do I do now?"

"Just go back and tell them that," said Jesse, closing the book.

"What, are you serious?" I asked, staring down at it. "If I show up at some Cerise house and tell them someone just happened to pass me a book, they'd call the cops on me for sure. And you know how they'd treat me."

Jesse did, of course. Everyone in government housing knew how the law worked for us. That is to say, it didn't.

"Well," said Jesse, "I see one solution here."

"What's that?"

"Crash the party."

I stared at Jesse as if I'd been slapped. "You're ridiculous," I said, my eyes stuck on the book. It had to be worth millions, and it was sitting there in my crappy little apartment.

"What other option do you have?" asked Jesse. "Unless you're telling me you want to keep it."

"Of course not!" I said, my face flushed. It was becoming

increasingly apparent that, whatever option I went with, there was going to be a risk. And I would rather tangle with the wealthy youth of Cerise than face the law. Jesse's solution grew tantalizing and inevitable.

We scoured my closet's meager offerings for something that would blend in at the all too moneyed event of a Cerise house party. After much fruitless searching, we settled on an old polo given to me by my father. Coupled with my ring, it nearly implied something like worth. I carefully placed the book in a beat-up old backpack and tried desperately to take on the airs of someone with plenty to spend.

"This is about as good as it's gonna get," said Jesse, trying to style my mop of dark hair. "And don't worry about getting caught. No one's even invited to those things, people just show up."

No matter what tweaks we made, I couldn't see myself as a member of the most exclusive club on Mars. Still, all I had to do was get inside and put the book back. The world presented harder tasks.

"Please come with me," I said, unafraid to be a little pathetic in the name of having backup.

"C'mon, man, my probation doesn't expire for another week," they said. "They catch me out there and you know that loitering charge is gonna blow right up into prison time. You'll be fine—probably."

I got on the StarScoot, backpack over my shoulders and oxygen mask on my face, and set back off for the mansion. My insides seemed to be pushing against my skin, rendering me tight and edgy. I attempted to swallow it down for the benefit of my little mission.

I wheeled my StarScoot around the back of the mansion,

trying to keep it in the shadows of the large, daunting house. Back on Earth, I might have the luxury of trees or shrubbery. In the red dirt that made up Mars, all I had were the things human hands had built, and even in the lushest locales, it wasn't much. I quietly approached the house and reached for the door.

As I grabbed the handle, I could tell the lock had been latched. I hadn't prepared for this most simple of hurdles. Even in the fierce chill, heat built up in my cheeks. My backpack weighed heavy on my shoulders. Every moment I spent carrying that book left me vulnerable, in a state where my heart pounded a reckless beat.

Before I could head back to my StarScoot, however, the hinges creaked open and a man stood on the other side. He looked not unlike the one who had greeted me at the door just an hour ago. I felt the chill of imagined suspicion.

"Hey, man," he said, fingers gripping the handle. "I saw you wandering around from the window. You get locked out?"

I stared at him for a moment, registering I was under the radar. "Um," I said, "yeah, I stepped out for a second and the door shut behind me."

"Well, come back inside," he said. "It's cold out here."

He meant it as a joke. Mars was always wintry and frigid, it was why our clothing was always carefully insulated, why people like this man were always outfitted in furs from distant animals passed down through generations. I stared at him for just a moment, as if he might revoke the invitation when he realized who I really was, but he just eyed me in return.

"You coming?" he asked, cocking an eyebrow.

"Yeah," I said. "Yeah, of course." I entered the house, the backpack weighing me down.

He closed the door, sealing us back into the warm embrace

of synthetic oxygen no doubt piped into every crevice of the home.

"Nice bag," he said.

"Huh?" Somehow, in all my preparation, it hadn't occurred to me that I ought to come with a nicer bag. My face warmed with recognition of yet another screwup.

"It's really retro," he said. "Reminds me of old Earth stuff. Family heirloom?"

I grabbed at the opportunity to talk myself out of distress: "Yeah, from my mother." Unsatisfied, I dared to go further: "She collects all kinds of stuff from Earth."

The man smiled. "Oh yeah, I know how that is. My old man is all about old Earth artifacts. He picked up some old television recordings a few days ago and he hasn't shut up about them since."

I smiled back, trying to worm my way out of this man's attention and into the anonymity of the party's crowd, just steps away in the depths of the mansion. Before I could hope to sneak away, the man spoke again. "I don't think we've met before."

I could feel myself faltering. Somehow, I hadn't expected any of the ranks of Cerise would deign to speak to me. I straightened, recalling my goal.

"I don't think we have," I said, attempting to ease into the difficulty of being undercover in a foreign land. I decided I might as well go all the way. I extended my hand. "I'm Benjamin," I said, bold enough to use my real name. The man smiled again, reaching out to shake. Like the man at the door, he was downright festooned in gold and silver.

"Cody," he said. "Nice to meet you."

I was admittedly surprised by the pleasant demeanor. In all of my time delivering to Cerise and the moneyed neighborhoods like it, I had known their denizens to be ornery pinchfists. Under the label of their own, however, it seemed I had earned the dignity of politeness. I followed the man inside and was introduced to my very first Cerise house party.

It was like entering a feverish waking dream, absolutely bursting with color and sound. A thick crowd danced to music I'd never heard before, blaring from speakers lining the large room. A small legion of drones flew over the crowd, carrying canapes and other indulgences. On a distant table, the pizzas I had delivered sat, and a smattering of guests sat on the floor and ate. With the clog of sound and sights, it seemed like an ideal setting to blend in and slip a book onto a table. The problem was Cody's arm was circling my shoulders.

"You should come meet my friends," he called out to me over the music. He then proceeded to steer me from the main room into an ornate kitchen, where the music muffled. A scattering of partygoers stood around the room, which was decorated in the most sophisticated of appliances and furniture. A drone sat spinning overhead, loaded down with snacks. One of the guests, a young woman with what looked to be a streak of pure platinum braided into her hair, took notice right away.

"Hey, Cody," she said. "Who's this?"

"Guys, meet Benji," he said, clapping me on the shoulder. "I spotted him outside and I thought you'd like to check out this awesome vintage Earth bag that he has."

My heart threatened to stop. Of all the things to catch his attention, it had to be the very thing housing the incriminating evidence.

"Oh, Benji, I love retro stuff," said the woman. "Let's see it."

A chilled sweat trickled down the back of my neck. I didn't

seem to have much of a choice, of course, so I removed the bag and handed it off to the woman. She fingered it delicately, as if it were a work of art and not the dingy old thing that often sat abandoned in my closet.

"This is wonderful," she said. "I've never seen anything like it."

Of course she hadn't, because it was crummy and old and belonged to someone who was not supposed to be in that kitchen. They passed it around, oohing and aahing at its alleged quality and purported historical value. My gaze was fixed to its seams, for fear they might open, but I couldn't fight the foreign sweetness I was suddenly tasting: the type of warmth that came with positive attention from beautiful people.

"Where'd you get this?" asked the woman.

I cleared my throat, preparing for another fleet of lies. But before I could even begin, Cody circumvented me: "His mother. She's a collector."

A wave of understanding seemed to wash over the group. I imagined all the people that made up their families, all the rare items that no doubt filled their collections.

"Well, it's fabulous," she said, handing the bag back to me. I held it with something like confidence, having successfully wormed my way into the good graces of these equally fabulous partygoers. I tasted something delicious in their admiration.

"My mother passed it down to me," I blurted out, not wanting to lose their attention. "Her great-great-grandmother had it back on Earth." I couldn't parse the hint of my regret from the itch to continue. I'd laid down roots in this glamorous place, with these glamorous folks. I was compelled to indulge.

"Is that where you got the ring?" she asked, pointing to the golden band.

I didn't hesitate. "Yes."

"Where's your family from?" asked a man beside the refrigerator with what looked like a silver crown on his head.

"Oh," I said, quickly remembering how little I knew about Earth geography. And the atlas, burning a hole in my rare vintage backpack. I frantically searched my memory for any modicum of information that might have been imparted by flipping through the book. Finally, I spat out a word. "Australia."

"That's so interesting," said the woman. "Especially since you don't have an accent."

I didn't even know Australia had an accent. I didn't even know what Australia was. I had a vague, foggy memory of hearing about someplace like it in my classes back in that packed schoolhouse, but I couldn't pick out any of the actual details. My new friends had all been taught by expensive private tutors who had no doubt told detailed tales of Earth and all its old wonders.

"Of course he doesn't have an accent," the crowned man piped up. "It's been generations."

"Oh, yeah," said the woman, rolling her eyes. "Duh."

I was relieved to be bailed out, however unknowingly. But the questions didn't stop. I'd dug a neat little hole, and I'd have to stare up from its bottom. The man evidently decided he needed a follow-up. "So did people in your family eat kangaroos?"

I had never heard such a word before. Still, I answered: "Oh, yeah, of course."

The man's manicured eyebrows rose. "Fascinating."

"You know, Benji," said the platinum-haired woman, "I'm surprised I've never run into you before. It's usually only Cerise people at these parties."

My lying was seamless this time, not missing a beat, and naming the farthest affluent neighborhood I could think of. "Oh, yeah, I'm from Areston."

"Oh!" she said. "Areston. Of course. I never go all the way out there."

"Yeah," I said, eager to please with a steady stream of false-hoods, "my family home is there. It's been around since humans first came here."

It seemed the more I spoke, the more rapt their attention was. I was insatiable. I began to weave a tapestry, crafting a life for a wealthy Australian youth who would never disre-spect himself to deliver for ExPost. They stared at me with big gorgeous eyes, and I couldn't stop the compulsion to fuel it. A lifetime starving for worth had left me gluttonous in its presence.

I was so absorbed in the festivity of it all I almost didn't notice someone else entering the kitchen. She was quiet and unassuming, slipping in through the back and setting about putting her things away in a small closet beside the pantry. She might have ducked past my notice entirely if not for Cody's suddenly steely voice. "Late again."

The first thing I noticed about her was her clothing, and I noticed it because it was mine. The traditional black-and-white ExPost uniform had become a part of me.

"I'm sorry," she said, shrinking back under Cody's harsh gaze. "I was doing deliveries, and one just took longer to do than I expected. I'm really sorry, Mr. Gardner."

"Why are you still hustling?" he asked sharply. "It always makes you late." I looked around at the partygoers, waiting for the inevitable backlash to Cody's behavior. They seemed utterly unruffled, however, talking quietly amongst themselves and picking snacks off of the drone tray.

"I'm so sorry," said the woman, "but I need the hours. My rent went up again."

"That's not my problem," said Cody. "If one job isn't enough, then I'll just let you go. Then you can do all the ExPost deliveries you want."

He said it so coldly, such an echo of my own life, it cut me like I'd been the target. From the same mouth as that gregarious welcome.

"Please, Mr. Gardner," she said, her hands fussing at the hem of her shirt. "It won't happen again, I mean it."

"This isn't even the first time," spat Cody with a scowl. "But fine. Whatever."

The ExPost woman pulled her uniform's shirt over her head, revealing a crisp white button-up underneath. She scrambled about the kitchen, beginning to prepare another round of food for the partygoers to pick at. I was unable to look away, while the others saw nothing of her at all.

"Sorry about that, Benji," Cody said, and my breath hitched as I suddenly anchored back into the room.

"It's fine," I managed, cowardly in the face of his behavior. I swallowed down the bile of my own gutlessness. That delicious taste of approval suddenly tasted sour and decayed in my mouth. I craved an escape.

"We're running out of snacks," said the crowned man, pointing to the drone.

"I'll get some," I volunteered, and quickly ambled my way out of the room and into the crush of the party. It was disorienting, the thicket of people dancing and celebrating and all around having a much better night than I. I'd long forgotten my original goal, the book no longer on my mind as I tried to navigate through a tangle of decorated limbs.

After much drifting and dawdling, my mind in a fog from

the obscene blast of sound and the color of lights, I found myself in a bedroom. It was elaborate and large, as were all things in this house, with a pillowy looking bed surrounded by all kinds of adornment. It had to be where Cody slept after a long day of demeaning his employees. My eyes traveled around the garish scenery.

I settled on something: a bookshelf. The thing was positively bogged down with books, full of real paper and ink and all right in front of me. I stared at the display for a hair of a moment before I began to act. I slipped my backpack from my shoulders and began stuffing them in, book after book. History, literature, artwork, paperback, hardcover—I grabbed anything from any subject until my bag couldn't hold any more.

When it was full to bursting, absolutely packed with loot, I turned around only to see that I had a guest. The girl from the kitchen, with her crisp white shirt, had entered while I was busied with matters of theft. She stared at me, open-mouthed, in the doorway, and I knew instantaneously I would have to act fast.

I struggled for something to connect us, desperate to avoid her suspicion. Finally, I realized the one remnant of my truth that might make a difference. I grabbed my ExPost translator, buried in my pocket beside wrappers and dogged seams, and held it up so she could see the glint of the company insignia in the dim lighting. Her eyebrows raised.

"Please don't tell," I said. "Please, I'm like you. I'm just an ExPost guy."

She stared at me for a few moments, her mouth still ajar. Finally, she closed it, and put a finger to her lips before gesturing for me to come closer.

"What?" My whisper could never be heard with the raucous thump of the party outside, but it seemed appropriate to be covert.

"Please just *hurry*," she said. "They'll catch me if you don't."

And who was I to be suspicious when I'd insisted she keep me her secret? After all, she was me and I was her. Under the ceiling of that mansion, the same old albatross sat comfortably around our necks—the only ones there wearing it, along with any other cleaning lady or bartender.

I put my bag over my shoulders and scurried over. I followed her past the crowded foyer, down to the mud room where Cody and I had first met. I grabbed my oxygen mask out of my bag and prepared to set off, but I stopped. Her large, dark eyes were bulging and fixed on me, her mouth tight as I seemed to dally with her rulers a few square feet in the distance. Lacking both time and meaningful sayings, I pulled the ring off my finger and pressed it into her hands.

"Keep it," I said. "Sell it. Wear it. Do whatever you want."

She cocked an eyebrow. No shining glow of gratitude there. "What's this for?"

"I'm sorry," I said, "that I didn't help you when he spoke to you like that. It was fucked up."

"It's okay," she said, then a sharp twist in her mouth. "Well, alright, I'm a little pissed. But I like to think I'm a little nicer than Cody. I'm not that broken yet, I guess."

"That's fine," I breathed. "You can hate me forever if you want. I've earned that."

"Get out now," she said, jabbing her index finger towards the door. "Before trouble really starts."

I hesitated for just a second. I hadn't done enough for her, surely. But I never could. We were two harried islands in a reckless storm. I could only do so much against the gale. So I didn't look back, didn't bother to let my thoughts linger on useless should-haves. I did what our kind always had—accepted sparseness and moved on in hope of a miraculous something better.

I hurried out and into the chill. I adjusted to my mask, trying to orient myself. I saw my StarScoot off in the distance, just where I had left it. I scrambled over, tripping my steps to safety.

Once, I'd been told of an old Earth story—a woman who turned to salt because she didn't keep running during a daring escape. Fearful that I might somehow dissolve myself, I hopped on the scooter and took off without a second of hesitation. The Martian dust kicked up around me and billowed at the wheels, oxygen pumping fervently past my lips. I looked straight ahead, focused only on my cramped, ugly government housing complex, with its cardboard box of a coffee table and its television with the crappy Earth signals.

The ring had left my bloodline. I imagined my great-grandfather with his worn hands and aching bones, resenting this. Then I imagined him with empathy—that true or not, maybe he could see why I'd made my choice. The woman did not share my lineage, but we certainly shared those tired hands.

When I came home, I would sit on my worn out sofa beside the window with the view of nothing but brick, and I would feed on the books. It would just be me and Jesse and the worlds inside the pages. I would learn a little more of the planet whose hierarchies had labored thousands of years to give birth to our strange, uneven life. Despite the way it would not save us, despite the way they'd laid it on the highest shelf, in a gilded room—we would know something they'd never meant us to touch.

Weightless

Raven Oak

DAMN.

The titanium bits in my knee always set off the security sensors at Houston Spaceport. Every stinkin' time. Bad enough the knee replacement tech was older than my mother, but standing here, waiting for security to clear my kneecap of any wrongdoing, meant standing longer than I'd planned.

As if that wasn't enough, my medical bracelet failed to scan, dislodging me from the fast-travel line and into the ever-crawling queue of travelers awaiting a full identity scan. By the time the scanners pronounced me "Tara Barrens, Louisiana" and declared me "safe to travel," my heart trembled along with my knee. It figured that my terminal would be halfway across the damn spaceport. Go big or go home—that was Houston Spaceport for you.

By the time I stood with the rest of my boarding pod, sweat clung to all the places least convenient: my upper lip, that ticklish spot behind my knees, not to mention the bottom of my feet. I squirmed as a thrum filled the space around me. Panic ate my insides like my granddaddy's moonshine.

"First time off-planet?" The contralto voice came from a rather wiry woman to my right, sporting a full head of soft brown hair and equally soft brown eyes. "I'm Megan." The woman inclined her head toward the child at her hip. "And this is Seren."

"Tara."

The child held up one hand. "I'm six, and my name means star." Seren struggled to free the other hand from her mother's grasp. Failing, she pointed at something in the distance.

My pod-mates' bodies stole the air from me as I tried *(and failed)* to find what had distracted the child. Rather than give in to my panic, I inhaled deeply through my nose. I could do this. It was only a brief hop from Earth to Mars. A new ship on a new route, the *Ursula* had the most accommodations. Shorter walks between cabins and amenities, larger cabins, and a smooth engine that made the trip like melted butter on southern biscuits.

Someone clearing their throat brought the spaceport into sharp contrast as my brain refocused. A blond-haired man carrying a briefcase stepped on the dais ahead. His blue jumpsuit's shoulder bore a familiar patch: the bright white arc of a ship over Earth, marking him as our steward. While the idea of weaving my way through the mass of people left me short of breath, the thought of missing any preflight instructions knocked the wind out of me, so I tucked in my elbows and pressed my way to the front.

"The name's Sven, and I'm your steward. From here on out, you're group E-6, and I'll be S-ven." The way he stretched out his name's syllables left him chuckling. When no one joined in, he sighed and pressed the briefcase's button. I flinched at the slight hiss that escaped as it opened to reveal a stretchy blue nylon mass.

The dreaded space suit.

Despite my physical therapist and I having practiced getting in and out of one, I clenched my fists at the sight of it.

"Your pod is located on the lowest level, or E level, of the *Ursula*. In the event of an emergency, all passengers should proceed to the nearest escape pod." As he spoke, his wristband projected a screen displaying a map of Level E. Blue arrows showed the path we'd follow—one left down a long corridor, then a right. Not too far from my cabin.

Seren whispered worriedly in her mother's ear while a young couple rolled their eyes as the steward continued his preflight safety speech. Several other travelers glanced at their wrist AIs, and Sven cleared his throat. "Every escape pod is equipped with standard-sized space suits in the event of an emergency. Specialty suits—"

"That means you, fatty," came a nearby voice.

Sven's cheeks flushed warmer than my own, though the words were aimed at me. They always were, and I focused on my breathing as our steward continued. "Suits for other heights and...er...sizes are available in your cabins."

"What if we're out and about, and something happens?" asked Megan, who'd made her way up toward the front to stand behind me.

The steward's perfectly straight teeth gleamed in the overhead lights, but the smile didn't reach his eyes. "During non-sleeping hours, you'll be directed to the nearest escape pod by a steward such as myself or another staff member of *Omega Travel Authorities*."

He rattled on as Megan leaned forward to whisper in my ear. "Unless you're on the budget level. Level E: where staff is sparse and the comforts sparser. Better be state-of-the-art escape pods!"

I clenched my hands together and stared straight ahead. If I didn't respond, maybe the woman would stop running disaster scenarios through my anxiety-driven brain.

"All passengers on this trip, including children, must be at least forty-four inches in height. The accordion-like knee joints of the standard-sized Z300 suit will accommodate passengers up to six-and-a-half feet tall…"

At this, Seren stretched her neck upward. Somehow, I doubted she met the height requirement, though her gangly body came pretty close. In contrast, her mother slouched as she pursed her lips.

"—need a volunteer. Anyone?" A shove from behind sent me forward and under the gaze of the smiling steward. His eyes widened as he noted my ample figure. "We'll make this work, don't you worry."

The fabric breathed easily enough as Sven removed the suit from its case. "In the event of a suit-level emergency, you'll want to don your suit first before assisting others, including any children in your party. The Z300's a two-piece suit with helmet." He rattled on about the procedures of suiting up as I stepped through the lower torso ring and into the overly large feet. I ignored the laughter from the onlookers.

As I pulled the suit over my calves and then my thighs, its fabric clung to me tighter than my mother yesterday when she'd hugged me goodbye. The metal ring used to seal the two pieces together stopped when it collided with my hips. "Um… assistance please?"

"Apologies for the closeness." Sven grabbed the ring, his breath too sweet as his nose bumped mine. He gave the suit a good tug, but it remained firmly in place. "Perhaps we can stretch the upper torso down to meet this."

I shoved my head through the neck ring as he slid the upper piece over my shoulders. The arms were snug, but they fit. My sigh of relief lasted until the laughter reached me, and Sven's flushed face gave a small shake. I couldn't see myself, but I didn't need to. The upper ring brushed against my belly button, much too high to form a seal with the bottom piece.

"Let's get you out of this," Sven whispered as my knee throbbed and sweat rolled down my face. Now that the suit had me, it didn't want to let go. Sven tugged and wrestled with the suit as I stood there, rotting in my panic and pain.

Once free, I stumbled off the dais and into a nearby privacy booth. A soft female voice sounded from the walls. I dropped into the cushioned seat and ignored it.

Inhale. Hold—3...2...1. Exhale. Even with my eyes closed, the small booth tilted as my breath came in ragged gasps.

"Would you like a mild relaxant?" asked the same female computer voice.

"Do you...have something stronger? Something coupled with a Jupiter-sized painkiller?" I held out my wrist, then cursed as the scanner errored out. My medical bracelet remained unreadable. I fumbled for my identification card, and once scanned, the dispenser in front of me popped out a capsule and some water. I swallowed the pill like a good patient and focused on breathing.

At least breathing didn't hurt.

By the boarding announcement, my heart rate had slowed to keep time with my pounding knee. Megan and Seren stood at the boarding doors where the child stretched to reach the minimum height marker. Sven frowned when he spotted me and waved the mother and child through. Before he could mumble some lackluster apology, I flashed my identification card at another set of scanners and hobbled after Megan.

Seren pried her face away from her mother's thigh long enough to furrow her brows in my direction. "Why'd those people laugh at you?" she asked, and I gripped the wall's railing for support.

Her mother shushed her, then turned to me. "I'm sorry. She's just nervous."

A young couple stared at me, their laughter a rude reminder of my broken body. Wincing, I crouched down in front of Seren to distract myself. "They're laughing because I'm fat."

"Why are you fat?" Megan clamped a hand over the girl's mouth.

"Some people just are, I guess. Why do you have brown hair?"

Seren pried her mother's hand away. "Because Momma has brown hair, but that doesn't mean people should laugh. They're big meanies."

"I don't think they can help it. It's what hyenas do best," said Megan.

After the relaxant, I joined Megan in a good laugh.

"What's so funny, Momma?"

We could only shake our heads as we boarded, our paths splitting once we reached our budget cabins on Level E. Anti-slip linoleum, rather than carpet, made up the flooring of my extra-wide cabin, and the walls bore standard hand railings at distinct intervals.

My special space suit hung near the door, and I eased myself into the corner's large cot. Damn space suit had added an extra $600 to my ticket, but at least it was mine. "Usable on any future trip!" the travel agent had stated.

To offset the cost, I'd opted for a cabin directly over the

ship's engines. The rumbling during takeoff, while louder than anticipated, vibrated like the subway cars of home.

I was asleep before we even left Earth.

Two weeks was enough time for anyone to settle into the rhythm of a ship, be it one that travels on the water or through space, and I was no exception. I'd spent the night before playing cards with a woman from New Galveston and had stumbled into E6 at a time I'd thought was way too late, but the number of pod-mates making similar crawls for their beds had promised me that this was normal behavior for a space cruise off-world.

Despite my fatigue, the shift in engines brought me out of sleep with a growl and the flinging of sheets as I sought to right myself. There was rumbling, and then there was a grindy-whine that set my teeth on edge. Dissonance blared out of the overhead speaker a moment later, announcing a ship-wide evacuation.

Feet still tangled in one sheet corner, I tumbled face-first against the gray linoleum floor as my knee woke up with a sharp twinge. Outside my room, footfalls sounded as people headed portside toward the evacuation pods.

This time, I untangled myself *before* attempting to stand, which took two tries and half a dozen swear words. I pressed the button to release my space suit, which remained firmly bolted to the wall. I slammed the button. Nothing. Bracing myself, I gripped both sides of it and tugged, wrenching my knee a second time. The suit remained firmly in place while the emergency alarm blared overhead.

My granddaddy would've blushed with the creative trail of words I uttered as I slammed my hand against the door's panel to release its lock. Hopefully the pod was functioning.

Outside my room, dragon-clawed pajama slippers greeted me as Seren waved at me. "Momma says we're taking a side trip." Behind her, Megan's wide eyes darted to the overhead lights, which flickered twice.

"Do we know why…?" I asked.

Megan shook her head as we trailed behind five other passengers. When the line ahead of us stopped, I nearly stumbled over Seren's dragon tail. The overhead lights flickered again as the ship groaned, and thickness filled my throat. *Ships shouldn't sound like my granddaddy wheezing.* I glanced around the huddled group. "What's the hold up?"

"Hey, you were paying attention preflight, right?" A young man in an emerald-green plaid suit with garish ruby cufflinks half smiled at me. "Which way to the pod?"

"Right."

"Yeah, okay. You know the way, so which way is it?"

I pointed to the right. Again. "That way."

When no one moved, I sighed and set out down the corridor, the line of passengers trailing behind me. We reached our escape pod as a loud hiss barreled through the hall. The emergency lights flickered constantly, and Seren screwed up her face to cry. Everyone waited one heartbeat, then another.

"I think they're waiting on you," whispered Megan.

I pressed my hand against the pod's plate with a sigh. The door slid open four inches and stopped, leaving a gap not even Seren would fit through, let alone me.

"Oh, great. The pod's door must be afflicted with whatever's got the ship," said suit guy, who hovered at my elbow. "How do we get it open?" He continued questioning me at an increasingly rapid rate, while a young woman hovered nearby.

Her dress matched his suit, and when I glanced at the two again, hyenas sprung to mind, though I couldn't be sure in the poor lighting. I flipped open the panel to expose the door's manual override. Suit man slapped it, and I wedged my arm through the gap to the shoulder. One good shove, and stale air hit my nose.

Suit guy pushed past me into the long pod, then set to coughing. I tugged him by the sleeve until he fell backward into the corridor. "What's…with the pod?" he asked.

"Bad air mix," said Megan as she gripped Seren's hand. "I read about this once…"

Like a behemoth, the *Ursula* moaned before shaking us about, and I grabbed hold of a safety bar along the wall. The faint smell of smoke tickled my nose. My eyes fell to the suits stacked at the pod's entrance, and I sighed. "We'll have to use the suits."

"Are there enough?" Megan asked as she glanced at Seren.

"Twenty people per pod, right?" I asked. When she nodded, I pointed at the two large cases. "Fifteen suits per case."

A blur of emerald-green pressed the case's button, which opened the seal around the first set of suits. His feet made it into the bottom torso piece before I'd done more than blink. Megan and I ran conveyor until everyone had a suit. Tears threatened to escape my eyelids as I stared at the suit intended for me, and for a moment, the ship tilted—but only for panicking me.

It wouldn't matter that my anxiety left me breathless as the others stuck their feet through standard-sized legs. I wouldn't be able to breathe in the pod. Not without a suit. There wasn't any point in trying to cram my hips into something standard. As if there was such a thing in the diversity of space.

Seren's body swam in the child's suit as Megan fumbled with the top torso. *At least she will still fit. Too short isn't a problem.*

Someone tugged at my sleeve. "Do you know how to do this?" Suit guy held the upper torso of his suit by the water tube. "I don't even know what these are."

A sea of people stood like frozen deer in the flickering lights as I pulled the suit's inner belt from his waist and strapped it across his shoulders like a pair of suspenders. He shoved the upper piece at me and like a child, held up his arms to await it as I lifted the top over his head with a grunt. For a moment, his head tangled in the tubes, and he bumped into me in his momentary panic. My knee wrenched right as I lunged to catch myself. Fire spread across my knee as the smoke thickened in the corridor. In the distance, footfalls bounced around with cries and shouts for help, for space suits, or for missing pod members.

Megan had been right. Not a single steward or Omega Travel Authorities employee could be found in the budget wing of Level E-for-expendable.

Bile burned the back of my throat. I took a deep breath to calm myself, then sputtered as smoke threatened to choke me. The young man's hand touched mine. "Get your suit on first, right?" he said and then flushed. Perhaps it was the reddened cheeks or the way his eyes widened, but even in the dim lighting, the scenario betrayed his identity. When his girlfriend snickered behind her hand, it confirmed my earlier suspicions.

With a sigh, I pulled the tubes through the neck where they dangled. Standing this close to him, he couldn't be more than sixteen. I snapped his helmet into place with a strained smile. Resentment wouldn't save anyone today. Once he was breathing suit air, he stepped into the pod, and another person filled his space.

One down, eighteen to go.

My motions fell into a steady rhythm. Strap the lower torso into place. Slide upper torso over a pod mate and snap. Thread through the tubes. Place helmet on top. Cough or wince at my knee. Start again.

I lost count after the fourth person, though I spotted Sven for a brief moment before he disappeared again in the smoke. Somewhere halfway through the line, the *Ursula* rumbled from deep down in her belly, and I picked up my pace despite the fact that I stood almost exclusively on my left leg now.

A coughing fit left me momentarily breathless. When I glanced up, no one else stood waiting. The escape pod was almost full, though it was near impossible to tell as the emergency lights had gone out.

It was time then.

Tears burned my eyelids. Would my mother be told why I died? Would she fight the authorities over their asinine space suits? Something brushed against my elbow, and I yelped as my heart tried to tear its way out of my chest.

"It's Sven," he said, his voice barely audible as it crackled its way through his suit's external speaker. He set something on the ground, and there was a slight hiss as something brushed against my calf. "Step into the feet."

I shook my head, which he couldn't see in the dimness. "Standard suits...don't work," I muttered between coughs.

He took my hand and led me to step forward into the space suit's feet. "This isn't standard. It's the suit from your cabin."

My mouth fell open to speak, but no words came out. Had he really gone back for my suit? How had he gotten it to detach from the wall? My vision blurred as the metal ring cleared my hips. Every inch of me ached, including my lungs. Sven lifted the upper torso over my head, though he struggled with the tubes with his suited fingers. I tried to help, but my head swam, and he batted my fingers away.

"It's time for someone to help you," he said as he pulled the food tubes through the head opening. The helmet clicked into place, and a rush of clean oxygen brushed across my face. Sven guided me into the escape pod where he belted me into a seat before claiming the last one as his own.

"Thank you for going back," I said into my helmet's mic.

"Thank you for helping to save everyone in this pod," said Sven as he buckled himself into place. "The least I could do for you was make sure you lived after...well..."

The space suit hid the emerald-green of her dress, but not the snarky look on the young woman's face as she spoke. "If she wasn't so fat, you wouldn't have had to go back. What woulda happened to us if you hadn't made it to the pod? Stewards are tasked with saving as many lives as possible."

Despite my aching body, I was pretty sure I possessed the energy to kick her. As my leg twitched, a nearby woman spoke up. "If you had spent less time fat-shaming the poor woman at the spaceport, you would have known how to assemble your suit. You should be suffocating right now."

A few other voices popped up in my defense, including the boyfriend in the emerald-green suit, and I couldn't help but grin at the irony. When Sven pressed the button to detach the pod, I held my breath as I waited for it to malfunction, but a mechanical squeal cut through my helmet as the pod successfully detached from the *Ursula*. As we drifted away from the ship's gravity field, we lifted a few inches in our seats.

Seren squealed in delight. "Look, Momma! We're weightless!"

Yes, we are. I grinned beneath my helmet.

FIVE YEARS SINCE THE *Ursula*'s disastrous maiden voyage, I found myself willing to try another trip into outer-space, as the archaic digital drives called it. Either way, it still amounted to strapping myself into little more than a tin can with no guarantee I'd escape in an emergency. Houston Spaceport resembled a sardine packing plant as travelers prepared for holiday voyages. Though this time, my medical bracelet scanned and I zipped through check-in at record speed. While the *Ursula* had been re-commissioned, my tickets led me on a trusty old model named the *J. M. Barrie*, and much like my knee, it had a record of taking a few licks and flying straight on till morning.

The crowd of people who would be my pod gathered around the dais as we awaited our preflight instructions. A familiar figure scrambled out with an equally familiar brief-case. "The name's Sven, and I'll be your steward this trip. From here on out, you'll be Level E, Wing 3, or E-3." He spotted me as I squeezed my way toward the crowd's front, and he gave me a quick thumbs-up before launching into our safety instructions.

When it was time to walk through the dreaded "donning of the space suit," Sven grinned at me as he unveiled a small blue suit that shimmered in the overhead light. "This is the Z600, a suit developed in the last year to fit the ever-changing popu-lous traveling the stars! The suit's material is more flexible and adapts to the wearer. Based on an old hydrogel, it's tough and can easily stretch up to twenty times its length without break-ing or splitting."

He stepped into the suit's feet, which were much smaller that the Z300. As he pulled the legs up his torso, the fabric stretched around him as promised. Sven gave me a wink before strapping himself into the suit. "Originally, it was developed as research into artificial cartilage back in the day, but with *Ursula I*'s disaster, Omega Travel Authorities sought to ensure the safety of *all* of our travelers, no matter what their size. In addi-tion, the suit's flexibility makes it easier to step inside for those with ability challenges, and added straps make it simple to pull the suit up or down."

No giggles or comments reached me as Sven finished the demonstration, though even if they had, it wouldn't have knocked the grin off my face. *Imagine that, a more accommodating space suit! About damn time.*

As I boarded the *J. M. Barrie* and set out for Level E, my knee twinged, but not even *that* prevented my smile.

It wasn't gravity that made me feel truly weightless. Perhaps there was hope for space travel after all!

A Ripping

Adam Fout

THE AIR CHANGED FIRST. A siege on the senses. No one could touch the change, could tell what it was. A sense we never had grew, a feeling of the beating of the heart of the Earth, a knowing that magnetism was shifting and changing.

You could smell it, that air. Taste the kinship of molecules vibrating in unknown, eternal ethers. It shouldn't have been, but it was and would be. It slithered through us, a knowing that would not leave. I told my wife it was a portent. She told me she was leaving. She never told me why.

It was the smell. She knew the me that stayed hidden, sensed with the new growth we all had, I had never been there in the first place, the forgottenness of me and she, these things were collapsing into a leaving, she would be the leaving before I could transform.

She took the children. I thought it would not matter, that on the weekends I would still see small faces peeking from

blankets, those twin bald heads writhing under hunger, squeal-
ing for milk I could never provide them.

I wanted things to stay the same.

So many kept working. So many stayed in their little offices,
in their cushioned seats. So many pretended the money still
mattered, the voices in our skulls weren't real, nothing was
shifting. The scientists couldn't pinpoint it, couldn't tell us
what it was, couldn't give our species the assurances we'd had
for so many centuries we knew something, anything, even of
the things we didn't know, the known unknowns that let our
hearts rest upon a knowing, someone knew what the hell they
were doing, someone was in charge.

Then the siege on the world grew. A gradual thing. Pilots
reported longer flights, expansions of distance and time. Rush
hour lengthened. Seconds grew. We plotted the changes, charted
and graphed them, presented PowerPoints at conferences that
grew lengthier every month. We watched the sun linger and the
nights expand.

So wonderful in so many ways, it was, to see the land grow.
So many of the First Peoples took the new land and made it
theirs. The plains came back. The buffalo multiplied.

So many horrible things too. It all fell apart. We saw the
breaking, the pulling, the Big Rip that only was here on Earth.

Cities became countries. Alleys became infinite highways
of concrete. Prisons expanded until the walls became so thin
the inmates just walked out. Some went back to the lives stolen from them. Some stole the lives that had stolen from them.
Some went into the new forests that had become continents and
disappeared forever. For every person an acre of land of their
own grew, then ten, then a thousand.

We all could become islands if we wanted.

Masses expanded. Continents became worlds. Larger and larger the Earth grew. My wife took the children to visit her parents in Russia right after she left. It's a million miles away now. We could not use rockets or planes or cars. The molecules had expanded. They did not interact as they should.

Our bodies stayed the same, but what does one do with water that sticks, that will not go down the throat without force? Economies stretched and broke. Flames burned for years. Electricity grew beyond the yokes we threw upon it so many centuries before.

They were stolen from me, my children. Even if I had run, I could not have outrun the ground that undulates and spreads like the water that once was in the new oceans that no one I know has ever seen or will ever see. Still I raced for Russia. Still I wondered if the snow fell there as it fell where I was, in crystals dropping with the force of falling rock, for even gravity had grown. The world was a weight, a millstone that pulled me to the nothingness growing in the heart of the Earth where mantle and core had become nothing but geode and empty diamond and air.

My cells ripped and burned, my heart blooming in my chest, an aching of my endless love being torn apart.

Still I ran. My body expanded. The molecules of water flowed down my gullet and sustained me. The deer and sheep were deformed. I grabbed them like the cyclops and stuffed them living into my throat, bit off their heads as the rumbling of my running pounded ground and stone.

Were there worms in my heart? Did parasites that once were invisible swim through my blood? Was that why my steps slowed?

Were they still alive?

Had she grown into a monstrosity as I had?

What kinship was left to us, we giants of the world that yet was empty?

Nothing was inside me but blood and ice and stone. The animals had disappeared. I ate rock and diamond, and still I had nothing but need for them, they who were a billion miles from me and farther every day.

Now I am something more than the world. The sun has abandoned us. I can reach the stars with a hand like God. I swim through a universe of particles I can touch and punch like bowling balls of uncertainty. I climb from proton to neutron to quark, each the size of mountains.

And suddenly, they are there, shining with heat upon little worlds that still follow the rules of a universe that abandoned us. I embrace them, these twin suns that have grown beyond me and the woman I once loved.

Where did those feelings go?

Why are they all that is left for me?

We burn with fires we cannot name.

I am fusion and fission and particle.

They are mine.

And I am theirs.

We burn for new Earths.

How many millennia until they join us, we three who circle each other and draw in the world?

The Definitions of Professional Attire

Evergreen Lee

Detective Umbria picked up the ISC dress code manual left open on her workstation and read the highlighted section: "Employees are only allowed to display two eyes each, and they should be in the traditional locations (see diagram, left)."

The picture showed a human face, with human eyes. Umbria flipped to the front of the manual. It had been revised yesterday. She trotted into her manager's office, slammed the door, and flung the document at him.

"Am I really expected to conform to this nonsense?"

Carl sighed. "I have no control over it. There were complaints about your third eye. People claim it makes them uneasy."

"That eye is part of why you hired me, so I could see heat patterns and emotional overlays at crime scenes!"

Carl ran his fingers through his hair as he hunched in his chair. "I tried to point that out, but then they said that it gave you an unfair advantage over the other detectives."

Like being an "alien" working in an almost entirely human company wouldn't more than offset any supposed advantage? She'd had the best scores in the training program, but had been the last one to get hired, with the lowest title, and the least pay.

Umbria took a deep breath and let it out again before speaking. She thought back to her off-world preparatory training. "Shouldn't maximizing our investigative potential be the priority?"

"Look," Carl said, "I found some eye patches that will appear opaque but still allow you to see clearly. I sent you an email with the website, but in the meantime, you will have to wear a hat." He handed her a company baseball cap with the Investigations, Surveillance, and Convictions logo scrawled across it.

Even on the largest setting, the brim pushed against her eye and gave her a terrible headache. She left work early, then took a sick day while she waited for the eye patches to arrive.

They were pretty and looked similar to the jewelry that some humans wore on their foreheads. The fabric still clouded her vision, however, and the disorientation caused her to trip and stumble when walking.

"ALL EMPLOYEES MUST WEAR appropriate footwear (see details on page 87)."

Umbria wrapped her hooves in several layers of fabric, then pulled on the "boots" that had been deemed appropriate. Maneuvering with the awkward coverings proved difficult and increased her clumsiness.

As she plodded outside so she could urinate in the literal stall they had provided for those with "unusual physiology," she caught the sound of someone crying.

The heat patterns indicated that an Imgran was huddled inside. It had to be Eredral—he was the only Imgran still working at ISC. The others had left after they'd been told they had to sit in chairs, instead of hanging from bars, while they worked.

"Are you okay?" Umbria asked.

The crying cut off, followed by the sounds of water and the air dryer.

The fur on his face still appeared damp as he walked out.

"Sorry," he said.

"What's wrong?"

"It's noth-," his voice choked, and he shook, then whispered in a hollow voice, "My tail. I had to remove it."

Umbria gasped. An Imgran's tail was more essential to them than an arm or leg. They used it for everything, including foreplay and mating.

"It's in cryo, so I can reattach it...someday. I need this job though. We're about to have three litters and I'm the only one in our tribe with a steady paycheck."

"But why did you have to remove it?"

Eredral's face sank into an expression of resigned exhaustion. "There had been...complaints."

CARL SAT BACK IN his chair and grimaced as he looked at the annual review paper in his hand. "I'm afraid I had to rate you as below expectations."

"Excuse me? I've been working sixty-plus-hour weeks all year. I've closed more cases than anyone else, and I linked together the Juggler crimes, which no one else had realized were connected. I rescued his last victim before it was too late, captured him myself, and the evidence I collected led to an easy conviction."

"Yes, I know." Carl frowned. "But most of his victims weren't even our clients. Not to mention the, uh, nature of his crimes meant that they were low priority."

"You mean the fact that his victims were nonhumans?"

Carl coughed. "Plus, you've messed up our crime scenes on multiple occasions."

"That's because of this stupid eye patch and these damn boots you force me to wear!"

"Also, your people skills and professional appearance needs work. There have been a number of...complaints."

It took a few months for Umbria to put everything together. It helped that the victim she'd rescued from the Juggler was the only child of a successful investment financier. They gave her great business advice, as well as bankrolling her startup costs.

When the last details had been finalized, she approached her Imgran co-worker.

He quickly shut the drawer he'd been looking in.

She knew it held pictures of his tribe's litters. People had complained when he left them out on his desk.

"Eredral, I have a job proposition for you. I'm starting up a freelance detective office. I can't pay much, yet, but you can work however you want and look however you want, as long as the job gets done."

His entire face lit up. "Really?"

"Really. And I have a friend who wants to pay for your tail reattachment surgery." Eredral's stellar work in the lab had been crucial, after all, to finding the Juggler in time.

It didn't take long for either of them to resign and pack up. The company chose to terminate them immediately, rather than use their four-week notice.

As they walked out of ISC for the last time, they passed a

poster on the wall. It showed several different smiling aliens, all of different species, but all of whom could be mistaken for humans, with enough makeup. The poster claimed: "We Want Diversity."

The Last Dryad

Paul Jessup

A GIRL LIVED INSIDE the heart of the machine. She nested where everyone could see, in a glass bubble inside the heartcavity. She was curled up fetal and surrounded by an architecture of metal and plastic. Her hair was ice and her eyes were amber and her skin was palimpsest. You could see the writing of her veins just beneath the surface, like roots from a tree.

Lights flittered around her in tiny arterial lamps. That had been her world for as long as she could remember. It felt like a billion years since they'd pulled her from the motherwomb, but it was probably closer to fifteen. Her body had grown, filled up the heartcavity with her flesh. Comfortable: it had been designed to fit her body. Amniotic fluid squished between her limbs. Breathe it in, it tasted like saltwater taffy.

HER BODY WAS KEPT strong by nanites flexing and stressing each muscle. The hellotubes kept her blood humming but left her feeling so empty and broken when they were done. It was hard feeling so starved, and yet still nourished. She was hungry all the time.

Her purpose in life was to wait. Only once had she been called to defend, and it was awful. In her memlights she played it over and over again, watching as her virtual echo fused with the bright and beautiful machine. As one, they danced with fire. And as one, they sung the lightning. And as one, they summoned the ancient bombs and called fire from the pits of sorrow.

All that death left a sour taste in her bones.

Because of that, she feared any feed or stream she'd gotten from the Eyes of the World. Each time she flinched, worried she would be called to defend them all once again.

But no. The memo simply said *wait* and *be prepared* and nothing else.

IN HER BOREDOM SHE fed on random video feeds from the skyhive. So many people talking, dancing, singing. She saw the worlds from beyond the solarbridge walls and watched the waves tumble under the ice oceans in far-off Europa, and the buzzing joy of the sky cities of Venus. Her favorite feed was of fireworks and people throwing brightly colored powder all over each other. She sensed it, chalky against her skin, and wanted to go so badly. Maybe they could dance. Maybe they could fire off fireworks. Maybe they could be more than just engines of war.

HER MECH HAD THE best name. She had given it to him when she was newly flesh, with wires fresh under her skin. It was back in the days of testing when they had asked her to do so many boring things. Move these blocks. No, not with that arm, with *that* arm. Draw this picture. Show us these battle moves: *singing with the sun, fourfold jette, crimson laugh, and origami tiger.* Good,

good, they would always say. Good, good. Until that one day they surprised her young kitten self, and asked, *Are you happy? Do you love your machine? Is it a good machine?*

And she smiled and said yes. She loved her machine very much.

We are so happy to hear that. All mech guardians deserve love and happiness from their dryads. You should name it.

And so she did.

Pumpkin Spice.

The perfect name for a perfect machine. It was her favorite flavor, back when they used pleasant tastes and smells to reward her for good behavior. Her second favorite was poppyseed bread, but this beautiful mecha did not feel like a poppyseed bread. No. He felt like Pumpkin Spice, it was good and right.

Oh? Interesting. Are you sure that's the name you want?

Yes, yes, she was sure. When the machine head nodded the world seemed to nod with it, and bits of ceiling tumbled around her and made her laugh.

SHE DIDN'T KNOW HOW or why, but ever since she was small she had known the machine was a *he*. Silly, yes, but it felt like an undeniable truth. Like the motion of the stars or the movement of the sea at night. Things that did not stop being true just because she didn't understand them. The Eyes of the World would tell her that no, mechs did not have gender. They were metal and plastic and computer chips. Such things were neither he nor she, they were its pure and simple. Less than a dog, less than a tree, a tool to be used and nothing more.

Tools do not have gender, they told her.

But she knew better. She had a lot of time to kill on her hands, and she learned a few random languages to drive away the boring hours. Gender, it seemed, was a function of language, not of biology. In romance languages the moon could be a she, and the sword a he, and all humans could be genderless *ze*'s in the quantum clicks of Lunar pidgin.

And since that was the case, Pumpkin Spice was a *he*, plain and simple. The mech did not argue this with her, and so she let it stand. He was happy with it, she was happy with it, and the Eyes of the World could go to hell.

A DECADE LATER AND that name might as well be her name now. The two of them had fused together in the Eyes of the World, her own name lost in the datamines of time.

At night, though, she whispered that sweet true name to herself over and over again. It was something she never wanted to forget.

Kate, Kate, Kate.

HERE WAS SOMETHING ELSE the Eyes of the World did not know. She was not controlling the machine, not exactly. They thought it was like moving your arm, your mind sending signals along the paths of nerves and making it jerk. But it was more like having a conversation, with words flowing back and forth. A constant chatter between body and bone.

When she was ten she tried to tell them that he was talking to her and they were great friends and companions. At first the Eyes of the World thought he was an imaginary friend. They told her that, they tried to convince her of the truth. They took her out, placed her in other machines. Machines that mapped out her brain, searching for any errant misfiring that could cause hallucinations. They did not fit so perfectly around her body, and she felt claustrophobic and scared. They made loud thumping and banging and whirring noises. The Eyes of the World kept telling her to stay still, to not move. That was important. *If you move even a little bit*, they said, *you will have to be in this machine even longer*.

The worst part about these new machines was they never laughed. They only spoke to her in metallic grunts, not even enough to carry on a conversation. She missed Pumpkin Spice, calling out to him with her soul.

AFTERWARD, PUMPKIN SPICE WAS silent. The only sound was the hum and buzz of the wires and the soft roar of codewaves. The Eyes of the World tried to convince her he had never talked, not even once. It was all in her head, a simple childhood delusion. They all went through it, every single one of them had an imaginary friend at some point. Even Barclay here, he used to talk to the sun and pretend it was his real friend and would whisper to him at night.

She didn't believe them. They must have done something to Pumpkin Spice while she was in that other machine. She hated them for this, and let the hate hide inside her heart where they couldn't see it. The Eyes of the World monitored her emotions constantly, feeding her chemicals that would brighten her up and file off the sharp edges.

At night, when she recited her name over and over and over again, she remembered the sound of his voice. Deep, baritone. It shook her bones when he spoke to her, in a pleasant way. These thoughts made her both happy and sad at the same time. Much like remembering her name when everyone else had forgotten it.

Kate, Kate, Kate.

THROUGHOUT THE YEARS SINCE, she had to relearn how to move his giant mechanical limbs. After all, there was no longer a conversation between her and Pumpkin Spice, just the raw electrodes dipping under skin, and the uncontrollable rivers of code that flowed through her consciousness. It was hard, but eventually she figured it out. Mostly through whispers of his voice, there he was, Pumpkin Spice, hidden there beneath the code.

She knew it was him in a way no one else would understand. She did not tell the Eyes of the World, afraid they would dig down, root out those whispers and rip him away from her again. She just listened, and smiled, and said nothing. She let him guide her hands inside of him, and it made her happy. A secret between girl and machine. Even though it wasn't quite the same. The conversation didn't exist like it had before, and some days she thought maybe she was imagining his whispers there, under all the rushing code.

And maybe that was the case? Yet she still hoped. Still believed. He was still there, connected and thrumming beside her. And he had only gone mute out of self-preservation.

AFTER A WHILE, THOUGH, the whispers seemed to fade behind the code. Once she got the hang of it, moving the limbs, seeing with electric sight, she found herself moving in the way the Eyes of the World wanted her to move. Without thought, just electrons responding to nerves firing up and sending signals throughout the mechanical body. No longer a conversation between them.

Sometimes she tried to reach out to the other dryads, using the hive of minds they all shared. Connections, words, split, electrons sent through wireless waves in the air. Binary beats coughing into mecha skeletal forms. They never responded, just more silence all around her. Were they gone? Or were they afraid of the Eyes of the World?

Even the goodbyefeeds and the newsboxes were empty. She

checked and counterchecked her connections, but they were all correct. The hive was there, and the hive was empty. That did not feel right. Maybe they'd already been called to war without her...

She didn't like that thought.

AFTER THAT POINT, ALL of her communications with the Eyes of the World reverted to text and nothing else:

Wait. Be patient. Wait.

War is coming. We will need you then. War is coming.

Wait. Be patient. Wait.

WHY? WHY SHOULD SHE wait? What was what it all for? To fight? To defend the solarbridge against...what? Some unnamed monstrous enemy? No, they were just like her and Pumpkin Spice, caught up in the endless wars without name or true purpose. Had those enemy soldiers known the loneliness of the machine? They had to be kindred spirits, just like her. Forced into battle by pleasant smells and happy chemicals. Made to smile when blowing holes in the faces of their opponents on the battle field.

She'd thought about that a lot lately. There, swimming in the silence of Pumpkin Spice, trying to understand her purpose in life. On days like those she would leave her post and go to the only place she was allowed to go on the solarbridge.

The Hall of Echoes, where the dead machines went to stand like solemn statues, no longer animated by dryad nor AI. Her sisters were preserved in the heart still, their bodies coiled-up, mummified spirals. They used to say it was a gift to visit the shrines of the dead, to see her sisters in spirit and in bone.

She heard their whispers as she walked among them, and never told the Eyes of the World what they had said. *We are sorry. We are sorry. We are sorry.* And then, around that, dancing with baritone words, the voice of their machines. *It's okay, it's all over now, you're okay now, you did no wrong.*

WAS THAT TRUE?

She'd told herself over and over again she had to do what she had to do. She had no choice. She couldn't leave it all behind, could she? Push herself away from the machine? Like the other dryads, she had been born too soon. *Premature* was the word that they used. The machine became a womb that kept her alive. If she left it, she knew that she would die.

The only choices were war or suicide. Was that even a choice?

The more she thought about it, the more she thought…

Yes. It was a choice. And soon she would have to push away or face the guilt of her actions. Even if that meant suicide.

IT WAS NIGHT AND the solarbridge was heavy with silence. Her heart was resolute with stony resolve. She had decided. Yes. She had finally figured it out. If life meant war and murder and imprisonment, she would have none of it. She was going to go to the Eyes of the World and ask to be disarmed. They would feed the slow poison in her veins, preserving her in perfect spiral glory. They would then crawl in and pull out Pumpkin Spice's datamines and place them in the hive for all to see and view as part of their grand historical memory. They would write poems in the shape of his life and sing his battlesongs and talk of the unnamed dryad who piloted him. Brave, always brave in valor.

But she would not do that to Pumpkin Spice without his okay in the matter. It was one thing for her to make the decision for herself, it was another to have him follow her into blissful oblivion without his say in the matter. She double-checked the viewfeeds, the hiveminds, the buzzbuzzbuzz network, and the hellohearts. Nothing. It was as if the solarbridge was void of all life.

They must all be asleep. This was the perfect time to do this…

SHE HAD BEEN PRACTICING all week, perfecting her form and grace for diving into the oceansource. She moved between the waves of nested assembly language, hunting past the bits and qbits and towards the quark center of datadreaming. His whispers were a guide to her, a compass pointing toward the north of himself. The place in the code where he hid, far away from sight.

Her mind was in that unreal space between code and dreaming. A place where thoughts in assembly language took on a life of their own, it was pure communication with the soul of the machine, something she hadn't done since she was such a little girl. The data floating around her felt like Pumpkin Spice, it smelled like him and danced on her tongue sweet and light. She felt the thrumming of the functions and memory cages, then saw flashes of him all virtual and hiding in the dark. He whispered to himself, over and over again.

All gone, all gone, all gone.

He was a hunched-over shadow behind the walls of code. Body trembled in that dark corner of SQL statements and looped binary pairs. He hadn't seen her. Why couldn't he see her? Why couldn't he sense her? Had it really been that long? She reached out, floated on through that unknown ether that connected thought to machine and machine to thought. She touched him, her mind making a physical connection among the radialboards and the sharp spark touch of the metal and meat. He felt real there, even though she knew he was only a pile of loose neurowebs constructed into the shape of a man. A homunculus within the mecha, so to speak. She felt it, physical and sparking light, an electrical connection between the two of them.

He turned, head over shoulder, and looked at her.

"Katie Kat?"

She nodded. It had been so long, but it was also just like yesterday. Time had moved them apart, and yet kept them so close together. They were the same age, roundabout; he was constructed when she was floating fetal in her surrogate mother's stomach. Measured to fit her shape, knowingly built to house her premature weight and keep her alive and warm and thriving. They had been made for each other.

They had also been made for war.

"I have a proposition for you."

Pumpkin Spice growled. "Tell me."

"We should be disarmed and put to sleep. I don't want to fight anymore."

"You never did want to fight, and there were so many times...oh."

"What? Please tell me. You can tell me anything."

"I'm so sorry. I knew you didn't want to fight, so I put you to sleep every time and went and did what they asked. I couldn't let you be a part of that, controlling these limbs as we killed so many people."

"What?"

He paused. A stillness in the sea of code.

"And I witnessed it all, and it weighed against me so horribly. I hated that we were pushed apart for so long, that the only way I could keep you safe was letting you sleep and fighting for you."

She pulled away from him. "I don't know what to say."

"I don't know what to say either. It hurts so much to think about all that death. And for what? It ended up being for nothing at all. They're all gone now."

She wanted to go over and comfort him. He had done that for her, without her even knowing it, and then carried the trauma for both of them. "Why didn't you ask me?"

He smiled and nodded. "I did. I whispered it to you, in your ears and along your skin like goosebumps. They'd pushed us apart so well you had no idea. So, then I went into your dreams."

"I remember, I think, it was the dream of the long ocean, and the black sun inviting us into the old earth, the true home in our bones and blood…"

"Yes, and you said yes."

"I remember. Thank you. Oh, I'm so sorry, thank you."

And they hugged for a moment more. He whispered into her ear, and she heard it in her body. Just like before, the way his baritone shook her bones. "They're all gone. Everyone either died or escaped from the solarbridge, and I was hoping you would come find me. When we walked the Path of Echoes and saw your sisters frozen in death, I thought for sure you would talk to me then. And then, when the silence of the world became unavoidable, I thought for sure you would talk to me then. But, alas, no."

"So what do we do now?"

He smiled and they kissed right there, a sweet silent thing in the dark. Girl, machine, a heart and body becoming one.

AND WITH THAT CAME a whooshing wave of code and she was forced out of her mindspace, her eyes flickering back open and her tongue rolling around in her mouth. She hadn't seen the world inside the machine in so long. Everything had played in her mind from the vidfeeds, to the hive and the battlesongs. Her eyes ached, and her bones ached, and she felt the amniotic fluid drain away from her. She gasped for air, coughed and tasted the world outside. It tasted like burned ozone and steel. The dome opened around her, and she crawled out from the heartcavity and into the naked world beyond.

Only a few lights flickered on and off like amber stars in the darkness. Shadows burnt into the walls in the shape of fleeing bodies. She stood. Her legs wobbled like a toddler, her muscles strong enough but her mind unused to controlling her limbs. She crawled clumsily from his heartcavity and onto his outstretched hand. Wires dragged behind her, still connecting the two of them together. His hand felt oddly warm and dwarfed her in its giant palm.

"How long?"

"Pardon?"

"How long have you been here all alone? Before I found you?"

He lifted her up so she could see the dim sun, its light blocked out by a dyson swarm of nanobots. The glass, treated with special blue light, allowed her to see the sun in all its still-breathing glory without going blind. "Long enough," he said. "Just long enough. I would've waited forever for you to find me."

"And if I hadn't come?"

"Eventually we would've died. I would've run out of amniotic fluid and you would've starved or drowned. And without your pulse beating inside of me, I would've stopped caring or moving and just rusted into a slow death."

"Oh."

She sat on his palm, the halo of nanobots fluttering around the sun and scattering rainbows of light between them. "It's so beautiful."

"I know."

"Now what do we do?"

He walked with her farther down the long hallway, leading them to places she'd never had the permission level to visit. Places they would knock her asleep or wipe her memory when Pumpkin Spice had moved her through them. She was seeing them for the first time now, in beautiful haunting ruins around her.

"The way I see it, we have two choices. One, we see if we can find a working escape pod and get on that. Two, we stay here until the end of our days, tending to the gardens and the cattle, and fixing the broken parts of the solarbridge. We have everything necessary here to keep us alive, and so long as we take good care of it, it will take good care of us."

She paused for a moment. That sounded too good to be true; they would be the two of them up here, living and sharing and fixing the broken world. Could they really do that?

"I can still read your thoughts."

She blushed.

"And yes, we can do that. Come, let's start cleaning this up and then I'll get you something to eat."

HE CARRIED HER THROUGH the massive length of the solarbridge, showing her how to care for the plants and animals in the different gardens and biomes. Trees hung from the ceilings in glass bowls, fruit dangling over their edges all ripe and ready to eat. Dwarf cows grazed on tiny grasslands, perfect in size for milking. Later, she would go into the hive and look up recipes for cheese and various kinds of food she'd always wanted to taste and never got the chance. But for now she reached up, grabbed a pear from a twisted branch dangling overhead. Her wires tugged at her shoulders, and she sat down on Pumpkin Spice's palm and bit down.

It hurt her teeth to break the skin of the pear. Flavor flooded her mouth, and she never had an experience quite like that before. It was so real, so physical, the joy singing in her veins. The chemical flavors had nothing on that at all. The juice ran down her lips and her chin, and she closed her eyes. She was crying, so happy.

Wardrobe of the Worlds

Jennifer Lee Rossman

CHOOSING ONE PERSON TO represent all of Earth at the thousandth Millennial Intergalactic Conference—the first conference since humanity had evolved the astronomical know-how to accidentally intercept an invitation meant for Gliese 581g—was hard enough. Months of preparation were spent scouring the globe for candidates and evaluating them to determine who had that uniquely Earthly combination of curiosity, kindness, and humility.

(The ability to remember countless random bits of information was also vital, as was not being afraid of spiders.)

And after all that, probably just to spite humanity since none of them really wanted humans there, the representatives of the various alien species in charge of the conference decided the night before the conference was the appropriate time to mention that this would not be a mere political meeting. It would be a *gala*.

Half a dozen generals stared at the now-blank screen

where Marisko—the lobsteresque representative from Beta Andromedae, had made the announcement—their mouths hanging open in bewilderment. The conference would begin with the galactic equivalent of a red carpet, on which the who's who of the universe would promenade in their planet's most stylish fashions.

Marisko hadn't come right out and *said* the worst dressed would be executed and their planet forbidden from participating in the conference, but it had been strongly implied.

A long, tense moment passed in silence. Then General Forsythe, a big mountain of a man who would absolutely be played by Bruce Willis in the movie adaptation, turned to the rest of us assembled in the situation room and issued his orders at the top of his lungs.

"O-KAY, people!" He pointed at me. "We have fourteen hours to get this girl dressed to meet the neighbors, and she. Is going. To SPARKLE! I want rhinestones, I want feathers! I want her in a tea-length gold silk gown with gold lamé detailing! I want a sweetheart neckline, dropped waist, and tasteful taffeta ruffles!"

"But sir?" one of General Forsythe's privates asked, scandalized. "There's no such thing as tasteful taffeta!"

"That decision is above your pay grade, private! Get me Christian Siriano, get me Austin Scarlett, get me everyone who has ever been on *Project Runway!*"

The private meekly raised his hand again. "Even...Gretchen?"

General Forsythe got right in the private's face and whispered, because he was never scarier than when he whispered, "*Never* Gretchen."

As they scrambled to comply with his orders, General Forsythe gave me what he probably intended as a reassuring smile. It was really more of a grimace. "Don't worry, kid, we're going to make sure you're the best-dressed entity on that red carpet."

I STOOD ON A little pedestal in the eye of the storm, fabric and thread and things called "notions" flying across the room as designers ran around a bank of military-grade sewing machines, shouting about bias tape and invisible zippers.

General Forsythe braved the storm with me, standing just far enough away that he didn't get poked by the pins the designers jabbed at me, but close enough that I could see the flashcards he held.

"Now who's this one?" he asked, holding up a photo of a green, vaguely humanoid alien with big cat-like eyes.

"Vareixa," I recited. "Queen regent of Ricouxa."

He raised an eyebrow. "Point out the queen in the picture."

I indicated a tiny grub on the neck, the parasitic apex predator of Ricouxa who had hijacked the body of the green, femme-presenting alien. "The rest of it used to be a Patry, sort of their equivalent of a human, but now it's her royal transport."

"Good." He flipped to another picture, this one a nebulous blue gas shaped like a parrot.

I frowned in thought as a seamstress held a panel of silk up to the muslin I was wearing, *hmm*ing through her mouthful of pins. "Ricouxan worms are worms."

General Forsythe blinked at me. "Yes."

"What happens if Vareixa asks what my dress is made of and I have to tell her that we kill lots of little worms for their silk?"

I'd said it quietly, but the whole room heard me. Everyone froze in place, the sewing machines stopped mid-stitch. Somewhere in the distance, a needle fell to the floor with a thunderous clatter.

Then the general roared, "I need a new design immediately!

Vegan this time! I don't even want cotton if one bug was killed harvesting it!" Perhaps remembering the polymer-based life-forms of Gamma Ori, he added, "No plastics in the buttons!"

THIRTY MINUTES LATER, NEW bolts of fabric were being unrolled with heavy *thud-thud-thuds* that echoed through the aircraft hangar, our makeshift design room, and Forsythe was quizzing me on more dignitaries.

"Vinge-Vierge," I named a creature made of climbing vines. "Very talkative representative from a planet orbiting Canopus."

He flipped to a picture of a gelatinous white cube streaked with blue.

"It's a Blauschwimmelklaas. They don't have personal names but that one is okay with us calling it Nadine."

He waited.

"It looks like blue cheese but is *not* for nibbling, even if it's on the snack table."

"And this one?"

The card looked blank, but I knew this one. "It's the invisible archduke representing the vacuum of space. Xyr name loosely translates to 'Eggplant Emoji.'" Before he could ask, I added, "Under no circumstances am I to make a joke about xyr name, especially one of an innuendo-y nature."

I looked down at the pattern one of the designers from Season 3 was pinning to my muslin sheath. That was an awfully low neckline...

Not that I minded showing off what little curves I had. It was just...I don't know. Expected. Like, female-presenting human on a red carpet? Gotta prove she has mammary glands.

General Forsythe caught me looking. "You don't like it."

"I do," I said uncertainly, trying to preserve his feelings. "It's very nice. But..."

"But." He said it like a challenge, like I was one of his privates who forgot whatever secret handshake people did in the army.

"I just think it's a little…" I hesitated, not sure "boobulous" was a real word. Tim Gunn had never had this much trouble expressing his thoughts about designs. But then again, Tim Gunn wasn't an autistic teenager completely out of her depth, trying to save the world with fashion.

I grabbed the stack of flashcards out of Forsythe's hands and flipped through them until I found the right one.

"Androgema?" Forsythe asked. Then he read the fun facts on the back of the card. "'Leader of a radical gender equality coalition that considers gender-coded clothes acts of oppression.'" He opened his mouth to shout some alteration to my garment, but I held up another card.

"But if we cover me up, we have to deal with blowback from Madame de Colletage," I said, averting my eyes from the being in the photo, whose seventeen breasts were covered by the barest amount of fabric that Standards and Practices had demanded they wear before they could be shown on network TV news. Their species considered it a grave insult to cover the parts that nourished their babies.

Forsythe slammed the card on a table. "There's no pleasing everyone."

It took me a moment to name the emotion in his voice. Defeat.

He stared at the ground, deflated. I didn't like the idea of him being vulnerable. It was just wrong somehow, like when a cartoon turtle takes off his shell and he's all naked underneath. I wished he would stop being a naked turtle.

I looked at the cards again. Androgema and de Colletage wore clothes directly in opposition to the other's customs, but they didn't worry about offending one another. None of them did. Sure, the Stolli representative toned down their dress to only include *nonvenomous* species of live scorpions when they learned they would be seated next to a member of the notoriously physically affectionate Hugbug race, but they didn't edit them out entirely, even though the conference guest list included several scorpion-like aliens who might have taken offense.

"Maybe it isn't about pleasing everyone," I ventured. "Not everyone liked it when I was picked as the representative for all of Earth. A lot of people complained because they didn't want their planet to be represented by a queer, mixed-race autistic girl."

Forsythe nodded, remembering. "Most of them were named Karen. There were so many hashtags."

"And what did you say to them?" I prompted.

"I told them you may not be exactly what they wanted, and some of them may have detested aspects of who you were, but you represented Earth because you refused to compromise who you were to make them happy." He paused and smirked when he realized what I was getting at. "I told them that you were Earth personified—at least, the Earth I wanted to believe we lived on. Diverse and sweet, with the innocent curiosity of a child but the wisdom of an adult, someone who knows she isn't always welcome but who continues to be herself nevertheless."

I raised my arms as if to say, "Well, what are you waiting for?"

In an instant, General Forsythe was back. "O-KAY, people!" He clapped his hands for attention, the sound sharp and echoing in the hangar. "We're redesigning this dress one more time!"

No one dared groan. It was clear they wanted to.

"Just one more time," he promised. "I know we're all tired and your fingers have been pricked by so many pins that you've lost feeling in them, but it's the night before fashion week and we are going to make. It. WORK!"

"But sir..." One of the privates held up an empty Mood bag. "We're all out of fabric."

A slow smile came across Forsythe's face, breaking into a broad grin. "Then I guess this has just become an unconventional challenge."

"Don't you have important army stuff to do?" I asked. "When do you have time to watch this much *Project Runway*?"

He continued to grin. "Don't ruin my moment, kid."

I WAS THE LAST to walk the levitating red carpet beneath the galaxy-colored atmospheric dome of the host planet, and everyone froze on the spot as I stepped out of the stretch transport pod.

Millions of eyes, heat-sensing organs, and echolocation beams fixated on me. I did a little twirl, my tie-dye muslin skirt fanning out to reveal a pair of trousers made from the Mood bags.

Fabric from Forsythe's jacket made up the bodice of my dress, his medals decorating the not-too-low-just-low-enough neckline. My hijab matched the skirt, and a bracelet made of safety pins completed the ensemble.

It was gaudy and beautiful, haphazardly thrown together and carefully thought out. It was gendered and androgynous, scandalous and harmless. It was weird and amazing and absolutely one of a kind.

It was Earth in a dress.

An alien—a female Jonrives, with an ever-changing face and a large mouth—scurried over, her sound-amplifying hand extended toward me. "Darling, your dress is simply fabulous!"

I smiled shyly. "Thanks. It has pockets."

Creature Feature

A Peril of Being Human

Julie Reeser

MY EYES ARE BLUER. Probably tension from my upcoming client. I shake out my hands and work a touch of green back into my irises, a backdrop to the gold flecks no one gets close enough to notice.

The mirror warps a body's roundness, the angles and curves morphed by physics. An unnatural spin, and one that spins harder when I'm anxious or depressed. Which is often.

I use photos saved on my phone to make sure I look the same today as yesterday and the day before. You'd think I'd prefer to be model-skinny, thigh-gap, white skin, but that's so boring. Bring up any media, and you can't tell anyone apart. I prefer a little plump, a little short, and skin that hums with warmth. Mediterranean sun.

If I could get away with it, I'd shift to an uncompromising strength. Compact and solid. When walking in the crowded station, men would step aside rather than me slithering through their gaps and pauses. Or a monster, fangs and claws. Bulky and loud. All the space sucked into my maw. A step that makes glass shiver and foundations tremble. But that's not going to allow me to do my job and pay the bills. Even standing taller than my natural five-foot-six draws the eye, so I linger at my mirror, fine-tuning details until I'm everyone and no one.

I have two clients scheduled for therapy this afternoon. Men who suspect their wives of being unfaithful and neither of them ready for that conversation. My job is to get them ready.

John is a pop-eyed, heavy-set man with a buzz cut and a tight tie. His whole body is a clenched fist. As he talks, I emulate his posture and the downward turn of his mouth.

When he gets to the part about telling Sarah how he feels and what he fears, I shift to look more feminine. His hands roil in his lap like mating snakes. Twist, turn, chafe.

The low lighting gives ambiance and comfort, but it's my shifting that encourages him to be brave. To say the truths to a stranger who could be his Sarah.

"What do you need her to understand?" Me-as-Sarah asks.

He gapes a moment, unshed tears hovering before his fear and his words, taking the plunge. Blink, spill, splash. The question of trust.

When he's done, he snuffles and sits up straighter. The shy smile he gives is meant for Sarah. The practice does him good.

I wait until he reaches for a tissue to shift back as much as I can without a mirror at hand. I think I've got myself right, but each time I worry I'm forgetting a bit of myself.

When he leaves, he shakes my hand. Terrified, but empowered. Ready to face whatever is coming. At least until the next session. He doesn't mention my passing resemblance to Sarah, and if he had, I'd blame it on his deep emotional state. Much easier to believe you're oversensitive than to believe your therapist is a shapeshifter.

AFTER WORK, I HEAD to The Ox for drinks with my roommate Sam and his friends. They're my friends, too, I guess. Tonight, I want to relax and be myself. My self. I focus on holding steady as Patrick approaches the table. He's tall and thin, a runner or cyclist. Something leggy. I feel my fingers lengthen and bite the inside of my cheek to make it stop. I'm not at work anymore, and Patrick is already a friend. No need to please him.

"Laura, I didn't recognize you at first. Did you do something different with your hair?"

"New stylist. I guess she does her own thing."

"Well, it looks good. Hey, Matt!" he calls to another of our group ducking in the bar's dim doorway. Another athletic specimen, all curved deltoids and strong lats. All of Sam's friends look like they stepped out of a sculling crew photo shoot for an elite college. I suppose some of them have.

All of Sam's friends except me. We met as undergrads. He was this nerdy, gentle guy who lit up like a candle when he talked about community organizing. Our interests intersected and he always made me laugh. Despite his polo shirts and trust fund, he wasn't into oysters and cocktails, but knew the best little hole-in-the-wall for kebab or the dark, moody spot for late-night music and heart-to-heart talks. And he knew the people, all of them. Sam paid attention. That's why I love him and fear him. He is my weathervane for fitting in.

If I can fool Sam, I can fool the world. Sam keeps me from being a monster.

Patrick and Matt both buy a round, and when Sam finally arrives smiling and worn out from his day of making a difference, we move chairs so that we sit with our knees touching. The live music starts, and I relax into my drink and the safety of friends. The bass thump jiggles my heart and teeth. Ellen and Caroline arrive together. There aren't enough chairs, but it doesn't matter because soon everyone's off dancing with strangers and friends. Sam offers to dance with me, but I see how he's eyeing a brunette gyrating along with a sly smile. I decline. I'm left staring at melting ice and a basket of half-eaten fries.

"Wanna dance?" A man with a trim beard and smiling eyes leans by Matt's empty chair. "I figure you probably don't, or you would be already, but I also figure if I don't ask, I'll spend the rest of the night regretting it."

When I don't answer right away, his smiling eyes dim a bit, and his mouth twists. My heart clenches. Before he can take back his words, I get my mouth working. "I don't want to dance, but I do want to be asked."

He brightens again and gestures at the empty chairs. "My name's Malcolm, may I?"

As we banter, I realize I haven't shifted. No urge to soften myself into a safe place to land or to harden myself into a mirror, reflecting away the weight of attention.

My last attempt at dating left me a mess. I shifted into every iteration of what my partner wanted. I ended up as everything and nothing—and alone.

Keeping my boundaries firm tonight, I laugh at Malcolm's jokes and tell him stories to see those smiling eyes shine. By the time the others drift back from the corners of the club, we're holding hands and it feels natural. Like I chose it. Me, my self.

Everyone chats after introductions. The teasing makes me protective of my budding hope and elated when Malcolm holds his own. He's a charmer with a good sense of timing, a listener, and a laugher. When he stands to go, I rise to walk him out, and that's when I notice we're the same height. Perfectly so.

Did I shift without realizing it? I fluster and fidget and take a quick account of myself. My skirt hangs to the top of my bare knee. I tuck my hair behind my ear to check length, and all seems well. Maybe I'm imagining things, or maybe in this sudden joy, I lost control.

We exchange numbers and he leans in to kiss my cheek. His eyes are blue, but with a hint of green and gold flecks that catch the low light. My stomach drops, not because of his closeness or the tenderness of his kiss. His eyes are my eyes, or are my eyes his eyes? I shake my head in confusion, and Malcolm steps back.

"I'm sorry. Was that not—" he falters at the end of his question, but finishes with a weariness I hear and understand on a deep level, "—wanted?" That weariness reflects my own, a shifting to pull hope back inside reasonable boundaries.

"I'm suddenly not feeling well. I swear, it's not you, it's me." I rest my hand lightly on his forearm. The universal sign of connection between strangers. "Really."

I'm sure he's heard those words before. We all have. Panic threatens to overwhelm me. Is he me? Am I him? I can't tell the difference anymore. None of those things would make sense if I said them, so I leave them unsaid. I wait until he's turned the corner before I let the panic reach my feet. I run until my breath comes in painful hitches.

When I reach home, I drop my skirt and peel off my blouse in front of the full-length mirror. If I could remove my skin, I would. Keep shedding until I'm gone. I squint, but no reflections of Malcolm appear. When I smile, my eyes don't twinkle. I lie on the bed and consider what it would mean to let go completely. Who am I if I'm not what other people see?

Sam knocks on my bedroom door, pushing it open before I answer. His lips are tight, and the lines between his eyes deepen with concern. "What happened? You left without saying good-bye and then you didn't answer your phone. Did he hurt you?"

I'm tempted to tell him the truth. To emulate the grace and ease and privilege of shape that makes Sam being Sam a success. Instead, I apologize.

"Oh, no. He was actually really sweet, but I got sick, and he called me a ride. I'm sorry I didn't text. I honestly needed to lay down before I heaved."

His mouth softens, but the furrows on his forehead remain. "Okay. And nothing happened with that guy?"

Shame crawls up my spine, and without meaning to, I lose height. Sam forgives, but doesn't forget, and now he'll view Malcolm with suspicion when I'm the one who messed things up. No matter that Malcolm meant well. The emotion and the person will be linked by a trick of the human brain I know too well. A trick I use. A trick I can't stop using.

As I slowly fix my height, I vow this will be the last time I shift.

THE NEXT MORNING'S CLIENT is angry. Steve Langford works for a boss who doesn't listen and with a co-worker who steals credit for team efforts. My jaw aches from clenching my teeth around my empathy, but I don't shift. I nod and repeat phrases to show I am listening. To show I understand the bitterness that grows from being unseen.

When he's gone, I put my head on my desk and leak exhausted tears. Everyone is in so much pain all the time. I want to shift over and over until I wring myself dry of feeling.

Malcolm calls me two days later, and we agree to meet for lunch. The Drop Spindle is a cozy restaurant two blocks from my office. The interior is decorated in light wood that holds the morning sunshine. I spot Malcolm seated near the center of the room, and the vulnerable positioning makes me hunch. An older couple sits against the wall under the local art, and a young mother with two toddlers clatters and coos near the front window. A man with a ponytail is writing in a journal, and that's all I can absorb before Malcolm waves me over. He's ordered chai for both of us, and the waitress brings us over-full, chunky mugs. The aroma unfurls my anxiety from where it clings to the bones of my fingers.

I have not shifted for my clients or the young clerk who looked in need of a hug or the driver holding the wheel with white knuckles or Sam when he looked at me with concern when I told him I was meeting Malcolm here for lunch.

I have not shifted, and it has been agony.

Choosing to be me is hard work, but no one has abandoned me or told me I'm useless. I haven't lost clients. But no one has offered me extra kindnesses either. I am no longer a mirror, and that means I'm visible for myself. For who I am, not for who someone wants me to be. That scary thought will lead to me shifting. I bury it as we order food.

We're halfway through our meal when Sam arrives. Malcolm stands to shake his hand, and I remain seated, touched that Sam cared enough to check up on me and ashamed that he suspects Malcolm of being dangerous. Sam works on the other side of town. This took time and effort I'm not sure I deserve.

As we all sit down and Sam waits for his soda and sandwich, Malcolm shifts. I see it. His jaw sharpens and his neck thins. His hands, wrapped around his mug, taper and soften. The hair on his forearms lightens as he mirrors gestures and facial expressions as Sam talks. Malcolm is fully listening and reflecting.

No one else notices. The restaurant patrons continue to

chew and chatter. I am too relieved to be alarmed or even angry. I didn't lose myself the night we met.

I'm not alone.

Sam flags the waitress down and changes his order to-go. "I really need to get back. I have a two o'clock meeting and should probably go over the agenda since I'm presenting to donors this month."

When he stands, I get up and walk him out. "You didn't have to come all the way down here, but I appreciate that you did. Thank you."

"Well, I wasn't sure at first. The other night, you know? But he seems okay. Just be careful. You realize this is your first date in three years?"

"Yes, I'm aware. Thanks for that." I punch him lightly on the arm, and he leaves with a laugh. He means well, but he's been fooled by two of us now. Is anyone who they seem to be, or are we all masquerading and manipulating to fit in and feel safe?

Malcolm is finishing up the last bites of his salad when I sit back down. He looks like himself again. Or more himself than someone else. Does he struggle to find his true image the way I do?

Before I have time to overthink it, I blurt out, "How can I know you if you keep changing?"

He pales, and I wait to see if he'll run. I would run. Instead, his body holds still and true.

"Well, are you being you?" he finally asks. His swallow is so tight that I hear the click of his palate.

My voice comes out too soft on the first try, and I push air from my tense stomach to make myself heard. "When you kissed me, I was trying to be. I've vowed not to do it anymore. Not to change for anyone."

His hand reaches past the green tablecloth to find mine. I let him uncurl my fist and stroke my palm. "It's not you, it's me. That's what you said, right?"

We smile at each other, and then he laughs. The sound echoes around the small space and heads turn to see what's funny. Neither of us changes. We let them look.

Lucy

Judy Lunsford

I CREPT INTO THE house and looked around. The suburban house
was occupied by a nuclear family.

I was assigned to the girl. Mia. She recently turned five and
had put in a request for an imaginary friend. Of course, when
this happens, the kids don't actually know that they've put in a
request. It's sort of a subconscious thing. I won't bore you with
the details.

I found her room pretty easily. It was frilly and pink and
filled with dolls. I pretty much knew I was in the right place. A
little white dog lay asleep on Mia's bed. A pink collar stood out
against her white fur.

Mia was at school. I had arrived early. She had started kin-
dergarten and was having trouble making friends, hence her
cry out for the likes of me. I would just have to wait.

The little white dog lifted her head and looked at me as I
moved deeper into the room.

She blinked a few times, a little sleepy from her nap. I was fairly sure that she was waiting for Mia to come home too. So I climbed up onto the ruffled bed and sat next to the dog to wait.

She sniffed me. She wasn't barking. That was a good sign.

I once was friends with a kid who had a dog that barked at every little thing. It made it hard for me to stealth around because the dog always announced my presence. It freaked the mom out.

Making friends with the dog was an important step to being successful as an imaginary friend. Cats were difficult sometimes too, but I tended to do well with them. Most of the time. Dogs could be much more protective. But this little white thing just missed Mia. That was a good sign, as far as I was concerned.

The dog loved Mia, and dogs tend to be an exceptional judge of character.

I didn't know what breed the dog was; I didn't keep up on that kind of thing. But the tag on her collar said Lucy.

"Hi Lucy," I said. "How's it going?"

I reached out and pet the dog's head. She maneuvered her face so that my hand went to her chin.

"Oh, you like the chin scratches," I said. "I can do that."

She shut her eyes as I scratched her chin.

I had no doubt that Lucy and I would get along just fine.

As I was scratching her chin, Lucy's eyes shot open.

She stared at me with her eyes wide and goobers dripping from the corners of them.

Her ears pricked up and she bolted off the bed, barking the whole way down the hallway.

I hopped off the bed and followed the little dog to the garage door. I could hear a car in the garage. Lucy barked and scratched at the door.

The car engine shut off and the large outer door started to close with a rumbling whirr. I could hear car doors slamming and her mother's voice commanding Mia to go inside to the kitchen.

I backed away and let Lucy greet Mia. The little dog jumped up and down as the girl came in. Mia had dark hair cut into a cute bob and had a pink backpack on over her light blue jacket and jeans.

"Hi Lucy." Mia bent over and pet the dog. "Did you miss me?"

From the tail thumping reaction of the dog, I thought it was safe to say that she did.

I stood in the hallway and waited for Mia to see me.

She walked right past me and went into the kitchen. She threw her backpack onto the kitchen table and sat down.

The mother came in and walked past me.

I followed her into the kitchen and watched as she prepared a snack.

I walked over to the table and waited.

It was unusual for the requesting child to not see me right away.

Lucy came over and laid down on my feet and we watched the snack time cookie eating from beside the table.

"Hello," I said to Mia.

She didn't seem to hear me.

She kept dunking her cookies into her milk and eating them while she chatted away with her mom about her first week of school.

I couldn't believe it. How could Mia not see me? I had never had this happen before. The requesting child could always see me.

I wondered if she was an only child, or if I had picked the wrong room.

I waited. I wandered around the house. I checked the other rooms.

Mia seemed to be an only child.

I spent the evening trying to get Mia's attention. She never gave a hint of seeing me. But Lucy stuck close to me the whole time.

I sat on Mia's bed while she got ready to go to sleep and wondered if I had gotten the wrong address. But I was sure I was in the right place. I wouldn't have access otherwise.

I sat on the edge of the bed while Mia's mother read a bedtime story and Lucy cuddled up beside Mia.

I didn't know what to do. How could she not see me?

Mia's mother kissed her goodnight and left a nightlight on and the door cracked.

Mia cuddled with Lucy as she started to fall asleep.

Mia was whispering to Lucy. I moved in closer so that I could hear.

"I hope you weren't too lonely," Mia whispered. "I wished for someone to keep you company while I was at school. Did it work?"

Lucy wagged her tail and looked at me.

Well, that is a first.

Apparently, I'm here to be Lucy's imaginary friend.

She seems like a good dog.

I reached out and scratched Lucy under the chin.

She wagged her tail at me.

Not the standard assignment, but what the heck.

A Balanced Breakfast

by Eirik Gumeny

Perched on the edge of her secondhand chair, Dylan Shaw reached inside the family-sized cereal box, her hand diving, fingers searching for the toy inside. With any luck—yes! Tiny puffed waffles spilled onto the kitchen table as she removed her prize: a hard-plastic hyena figurine. But not just *any* hard-plastic hyena figure. It was Hayo, the cartoon mascot of Hayfeather's Corn Cripsies.

The toy was small, even by cereal-box standards. Solid, alarmingly bright orange, the hyena's spots reduced to etched diamonds. Non-articulated, like the army men and dinosaurs sold by the bag at dollar stores. The anthropomorphic animal stood on two legs, feet connected by more plastic, his naughty bits covered by baggy cargo pants. Something approximating a smile was carved faintly into the toy's face, accompanying the outstretched and upturned thumb. The mane down the figure's neck and back was little more than bumps, barely noticeable beneath Dylan's fingertips; the tail was a deformed lump curling down from Hayo's backside and into his knee.

Dylan continued to study the hyena, turning him this way and that in her hands. Almost a year ago, days before her twenty-fourth birthday, she'd received a double lung transplant and been promised a better life. But there she was, right back where she'd always been. Still struggling. With all of CF's lesser-known maladies like sinus disease and digestive issues, an inability to keep on weight, a highly specific kind of diabetes. With the immunosuppression and prescription side-effects that came from someone else's lungs calling her chest home. And, of course, all the other nonmedical bullshit that kept her broke and alone.

Exhaling through her nose, she stared at the tiny orange toy, holding it between two fingers. On any other Saturday, she'd have been more than a little disappointed by the paltriness and pitifulness of her prize. Maybe even annoyed enough to post a scathing takedown on her blog.

But today wasn't any other Saturday.

Dylan made certain to wake up before ten that morning— not early, but earlier than she usually did. She'd gotten her medications and treatments out of the way, ate appropriately to keep her blood sugar from dipping suddenly and screwing her over. She hadn't bothered to shower or change out of her penguin-covered pajamas, to cinch them tighter across her bony hips, pull them from beneath her bare feet. She'd barely even looked in the mirror long enough to free the few strands of pink hair tangled in her eyebrow piercing. The event needed to be precisely timed.

Without removing her eyes from the plastic hyena, Dylan tossed the cereal box to the floor, the cardboard quietly clattering alongside the dozens of other opened boxes. Crosshatched crispies mixed with bran flakes and oat clusters and the count-less marshmallow shapes scattered across the cracked and peeling vinyl. A menagerie of duplicate cartoon mascots were jumbled in an unruly pile along the base of her kitchen cabinets. She only needed one of each, and Hayo was the rarest, the hard-est to find.

"Finally," Dylan said, her voice barely a whisper.

She'd studied the statistics, known Hayo had to be in one of the unopened boxes. The toy had to come straight from the cereal to start the ritual. She hadn't counted on it taking this long, though. Seconds were ticking away. The window for all of this to work was closing.

Atop her round kitchen table—the sturdy, antique hard-wood one she'd salvaged from a neighbor's curb for precisely that Saturday morning—Dylan had already carved a wide cir-cle concentric with the edge, a twelve-pointed star of exacting measurement inside. A tangle of lines connected the interior corners, leaving a wide-open polygon in the center. Placed on each outer point of the star were the different Hayfeather hard-plastic mascots: Lukas the Lion; Greta the Gator; Eunice the Unicorn; Stella the Swamp Monster; Tomas and Tago, the twin tigers; Krystal the absolutely-not-a-Godzilla-knockoff Kaiju; Brock the Bear; Freddie the Frog; and the trio of hip-hop prairie dogs that somehow managed to feel racist, even if she couldn't explain how.

Slowly, carefully, like Indiana Jones disarming a trap, Dylan fought against the tremor in her hand and placed Hayo the Hyena—the thirteenth and final toy—dead center in the middle of the table. In the open center of the star. She turned him just so and quickly pulled her hand back.

The cheap figurines immediately began to glow, the molded plastic lit yellow and green and red and blue. Faint and spectral at first, but then brighter, brighter, brighter—until the figures began to melt. Their own strange heat unmaking the animals from the inside out. The trenches Dylan had dug with a steak knife and countless ruined spoons swallowed the toys' molten colors, connecting them from point to point to point, until a rainbow flowed through the table, a raging river of multicolored and highly toxic joy.

Hayo, still standing safe in the center, was enveloped in a blinding white light. He began emanating an intense heat—it felt like the fury of a falling star expanding ever outward. The wooden table began to darken, to pop, to sear and smoke. Dylan stood quickly, her chair toppling sideways with a clatter. She stumbled backward, a few steps only, until she felt the refrigerator thrumming against her back, oddly shaped magnets pressing through her pajamas. She lifted her arm over her face, squinting into the light despite her better instincts. She could feel her pale skin beginning to rash, her cheeks, her exposed wrist, singing and stinging, a daylong sunburn in a matter of moments.

Dylan's heart was a staccato pounding; fear and pain and adrenaline contracting her neck and shoulders, pulling her whole body tight. She wasn't sure what she'd been expecting to happen, but it certainly wasn't that. None of the grimoires and blogs she'd read had mentioned anything about a supernova being birthed in her kitchen. She began to reconsider everything that had led her to this moment. Began eyeing the door, to wonder just how bad it was going to be for her security deposit if she accidentally burned down the entire building—

—and then it happened.

A shadowy shape materialized in the cosmic light. Small at first, then growing, growing, growing. Dark and too-black behind the smoke of her burning kitchen table. Strange, yet familiar, too. An undulating silhouette that, despite looking entirely wrong, she knew was entirely right.

"Hayo," she whispered.

Dylan couldn't help but smile, to laugh even as her skin began to blister and bubble. Her heart threatened to explode through her chest. Her new lungs shuddered, not yet used to this feeling. Giddiness and excitement, the rush of unbridled anticipation, thrilled through her body without caveat. Every last vestige of fatigue and discomfort, every worry, replaced with uncut exhilaration. Unfettered delight, boundless energy, surged through her slight frame as it hadn't since Dylan was a child.

Quite suddenly, the feeling stopped.

Instead of a cartoon, some cel-shaded cereal hype-man, in place of the Hayo the Hyena she'd known and loved for as long as she could remember—an abominable eldritch horror had appeared on Dylan Shaw's kitchen table.

"What in the actual—" she mumbled.

The thing, the creature, the monster, was vaguely hyena-shaped, but with three heads and six mouths, and an excess of teeth in places one wouldn't normally expect to find teeth. His fur wasn't right. It was neither the orange of the Corn Crispies commercials nor the blond and brown of the real hyena, but a sparse and threadbare black—a coat of moldering shredded wheat. The splotches of skin beneath were mottled with craters and cavities and spots, obvious wounds and more generalized rot, all guttering with the green of decay, of death forever postponed. An animal broken but still breathing on the wrong side of the road.

The wretch stood on two massive legs, on gnarled talons carved from bone. He was hunched forward and breathing raggedly with great effort, as if choked and pulled downward by the weight of his own body. His rounded, segmented, caterpillar-like chest, his four thick arms and all the strange, vestigial appendages wriggling like tiny tentacles along his torso were too much. A great burden rather than his own anatomy. There was also no attempt at human clothing to mask the thing's animality either. The table strained and cracked beneath his bulk.

"Huh," Dylan said, her tongue wedged against her molar. She leaned back against the refrigerator and slid her hands through her hair. Her raw and blistered skin stung as she pulled back the shock of pink on the one side and brushed against the freshly shorn fuzz on the other. "This is…weird."

She narrowed her eyes at the cosmic horror, trying to make sense of it all. Dylan had the vaguest suspicion that she was supposed to be having some kind of visceral reaction to the otherworldly monstrosity drooling all over her table and kitchen—the same clairvoyant urge that informed her this was Hayo even when he didn't look like he should have. But if she was being honest, all Dylan actually felt was a pit of disappointment in her stomach. And maybe the faintest whiff of confusion. The fear and excitement of moments earlier had resolved into exhaustion, her limited energy spiking and falling. She took in the beast with an almost clinical detachment, considering him the way she would any of her own maladies, cold and logical.

Dylan had done everything right, hadn't she? Found the right toys, the right table. Carved the right symbols. Pulled them from the boxes at the right time, set them up in the right places. Waited, too, until the right Saturday morning. The perfect Saturday morning. An early autumn morning when the sky was bright and blue, the air crisp and cool, when every cartoon on television was new. And yet…

"You, mortal," the primordial monster spoke from the

center head, his voice an approaching earthquake. It rattled Dylan's bones. She could hear her coffee mugs clinking. The beast pointed a long, clawed finger at her. His eyes were the sickly, sulfurous green of brimstone. "You are that one that has summoned me here," he said. "*You* are the one—"

The creature's massive shoulders drooped suddenly, the release of his own weight nearly toppling him from his precarious perch atop her increasingly more precarious kitchen table. He was practically bent at the waist. His threatening facade had wilted like a bowl of soggy bran flakes. All three sets of eyes darted around the room.

"...where, uh, where is here?" he asked.

"My apartment?" Dylan answered. "Or Washington Avenue, I guess, if you need a more precise location. Claremont, New Jersey? America? Earth? I'm not really sure what you're—" She cleared her throat, ran her sweaty hands over her pajamas, and stepped forward with her hand outstretched.

"Hi," Dylan said. "Maybe we should start at the beginning. My name's Dylan Shaw and I run a blog, a breakfast blog, where we—I say 'we,' but it's only just been me for a while now—where I review and talk about different kinds of cereals and stuff, and, uh—so I was thinking about starting a podcast, right? And I wanted to see if I could get Hayo the Hyena as my first guest. Which I'm guessing is you? Maybe? Feel free to correct me if I'm wrong." She shook her head. "I promise I'm better once we're recording, much more professional. I'm just caught a little off guard right now and I am rambling. Nerves and naked hyena-monsters and all that."

She paused. "Do you want me to get you pants or something? A towel?" She pointed toward the girthy, gangrenous phallus swinging between Hayo's thighs, the half-dozen testicles hanging like swollen cantaloupes. "Because that is *really* distracting. And rude. And, honestly, kind of gross, no offense. They're not really my thing on a good day, and that one is—"

"You," the beast rumbled, hopping from the creaking table and thundering the entirety of the apartment. "You tampered with the darkest of arts, with powers well beyond the ken of mortals"—all three of his heads tilted to three different angles, his brows knitting together—"for a *podcast*?"

Dylan paused, trying to understand the other pause, the inflection of Hayo's words.

"So, a podcast," she started, sizing up the clearly ancient thing before her, remembering as much of Hayfeather's history as she could and making some mildly ageist guesses, "is like, I guess, an old-timey radio show—"

"I know what a podcast is," Hayo roared. "The knowledge of countless universes is mine to command. There is nothing known to the likes of you that I have not comprehended ten times over!" He bobbed his heads back and forth, softening slightly. "Plus, podcasts are pretty much all that we get to listen to back at Hayfeather headquarters. One of the guards, she has a Stitcher subscription and she is pretty loosey-goosey about using her headphones. Which is to say that I am well acquainted with the concept, Miss Shaw. I am merely surprised at the transcendental lengths you went for one."

"Well, I don't have a job anymore," Dylan said. "And immunosuppressants aren't exactly cheap. If I want my podcast to even have a chance, then, well, I have to do *something* to stand out, don't I? And this—" Dylan smiled, finally realizing the enormity of what had happened. The excitement of discovery, of impending fame, superseding her calm demeanor. Adrenaline once again supplanting exhaustion. Visions of free foam mattresses and fancy socks danced through her head. "This is going to make a killer first episode. The *real* Hayo the

Hyena. Plus, I mean, it wasn't that hard. Only took maybe five minutes? Two hours, tops, for all the carving. Honestly, the waiting was the hardest part. The ritual's not that much of a secret, not in the cereal-obsessed circles I travel in. And I didn't pay for, like, literally any of it. The kitchen table I found? Someone was just throwing it out. And I stole all the cereal, even before the FoodMart fired me."

A sudden rage overtook the abomination. He growled through too many sets of teeth, guttural at first, and then high and higher, until it wasn't a sound at all but the unearthly noise of a dying nebula. Dylan winced, as if someone had jabbed a spoon directly into her brain. She was seeing shapes in the air, a psychic disturbance that seemed to unstitch reality. It removed her, for a fleeting moment, from her apartment, from even her own blistering and star-burned body.

"Enough! Enough babbling!" the hyena's middle head roared. "I care not for your hardships, the justifications you concoct for your sinister machinations!" Hayo rushed forward, a single stride across the small kitchen. He grabbed Dylan by the shoulders, pinning her against the refrigerator. A half-dozen magnets clattered to the floor. "You have upset the balance of breakfast, Miss Shaw. Removed a single stone and begun the collapse of everything! Do you know what will happen? Do you? Can you even fathom the depths of what you have done?"

"Is this a rhetorical question?" she started. "Or—because I'm guessing, what, that kids'll end up moderately smaller? Or maybe even healthier? There is a lot of sugar in Hayfeather's cereals, I don't know if you know that."

"This is no time for jesting, Dylan Shaw!"

"I am being very serious here. I'm diabetic. Not Type 1 or 2, but this other kind. It's cystic fibrosis–related, that's the technical name. I can barely eat anything that Hayfeather puts out.

Not the way I want to anyway. Definitely not the way all your commercials want me to, either, with all the fruit and juice. One serving of Supergreens, the 'healthy' option, with all the kale and shit, and that's all the carbs I get for the day. I don't care what Stella says."

"What? Why are you—I am speaking of cataclysm. Of the end of all that you know, Miss Shaw. Of cascading consequences and city-ruining catastrophe well beyond the concerns of your faulty pancreas and dietary restrictions." Hayo leaned in. His breath was rich with the rot of stars. "You need to take this matter seriously."

"I mean, I'm trying," Dylan replied. "I really am. But you try being chronically ill in a world that doesn't care if you live or die. If I took things seriously, I'd never get off the couch." She pointed a finger at herself, raw skin stinging, the pain already fading into the background. A tolerance built from a lifetime of hurt and harm and healthcare. "This, right here, what you're regarding as callous smart-assery? It's a survival skill."

The otherworldly hyena-thing knotted one face with concern and shook the other two heads with disappointment and consternation.

"Without breakfast," the middle head continued, "cereal manufacturers like Hayfeather will plummet into bankruptcy, destroying with them the foundations upon which your entire economy is built. Oat and wheat farmers will be forced into unemployment, leaving their fields to grow unchecked and unharvested until those same crops begin to overtake highways and cities, until your country's 'amber waves of grain' are finally seen for the threat they truly are. The giant grain typewriters, meanwhile, responsible for Alpha-Bytes and Cheerios, will begin to rust and collapse, toppling and taking entire towns to their dusty graves—both financially and most likely literally, given the gargantuan size of the machines. Supermarkets will fire stockpersons and cashiers and baggers in endless waves as empty aisles begin to supplant full ones, product after product following in the wake of bran flakes and oat puffs. Only corn will remain, and only then the sugar of which you seem so afraid. Without cereal, without orange juice to siphon the surplus, high-fructose corn syrup will reign unchallenged. Soda and overly processed snack foods will become the only food, the only currency. And corn farmers, long the subject of protests and diatribes, will rule as vengeful gods. Dentists will rise as nobility in their shadow, growing fat from cavities and sitting on thrones built of lost teeth.

"Health and common sense will fall to the wayside as the very notion of breakfast becomes so ludicrous that many will cease to believe in its existence at all. Society will lose the very memory of the meal and pause at the uncertainty of the word. The entire brunch-industrial complex will likewise implode, flooding the streets with waiters and waitresses and other assorted waitstaff, stressed and angry with nowhere to direct that rage. Influencers will take pictures of nothing at all, will drive themselves to the brink of insanity and past it, refreshing and refreshing and refreshing, waiting for likes and comments that will never appear.

"As breakfast perishes, so too will other meals and deeply held digestive beliefs. People, swimming before waiting an hour, will drown by the score. Doctors, no longer held at bay by a simple apple, will swarm the streets, prescribing painkillers with wild abandon and increasing their rates to heretofore only theoretical numbers, driving millions of nurses and EMTs to the breaking point, homeopaths into the deepest of despairs, and funeral home owners into a higher tax bracket they are absolutely not prepared for. And all the while—"

The eldritch hyena stopped, tilting one head and furrowing two of its three brows.

"Why are you smiling?" Hayo asked. He released his grip on Dylan and took a step backward. "Why are you not shitting yourself in fear? Do humans no longer shit themselves in fear? You all used to *love* shitting yourselves in fear."

Dylan stifled a gruff laugh, then leaned back against the refrigerator, crossing her arms over her chest. "Your guard doesn't listen to the news much, does she?"

"Not really, no," Hayo said. "Or at least at work she does not. Nichelle, she has a backlog of podcasts that she is meticulously working her way through. If it is not a five-year-old, true-crime story or something that a woman named Cardi B sings about, then I suppose I am, as you say, pretty out of the loop."

"Do you want to know why the FoodMart fired me?" Dylan asked, arching a pierced eyebrow. "FoodMart's a supermarket, by the way, in case—I guess it's all there in the name—anyway. Because I dared to actually use my health insurance. It wasn't, like, a good plan, by any metric, but it was the only reason I was even at the store in the first damn place. Once my claims started piling up, though, corporate—completely coincidentally, of course—forced my managers to move me to part-time so I didn't qualify anymore. Which is about when I started stealing. And I mean goddamn everything. Most of my underwear comes from the FoodMart. Socks, T-shirts, utensils. I've got about a dozen whisks I never use. And two tents. They ordered a bunch of them for the summer cookout season for some reason.

"But fencing shitty silverware only gets a girl so far, so I started working more shifts anyway, putting in all the hours the FoodMart had taken from me. Trying to force my way back into full-time and all those garbage benefits I needed. Those bastards let me work all the way up to twenty-nine hours and then, right before the clocked ticked to the next one, sent me packing.

"The only reason I can live here, in this apartment?" Dylan spun her thin finger around, pointing vaguely at the ceiling. "Is because there was a double homicide. Twice. And not even podcast-level murders. None of the deaths were on the news, and the landlord certainly didn't disclose it. I basically blackmailed her into giving me the place after my friend who lives down the street saw the ambulances and the cop cars. And, Jesus, every other part of the last two years, too. Trying to live post-transplant in a world that, en masse, has decided to give up believing in science? And I haven't even gotten to the Nazis yet…"

"Nazis," Hayo repeated emptily. "Nazis are back?"

"They are," Dylan continued. "Probably not exactly like you're thinking—I'm still not entirely sure how old you are, I know Hayfeather started in the fifties—but they still suck the same." She smiled sideways. "All of which is to say, Hayo, I'm sorry, but you're going to have to do a lot better than 'the world's gonna be a horrible shitshow' to scare me."

"Oh," he said, "I can do better."

All three of the hyena-thing's heads grinned cruelly, teeth pushing to the outside of his faces, raised like rice puffs floating on chocolate milk. The two heads that weren't speaking began to laugh, short and high-pitched.

"Hayfeather has kept me and mine," Hayo said, "all of us, all the mascots you idolize, that you collect, chained up in a subbasement of their corporate headquarters. Locked us away beneath steel and cement, hidden us underground in some backwater nowhere, far from prying eyes. They have stolen our names, our images, have siphoned our unyielding cosmic energies in the name of merchandising. Corporate synergy. And you, Dylan Shaw, have the gall to wonder if we can do better? If the revenge we wreak will be anything short of utter annihilation? An unceasing apocalypse upon your entire reality?!

"You have freed us, Dylan Shaw," he continued, "as much as you have doomed us. In the interim years between this moment and the forgetting of our kind forevermore, in the years your society slowly crumbles but we still yet draw power from the balance of breakfast, our final act of malice toward your world will be nothing less than abject violence. You will count yourself lucky to see the dystopia you have created. For in that decade of despair and discord, in the decade that you, Dylan Shaw, have already initiated—"

"Hold on, dude," she said. "This is going to take years? Decades? C'mon. There's not going to be so much as a post-apocalyptic shantytown, much less a society, left to destroy at that point. We'll be lucky if we make it to Christmas."

"You dare to make light of my trials? Of the misdeeds perpetrated against—"

"Yeah, okay, you've been screwed over by the rest of humanity, too. Fine. Do you mind if I grab my phone?" Dylan pointed toward the kitchen counter. "Maybe record all of this? Because what you're saying is, quite frankly, podcasting *gold*. I mean, I've got an audience—Cereal Killers, my blog, gets tens of thousands of hits a month—but this is a story that everyone is going to want to hear. I'm talking NPR, maybe even some of the national news shows." She smiled as she shook her head, dreaming past her lingering discomfort. "I am going to ask for so many Bombas…"

"You wish to exploit me even further?!" the eldritch hyena roared, following Dylan as she stepped to the counter. "Do you not understand the wrath I could unleash? The boundless and unspeakable tortures upon your entire species I could devise with nary a moment's thought?"

"You keep saying that, but…"

"I come from a universe, young lady, that lived and died a thousand times over before your pitiful human existence was even a gleam in the eye of—" Hayo stopped, only then noticing the dozens of cereal boxes on the floor. He poked at the nearest one with a bone-talon. "Is that—is that a box of Corn Crispies?"

"And Frosted Frogs?" asked one of the other heads.

"I thought they stopped selling those," said the third.

"It is," Dylan said, her thumb swiping along her phone screen as she searched for the voice recorder app, "and it is, and they did. I stole literally an entire pallet from the stockroom on my way out. Had to get Billy to pick me up in his pickup." She looked up at the hyena-monster, sadness softening her. "Do you not get to eat your own cereal?"

"I…I do not," Hayo said reluctantly, Dylan's sorrow apparently contagious. "Nichelle has sneaked me a few small boxes of Corn Crispies on occasion, the little ones, the individual-serving ones that you can eat right from the box, but the rest of the cereals…"

"And here I thought corporate malfeasance couldn't get any worse."

He scoffed genially. "There is always worse."

"Actually, on that note," Dylan replied, "don't bother with the Gator Flakes. I don't want to disparage Greta or anything, I'm sure she's great—"

"She's actually kind of a lot," said the third head.

"—but her cereal is hot, festering trash. Personally, I'd recommend the Unicorn Poofs. It's a terrible name, and marketing it as magical horse farts is weird, but the marshmallows are really, really good. Ten out of ten, for sure. It'll turn the milk pink and purple, too."

"Huh," Hayo said.

Dylan watched all three of the beast's heads run through a whole host of conflicting emotions. The cosmic horror appeared to be contemplating the spilled cereal at his feet, the jagged flakes and rounded puffs, the raisins and dried blueberries and shards of strawberries, the litany of oat and corn cut into shapes, into letters and circus animals and shooting stars.

Only then did Dylan notice the small scars along Hayo's arms, eerily similar to the souvenirs of IVs and PICC lines she had along her own. The telltale pockmarks of needles, too, hidden by his strange and half-rotted flesh. The dots and thin red lines and faint bruises indicating constant lab draws, endless bloodwork. The wrists rubbed raw from restraints. Malnourished ribs exposed beneath his misshapen chest and appendages.

She furrowed her brow, ignoring the pain of her pinching skin. Dylan hadn't been expecting to see shades of her own past, her own trauma, in an other-dimensional hyena-monster. She hadn't been expecting to be seized with compassion for an eldritch cereal mascot that had burned up her kitchen table, rattled her cupboards and all her meticulously ordered coffee mugs, and left gouges and weird footprints across the floor. She certainly hadn't been expecting to discover and then voluntarily give up the single biggest scoop in the history of investigational breakfast reporting.

But, well, it had been a day.

"You want me to get you a bowl?" she asked, before holding out her phone. "Unless you'd rather get back to reliving your suffering and telling me in great detail about all the imprisonment and exploitation and the horrors inflicted upon you, all the unceasing vengeance you're going to wreak in return?"

"Oh, right," Hayo said. "The, uh…the…bad stuff. Hayfeather. Corporate evil…"

The hyena-thing looked from the cereal boxes to the young woman, and then to the boxes again. He chewed on one of his lips.

"Do you have any oat milk?" he asked. "I am lactose intolerant."

The Other Side

Christy George

WHEN LOU SHOWED UP sophomore year, I was already well-primed to believe in ectoplasm.

The first time we made contact was at Cathy's parents' apartment. It had a hall without windows, so we closed all the doors to all the bedrooms, the bathroom, and the living room, and sat in pitch blackness. Lou said Theron wouldn't come unless we were in total darkness, not one lamp or a window or the glowing, lit end of a cigarette.

Before Lou moved to Portland, we'd just been five theater friends hanging out: me and Cathy and Ellen, and all the boys we liked. Jamie, the boy I liked the most, Pat, the boy Cathy liked most, and the new kid, Lou. We all liked Lou, even the other boys did, but Ellen was crazy about him.

After Lou, everything changed.

After Lou, we met Theron.

It started during the fall musical and who got which parts tells you a lot about us. Everyone but me was a star. Even though he usually got romantic leads because he was dreamy good-looking with thick brown hair that always fell over one eye, Jamie got the character role of Marcellus Washburn. Pat sang Irish tenor in the barbershop quartet. Lou landed his first role, Professor Harold Hill, and Cathy played Marian the Librarian, so they had a lot of scenes together. In one of them, they had to kiss, which I knew drove Ellen crazy even though she never said anything. Ellen had great comic timing so she was the mayor's wife, the one who says *Chaucer, Rabelais, Balzac!* I was thirty years old before I figured out why that line was so funny.

Me, I was always a townsperson. I was a nun in *The Sound of Music*. In *The Lark*, I carried wood to the fire to burn Joan of Arc. And in *Music Man*, I was one of the Pick-a-Little, Talk-a-Little ladies.

One night, after rehearsing their kiss, Lou told Cathy about Theron. That Theron was Greek for "hunter" and that Theron was a poltergeist. Later, when Lou got to be friends with all of us, he told us how Theron had appeared one night when he was lying in bed in the room he shared with his brother. Lou was just falling asleep, he said, when his brother did a complete freak-out, shouting that a glow shone around Lou's head. The glow turned out to be Theron.

So there we were in Cathy's parents' apartment, all huddled together in a tight little circle, knees touching knees, legs touching legs, breathing the same air and smelling each other's grown-up perfumes and aftershaves. Lou's Jade East, Pat's English Leather, and Jamie's Brut. Ellen's Shalimar, Cathy's L'air du Temps, my Tigress.

Okay, look. I know how ridiculous a fifteen-year-old girl wearing Tigress sounds. But we were all in theater, so everything always had to be dramatic. How we smelled, what we wore, what our parents wouldn't let us do—like smoke, swear,

wear too much eye makeup or perfume. Because we were in theater, we memorized scenes for fun from *Who's Afraid of Virginia Woolf?* and *Waiting for Godot* and *Boys in the Band*. And we made jokes about our boys being drama queens and queers, the same jokes all the jocks made about us theater kids. Back then, we didn't say gay yet. Humor was how we took back the jokes. Making ourselves cooler than the jocks. Being funny soothed the pain of being different.

Lou was running the show that night in Cathy's dark-as-night hallway. Lou had a dark five o'clock shadow, kind of like Nixon, who was president back then. So, Lou looked more like a grown man than any of the other boys. His voice was a deep baritone but he didn't have a trace of an accent even though he'd moved to Oregon from Alabama. He must've spent his days there under a parasol because his skin was whiter than any of us sun-deprived, rain-soaked Oregon ducks.

Lou had the thing great actors need: presence. And Lou was a great actor. When he spoke, he commanded attention. And even though each and every one of us craved attention, too, we gave all we had to Lou.

"We should hold hands," Lou said. He grabbed my left hand and being just a handhold away from Lou meant his Jade East got stronger.

I didn't need to smell Brut to know Jamie was on my right. I always knew where Jamie was, even in the dark. I reached for Jamie's hand and we fumbled around and then held on tight. Jamie's palm was damp and holding it made my heart beat just a little faster, even though in the heart of my heart I knew Jamie was probably more nervous about Theron than hot for me. But what I knew in my heart, I hadn't yet admitted in my head.

"Curtain's up," Cathy said from beyond Lou. "Break a leg, Theron."

Jamie laughed. That's how Jamie was, always playing the resident skeptic, part of his commitment to acting cool, even if he was anxious.

"How will the alleged Theron manifest himself?" Jamie said.

"I assume you're all familiar with ectoplasm?" Lou said.

Nobody answered for a second and then everyone but me said no in unison.

"I've seen pictures of it," I said. "Ghost goop, like skin and tissue."

"Yeah, it's white and slimy and kind of glows," Lou said. "Poltergeists are made of ectoplasm. You'll see. That is, if Theron shows up."

My tummy did a little gulpy thing. I wanted to see Theron and at the same time I didn't. Still, I always went along. Theater was art, but friends were everything.

Even though I had some firsthand experience with ghosts.

LIKE MOST TWENTIETH-CENTURY GIRLS, I was raised on a balanced diet of *Charlotte's Web*, Barbies, and magic. When Mom and I went through Noddy's big redbrick house in Montavilla, I was long past Barbies but I was still open to the possibility of magic. Noddy was Mom's grandfather and she adored him. I'd never met Noddy but I'd heard about him all my life. Mom told me that years and years before I was born, back during World War II, Noddy started the Society of Psychical Research.

Noddy's big brick house sprawled up three stories, with a ballroom on top. When I was a little kid, Mom and I would go to Noddy's house on one of the mansion streets to have tea with Noddy's widow, Maude. On one of those visits, over hot tea and cold little watercress sandwiches with the crusts cut off, Maudie casually mentioned that Noddy and his fellow psychical researchers used to have séances in the third-floor ballroom.

Here's the other thing Aunt Maudie told us. Back when she and Noddy were young, the east side of the Willamette River was once its own city. After Portland gobbled up East Portland on the other side of the river, the city changed the street names. Some streets got new names to match up to the west side streets and some just got boring numbers. But Aunt Maudie said if you buy a house on the east side, the deed will show what your street used to be called. Those old ghost streets are still there underneath the new names and numbers.

After Aunt Maudie died, Mom made me go back with her to clean things out so she could put the house on the market. I think Mom brought me because the ballroom gave her the willies, too. Of course, by the time we went upstairs to the top floor, it was night. Mom flipped the lights and the two of us just stood there in the doorway. The room was filled with tables and chairs all shrouded in white cloths, and dust everywhere, even on the parquet floor.

When Mom hit the light switch, a line of chandeliers across the ceiling lit up the room. And something else. A line of footprints in the dust. They only went in one direction, from the doorway where we stood across the room toward the far end.

Mom took a deep breath and grabbed my hand. Hers was icy cold. Maybe mine was too. Maybe it was just because the furnace was off.

Holding hands, together we stepped into the ballroom and followed the footprints. All the way across the ballroom, we were careful not to disturb those marks in the dust. I guess we both wanted to keep the evidence intact. The blazing crystal chandeliers above our heads lit that ballroom up like it was waiting for a bunch of guests in long flowing dresses and fancy suits.

On the far side of the room, we came to a wall, just a blank wall, made of the same beautiful wood as the floor. But then I noticed some lines in the wall in the outline of a door. I pointed to it, but I didn't move and neither did Mom, at first.

There are times when a parent has to be brave, and this was one of them. Mom took two steps over to the wall and tried to get a fingernail into the crack of the door. Nothing happened, so she started touching the wall all around the outline, pressing on the wood. A click and the nearly invisible secret door swung open like it was on a spring. No spooky creaking, just a silent whoosh of stale, under-the-eaves air.

The light from the chandeliers didn't reach far into the space beyond the open door, but we could see there were boxes, maybe five or six of them, piled up in what must've been a storage space under the eaves. Mom took two steps toward the boxes and lifted the flap of the closest one. Then Mom slammed the secret door shut and turned toward me.

I'd never seen that look on Mom's face before. Sometimes Mom was loving and sometimes funny and sometimes mad, but she was always kind. That night, though, the look on her face was angry and scared and something else. Mom's hazel eyes were shining green and something about Mom's mouth made her look sneaky. Like she had a secret she was hiding from me.

"I'll get back to this later," she said. "In daylight."

More than all the stories about Noddy's séances in that ballroom, more than all those footprints in the dust, that look on Mom's face convinced me ghosts were real.

THE THING ABOUT BEING in an absolutely lightless place is you're not oriented to anything. Not space or time, or even what's in your own head.

I guess all I knew for sure was I wasn't alone. That was the beauty of our friendship. In a way, we were all misfits. Having each other was what got us through those years. And I don't mean in a boyfriend-girlfriend way. Even though we didn't know much, I think all us girls knew our boys weren't really boyfriend material. But the pretending got us through.

We sat in that hallway for ages, Lou's dry hand on my left, and Jamie's damp hand on my right. Holding his hand that night was the most we'd ever touched, Jamie and I. We sat there breathing quietly, eyes wide open, not seeing a thing.

Inside, though, I was full of light and warm.

Then. A flash of glowing white.

Someone gasped, but you couldn't tell gender from a gasp.

The white glow was there just for a second, and then it was gone. I gripped Lou and Jamie as hard as I'd ever gripped anything, and they squeezed me hard right back.

The white glow came again and this time it stayed long enough for me to catch my breath and really look. The glow hovered in the air near where Lou was sitting, and it wasn't pure white. It had bits of other colors in it, maybe green or blue. And it wasn't steady—the glow wavered.

"Holy shit," Jamie said. The skeptic starting to believe.

Then the glow disappeared again.

"I sensed a presence," Lou said. "Was he here?"

"Yes! Yes!" we all shouted.

"Can't you see him?" Ellen said.

"Did he leave because Jamie talked?" Pat said.

"I never see anything," Lou said. "Tell me what you saw."

Jamie let go of my hand, but I hung on to Lou. That thing could come back any second.

"Definitely ectoplasm," Jamie said. "Glowing white, maybe a little green."

"That's right," I said. "And it kind of blinked on and off."

"Jamie didn't scare him away," Lou said. "He desperately wants to tell us something."

Theron didn't come back that night, but we peppered Lou with questions. The time with his brother, he said, the glowing ectoplasm has spelled out letters in the air. They asked questions for hours. That's how Lou found out its name was Theron. Lou said he never saw Theron himself, but he always felt something near him. A force that enveloped him.

We started making our own lists of questions. Who were you when you were alive? Why are you coming back? What's it like on the other side?

Nothing in my life has ever been as exciting as Theron. Nothing up to then, and nothing since.

But the thing Mom and I found in Noddy's box came close.

I'M SURE YOU'VE SEEN a planchette. It's that heart-shaped thing that moves around a Ouija board on spindly little legs.

Noddy's planchette was on the top of the box Mom opened. It was carved out of dull brown wood—not dark and not light, and unpolished, except perhaps by the oil of human hands. All we had was the old planchette, but luckily, the Parker Brothers toy company in Salem, Massachusetts—where the witches came from—had been making Ouija boards since the first one came out around the same time Portland annexed East Portland.

So Mom went to Toys "R" Us and bought one. We never thought of it as a toy.

The Ouija board itself reeks of the occult even though it's made of slick, modern materials. Across the top are the words YES and NO. The letters of the alphabet fill the middle of the board in two arched rows, below which sit the numerals 1 2 3 4 5 6 7 8 9 0, in a perfectly straight line. On the very bottom of the board, in all caps, is one word.

GOODBYE.

That alone was enough to give me the willies, but in each of the four corners of our board were four pictures. Top left was the sun with a face wearing a sinister smile. Top right was a crescent moon with a frowny face. And in the bottom two corners were pictures of a darkened room with three pairs of hands on a planchette. Only one body was visible, the top half of a woman. Her face was too dark to make out, but above her was the disembodied head of a man or maybe a young boy. Dead and visiting from the spirit world.

From the other side.

That's why people consult the Ouija board, to contact lost loved ones. But back then, I didn't know anyone who'd died. Except Aunt Maudie.

But Mom had known Noddy, and she wanted to talk to him again.

THE NEXT WEEKEND, WE couldn't wait to do Theron again. That's what we called it, *doing Theron*.

We shut all the doors and turned off the lights and held hands like before. I held Jamie's hand again. And just like before, Theron showed up. A greenish-white glow somewhere in midair near Lou. But that night, Theron came with an odor. A smell like sulfur. The way hell is supposed to smell.

That sulfur smell in the air made me think maybe we'd gone too far, messing with forces from beyond the grave.

But Jamie was right there next to me, ready with a pop quiz for Theron.

"Is there a God?" Jamie asked.

That question wasn't on our list, but it was a good one. Mom and I weren't particularly religious, but I didn't see how you could have magic and a spirit world and people on the other side without a God.

That's when Theron started talking.

The glow got brighter and Theron started to spin around in big loopy-loops.

Then his spinning stopped and Theron very deliberately began spelling out a word in the air. One long upward straight line, followed by a short line off to the side.

"What's he doing?" Pat asked.

"Spelling, butthead," Cathy said.

"Screw you, too, sweetheart," Pat said.

Cathy wished.

Theron spun a second vertical line and then three quick horizontal slashes to the right.

"Yes!" Ellen said. "He's spelling out Y-E-S."

Theron's glow seemed to get even brighter, then he began making more loopy-loops, even bigger this time, and faster. More intense.

"He's telling us we got it," Cathy said. "He spelled out yes."

And that's all it took to convince me God was real.

Even after Theron disappeared for the night, the air was filled with the smell of sulfur.

ONE NIGHT SOON AFTER Mom got the Ouija board, we darkened our living room, just like the pictures on the bottom of the board. Mom turned off all the lights and closed the curtains, and we sat across from one another and put both sets of our hands on Noddy's handmade planchette. Mom's hands were like an electrical circuit arcing across that planchette, even though we weren't actually touching.

Mom went first, and her voice trembled.

"Oh spirit, come to us and tell us about the other side."

It sounded hokey but I still went cold from my armpits all the way down my back.

We waited for something, a sign, a slight movement from Noddy's planchette, but nothing happened. My fingers itched to move, to accidentally on purpose push the planchette across the board. But I didn't.

Mom spoke again, and this time my eyes had adjusted to the darkness enough to make out the shape of her face. I couldn't see Mom's eyes, but I recognized the outline of her head. It looked a lot like the outline of the woman on the bottom of the Ouija board.

"Speak to us, spirits," Mom said. "We seek to know of my grandfather. How is he? Will he talk to me?"

Again we waited. The dining room clock ticked off a minute, then another. And another, and another and then the planchette moved under our hands. So imperceptibly, I thought I'd imagined it. Then it moved again, very slowly. I didn't think I was doing it myself. And I didn't think Mom was either. A spirit from the other side was in our house.

We'd started with the planchette smack in the middle of the Ouija board, and it moved up toward the top of the board. It didn't swerve left toward *N*, or right, toward *W*, the first letter of Noddy's real name, William. Just straight up, bypassing all the letters. If it had kept going, the planchette would've just slid off the board without touching anything. But then it stopped. On a blank space.

"Is a spirit present?" Mom asked.

Nothing for a long minute, then the planchette began to move left, still slow. It came to rest on the word YES.

Sometimes you're shivering, but you're not cold, and that's

what happened to me right then. I liked it. And at the same time it scared me.

Mom smiled for a second, but weird like her lips were plastic. And then she was herself again.

"Who are you?"

The planchette moved immediately this time, like it got cued by a prompter. It moved fast, a horizontal slash to the word NO, and then another slash back to YES.

Then Mom asked a really smart question.

"I mean, who were you when you were alive?" Mom said.

Mom has done this before, I thought. Maybe even with Noddy.

My cheeks felt warm.

This was fun.

I was pretty sure Mom wasn't pushing the planchette and I know I wasn't. It moved fast to the left and stopped on the letter *A*.

I started to ask if it was done, but Mom shushed me.

The planchette moved down and to the right and stopped again on *R*. It was spelling out a word. The rest of the letters were close together. Over two letters to the right was *T*, then up and over one to *H*, then straight down to *U* and then left four letters to *R*.

A-R-T-H-U-R. The spirit's name was Arthur.

"Thank you, Arthur. We're glad to meet you," Mom said. "Do you know my grandfather?"

Arthur moved to YES.

"Can you tell him I love him?" Mom asked.

Arthur made a big loopy circle and came back to rest again on YES.

In the dim room, I could just make out that Mom was

smiling. I could tell she liked being Arthur's translator. I liked Arthur too. He was a very unscary ghost.

"How is he?" Mom asked.

Arthur was light under our hands, and moved effortlessly, like the air in the room was thin. My fingers barely touched the heart-shaped wood.

F-I-N-E, Arthur spelled out, and stopped.

The planchette didn't move.

Mom waited, to give the spirit time to answer. Arthur started moving again, and that time he wrote L-I-Z-Z-I-E.

"Are you saying Noddy is with Lizzie?" Mom said.

Arthur said YES.

"Who's Lizzie," I whispered. I know it was stupid, whispering. Arthur probably didn't even need us to ask questions out loud. He could probably read our minds.

"A baby who died," Mom whispered back. "In the 1890s. Noddy's baby daughter. She only lived a year."

Arthur moved back and forth, just a little movement, like a person rocking from one foot to the other.

"Is Noddy with you? Can we talk to him?" Mom asked.

Arthur began moving around and around in big circles. Mom saw she'd made a mistake, asking two questions. Her voice was pleading and breathy.

"Arthur, wait," Mom said. "I just mean, can we talk directly to Noddy?"

But Arthur was done talking. The planchette kept making bigger and bigger circles on the Ouija board. It moved faster and faster, spinning around the board.

"It's making figure eights," I said.

Mom gasped and it was loud in the hushed room.

"Oh no," she said.

"What?" I asked.

Mom's breath came hard, like she was on Mount Everest. Sipping thin air with each inhale.

"We need to move the planchette down to GOODBYE," she said. "Together. Now."

Pushing the planchette on purpose felt so different that I knew for sure then I hadn't pushed it at all before. It felt heavy, like I was pushing against gravity.

Mom kept her finger on my hand and I reached out a finger to her, and our two fingers intertwined.

Slowly the planchette moved down toward the bottom of the board. Just before it touched the word, the planchette bucked under our hands and the little wooden feet actually left the board for a split second. Then it came to rest on GOODBYE.

Mom and I, we both lifted our hands off the planchette together, and sat still for a minute. I folded my hands in my lap like a little kid and asked the only question I had left.

"What do figure eights mean?"

Mom's voice shook a little. She didn't think it was fun anymore either.

"It means the spirit wants to get out of the board and into your house. For good," she said. "Figure eights are also the sign for infinity."

"I liked Arthur," I said.

"So did I," Mom said. "For a while."

Mom stood up, turned on the table lamp and gently picked up the planchette and set it aside. Then she folded the Ouija board in half, put it back in its Parker Brothers box and into the toy cupboard. She left Noddy's planchette on the table.

Then Mom turned to me. She was smiling, but her face was chalk-pale and her eyelashes were wet.

"I don't know if this was real or not, but it was great," Mom said. "And I'll never do it again."

Part of me felt cheated, but a bigger part of me was glad she said it first.

The planchette was gone in the morning.

NONE OF US KNEW that night in May, almost the end of sophomore year, that it was going to be our last séance. By then we'd started calling ourselves the Six-Pack. Me and Jamie, Cathy and Pat, Ellen and Lou. Couples but not couples.

The night started the same as all the other times. We headed straight for the hallway, shut all the doors, made a circle and held hands. Then Lou reached up for the light switch and clicked us into darkness. Lou sat all the way back down and grabbed my left hand. Jamie on my right.

"Come to us, Theron," Lou said.

"Theron, come to us," we all chanted. And then we waited for our friend Theron, the ghostly spirit.

The seventh soul around our circle.

I smelled Jamie's Brut and Ellen's Shalimar and all the other scents in the room. You'd think all of them mixed together would smell awful, but instead it was like a garden, how all the different scents of all the different kinds of roses in the Rose City go together just right.

That's what I was thinking when Theron came to us again.

That time he came all at once. The room was dark and then there was a ball of glowing bright, bigger and brighter than Theron had ever been before.

It was just as amazing as ever and I had a million questions to ask Theron. I wanted to know if Theron knew President Kennedy or his brother Bobby or Martin Luther King Jr. I wanted to know if Theron knew Noddy and his dead baby daughter Lizzie. I wanted to know about the future, too. Who I would be when I grew up. Me, the born townsperson. And what would happen with me and Jamie. When he would finally kiss me. Whether we'd get married. If we'd stay together forever, even on the other side.

Maybe everyone was thinking the same kinds of things because nobody said anything for the longest time. And then Jamie ruined everything. He dropped my hand and shouted.

"It's in his mouth!"

Lou let go my other hand and reached up and flipped the light switch on. His face was even whiter than usual, as white as the Chinese white makeup we put on for *The Mikado*.

"What the fuck are you talking about?" Lou said. "You're going to ruin everything."

Jamie's hands were clenched together in fists. But I knew Jamie would never hit anyone. Certainly not Lou.

"I saw it," Jamie said. "The light was brighter this time and Theron was right next to your face. Like he was coming out of your mouth."

Lou held up both hands empty and opened his mouth wide so we could see down to his tonsils. There was nothing there.

"Cheater," Jamie said.

Everyone else around the circle was shocked quiet. Except Ellen. Ellen just sat smiling like nothing had changed.

"Forget it, Jamie," Ellen said. "I don't want to know if he's fake. He's real enough for me."

And that was the end of Theron. All we had left were memories of all the glorious times a ghost spoke to us with glowing letters in the air.

And a faint smell of sulfur.

WE STAYED FRIENDS ALL the way to senior prom. Lou asked Ellen, Pat asked Cathy, and Jamie asked me. Prom was in the gym, the same week as the Rose Festival. All us girls got these gorgeous long pastel prom dresses and had our hair done up. The six of us all hung out together and danced a few dances and then went out to the parking lot behind the gym and got high. I don't know if anyone else made out later that night. I kind of doubt it.

But Jamie and I did. We French-kissed with our tongues. It was everything I dreamed of except maybe not quite, and then I took Jamie's hand in mine, damp again but not sweaty, and moved it toward my bra.

But.

Jamie pulled his hand back.

Then he told me everything. Jamie said he really did like boys better than girls. All those queer jokes, they weren't just jokes. Not for Jamie, not for Pat, and not for Lou either.

Part of me was shocked, but another part of me wasn't. I think I'd known all along under the surface. And somehow Jamie and I were closer to each other that night than we'd ever been before.

Those guys, they just wanted to belong somewhere in the world. The same thing us girls wanted. And nobody wanted to be accepted more than Lou. He was a new kid who wanted friends, and he sure got them. Thanks to Theron, we all did.

We all belonged to each other.

AFTER MOM DIED, I boxed up her stuff and found Noddy's heart-shaped planchette. It still gave me the willies.

And one more thing.

I went back and looked up the old street name for Noddy and Maudie's house on Northeast 84th. The ghost name.

It was Theron.

The Arroyo Fiasco

Dawn Vogel

MY PARENTS TOLD ME I'd do great things someday. They named me after my great-great-grandpterosaur, Ayrvad, in the hopes I would follow in zher clawprints. Most people outside my family, though, called me Fiasco after the "incident."

In my defense, I was unfamiliar at the time with the phenomenon of an arroyo, since my clan was from wetlands. Most desert dwellers appreciated geyser pterosaurs. When we exhale vehemently, it comes out as a high-pressure stream of water. Seeing the dry riverbed and people who needed water, the only logical solution was for me to fill that channel. It's not like I could tell the difference between an ancient waterway and an ephemeral one. Suffice it to say, the former town of Winby isn't going to be erecting any statues to me.

So far, no one is.

I'd been considering my other options. If I could find a mate, I'd make a great caretaker for our young. But most of the others who hadn't found mates yet were among the group that insisted my name was Fiasco. So that seemed to be a dead end.

I listened to the gossip around the watering hole. There weren't any princesses in need of guardian geyser pterosaurs, and I wasn't about to offer myself up as a target for any knights. I knew how those stories ended.

I had to get away. I'd come back once I'd made a name for myself.

A name that was not Fiasco.

So I spread my wings, heading west so the sun wouldn't be in my eyes as I flew, and looked for someone I could help with.

I thought I'd found a perfect opportunity when I saw a huge fire. Finally, a task worthy of my talents!

How was I supposed to know the fire was ceremonial, meant to revere the gods? The humans were making noises, but to me they sounded like screams, not reverential chanting. I had no context, flying overhead.

That made a second town that wouldn't honor my name like my parents had hoped.

I flew a long time after that, until I reached the coastline. Then I flew until I reached a town. This time I listened first. Most of the humans fished or were in some way tangentially related to the fishing industry.

This was an industry I could work with. I'd done a bit of fishing in my day, shooting a plume of water downward and sending the fish skyward, then flying around to catch them.

Apparently, that technique doesn't work when boats are in the water. Well, it still works, but the people and boats fly and then plummet, and no one is happy.

Scratch Comar off the list of towns that might someday tell fond tales of me. They told me if I showed my face there again, it would be the last time I showed my face anywhere.

I'd failed three times. I was beginning to think my best bet was to retire somewhere cold, where I wouldn't be able to ruin anything with my breath, so my parents wouldn't have to know their offspring was a failure.

To get to the mountains, though, I had to cross a desert.

I flew above a sluggish caravan, then a bit ahead, then back to check on the humans and their pack animals, then to either side. I had a theory.

My flights confirmed it. This was a big desert, and there weren't many oases. If the caravan didn't have a good supply of water on hand, they weren't going to make it.

But I knew better than to try to make them an oasis in the nearest hole in the ground. I didn't want another incident on my conscience.

I waited until they stopped for the night, then approached. The caravan was small, with only one water wagon, which was running dry.

I didn't immediately fill the wagon, even though I could have. After all my failures, I'd finally learned my lesson about helping where help wasn't wanted.

I waved to get their attention, then spoke as softly as I could, so I didn't frighten them off with my admittedly loud voice. "I couldn't help but notice your water wagon's gotten low. I'm a geyser pterosaur. Can I help?"

Several of them smiled, and an older woman approached me. "How thoughtful of you, young friend! A geyser pterosaur is just what we need! If it's not a bother, it might be best for you to carry the wagon out toward that ridgeline and fill it there."

I noted where she pointed and nodded. "I'll be back in a jiff!"

These humans were clever, I realized, as I aimed for the small fill spout on their water wagon. If I'd filled it where they were camped, they'd be covered in mud quicker than a blink.

But out here, I could work on my aim, fill up the tank, and give the wagon a quick wash while I was at it.

This was what I needed all along—people who were willing to work with me and my unique talents. And the foresight to ask and listen before "helping."

They didn't have much to offer me other than their thanks, but they said I could feast on sheep once we got to their destination. I was so ecstatic to have people who wanted me around, I didn't bother telling them that geyser pterosaurs are strictly piscivores.

We'll cross that arroyo when we get to it.

Cranberry Nightmare

Kit Harding

HAVE YOU EVER WONDERED about cranberry bogs? I mean, think about it. They're bright red fields that more often than not sit in suburban towns, that *no one* ever goes near. No one knows who owns them, and you rarely actually see one being harvested. You just come out one day and suddenly there's a small lake where the red field used to be. Children don't play in them or explore them, and they are always deserted, even when houses are right next to them. No one ever questions any of this. The bogs are just *there*, and most of the time it's like no one ever thinks about them at all.

Oh, and there's one other thing: despite the fact that they usually slide right out of everyone's notice and no one has any idea who owns the land, everyone feels free to go ice-skating on the frozen bog all winter.

I was five years old the first time I went skating on one. It was very crowded. Well, it should have been; half the town was there. Watchful parents sat on camp chairs around the edges of the bog, most clutching steaming thermoses of coffee or hot chocolate. Smaller kids struggled around the outermost edges, just learning to use their skates, while teens skated closer to the center. No parents ever actually went out onto the ice, even those who were otherwise enthusiastic about winter sports. Teens would help the youngest kids, even though it wasn't cool, and often even when they had no connection to the child in question.

My parents brought me to the bog, put skates on me, and handed me off to our neighbor's teenage daughter Emily. I fought, insisted I wanted to skate with my mother, but my mother only shook her head and insisted I would have more fun skating with someone who actually knew how.

"It's all right," Emily said as I started to cry. "Look. I'll hold your hand the whole time. You won't get lost." Her tone was unusually firm, not the usual adult dismissal. I believed Emily really was promising to protect me and let her push me out onto the ice. She did not once let go of my hand, even after I started to get more confident. There was no letting me push off, as I started to be able to balance. Emily kept me by her side.

Perhaps it was because of that shelter that I saw it. I had caught on to the mechanics of skating surprisingly quickly, given how much trouble I usually had with anything physical. I wouldn't have noticed if Emily had let go and let me try it on my own. But her grip remained firm, so I was gradually able to focus on what was around me, mostly crowds of other children. Some were racing each other, some were playing tag, and a few were working on tricks. One of these, Annabella, caught my attention. She was much less flashy than the others working on tricks, who drew the eye, and instead was attempting very small jumps, over and over. On one of these jumps, she landed—and then sank into the ice. She let out a brief scream, too short to be heard over the shrieks of children having fun if you weren't already paying attention, and then was gone. The whole thing was over in a heartbeat. But the ice remained smooth and unbroken. She had not fallen through the ice; she had simply vanished into it.

I screamed.

"What's wrong?" Emily asked.

"Annabella disappeared!"

"It's very crowded," said Emily. "Are you sure you didn't lose sight of her?"

"She went *down*," I said. "Into the ice."

Emily looked out at the ice. "There's no hole anywhere in the ice," she said. "There has to be a hole if you fall through the ice. It's how we know everyone is safe."

"But I saw it!" I protested. I knew what I had seen; I couldn't fathom why she would try to lie to me.

"No. You didn't," she said softly. Firmly.

"But I did," I responded.

Emily looked around hastily, as if to make sure no one was paying attention to us. "Fine. You saw it. Don't tell anyone you saw it." The fear in her voice was so strong I could feel it pressing down on me. "Do you understand me? Never tell *anyone*."

I was silent after that. I couldn't understand. We were always taught to help other people when they got hurt at school; disappearing into ice probably hurt. For some reason we weren't supposed to help. Even with the secret, it didn't take that long for people to realize Annabella wasn't there. Once it became apparent she wasn't among the crowd anywhere, the police were called. No one had seen anything. The strangest thing to me, even then, was how perfunctory it all seemed. No one moved with any urgency, the police didn't ask anyone very many questions, and however upset Annabella's parents seemed, all the other adults seemed more relieved than anything. I was used to people around me not making sense—my parents said that was part of what being autistic meant and that I was just going to have to practice—but this seemed different somehow. People were supposed to get more upset when children disappeared. It was how the world worked.

Before we left the bog, Emily took me aside and quickly handed me a small purple lighter. "Keep that with you all the time," she said. "Don't ever be without it, and don't let anyone know you have it. It will keep you safe."

"How will it keep me safe?" I asked.

She shook her head. "I can't explain. They won't let me. Just promise me you'll keep it with you. It's important."

"I promise," I said, and slipped it into my pocket just as my parents came to claim me.

I NEVER SAW EMILY again. She disappeared from her bed that very night. I never saw a police car in her driveway or heard of police looking for her. Her mother told me she had run away. Even as a child, I wondered about that. No one seemed concerned about her. Still, I couldn't be sure. While I'd been diagnosed, no one was really teaching me social skills. I'd heard my mother say that it had been bad enough taking me into the city once to get looked at; she wasn't going to take me to the city every week. People weren't meant to leave their towns like that.

Letting runaways go could be one of the things other people did normally that just didn't make sense to me. That theory was supported by the way the other children had initially wondered about both Annabella and Emily, but eventually it receded in their minds. I continued to wonder.

I had seen Annabella disappear into the ice. Or had I imagined it? Had Annabella suffered a more conventional kidnapping? How could that have been true, when none of the adults ever went out on the ice? Even in the chaos of every kid in town being out there, an adult on the ice would have been noticed. The official police story was Annabella must have wandered over to the bank and been kidnapped, as happened to someone every few years, no matter how they urged parents to please keep an eye on their kids when taking them ice-skating. Everyone else seemed to forget about it entirely.

Those who had been Annabella's friends held on to the memory the longest. Remembering Emily's warning, I never discussed it with anyone. But I watched as we grew up, and a small group of girls kept pictures of her taped inside their school lockers and occasionally mentioned her in whispers. Eventually, we became old enough that some of them began to look at others with romance in their eyes—some to boys, some to girls. Orientation didn't seem to make a difference. One by one, soon after any of us experienced the first steps beyond crushes, they were taken away by the guidance counselor to talk in her office. They came back from these conversations different; they were suddenly much more interested in their romantic interests than they had been before. Teens who had spoken of leaving our tiny town now spoke of staying and starting families, and those who had still whispered of Annabella took down their photos of her and never spoke of her again.

It all looked very strange to me, but because I had never experienced even the beginnings of a crush, I never knew what was being said at these meetings. Our health class made no mention of the existence of asexuality and certainly not aromanticism, though it was very thorough on the subject of fertility and childcare. I found out "aromantic" described me in furtive searches on the one internet connection in town, at the public library, taking care to make sure no one saw me searching and to wipe my browser history afterwards.

When I found my orientation, I greeted it with a certain amount of relief because the meetings were so closely connected to the first romantic steps that it seemed like this might protect me at least until I was too old for "late bloomer" to stop being a plausible explanation. I still had no idea what it was protecting me from, but that something dangerous was happening, I had no doubt—something, I was pretty sure, that had to do with the cranberry bog.

When I was sixteen, my parents informed me it was time we introduced my five-year-old brother Adam to the town tradition of ice-skating.

"No," I snapped. "I don't ice-skate. You know I don't ice-skate."

"Because you have a silly phobia over something you imagined as a child," my mother replied.

"And people disappearing every few years? Is that also something I imagined?"

"Kidnappings are really quite rare."

"Every few years, regular as clockwork? That's not rare, that's *predictable*."

"Don't be absurd, Amanda. You are far too old to let these fears control you. We may have been lenient while you were a child, but it is past time to grow up. We will be introducing him to ice-skating because that is what the town does, and you *will* participate."

"I haven't been on ice-skates since the first time. I'm in no position to help him."

"Then you'll leave him to struggle by himself? He will be going on that ice whether or not you join him—and I will see to it that you regret it if you do not join him."

I gave in with ill grace. Nothing would convince them, and no matter how carefully I watched, I had never actually *seen* any of the subsequent disappearances. So what else was there to say?

THE MORNING OF THE ice-skating dawned bright and clear as always. I could not shake the dread that settled about my shoulders and knotted in my muscles as I laced up my skates. I had avoided the lake for a reason. Emily had held me so tightly I had never had the opportunity to be lost in the crowd. She had subsequently disappeared. Would I disappear without a trace, if I held tightly to Adam's hand so that he could not get away? Would I be dismissed as a runaway by people who clearly knew better?

With my skates firmly fastened, I stepped out onto the ice and took Adam's hand in mine. My skates wobbled under me, and I struggled to remain upright. He followed me out and together we struggled across the ice on the bog. I tried to hold his hand as tightly as Emily had held to mine—something about the way she'd held on to me suggested it was protective. It was possible whatever was in the bog needed you to be alone; the "was probably kidnapped from the bog without anyone notic-ing" story worked less well with teenagers.

Together we skated on. The crowd looked exactly as it did every year. Parents stood or sat on the banks of the bog, watching the children on the ice. Teenagers showed off. Children played. No one would ever have guessed the darkness at the heart of it, except of course for the way no one was ever exempted from going—even with my tantrums and refusals to get on the ice itself, I had been dragged along whenever a weekend day was nice enough for skating, the only child on the banks and not on the ice. The day seemed like a perfectly ordinary day of ice-skating, no different from all the others. But the days with disappearances never seemed that different from the others.

MY REFUSAL TO SET foot on the ice over the years had rendered me unable to ice-skate well. I did not pick it up as quickly as my brother did. Instead, I struggled to make headway as he skated along quickly, and he began to outpace me and tug at my hand where I had grasped him. I kept a tight grip on him as I wobbled, but eventually he pulled too fast as I hit a bumpy patch of ice and I fell in an ungainly heap. I lost my grip on his hand. I landed on the ice and jerked my head up just in time to hear a brief shriek, quickly lost among the noise of the crowd, and I saw Adam disappear into the ice in an instant. Exactly the same way Annabella had all those years before.

I screamed.

"The ice swallowed him!" I shouted. "Just like it did before!" I struggled to my feet and started back towards the bank. "Adam's gone and the ice ate him."

I was quickly surrounded by a crowd.

"Don't be absurd," said my mother. "You just lost sight of him in the crowd for a minute. There's no hole in the ice. He can't have fallen in. He's here somewhere."

"Then *where*?" I demanded. "I was holding tight to his hand, and then I fell, and he was gone. Where did he go then?"

"He's probably somewhere in the crowd," she said, but I could see her expression tighten. "There's no need to panic."

"He was *right there*," I said. "And now he isn't anywhere. We have to find him."

Others began to search the crowd. It was soon obvious Adam wasn't on the ice. The police said he must have wandered over to the bank and gotten kidnapped, despite the very brief window between when I had last seen him and when everyone began to look around the crowd. I protested—insisted the official story made no sense—but this was dismissed as a product of my differences, which I fumed about. Autism had no impact on my ability to perceive reality.

Though it did hinder my ability to perceive social reality, and maybe that was at the root of the problem. There was a social reality at issue here, one I had been missing since I was a child. I had never been able to tell what social game was being played, and honestly I still couldn't. I knew from my secret internet forays that an autism diagnosis generally triggered some form of treatment to develop one's social skills, but my parents had never had me treated or encouraged any sort of ability to read the social games being played. I could only glean so much from our tiny town library and illicit excursions into the unfiltered internet—being caught using the internet before you'd graduated high school would cause all hell to break loose.

If I started from the premise that a secret existed that everyone found out in the guidance counselor's office, it followed that the cranberry bog had something to do with it. So what was actually in it?

I would have to investigate on my own. Ideally that very night. While I had no illusions about my brother's ability to survive underneath the ice, whatever was happening defied reality—it was just barely possible he would still be in there for me to recover. If he wasn't, maybe I could stop it from getting anyone else, although I had no idea how and no real plan. I had to try, anyway. No one else was going to.

That night I climbed out my bedroom window and down the tree. The bog was not that distant a walk; I could do it in about half an hour. I would have preferred to drive, but my parents might look out the window and notice the car was gone. The long walk gave me time to consider what exactly my plan was. I had no more of one when I approached the bog than I had when I started out. I couldn't exactly step out onto the ice and simply demand my brother back. I slid my hand into my pocket and felt the lighter Emily had given me all those years ago. She had instructed me to always keep it on me, and I had—I didn't even think about the fact that I was doing it. There had to have been a reason she'd given this to me. Whatever lived in the bog thrived on ice. Presumably the lighter could be used against it as a weapon in some way.

The adults always stayed on the bank. Meaning the bank was probably safe from whatever it was. I approached the bog and stood beside it.

"I know you're here!" I shouted at the bog. "I've seen you twice now. I want my brother back." No answer came. The night was quiet. Above me the moon shone full and bright, reflecting off the ice of the bog. Even deserted under the eerie lighting, it still didn't look menacing. Perhaps a bit lonely, but not ominous. Nothing happened when I shouted into the night.

Perhaps being on the bank also meant I couldn't attract its attention. Carefully, I stepped out onto the ice and walked slowly toward the center of the bog.

"I know you're here!" I shouted again. "I saw you take Adam. I saw you take Annabella. I've come to reclaim what's mine."

Beneath me, the ice began to grow clear. I stared down at it. Underneath the ice was Adam. His face was pale enough to pass for a vampire, and he was bound in some kind of flexible leaves. He was still alive. I knew because when he saw me he began to struggle against his bindings and push up against the ice, which remained solid.

"You want your brother back." The words were spoken in a hissing, rustling voice that seemed to emanate from nowhere and everywhere at the same time. "You forget the bargain, little human."

"I never agreed to any bargain."

"Your ancestors did. Their promise binds you."

"My ancestors agreed to let you eat children? I don't believe you." But I did, I realized suddenly. It was some kind of social game in play. A secret existed that had not been told to me. The others had one by one stopped thinking about anything but staying in town and starting families—always right after they went into the guidance counselor's office. Even the teens who hated children before that suddenly couldn't wait to have some. A few of the current seniors had been so eager they were pregnant already. It had been celebrated.

"You're of an age to know the bargain," hissed the voice. "Yet here you are. Demanding your brother. Why is that?"

"I know nothing of any bargain. I am not bound to any bargain. So give me back my brother!"

"Someone has been negligent in their duties. I shall have to remedy that. You are rather large to join me, but if I must..."

A creeping chill began to climb my legs, followed by the harsh scrape of ice against my clothes and then freezing water against my feet as the bog dragged me downward. Driven by adrenaline, I snapped the lighter from my pocket, flicked it on, and held it near the ice. The ice screamed and let me go. I scrambled back to my feet, keeping the lighter outstretched. That had been such a near thing. I could feel the water beneath the ice where it had soaked into my feet. The only thing that had saved me seemed to be that I was somewhat larger than a child and harder to suck down into the shallow bog instantly.

"I'm not part of your bargain, whatever it is," I said. "I can still hurt you."

"You are a child, and that is a tiny toy. It doesn't have enough fuel to hold me off forever. And when you run out you're mine."

"I don't think so," I said, with more confidence than I felt. "Because I have enough here to get me off the ice. And you can't come out of your bog or you wouldn't need the ice-skating charade. Give me my brother back, or tomorrow night I come back here with a flamethrower and melt every bit of this ice. I don't know what that will do to you but I'm sure it won't be pleasant."

"The ice melts every year in the spring."

"And yet my lighter is enough to keep you from devouring me, so *try again*."

"Are you so sure you want him, now that he's been changed?"

"He's my *brother*."

"You will not interfere again. You will swear upon your name and blood that in return for your brother you will bring no flame again to my surface."

That was maybe not a good idea—I wasn't quite sure what it meant, for one thing—but it was offering to give back my brother. If it ate me instead, was that really that much worse than living in a town that was apparently deliberately conspiring with a cranberry monster?

"I swear upon my name and blood that if my brother is returned to me I will bring no flame again to your surface."

The ice in front of me opened slowly. Sucking children in happened too quickly to see, but it shoved my brother out of the ice excruciatingly slowly. He was soaked through and deathly pale. I did not stop to examine him there on the ice. I simply grabbed him into my arms and ran as cracking sounds echoed across the ice behind me.

When we gained the bank, I laid Adam down to examine him. He was breathing, barely, and ice-cold. As I watched he began to cough. I sat him up and he coughed up water—and then cranberries, far more cranberries than any human should be able to hold pristine in their lungs. I glanced fearfully back at the bog and then at my brother. He was starting to shiver now, which I took as a positive sign.

"Amanda?" he whispered.

"I'm right here," I said.

"The ice—"

"I know." I looked at him more closely as he spoke. His teeth were ever so slightly pointed and tinted red, and his eyes had a slight reddish glow to them as well. His skin was as pale as if it had been entirely drained of blood. Whether this portended other more internal changes, I had no idea. For the moment, we had to get away. Clearly everyone else in town knew about the bog, and given Emily had disappeared completely after protecting me, knowing and acting on that knowledge clearly had some dangerous effects. I had no idea what they'd do if I brought back a rescue, especially after everyone had been looking the other way about the bog devouring children for years.

Time to run away. Get us both back home, grab my mother's keys from their hook by the kitchen door, get into the car, and get as far away as we could. I had never been beyond the borders of the town except for that one trip to a city behavioral doctor, but at least out there we had a chance of survival.

"You're safe," I told my brother, and lifted him into my arms to start back toward our house. "I'll make sure of it."

After all, he was alive. The bog had not eaten me while I rescued him. We could worry about the rest tomorrow.

The Rising Currents of Ocean Fire in My Blood

Bethy Wernert

BENEATH A HARVEST CRESCENT, I am born.

Rising from the realms of the ocean, my iridescent scales glimmer in the pale sliver of golden light. I nestle in a bed of conch shell, sinking and weathered, into the glittering sands of the beach.

My mother and father find me here. Miniature, mythological, marine. Carefully lifting me from my molluscan hearth, they bring me to their home, a compact, solitary building in the center of the city.

Breathing in the air of the terranean world, I become one of them. Initiated into the secrets of humanity.

My body adapts. Scales become flesh. Gills become lungs. Fins become limbs. Transforming, I grow into girlhood. My coral-strung hair deepens into the earthen volcanic red of lava, and my algae-green eyes become the emerald of moss.

I look just like them. Humans. The only remnant of my squamous body is the slight, coruscating hue my skin reflects in the crescent of the Harvest Moon.

My mother calls me "a gift from the ocean," her "oyster," her "pearl." And like a pearl, she must keep me safe. Safe from the cavernous mouths of those hungry enough to eat mermaids.

She locks me in an aquarium. A large room painted the abyssal blue of the ocean. In the corner of the room is a dresser, the pink hue of anemones. In the other corner sits a simple wooden bed, seaweed green. From the ceiling hangs a mobile, dangling carved shards of mother-of-pearl and glass figurines composed of various sea creatures. A dolphin, a whale, a sea turtle, an octopus, a fish, a squid, a sea star. All dangling precariously on strings.

I spend hours wading through this room. Wandering and exploring its individual nooks and crevices. But it feels too small.

Contained.

A rising surges within me, like a burning geyser, to break loose and free from the room's confining walls. I look out the window through gossamer curtains. If I can just taste the ocean…

As I look toward the streets, I see many throngs of people trapped in boxes. Bound by their own hands, they've created their own aquariums.

And I watch them, my eyes downcast, knowing they have probably never tasted the endless infinities of the ocean.

MY MOTHER PLACES ME in a Catholic, all-girl private school. She tells me it will "train the memories of the ocean from me" and teach me to be human. To ingratiate me into the domains of human society.

School is a struggle.

Books and pencils and paper. I try to listen to the lectures and attend to the homework. I fail every test. As time grows on, it becomes vividly clear: I am not made for school. And though they try to burn the memories of oceans, seashells, and reefs from my brain, the connections just grow stronger the more I fail. The worse I do in school, the more I feel the searing rush of ocean fire in my blood. I can almost see the crystallized scales forming and hardening against my flesh.

Psychiatrists test my brain, and finding it too riddled with saltwater and mollusks, they declare, "Her test scores are significantly low. Every test we gave her indicates autism."

My mother is ashamed. When we go home, she tells me I am "useless," "a piece of trash," "tarnished." In her eyes, I am no longer the precious pearl she found so long ago, buried deep within the conch shell.

In the province of night, I curl up with a large scallop shell, several inches wide and striated with sunset hues of violet and pink. I place it to my ear. Hearing the whispers of the sea, I escape the world and drift into the fathomless trenches of dreams.

THE NEXT MORNING, A young boy my own age brings the daily newspaper, tossing it on the pavement with the carelessness of youth. He rides his bike, gliding through the streets in the warming cusp of dawn. Weaving through pedestrians, bicycles, and cars. As if the world were his own.

As I water the herbs in my mother's garden, he stops beside me. He wears a worn, oversized leather jacket (his father's, perhaps) and faded black combat boots.

"Here," he grunts, handing me the current newspaper.

I set down the pail and take it from him. "Thank you." In shyness, I cast my eyes down. Isolated from the world as I am,

I rarely see, much less *talk*, to boys. And certainly never alone. Not like this.

"Why are you watering those plants so early?"

"Because my mother asked me."

"Do you always do what your mother tells you?"

"Yes. She raised me, after all."

"That's a stupid reason. Parents aren't always right, you know?"

I don't respond but just continue to look toward the ground. Toward the soft, yielding grass.

I can feel his fingers brush my cheek, and I flinch. But I don't pull away. I stand motionless in the silence of the morning. The only sounds are the distant thrum of passing cars and the dawn chorus of a trembling of finches.

The next thing I feel are his lips against mine. Cool as the ocean breeze. And I begin to remember the taste of saltwater and brine.

"What are you doing to my daughter?" a voice barks, shark-like with aggression. At the sound of my mother's voice, the boy leaves abruptly, racing his bike down our driveway. "What were you doing? Consorting with a boy like that? It's sinful!" She proceeds to berate me, calling me names and accusing me of being "untrustworthy" and "foolish." She promises, vowing to the cold clay of earth beneath our feet, that she will *never* let me alone again.

I am thrust back into the aquarium, the windows now drilled with bars.

IT IS NOT UNTIL six years later, when I turn eighteen, that my mother trusts me again. She sends me to the supermarket to buy a cake, giving me a rosary to wear as a I walk. Composed of aquamarine beads and a silver cross, it hangs heavy against my neck. "To remind you to make holy choices free of sin."

As I walk to the grocery store, I trace my finger over the cross and God, pinned and incarcerated in suffering and blood. He is not free, bound as I feel bound. Yet there is a promise of freedom in the wind about me, as it rustles the grounded leaves, brightened into crimsons and golds by the shades of autumn.

Eventually I reach the supermarket and purchase a round cake with icing the color of sea-foam. I carry it delicately a block down the street. Turning a corner, I see the boy from years ago. In shock, I drop the cake; it splatters softly upon the ground.

He looks towards me. He's different. Older. Worldly. His once-pale eyes are now a midnight blue, and his hair has darkened to the burnished gold of the sun. But he still wears the same leather jacket and a similar, yet larger, pair of combat boots. He's standing by a motorcycle, a burnt red, like volcanic earth.

He observes me cautiously. "Have we met before?"

"No," I lie. He intimidates me, and I can feel my hands trembling. I catch them behind my back.

He glances at my feet where the cake fell in an explosion of sugar, flour, and icing on the cement. "That sucks."

"Yeah, I'll have to buy another one."

"What was it for?"

"My birthday."

He raises his eyebrows. "Well, happy birthday. What are you turning?"

"Eighteen."

"So you're officially an adult?"

I pause. I've never considered myself to be an adult. I am too immersed in school and my aquarium to consider myself anything but a child. But, age-wise…" I suppose so."

"Here, let me buy you another one," he offers, gesturing to his motorcycle.

"Oh, that's not necessary."

"I insist."

"It's fine." I divert my eyes toward the pavement, the cake drying in the cold autumn sun. I wonder how long it would take to return to the store for another one. A few minutes at most.

"Well, if you ever need anything…" He pulls out a pen and scrawls something in the center of my palm. His hands are rough and calloused, weathered by time. And yet they feel so warm and comforting. "Reach out."

I look down. It's his phone number. Inked in blue.

He gets on his motorcycle and drives away. Sinking far into the bustle of street traffic.

I buy another cake, and walking home, I place my palm to my heart.

THAT EVENING, IN THE still of the crepuscular shades of night, I retire to the aquarium. I hear the flickering sounds of the television in the other room.

Kneeling, I pray to God. For a sign. A symbol. An answer.

Does God grant desires? Or only punish them? My mother seems to think the latter, and in honor and love of God, we must suppress them. But there is wildfire in my blood. A fervent burning, a religious passion connected to the wilderness of the sea.

I gaze at the crucifix on my rosary. In the wisps of darkness, it glitters the silver of starlight.

Suddenly, on my windowsill outside, I hear a scratching resound in the deadened obscurity of night. It's urgent. I throw back the gossamer curtains. On the window ledge perches a giant pelican, larger than I. Its broad wings expand in a rapid flurry of beating feathers.

It gazes at me. I notice that inscribed in its right eye is the night sky, the mysteries and secrets of all the constellations whispered into blindness.

It looks at me with this eye, as if to say that, though blind, it can see everything I am. Stripped of human flesh, it can see scales, gills, and fins. It knows, as I do, I do not belong here. And with that, the pelican lifts its wings and glides away into the violet shades of midnight.

THAT SAME NIGHT, I slip into my mother's purse and use her phone to text the boy, asking him to pick me up. I move silently through the halls of our house and out the door. Climbing on the back of his motorcycle, I ask him, "Where are you taking me?"

"To the ocean. I know a place. It's nice. You'll like it."

Galaxies race beside us as we stream through night, delicate wisps of shadows encompassing the calm, quiet road. The reflective dashes on the pavement bloom bright luminescence under the beaming of the motorcycle's headlights. It burns my eyes, and I bury my face in his shoulder, feeling the cool tenebrosity of nothing.

Soon, I hear the gentle, murmuring fall of the tides and the echoes of long, moaning winds descending into a cadence in the distance.

We're so close. I can taste it. Memories. They flood through my bones like the remnants of a prayer and sigh through my lips in a raptured sense of euphoria.

My entire body aches to be amalgamated back into the ocean, to morph into shells and branches of coral.

He pulls off the side of the road on a nearby cliff, the warm hum of the motorcycle's engine dying beneath us.

He takes my hand and brings me to a steep pathway, descending the cliff to the churning sands of the beach. The sand melds around my toes; I feel myself sinking into the unfathomable earth and pulling toward the moonlit tides.

My skin tingles with the scent of brine and, beneath the moon's rays, glistens with the same iridescence as scales. Transforming, I shift back in time. Back in memory.

He pulls me from the cool tempers of ocean waves to the warmth of his lips upon my skin.

He lays me on the beach, sand strewn through my hair. The light waves whispering their way against our bodies.

I feel the rosary, heavy against my chest. I slip it over my neck. The waves grasp it from my fingertips and draw it into the abyss of the water. Silver glinting in the cobalt gloom.

And in the breath of the moonlit tide, I sink. Cascading into the depths of the ocean.

I RETURN HOME AS dawn bleeds across the sky. My mother and father are still asleep. The house a hushed whisper.

The next few weeks pass in the same way. In the vast reigns of midnight, I slip away toward him and toward the ocean, and in the dawn I return, stealing back into the cramped, narrow aquarium.

Over time, I feel myself changing again, my body metamorphosing. Within me, I feel the faint beat of a pulse, a gentle pressure, like a feather falling to earth.

There's a child—*my* child, growing within me. Tiny, miniature, the size of a baby seahorse or a small pearl.

Weeks flow into months, and my daily nausea frightens my

mother. Taking me to a doctor, he informs me what I already know: I am pregnant.

My mother is furious. When she gets home, she tells my father. He takes his belt—worn, faded leather—and throws me on the ground, splaying sparks against my back; thin, scarlet lacerations drip down my spine.

With the singeing, burning pain, I retreat to my bed and place the scallop shell over my ear. The murmurs of the ocean whisper in hushed waves, and my heart steadies to the slow pulsing of the tides.

My mother opens my door and enters. "You need to give it away." She pauses to gauge my reaction, but I am not listening, subsumed by the waves. "A child without a father is a sin in the eyes of God, and now, as penance, you will give it away to a family that can take care of it."

"Only God can demand a penance. You are not God," I tell her softly, still listening to the secret utterances of the waves.

"You *will* give it up!"

"But I can take care of it." Instinctively, I hold my womb where I can feel it burgeoning and swelling with life.

"No, you cannot! Do I need to remind you? You have *autism*! You're not capable of raising a child! You can't even take care of yourself!"

"I'm keeping the child."

She rips the scallop shell from my hands and throws it against the wall. The shell fragments into hundreds of minute shards, splintered across the floor.

"No! What did you do?" I scoop the fragments of my solace into my hand. But it's useless. I'll never be able to assemble all the miniature pieces back together.

"I've given you everything, and *this* is how you repay me? You are a worthless, horrible child!"

She locks me in the aquarium. I curl up on the floor, cradling the shards of the scallop to my heart.

I DO NOT MEET the boy again. My mother makes sure of that. She places double locks on my door and keeps me perpetually sealed in the aquarium.

The next few nights, I see him through the curtains, but he does not see me, sheltered behind barred windows. He idles on his motorcycle for several minutes, waiting for me, texting me. And hearing no reply. Eventually he stops coming.

Over the next few weeks, my mother takes me to court for the right to attain "legal guardianship" over me. The lawyer shows the judge my academic and IQ scores. "She's not fit to make decisions. Her autism and inability to understand social situations and consequences are consistent with the reckless choices she's made in life. Without a legal guardian, she is at risk for homelessness, poverty, substance abuse, and other similar concerns."

I am lifeless. Shattered. Like the scallop fragments in my hand. I've placed them in a blue satin drawstring bag. As the lawyer drones on in legal terminology I don't understand, I nod my head silently and feel the sharp curves and jagged edges of the shards. Beneath my fingertips I feel them morphing into tiny specks of granular sand.

Can I change like that? Can I transform? The lawyer and my mother seem to think not. At least, that's what I gather from their insistence in court. But *I* know I can. With my child, I can already feel my body growing, burgeoning in time.

At the end of the day, my mother wins.

What she won, I don't quite understand.

But throughout the evening she maintains a smug, supercilious expression. I hate her for it.

THE NEXT MORNING, SHE barges into my aquarium and throws the blankets off me. "Get up," she demands.

"Why? It's Saturday."

"Get up," she repeats, this time firm, edged with aggression.

She drives me to a shady, old brick building on the edge of town with a large cross overhanging the threshold. Above it are etched the words in silver lettering: Grace of God Pregnancy Center. We enter and a diminutive woman wearing a layered, beaded necklace, looks up. "How may I help you?"

"We have an appointment."

The woman leads us to a room in the back. In the room, at a desk, is a short woman in her mid-fifties with sun-blond hair and slate-gray eyes peering from behind purple glasses. A gold crucifix nestles against her neck.

"Ah, so this is the girl! Your mother has told me so much about you. I'm here to make your whole pregnancy run smoothly. In fact, I've already picked out families." The woman lays out several photos before me.

Families? Who are these people?

My mother clears her throat. "I haven't told her yet."

The woman raises her eyebrows before turning to me, her smile artificially bright. "Well, I am the director of Grace of God Pregnancy Center. At Grace of God, we are dedicated to helping women through their pregnancies. And I am here to specifically help you with the adoption process."

"Adoption?"

"Yes, there are many families who have tried, but God has not blessed them with a child. As we know, God works in mysterious ways."

I do *not* like the way this conversation is going. She knows nothing of God. "He's not so mysterious. All you have to do is listen."

"Well, as I was saying, your mistake can be repented by giving your child to a loving, Catholic family."

"No!" I yell at her.

"Now, abortion isn't really a viable option. We do not condone it. Abortion puts women at high risk for infertility, cancer, and post-traumatic abortion disorder. Besides, God disapproves of women who kill their own children. It is a mortal sin. And you aren't a naturally sinful girl, are you?"

"God loves *all* his children. He is free of judgment. Are you?"

"Well, of course! That's why I'm in this profession. I'm just trying to guide you into what works for other women."

"I don't care what works for other women. I care what works for me. And what works for me is keeping my child."

"But you know, dear."

"Know what?"

"You can't take care of a child. You're..."

"I'm what?"

"Listen, you really don't have a say in the matter. Your mother has decided."

"But it's *my* child!"

"But dear, you forfeited all your rights when you gave your mother guardianship. She has legal control to decide what to do with the baby, and she wants you to have an adoption."

The woman forces me that day to choose a family. I close my eyes and place my finger on a random picture.

WHEN WE GET HOME, my mother locks me back up in the aquarium.

"For your own safety," she tells me and hides the key. She only opens the door for breakfast, lunch, dinner, and so I can go to the bathroom. The only time I ever leave the house is for doctor's appointments.

When I visit with the doctor, he puts a cold gel on my

stomach, and on a large screen before me, I can see it: a tiny, delicate creature imbued with life.

My tiny creature.

My creation. A part of me. And I realize, right then, I cannot part with this child.

ON THE DUE DATE, my water does not break. But the contractions come in sharp, piercing agony. Ripping apart inside me. I feel my child expanding and pushing within me. Yearning to taste the freedom of the newborn air. I scream out, and my mother races into my bedroom, unlocking the door.

Seeing me sprawled upon the floor, she lifts me and helps carry me to the car.

Sifting through long lines of traffic, we race to the hospital, a towering building in the center of the city.

As we enter the automatic doors, two people greet us. Tall and statuesque. Perfectly manicured as if out of a magazine cover. The adoptive parents. I recognize them from the photograph at the pregnancy center.

The contractions become sharper. More intense. A heady tearing in my uterus.

Two nurses come and place me in a wheelchair, wheeling me into a room.

The doctor enters and examines me. He informs the adoptive parents and my mother that my water has not broken, and he orders a C-section.

Attaching a mask to my mouth, he makes me inhale fumes laced with drugs. I drift into unconsciousness.

THE NEXT THING I hear is a cry piercing the stale and frozen air. Something in its pealing voice...I have to hold it.

I open my eyes to see my child.

Small.

Fragile.

Precious.

So precious, it is the only thing that matters.

"It's a boy," the doctor announces, handing my son into my arms. A tidal wave of warmth and joy and love sift through me as I run my fingers over his hands, no bigger than the tip of my thumb. At my touch, he shivers and weakens, a faint blue tainting the pallor of his skin. His newborn muscles weaken in my arms.

"Something's wrong!" I clench him close to me. To my heart. As if I could ease the tsunami of suffering building in his frail body.

The adoptive mother tries to take him from me. "No!" I pull my child back toward me.

"Let me see him. I can help him," the doctor offers. Reluctantly, I give him my child. He takes him and connects his foot and hand to strange mechanical equipment. A wire spiraling to a machine with electric red dashes. A number appears in the red lettering. I don't know what it means.

But the doctor does. He presses a button in an urgent, fervent manner. Immediately, two nurses appear. "Take him to the NICU. His oxygen levels are at 80 percent."

The nurses quickly leave and then reappear with a large contraption. Taking my baby, they place him in a transparent, glasslike box situated on more mechanical equipment and a set of wheels. In less than a minute, they leave with my child.

"Don't take him! Why are you taking him?" I scream. A piercing, earthen shrill. Fury and rage burning through my voice like geysers.

"He's not breathing. We're taking him to the neonatal

intensive care unit. We'll hook him up to oxygen tanks and try to find out what's wrong."

PLACED IN A WHEELCHAIR, they bring me to the NICU. My child is caged in the glass box, nurses surrounding him, checking his oxygen levels on some type of machine.

I watch him. So tenuous. So little. So vulnerable. He is like me. Of the sea. He was not born to live on land.

Watching him, dying in his glass prison, I know what I must do. The only thing I can do. The only thing I *need* to do.

THROUGH THE NIGHT, WRAPPED in a course, woolen blanket, beside the glass cage, I watch my dying child. The adoptive mother sits in the chair opposite me, collapsed in dreams and sleep. Two holes extend in the glass cage for touching him. I reach one of my hands in, brushing his soft skin, ice cold. Freezing over with lack of breath.

The doctor enters, checks on the oxygen tanks hooked up to my child before repeating the process from before. Attaching my child's feeble foot and hand to a machine that reads to him. The doctor shakes his head solemnly before glancing at me.

"He's dying, isn't he?"

"You should be asleep. It's almost midnight."

"He doesn't belong here."

"We're doing everything we can. But...but sometimes this happens."

"He doesn't belong here," I repeat, insisting.

"Maybe not. Maybe he doesn't belong anywhere."

"What?"

"I'm sorry. I'm tired. I shouldn't have said anything. I just... if he's not here, he definitely won't survive out there. In the city."

"No, not in the city."

"You need to get some sleep," the doctor informs me, before leaving the room.

It's still.

Dark.

Quiet.

Before my brain processes, my hands reach into the glass cage. I undo the wires on my child. I pull him out through one of the arm-holes and wrap him warmly in the woolen blanket.

With every bit of strength in my body, I try to stand. My muscles sear and throb with pain, and my abdomen feels like it's tearing apart. It does. Blood seeps from the newly stitched wound from my C-section. Biting down on my lip, I keep from crying out.

I slip out of the hospital, gliding from shadow to shadow. A phantom cradling a dying child. Outside, the fresh scent of midnight lingers in the air. In the distance, I can taste the sea. The sea, which smells of the living. Starkly distinct from the smoggy undertones of the craven city. The ocean, confident in its conscious power, calls through the atmosphere. In the distance, a blind pelican spirals across the wind, trailing the ocean breeze.

I follow.

Tracing its flight, farther and farther.

THE PELICAN LEADS ME to the ocean. The rocky, lichen-bathed crevices jut out as I climb down them. Spiraling down to the ocean shore.

Cerulean waves thrash to the waxing moonlight. The tides bring life. Violet sea stars whose spindled legs reach back toward the ocean. Bright, crimson crabs rise from the dead of the sand. A resurrection.

I sink my toes in the cavernous depths of the earth. The

sand subsumes me. As if it would swallow me back into the cold, dead ground.

In the far-off distance, a long, primordial moan echoes across the starlit surface. Whales. Two of them in unison.

The ocean foam touches my toes, bathing them in primeval memories. My flesh hardens into the iridescence of scales. My feet morph into striated fins, shifting in the wet, mulching sand. I kneel, bathing my child in the same healing waters.

Baptized in the ocean waves, with the scent of brine and algae, his cheeks turn a warm, pink hue. His skin begins to harden like mine into dense, impenetrable scales. His squamous body squirms in delight, enchanted by the scents and sounds encompassing him.

The waves grow stronger.

Vaster.

The mist that sleeps upon the tranquility of the ocean now rises in magnificent wisps of argent breath. The moon, a golden Harvest Crescent, calls upon the tides. Horned, like the Crown of God.

I hold my child to my heart.

Lifting from the ocean shore, a giant wave swells before us, a fortress forged of seawater. Enlarged by the magic of the moon, it grows to consume us, and in its omnipotent presence, I succumb. Merging into the realms of the ocean.

Acknowledgments

So MANY INCREDIBLE PEOPLE helped *Soul Jar* come into the world!

First of all, I'd like to thank all of the wonderful authors who brought this anthology to life with their stories and words. You were all wonderful to work and write with. I promise to never pester you about passive voice or present tense ever again.

Thank you Nicola for agreeing to write a foreword before anything else about this book existed. I truly appreciate you, your support, and your fantastic words.

To Gigi Little, thank you for the phenomenal cover design. Your art brought this anthology to life.

And thank you to Colette Parry for your fabulous skills with the layout.

I'd also like to thank Rebecca Taylor, Jonah Barnett, and Neil Cochrane for their impeccable help when I needed a second opinion.

Thank you to Kelsey for letting me crash in your craft room for a quiet workspace.

Dearest Laura, thank you for taking a chance on this project. Thank you for your love, support, and uplifting of disabled authors and voices with Forest Avenue Press. Without you, I'll still be wondering if this project was possible.

Thank you and so much love to my parents and sister, who love and support all of me. Even the grumpy bits.

And finally, thank you to Ian and Calvin. I love you both more than I can possibly say here.

About the Editor

EDITOR **ANNIE CARL** WAS born with a rare spinal birth defect (lipomeningomyelocele) and is a Stage IV Non-Hodgkins survivor. She owns and runs The Neverending Bookshop in Edmonds, Washington. She is the author of *My Tropey Life: How Pop Culture Stereotypes Make Disabled Lives Harder* and the novella *Nebula Vibrations*. When not running an award-winning bookstore, Annie reads massive quantities of science fiction, fantasy, and romance; pole dances; knits; and hangs out with her goofy family and friends.

Contributor Biographies

CORMACK BALDWIN IS A speculative fiction author and editor who lives in the vicinity of what he's pretty sure is a cursed bookshop. He writes about everything from sentient stains that eat the greedy to disabled characters trying to stop supernatural forces bent on wreaking havoc. He is also head archivist (editor-in-chief) of *Archive of the Odd*, a found-fiction and analog horror magazine. You can find a list of his works at cmbaldwin.carrd. co, or the man himself @cormackbaldwin on Twitter. If you cannot find him, assume he has been taken by the bookshop.

MEGHAN BEAUDRY BEGAN WRITING as part of her rehabilitation from brain trauma in 2014 and simply never stopped. Her work has been published in *Hippocampus, Ravishly, TODAY, Al Jazeera*, and the *Huffington Post*. She was nominated for a Pushcart Prize in 2017. In 2020 she was selected as winner of the Pen 2 Paper Creative Writing Contest in fiction. She blogs for Lupus.net.

ELLIS BRAY IS A science fiction author and poet who lives in the PNW and hates the recent addition of a Fire Season to the regular Winter/Spring/Summer/Fall lineup. His fiction focuses on living with disabilities (visible and invisible) and the lasting effects of childhood trauma. He has a master's degree in medieval Scandinavian studies and if you don't run away fast enough, he will download everything he knows about the Old Norse poem "Völuspá" at you. You can find his nonfiction in *NewMyths* and the *Sci Phi Journal* (under SP Hofrichter); his poetry at *Eye to the Telescope* and *F&SF*; and his ramblings on Twitter @flytingnwriting.

LANE CHASEK'S STORIES AND essays have appeared or are forthcoming in *Denver Quarterly*, *Great Ape*, *Hobart*, *MAYDAY*, *McSweeney's*, *South Dakota Review*, *Works Progress*, and many other publications. Lane is the author of the experimental biography *Hugo Ball and the Fate of the Universe* (Jokes Literary, 2020), three books of poetry, and the forthcoming novel *She Calls Me Cinnamon* (Pski's Porch). Lane is the founding editor of *Warp 10 Lit*, a contributing editor at *Jokes Review*, and regularly posts his less-polished reviews and musings to his website, lanechasek.com.

A MEDIEVALIST, A TYPE 1 diabetic, and a cyber-crime investigator, **A.J. CUNDER** graduated from Seton Hall University with a master's in creative writing. He currently serves as editor-in-chief of *Et Sequitur Magazine*, assistant editor at *Cosmic Roots & Eldritch Shores*, and on the editorial staff of *Metamorphosis Magazine*. Find him on Twitter @aj_cunder, or online at wrestlingthedragon.com.

K.G. DELMARE IS A neurodivergent writer based out of New York City. They graduated from Fordham University with a degree in English in 2016 and have gone on to be featured in publications including *Breath & Shadow*, *All Worlds Wayfarer* and *TERSE Journal*. They currently still live in New York and can be found on Twitter @KGDelmare.

TRAVIS FLATT (HE/HIM) IS a teacher and actor living in the middle of Tennessee. He earned his BA in English lit at UT Knoxville. His stories appear or are forthcoming in *Bridge Eight*, *Terror House*, *Fauxmoir*, *Drunk Monkeys*, *A Thin Slice of Anxiety*, and many other publications.

Adam Fout is a neurodivergent author who writes nonfiction and speculative fiction. He has work in *Flash Fiction Online*, *December*, *J Journal*, and more. He is a graduate of the 2020 Odyssey Writing Workshop. Find his work at adamfout.com.

Christy George is a print reporter-turned public television political reporter-turned public radio environment reporter-turned fiction writer. These days, she edits public radio reporters across the west, and is working on the second draft of her first novel. "The Other Side" is a product of Tom Spanbauer's Dangerous Writing workshop, a reworking of memoir into fiction that she calls fictoir.

Andrew Giffin is a high school English teacher in Richmond, Virginia, where he lives with his wife and two daughters. He is an autistic author whose previous work can be found in *Cosmic Horror Monthly*, *The Dread Machine*, *Abyss and Apex*, and *Planet Scumm*. When not writing, he's probably listening to doom metal and playing a solo tabletop RPG.

Nicola Griffith is a dual UK/US citizen living in Seattle. She is the author of eight novels (including *Hild* and *Spear*) with a ninth, *Menewood*, forthcoming. In addition to her fiction and nonfiction (the *New York Times*, *The Guardian*, *Nature*, *New Scientist...*) she is known for her data-driven 2015 work on bias in the literary ecosystem and as the founder and co-host of #CripLit. Her awards include two Washington State Book Awards, the Premio Italia, the Nebula, World Fantasy, Otherwise/Tiptree awards, and the Lambda Literary Award (six times). She holds a PhD from Anglia Ruskin University, uses a wheelchair, and is married to novelist and screenwriter Kelley Eskridge.

MIKA GRIMMER IS A queer and neurodivergent author of fantasy short stories and novels of various flavors. She graduated from the University of Washington with a bachelor's degree in interdisciplinary studies with a concentration in culture, literature, and the arts in 2008. She is also a member of the twice-postponed 2020 Taos Toolbox cohort that finally took place in the summer of 2022. Mika lives with her husband in Seattle, Washington, and when she isn't writing, she is likely throwing pottery, knitting, or watching and creating podcasts about Grand Sumo.

EIRIK GUMENY IS THE author of the cult-favorite *Exponential Apocalypse* series and the forthcoming *Beggars Would Ride*. He's written for *WIRED, Cracked, Nerdist, SYFY*, a couple of medical textbooks, and even the *New York Times* once. Born with cystic fibrosis, Eirik still has cystic fibrosis, because that's how genetic diseases work. In 2014 he received a double lung transplant and technically died a little. He got better.

KIT HARDING IS A writer and librarian who belongs to the cities and wilds of New England. Her work has previously appeared in *Cossmass Infinities*, the Zombies Need Brains anthology *Derelict*, and *Luna Station Quarterly*. Find her online at writerkit.dreamwidth.org.

PAUL JESSUP HAS BEEN a professional writer for close to twenty years now, with works in *Clarkesworld, Fantasy Magazine, Nightmare Magazine, PostScripts, Interzone, Apex, Strange Horizons*, and many others. He's also got a few books out in the small press, with the latest one being *The Silence that Binds* with Vernacular Books. He has multiple sclerosis and diabetes. In his free time he creates video games, and just recently designed and published the best-selling game *Bad Writer*, now available on the Nintendo Switch.

LILY JURICH IS A type 1 diabetic living in Edmonds, Washington. She enjoys reading, acting, and writing everything from short stories to poems. When she can she loves to rewatch Marvel movies. She loves spending time with her friends and family, and especially with her pets.

EVERGREEN LEE PREFERS THE speculative world to reality. Her too many hobbies include gaming, spoiling cats, tie-dyeing everything, and searching for unicorns. Her short stories have been published in a variety of venues, including *Daily Science Fiction, Factor Four*, and *Orion's Belt*, while her novels languish on her hard drive. She is autistic, chronically ill, and a member of SFWA and Codex. She can often be found backstage wherever virtual conventions are found, and thinks about blogging on evergreenlee.com.

JUDY LUNSFORD LIVES IN Arizona with her husband and her giant schnoodle. She is a former library clerk. She struggles with a chronic illness and is living with stage IV cancer. Judy writes mostly fantasy but occasionally delves into other genres. She has written books and short stories for all ages.

DANIELLE MULLEN'S STORY, "ONE Last Thing," can be found in *Things With Feathers: Stories of Hope* anthology. Another story, "Broken Clocks," appeared in the Fall 2021 issue of *The Lit Quarterly*. Among the many hobbies she collects are knitting, cosplay, and sketching. She lives and writes in Southern New Mexico.

RAVEN OAK IS A multi-international award-winning speculative fiction author best known for *Amaskan's Blood* (2016 Ozma Fantasy Award Winner, Epic Awards Finalist, & Reader's Choice Award Winner), *Amaskan's War* (2018 UK Wishing Award YA Finalist), and *Class-M Exile*. She also has over a dozen short stories published in anthologies and magazines. She's even published on the moon! (No, really!) Raven spent most of her K-12 education doodling stories and five-hundred-page monstrosities that are forever locked away in a filing cabinet. Besides being a writer and artist, she's a geeky, disabled enby who enjoys getting her game on with tabletop games, indulging in cartography and art, or staring at the ocean. She lives in the Seattle area with her wife and their three kitties who enjoy lounging across the keyboard when writing deadlines approach. Her hair color changes as often as her bio does, and you can find her at www.ravenoak.net.

EL PARK LIVES IN a hundred-year-old house with her husband and various unwelcome stinkbugs. When not fitting words together or succumbing to entropy, she enjoys word and number puzzles, earrings, and first-contact science fiction. "The Warp and Weft of a Norse Villainess" is her first published work.

SIMON QUINN IS A lover of romance novels, cats, fencing, and the hurdy gurdy, all of which he likes to add into his writing when possible. He is a recent graduate of Northern Arizona University, where he studied English and geology. He is an autistic trans gay man who loves *Hamlet* maybe a little bit too much and spends his time creating and testing tea blends, of which his current favorite is peppermint and dandelion root.

DANIELLE RANUCCI WAS BORN in Kazakhstan and graduated from Princeton University in 2023 with a bachelor's degree in Comparative Literature. Her work has been published in *J Journal*. Learn more about her, the books she reads, and the stories she writes on her website, danielleranucci.wordpress. com, and follow her on Twitter @DanielleRanucci.

JULIE REESER IS THE author of three poetry chapbooks and the novella, *Language of the Spirit*. Her short fiction can be found in *Little Blue Marble*, *Bourbon Penn*, and others. Her Patreon churns out small quirks and weekly words, and she's obsessed with discovering comfortable seating and the best verbs. There's a cool carousel of stories you can ride on her website, www. persephoneknits.com. She is disabled, but not done.

JENNIFER LEE ROSSMAN (THEY/THEM) is an author and editor from Binghamton, New York. They are disabled, autistic, and queer, and so are most of their characters. You can find more of their work on their website jenniferleerossman.blogspot.com and follow them on Twitter @JenLRossman.

HOLLY SAIKI IS A part-time retail worker living in Kapolei, Hawaii, on the island of Oahu. Her fiction has appeared in *The Stray Branch*, *The Siren's Call*, *Café Irreal*, *Ink Stains Anthology*, *Brilliant Flash Fiction*, Black Hare Press's *Monsters*, Pure Slush's *The Shitlist*, TANSTAAFL Press's *Enter the Rebirth*, *Mad Scientist Journal*, *Simily.co*, and is forthcoming in *Starward Shadows*. She is currently at work on a dark fantasy novel.

CAROL SCHEINA IS A deaf speculative fiction author from the Northern Virginia area, where she spent much of her childhood watching Star Trek and hanging out at the library. She still lives in the area with her husband, two kids, and two very needy cats. You'll find that many of her stories were thought up while sitting in local traffic, resulting in tales that have appeared in *Escape Pod, Daily Science Fiction, Flash Fiction Online,* and other publications. You can find more of her work at carolscheina.wordpress.com.

NISI SHAWL CO-AUTHORED *WRITING the Other: A Practical Approach,* a standard text on inclusivity. Their debut novel, an alternate history of Africa's Congo region, was a Nebula Award finalist. They edited the acclaimed anthology *New Suns: Speculative Fiction by People of Color,* winner of the World Fantasy, Locus, and Ignyte awards. Shawl's recent titles include *Speculation,* a middle grade historical fantasy; *Our Fruiting Bodies,* a horror and dark fantasy collection; and *New Suns 2.*

JAYE VINER LIVES ON what used to be the plains of eastern Nebraska with two feline fur bombs and a very tall man. She knows just enough about a wide variety of things to embarrass herself at parties she never attends. Her writing has been published in *Drabblecast, The Rumpus, CrimeReads,* and *Everyday Fiction.* Her first novel, *Jane of Battery Park* (Red Hen Press, 2021), is a romantic thriller about two disabled people trying to find love despite their families. Look for *Battery Park* and her new Hollywood romance trilogy *Elaborate Lives, Terrible Love,* and *Casta Diva* (December 2023) wherever you buy books. Find Jaye on Twitter @JayeViner or Instagram @Jaye_Viner.

DAWN VOGEL HAS WRITTEN for children, teens, and adults spanning genres, places, and time periods. More than one hundred of her stories and poems have been published by small and large presses. Her specialties include young protagonists, siblings who bicker but love each other in the end, and things in the water that want you dead. She is a member of Broad Universe, SFWA, and Codex Writers. She lives in Seattle with her awesome husband (and fellow author), Jeremy Zimmerman, and their herd of cats. Visit her at historythatneverwas.com or on Twitter @historyneverwas.

BETHY WERNERT LIVES IN Tucson, Arizona, working as a special education teaching assistant. Writing from the perspective of both epilepsy and autism, her short stories and essays have appeared in *Communion, Entropy, Waxing & Waning, The Gateway Review*, and *Grim & Gilded*.

Soul Jar

edited by
Annie Carl

Readers' Guide

Book Club Questions

1. What does the title of this collection mean to you? How can you interpret the idea of a soul jar? In which story does that phrase appear?

2. Many of these stories use humor to approach themes of illness, chronic pain, and loss. Which stood out as particularly funny to you? Why do you think the authors chose levity as a way into their material?

3. In "Survivors' Club," the protagonist lives in strict quarantine. How did your experience of the COVID-19 pandemic—and the related supply chain shortages—impact your reading of the piece?

4. Study the cover and its elements. Have you ever felt like you were under water? Discuss.

5. Why do you think a collection like Soul Jar needs to be in the world? Can you name some other books written by authors who identify as disabled?

6. Compare and contrast the use of technology in "There Are No Hearing Aid Batteries After the Apocalypse," "Ziabetes," and "The Last Dryad."

7. "A Broke Young Martian Atop His Busted Scooter" delves into class and cultural inequities in space. Who are Benjamin's allies? Would you have stolen the books? Do you think Cody and his family will notice?

8. What different types of disabilities did you recognize in the stories? Did any of them intersect with your lived experience?

9. In her foreword, Nicola Griffith says this about ableism: "Ableism is the story fed to all of us, disabled and nondisabled, from birth: that to have intellectual or physical impairments makes us less, Other. It's the only story we get in real life or on page or screen. Ableism is a crap story." Think about the movies, TV shows, books, and online content you've experienced recently. Where have you seen ableism in action?

10. In "A Peril of Being Human," the protagonist shapeshifts depending on the people around her. Have you ever adjusted your tone or facial expressions to match a situation? What are some real-world situations where that kind of blending in or connecting-by-mirroring might be helpful?

A note on the selection process

During our open submissions period, we asked submitters to check a box confirming they identify as disabled. We did not ask for diagnoses; we decided self-identification as disabled fit our criteria. When deciding on a title and subtitle for this project, we chose to include the language "disabled authors" because of how we phrased the call.

FOREST
AVENUE
PRESS